SHADOW & SOUL

The Night Horde SoCal Series
Book Two

Susan Fanetti

THE FREAK CIRCLE PRESS

Shadow & Soul © 2015 Susan Fanetti
All rights reserved

Susan Fanetti has asserted her right to be identified as the author of this book under the Copyright, Design and Patents Act 1988.

This is a work of fiction. Names, characters, places, and incidents are a product of the author's imagination. Any resemblance to actual persons, living or dead, events, or locales are entirely coincidental.

The Night Horde patch design by C.D. Breadner

ALSO BY SUSAN FANETTI

The Night Horde SoCal Series:
(MC Romance)
Strength & Courage, Book 1

The Pagano Family Series:
(Family Saga)
Footsteps, Book 1
Touch, Book 2
Rooted, Book 3
Deep, Book 4

The Signal Bend Series:
(The first Night Horde series)
(MC Romance)
Move the Sun, Book 1
Behold the Stars, Book 2
Into the Storm, Book 3
Alone on Earth, Book 4
In Dark Woods, Book 4.5
All the Sky, Book 5
Show the Fire, Book 6
Leave a Trail, Book 7

All of my books are dedicated to the Freaks, because my books wouldn't exist without them. Some days I think I wouldn't, either.

This story is also dedicated to the children no one looks out for, and to the adults they become.

*I love you as certain dark things are to be loved,
in secret, between the shadow and the soul.*

~Pablo Neruda, Sonnet XVII

CHAPTER ONE

Faith saw Bibi come through the automatic doors into the Emergency Room. She sat and watched as the older woman strode with purpose to the curved reception desk. She was dressed yet, or again, in her signature snug jeans, low boots, and leather jacket, probably with a v-neck sweater underneath, and her bittersweet-chocolate-brown hair was down, just over her shoulders, and perfect. Even at one o'clock in the morning, Bibi Elliott put herself together if she was going to be seen.

Faith Fordham, on the other hand, was wearing ancient UGGs, white sweatpants, and a gigantic black hoodie left behind by some guy or another, and she couldn't remember the last time she'd even brushed her hair.

She couldn't hear the exchange, but she could see in the set of Bibi's back that it was about to get heated, so she stood and took a few steps toward the desk. "Beeb. I'm here."

The receptionist or whatever she was forgotten, Bibi spun on her heel. "Faith! Honey!" Her arms extended, she crossed the waiting room. Faith met her halfway and allowed herself to be hugged hard and enthusiastically. She'd spoken to Bibi regularly over the years, every few months or so, but she hadn't actually seen her in…fuck. A decade.

"Oh, honey! Oh, I'm so sorry. What a way to come back home. Is your mama okay? Are you okay? What the hell happened?"

None of those questions had easy answers, so Faith pulled back and took Bibi's hand. "Let's sit."

As she led her over to the empty row of thinly padded chairs—it was quiet in the ER on this midweek predawn—Bibi asked, "What happened, honey?"

"I don't know much yet. They took her for tests."

"Didn't they let you go with her?"

Faith took a deep breath and met Bibi's eyes. "I couldn't, Beeb. This all is…my head's going a thousand miles a second. And she was yelling, and they had her in restraints, and I just—"

She cut off abruptly, realizing that she was about to burst into tears. Bibi was still clutching her hand. With the other, Faith pinched her arm as hard as she could. She'd learned when she was a kid that doing so would make the tears die where they were. It worked, and there were times in her life that she'd pinched herself black and blue trying to maintain her composure. "I haven't laid eyes on her in almost ten years, Beeb. I don't even know what I'm supposed to do now." She squeezed her mother's best friend's hand. "Thank you for coming."

"Oh, my God, Faith. Of course I'm here. *Of course* I am." Then Bibi got a look that Faith remembered vividly from her childhood. It meant that Bibi was on the job, and the relief Faith felt at that almost started the tears again. "Let's start with what happened and work out from there."

"I got a call. I guess when Sera got transferred to Tokyo, she set me up as Mom's emergency contact. I don't know why it wasn't you."

"Has to be kin, honey. Blood kin."

Faith nodded; that made sense. "Okay. Anyway, I got a call that she'd been brought to the ER and they needed me here. She got hit by a car. She ran out in front of it."

"Oh, lord!"

"It's worse, I think. The driver had just left a stop sign, so she has a broken leg and some bruises and scrapes, but it's not that bad. The worst part is that she was out on the street naked and completely incoherent. She's still totally raving—or she was until they put her out. And they don't know why. Fuck, it should be Sera dealing with this."

Sera—her full name was Serenity, but she'd decided she was Sera when she was in seventh grade—was the oldest of the two sisters, a Type-A do-gooder. She was their mother's pride and joy. Faith, a rebel from the time she'd learned to say 'no,' had preferred the bike shop to school, or anywhere else, and she'd found her home in her father's heart. Until they'd both torn it all apart. Her mother, too. Maybe her mother most of all. Or maybe not. When Faith thought of that time, she assigned blame variously and had no idea where it truly belonged.

But when the dust had settled, Faith had moved on, alone and away from the rubble of her life and her family.

Bibi gave her a little shake. "Well, it's not Sera. It's you. And me. We'll figure this out together, okay?"

Faith nodded. "Okay. I guess…I guess we wait. Will you stay?"

"I'm not goin' anywhere, baby. I'm right here." Bibi wrapped an arm around her and pulled her close. It was the most familial affection Faith had felt in years, and her throat clenched again.

She sat with her head on Bibi's shoulder for a few minutes, finding calm in that motherly embrace. Then she said the thing that had really started her head spinning like a centrifuge. "She didn't recognize me."

Bibi had been rubbing a soothing circle on Faith's arm. At that sentence, she stopped, and they were both momentarily still.

"From what you said, honey, it didn't sound like she knew much about anythin'. Don't wrap yourself around that axle. Your mama knows you. She's been missin' you all this time. I know."

And that didn't make Faith feel better at all.

~oOo~

There was a television on the wall, set to a channel playing back-to-back-to-back episodes of one of the *Law and Order* shows. The sound wasn't on, but the closed captioning was. Faith leaned on Bibi and stared at the television, not really watching, not really paying attention to the captions, and not really thinking, either. All of her thoughts wanted to be thought at once, so she had put them on time out until they could take turns.

Bibi's hand was back to rubbing her arm, but otherwise they were both quiet and still, except each time the doors back to the treatment rooms opened, when they both swiveled their heads. For a long time, a couple of hours at least, no one she recognized came out, and no one came looking for her.

And then, the doctor who'd invited Faith to follow them up to Radiology or wherever they'd taken her mother came through the doors, scanned the room, and headed for her.

"Miss Fordham."

Bibi had already taken her arm back, probably sensing in Faith's posture that it was time for them to stand, which was what they did.

"Yeah, hi. How is she?"

The doctor seemed young, about Faith's age. He was short and sort of doughy, but he had a kind face and a gentle demeanor. He was probably great at emergency medicine, where people came in frantic and needed a calm, kind presence.

"She's sleeping quietly now. Why don't you come back with me, and we can sit and talk with some privacy."

"Um, okay. Can...can Bibi come back? She's my mom's best friend."

He smiled warmly. "Of course. Right this way."

The doctor—Faith reminded herself to try to read the name embroidered on his coat—led them through the swinging double doors and then off to the side. There was a little room with a comfortable sofa and a couple of upholstered chairs. The color scheme was blue and pale grey, there were quiet seascape prints on the walls, and there were boxes of tissues on all three little tables near the seats.

Jesus, Faith thought. *This is the death room.* She stopped in her tracks. "Wait. Is she—is…you said she was only sleeping, right?" She had no idea how she'd feel if her mother was dead. And that thought was on a *long* time out.

The doctor—Reid, no Riedl, was his name—indicated the sofa. "She's sleeping, yes. Please, have a seat."

They sat.

"We'd like to admit your mother. Until we fully sedated her, she was still agitated and disoriented, and the test results we've gotten back so far aren't showing us why. There are no drugs in her system, other than those we've administered. Her vitals are strong, if a little elevated from stress. The only signs of trauma are a result of the accident. Has she been acting oddly lately?"

Faith looked at her feet. The toes on her old suede UGGs had been worn shiny and dark, and she stared at the pattern of wear. Her mind had always sought out patterns and shapes, and she felt a little more centered as the part of her that wanted to turn shapes into things made its attempt to see something on her toes. A bear, she decided. A bear on a sled.

"I don't know," she answered. How could she know?

Bibi spoke up then. "I don't think so, Doctor. I saw her a few weeks back, and she was fine."

"No forgetfulness, or unexplained anger, outbursts of any kind?"

"No." There was something in Bibi's negative that Faith heard, though. She turned and gave her a look, and got a reassuring smile in return. "Nothin' unexplained. She was a little upset. We'll talk later, honey. Don't have anythin' to do with this."

Dr. Riedl looked from Bibi to Faith and then nodded. "Okay. Well, I brought in a neurologist to consult: Dr. Tomiko. She'd like to do a complete workup, so we can see what might have caused this. With no signs of drug or alcohol abuse, then this is either something physiological or psychological. We'd like to rule out any physiological causes before we explore the psychological."

Her mother had always been high strung and dramatic, but she wasn't nuts. "If she's not crazy, then what could it be?"

He shook his head. "Speculation at this point is premature. Let's get some tests done. Dr. Tomiko will talk to you in the morning and walk you through everything. For now, we're going to move her up to Neurology and keep her quiet and comfortable. Visiting hours are obviously long over, but if you'd like to stay with her down here until they take her up, that's fine."

Faith started to shake her head, but at her side, Bibi said, "Yes, thank you, Doctor." The forceful insistence in her voice stopped Faith's refusal and turned it into acceptance. She nodded.

Dr. Riedl smiled and stood. "Of course. She's in Room 3, like before. You can stay as long as she's there. She won't wake, but you can sit with her."

~oOo~

Margot Fordham was still beautiful, even bruised and scraped, her blonde hair matted. She was fifty-six, a few years younger than Bibi, but neither of them was ever going to go grey or get especially wrinkly. Or fat. These were women who intended to keep themselves together all the way to, and probably beyond, the grave.

So it was weird, and difficult, to see her looking pale and frail, in restraints, sleeping on the white hospital linens.

Her leg was set in a cast that went over her knee, and she was in a traction device the lifted it up a bit from the narrow bed or gurney or whatever it was. Faith and Bibi stood side by side and held hands, looking down at Faith's peacefully sleeping mother.

She'd been screaming and cursing and begging when Faith had been led back to the room earlier in the night. They'd tried to calm her by telling her that her daughter was there. She'd calmed for a moment, asking "Sera? Serenity? Where's my baby?"

When she'd seen Faith, she'd said, "That's not my baby!" and gone even more wild.

Faith supposed that was fair. But it made it hard to feel like she should be here, waiting. Sera hadn't even said she'd come home. She wanted Faith to 'keep her posted.' Okey dokey.

"Why was she mad at Christmas?"

"Hmm?" Bibi sounded like she'd been far away in her head.

"You said she was upset but it wasn't unexplained. How come? You said club stuff?"

"Oh." Bibi sighed. "Yeah. The club is…getting into some stuff again. Your mama found out at Christmas, and she was pretty unhappy about it."

Faith had no reaction to the idea that 'the club' was going outlaw again—which, she knew, was what Bibi had meant. 'The club' wasn't the club Faith knew from her childhood. That club had been outlaw her whole life. Her father, whom everyone, including her mom, had called Blue, had been the Sergeant at Arms of the club she'd known. But he was dead, killed doing club business, and that club was dead, too. Now the men who'd been her father's brothers wore a different patch. They were the Night Horde now. And Faith was no part of them. Even if they'd still worn her father's patch, she'd left that life behind the minute she'd turned eighteen.

Literally—she'd been packed and ready at midnight on her birthday. By the time her family had woken that morning, she'd been well on her way to San Francisco.

"Why'd she care?" Blue had been dead more than five years. She didn't see how a club her father hadn't even been a member of factored into her mother's mental state at all.

But Bibi grabbed her shoulder and made her turn so they were face to face. Her expression was pointed, almost angry. "We're your mama's family, Faith Anne. She moved here to Madrone to stay close to us. She's a part of us. So're you and your sister. I know you know that. Deep down, you know you're still part of us, and we're part of you. It's not the shape of the patch that matters. It's the family. And your mama was upset that things could get dicey again for her family."

Faith didn't like the way guilt was making her stomach feel sour. *She'd* been the wronged party. One of them, anyway. If she didn't want to forgive and forget, that was her prerogative. But Bibi was serving her up a big ol' helping of guilt pie, and, standing at her mother's bedside in the hospital, Faith was lapping it up.

The door opened, and a nurse stepped in. "We're taking her upstairs now. Room 562. Visiting hours start at eight in the morning."

Faith and Bibi stepped aside and watched as her mother was wheeled out. Then they were standing in an empty trauma room, which seemed strangely huge without the bed in it.

And Faith realized she had nowhere to go. Driving all the way back to Venice Beach just to return in the morning seemed insane. She couldn't stay at her mother's house—she didn't even know where that was. And the thought of a motel room tonight made her ache with loneliness.

She turned to Bibi. "Can I come home with you?" Bibi would let her, she knew that for sure.

But the look on her face was uncomfortable and almost panicky. "Oh, honey, I…"

Faith felt panicky then, too. "Please? I'll just crash on the sofa for a couple of hours. I promise I won't be in your way, and I'll clear out right away in the morning." She had not at all expected not to be welcomed at the Elliotts' house.

"It's not that, honey. You know I'd be happy to have you stay, and we have plenty of room. It's just...oh, hell. Honey...things are complicated."

Whatever had happened to her mother—that was bad. Being back in the midst of all these family memories and feeling absolutely besieged by them all—that was worse. But having Bibi tell her no—that was unbearable.

But she bore it. She swallowed and tried on a smile. "Hey, no. It's cool. I'll find a room. I saw a motel right by the ramp I took to get here."

Bibi was shaking her head. "Faith, listen. I'm not sayin' no. But you need to know...Demon—Michael—is there. He's stayin' with us. Has been for a few months now."

All at once, all those thoughts that had been wanting to get thought, they all died. Faith's brain was a ghost town. She stared stupidly at Bibi, only one word in her head, rolling through like a tumbleweed. Michael.

Michael.

Michael.

Bibi picked up her hands and held them both. "He's...he's got a little boy, honey. Tucker. He's two. Hooj and I are helpin' 'em out."

Michael. Had a child. Michael was at Bibi and Hoosier's with a child. His child.

Michael was the other injured party in the reason she hadn't seen her parents since she was eighteen years old. More injured than he even knew.

It had been even longer since she'd seen him. Since she was seventeen. And a half.

"Faith?"

She made an effort to pull herself together and put another smile on. "It's been a long time, Bibi. If you're okay with it, I am."

Bibi gave her a long, considering look. Then she sighed. "Okay, then. What the hell. We live in interestin' times." She hooked her arm around Faith's and led her back out through the ER.

Faith went along, lost in memory.

memory

Several of the men were standing near their bikes when Faith pulled into the lot at Cali Classics Custom Cycles. She saw her dad and Uncle Hoosier talking together at the heads of their bikes, their helmets in their hands. Looked to her like something was up.

She honked, and all the men waved. As she parked, her father came up to the door and opened it. "Hey there, kitty cat. Did I know you were comin' by?" He held out his hand, and she took it and happily let him close her up in a quick hug. He smelled like he always did, the scent she thought of as her daddy—leather, tobacco, and motor oil, a hint of British Sterling aftershave underneath.

"Poppy called and said he had a box for me." She looked over the hood of her car at the men waiting for her father. "You're heading out." It wasn't a question, just an observation—it was obvious that he was. "Does Mom know?"

"She's out with Bibi. I left her a message." He gave Faith a sheepish grin. "Guess you'll have to tell her for me. I'll be back tomorrow."

"Daddy!" That meant it would just be Faith and her mother at home tonight, and that was a terrible combination. Since Sera had gone off to college the year before, their mother had noticed Faith and decided she was really lacking in the daughter department. Without her father as a buffer, all Faith and her mother did was bicker and glare.

But her father wasn't paying her any attention. His eyes were focused on the hood of her car, the area between the two wide, black stripes down the center. "What the fuck, Faith Anne?"

As was always her immediate reaction to censure, Faith got combative. As he leaned over for a closer look, she crossed her arms and set her heels. "It's Sharpie. I'm gonna cover the whole thing."

Her dad turned and stared at her, his expression cycling from shock to anger to bemusement and back around. She thought there might have been a quick flash of pride in there somewhere, but maybe that was just wishful thinking. "Do you know how fucking long I worked on this damn thing?"

She did. She'd watched him do a lot of it. Faith wasn't much interested in mechanics, but she was deeply interested in shapes and patterns and the way things fit together, so she liked to watch her father, and all his brothers, work, even though she didn't want to learn how to do what they did.

This 1970 El Camino, white with black hood stripes, had been in the garage for about four years. She'd had no idea until she'd gotten up on her sixteenth birthday, five months ago, and found it on the driveway with a big orange bow, that he'd been restoring it for her.

It was the best present ever in the whole world.

A few weeks before, she'd cut school and driven out to San Pedro with her best friends, Bethany and Joelle. They'd been parked on a bluff, sitting on the hood, drinking from a bottle of peach brandy that Bethany had lifted from her grandma's cupboard. Faith had been drawing with a Bic pen on Jo's white Chucks. She'd looked down between their legs and had seen that white space between the black stripes, and it had been a beautiful, gleaming blank canvas.

She'd had a couple of Sharpies in her backpack. So they'd all drawn in that white space. And then, later, Faith had gone back over it all, connecting and shaping the graffiti into art. Since then, she'd filled in the whole space. Now she was working on the rear end, too. No rhyme or reason. Just the next place she'd seen where art should be.

Eventually, she'd get metallic Sharpies and fill the black stripes with gold and silver.

Her father's face finally settled on bemusement. "Fuck, kitty. That finish took weeks to get right."

Now that he wasn't mad, she relaxed her battle stance. She grabbed the edges of his kutte and smiled up at him. "I know, Daddy. I love Dante so much." She'd named her car Dante. She had no idea why, but he felt like a Dante to her. Also like a 'he.' "But this is how I make him mine and not yours. Please don't be mad."

He stared down at her, his brown eyes crinkling, and she knew he'd get over it. Finally, he sighed. "Your mother is gonna have a stroke."

Faith scoffed. "I've been doing it for weeks. Nobody even noticed until now. She doesn't pay me any attention unless school calls. She couldn't care less what I do."

Her father shook his head. "That ain't true, kitty cat. Your mother loves you. She wants you to do good is all." Before Faith could give that statement the derision it deserved, he looked over Dante's roof. "Gotta go, kitty. Sorry about tonight. Be good for your ol' dad tonight, okay?"

"Good is hard," she pouted.

He laughed and kissed her cheek. "Don't I know it. Love you love you."

"Love you love you. Be safe."

He winked and trotted off. Faith watched as the men mounted their big Harleys and rode off the lot in a roaring rumble of black thunder.

Then she turned and headed into the work bays, knowing she'd find Fat Jack back there.

On her way in, she saw a guy she didn't recognize rolling a Street Glide up to Diaz's station. He was young and super cute, tall and lean, with shaggy, light blond hair. His coverall was folded down around his waist, and his plain white t-shirt was snug and showed off wonderful, muscular arms. And he was wearing a Prospect kutte—which was what she'd noticed first.

Her dad hadn't said anything about getting a new Prospect, but she'd been around home and the clubhouse a lot less since Dante had entered her life, so maybe she just wasn't up on the news. If he was a Prospect, that made him at least twenty-one. But that was only five years older than she was. That was nothing.

She sighed. Yeah, right. She was going to die a virgin. Unkissed and untried forever. Her father would see to that. And Uncle Hooj, and Poppy, and every other man in black leather.

"Get your skinny ass over here, short stack." Fat Jack had bellowed across the bays, and the cute blond Prospect, who'd just stood the Glide on its stand, turned, looking like he thought maybe it was him Jack had been calling. He saw Faith, and their eyes met for just half a second. Oh, damn. He was way more than just cute. But then his eyes cut away, and he went back to whatever shit job he'd been assigned.

She sighed and sauntered over to Fat Jack's station. "Hey, Poppy. What you got for me?"

The man who was, for all intents and purposes, her only grandfather, despite their lack of blood relation, gave her a quick hug and a kiss on the cheek. "A strong word first. You leave that boy alone. He's got enough trouble without you making more."

Faith thought that was ridiculously unfair. She'd never caused any trouble for the guys in the club. She'd grown up with the members. She barely even noticed the hangarounds, and she didn't think they'd ever had a Prospect that was worth a second look—certainly not since she'd been looking.

"What? I just noticed he existed. No big."

"I'm old and fat, missy. I am not blind. If you'd been a Looney Tune, your eyes would have bugged out of your head about a mile. Don't get no ideas. You are jailbait, and he needs a steady place to be. A home. So keep those new little titties to yourself."

Well, that was weird and kind of gross, having Fat Jack talk about her boobs like he'd noticed them. She knew she was pretty cute, and, though they'd been slow to make their appearance, she thought these newish boobs were not too shabby—not huge, but not teeny, either. But he was not somebody she wanted to notice them.

Although it would be totally awesome if somebody somewhere that she did want to notice would notice. Not that that was ever going to happen. She was pretty sure her father had put the word out in the Greater L.A. Area that any man who even thought an impure thought about his baby girl would die a bloody death.

She knew for sure that she was going to graduate high school without even holding hands with a guy. Her father had seen to that on the first day of ninth grade, when he'd taken her to school on the back of his Softail, and the entire fucking club had ridden in formation behind them. Then they'd all sat there on their damn bikes in their damn kuttes wearing their damn black sunglasses, with their damn inked arms crossed over their damn chests, and stared until the bell rang.

Her father might as well have locked her in a steel box. No boy would even talk to her. They panicked if they got assigned to a group project with her. Even when a new boy came in, not knowing who she was, she'd get maybe one flirt, and then somebody would say something to him, and there she'd be again, alone in her force field of threatened biker aggression.

They'd done nothing of the sort when Sera had started high school. But then, Sera had been a mathlete and in Model UN and on the student council and shit like that. She was hot, but not interested. And, anyway, Faith supposed she hadn't attracted the kind of boys their father felt the need to guard against.

Apparently, he was sure Faith would. It would be cool to know if he was right.

While Fat Jack had his nose buried in a bike engine, Faith sneaked another look at the Prospect. Diaz was yelling at him, and his face was getting bright, bright red. Then he nodded and slunk off in the direction Diaz was pointing. Faith felt sorry for him. Prospects got treated like shit, that was the way of this world, but still she felt bad. He'd been blushing so hard.

"What's his name?"

Fat Jack sighed heavily and plunked a wrench on his worktable. "Michael. For now, he's just Michael."

Michael. That was a good name. She hoped he wouldn't do something to get saddled with some obnoxious road name. She knew how her father, who'd been born Alan, had ended up Blue, and it was gross. It had to do with a misapplied cock ring and an ER visit, and she would have given up a lot never to have overheard *that* drunken story.

"Box is under the table."

Faith looked around to see Fat Jack giving her a sharply pointed look, one bushy white eyebrow high on his forehead. She grinned and pulled on his long beard. "Chill out, Poppy. Jeez. Let's see what's what."

She squatted down and dug through out an open carton that had once held motor oil. Inside was a treasure trove—all different kinds of old sprockets and chains and washers and who knew what-all, a lot of them rusty. "Oh wow! This is fantastic! Thank you, thank you!"

She stood and hugged him, and he gave her one of his signature bear grapples, lifting her off the floor and leaning back a ways, so she was resting on his big belly. Then he set her down and clutched at his back. "I'm gettin' too old for that, even with a little shit like you." He nodded at the box. "Make me somethin' cool."

"I will, Poppy. It'll be the coolest." Faith didn't care a whit about making an engine run the way it was supposed to run. But she thought the parts that made it work were fascinating and beautiful. She saw other things in them than engines or brake assemblies or whatever. She saw people. Or trees. Or sunsets. Or just shapes, big and elaborate and weird. She would dump a box like this out on the garage floor at home and wait to see what it showed her.

She had a soldering iron. Someday, she wanted to have a blow torch. A big industrial one.

She squatted again and took hold of the box—but when she tried to lift it, she ended up dropping to a knee. It was *way* heavier than she'd expected.

"Fuck! It's heavy!"

Fat Jack laughed. "It's full of metal, goof." He looked down at the box, and Faith saw him realize that he probably wouldn't be able to lift it, either. He'd been big and strong once, but he was somewhere past seventy. He still did his miles and kept his VP patch, but he was, as he said all the time, 'getting too old for this shit.'

He sighed and then yelled, "PROSPECT! GET YER ASS OUT HERE!"

The new Prospect—Michael, Faith reminded herself—came back out through the door that led to the clubhouse, moving at a hurried clip. "Yeah, Jack?"

Oh, he had a nice voice. Soft and deep at the same time.

"This here is Faith. She's Blue's little girl. Take this box and put it in her car. Then get your scrawny ass back here."

Michael met Faith's eyes again, and then cut away again just as quickly. Lifting the box like it was filled with bubbles instead of engine parts, he said, "Sure thing. Lead the way."

Fat Jack gave Faith another pointed look. She rolled her eyes and kissed his cheek, then headed toward Dante with Michael in tow. He hadn't even bothered to look her over, so she honestly had no idea what powerful sorcery Jack thought she had that was going to get the guy in such trouble.

"You can just put it in the back. Thanks."

Michael tucked the box in the corner of Dante's bed, just behind the driver's seat. "Nice ride."

"Thanks. My dad fixed it up for me."

"That's Blue, huh?"

"Yep. That's him."

He nodded. "Okay. See ya." Halfway through his turn toward the shop, he stopped. "What's goin' on there?" He pointed to the center of Dante's hood.

She shrugged, but he wasn't looking at her to see it, so she said, "Just something I felt like doing. I figure I'll do the whole thing like that eventually."

"It looks good. That'll be rad. They have these metallic markers, too. You could do the stripes with those."

Faith looked hard at him. His left ear was pierced—just a thick ring through the lobe, with a hematite ball at the connection point. "Yeah. That's what I was thinking."

He turned and finally really looked at her. His eyes were a crazy-intense kind of blue. Her mother loved these dumb romance novels, the bodice-ripper kind, where the women were all virgins with heaving, alabaster breasts wedged into miles of heavy brocade, and the men were all pirates or highwaymen who were really nobles in disguise, the rebellious second sons of dukes and earls or whatever—Faith knew this because she'd read just about all of them in middle school, sneaking them from the box under her parents' bed and devouring them in the corner behind her own bed as if they were the best and sickest kind of porn. To her twelve-year-old eyes, that was exactly what they'd been.

Before she got boobs, she got hormones, and she'd had a few fantasies about being one of those heaving-breasted virgins getting accosted by dashing highwaymen.

All the heroes and heroines in those books had gemstones for eyes—jade and emerald, aquamarine and amethyst. Even at twelve, she'd thought that was a dumb way to describe eyes. She'd never seen a single pair of real eyes that looked remotely like emeralds, and she was pretty sure real eyes the actual color of amethyst were a physical impossibility.

Her own eyes were a weird combination of brown, blue, and green that her mother called 'hazel.' The closest they'd come to a gemstone would be like a slimy, algae-covered rock on the beach.

But Michael's eyes—they were exactly the color of lapis lazuli. Exactly. That was her story, and she was sticking to it.

He smiled. And Faith had no idea what kind of mystical power she might have over anybody, but at that moment, she herself was completely ensorcelled.

She smiled back, and for a timeless second, they just looked at each other.

Then his eyes fell, and the moment was gone. "See ya," he said again, and this time when he turned, he didn't pause. Faith watched him walk back to the shop.

She knew he'd never touch her. No man ever would, not as long as her father was anywhere within striking distance—and certainly no man in the club would come near her, even if she were of age. But if anybody ever would, she knew she wanted it to be him.

Michael.

CHAPTER TWO

"PA! PA! PAPAPAPAPAPAPA! PA!"

Demon's eyes flew open at the sounds of his son's shrieks, magnified by the baby monitor sitting on the bedside table. He didn't really need the monitor; his room and Tucker's were separated only by a bathroom, but Bibi had bought it, and he felt better having it around.

Without bothering to put on a shirt, Demon stumbled through the walkthrough bathroom—Bibi had called this a 'Jack and Jill suite,' but he didn't know why—and into his son's room. He was standing in his crib sobbing, his face red. The room reeked of urine and sweat.

Fuck. Another night terror. What was going on in that two-year-old head that had made this happen? What had he seen already?

Demon knew the horrors a foster kid could see and experience. He knew them firsthand and intimately. But Tucker had only been away from family for a few weeks, and Sid, Muse's old lady, who was a social worker and had once been Tucker's caseworker, had told Demon that his first placement had been a good one. His second placement was here, with family. Until Demon could get custody of him himself.

Tucker's worst home had been with his own junkie gash of a mother. If he'd seen anything to break his little mind, it had been with her.

Seeing his father, Tucker raised his arms, and his shrieking intensified. Demon went to him and picked him up, holding him close, ignoring the sopping wet that had maxed out Tucker's diaper and soaked his pajamas. Once he had his arms around his son, the shrieking settled into hiccupping gasps, and Tucker let his head drop to his father's shoulder.

"Hey, hey, Motor Man. It's okay. Pa's here." He'd thought he'd be 'Dad' or 'Daddy,' but Tucker called him 'Pa.' Since Tucker hardly talked at all, Demon wasn't about to try to change it.

"Pa," his son sighed.

"Bad dreams, buddy?"

Tucker nodded, his sweaty hair ruffling against Demon's bare shoulder. His little body was still racked with those hiccupping gasps.

"Okay. Let's get you into the bath and get you cleaned up." He carried Tucker into the bathroom and set him on the floor, then turned the tub faucet on and massaged the taps until he had a good temperature. Tucker busied himself in the cupboard under the sink, pulling out plastic boats and rubber ducks and other animals.

"C'mere, buddy. Let's get that thing off you."

Tucker shook his head, giving his father a determined look. His eyes were still wet from his tears, but his heavy gasps were fading out. His terror was behind him.

"Boa*t*s." He hit the 'T' extra hard. His speech therapist was working with him on completing his word sounds or something like that.

The thought of his kid getting worked over by a 'therapist,' even a 'speech therapist,' made Demon's stomach hurt. No 'therapist' had ever done anything for him but make his life harder. And it had never been a walk in the fucking park to begin with. But Tucker's new caseworker, Rex, said it was 'strongly recommended,' and Bibi, who was Tucker's official legal guardian, told him that he really wasn't talking like he should be, and that doing what the caseworker recommended would help Demon's case to get custody for himself.

So twice a week either Bibi or Demon took Tucker to 'go play with Miss Kathy.' And Demon supposed maybe it was helping.

He did have more words now, anyway. Sometimes even little sentences.

He turned off the faucet and added a couple of drops of lavender oil, which smelled weird, but not exactly bad, and Bibi had said it would be soothing after a night terror. As he swirled his hand in the warm water, moving the oil around, he said. "Okay. Bring your boats."

Tucker grinned at him, and Demon's heart did a thing it only did when his son looked at him like that—like he was a good guy. Like Tucker loved him. Like he trusted him.

He was sure he didn't deserve that. He knew he was loved—by Bibi and Hoosier, by his brothers, by his son. He held that knowledge, and the love he felt for all of them, close. But most people, even those who loved him, kept a shade of wariness in their eyes, too. *That*, he knew he deserved. He had trouble controlling himself when he got emotional. He'd only ever really hurt one person he cared about, physically at least: Tucker's mom. And by the time he'd hurt her, they hadn't cared about each other at all. But still, he'd almost killed her.

It didn't matter that she'd known she was pushing all his bright-red buttons over and over; it didn't matter that she'd done it to fuck him up, that she'd hated him so much by then that she'd been willing to take the weight of his fists just so she could bring him down. He'd beaten her almost to death, and that was the biggest reason that he was sitting on the floor in Bibi and Hoosier's 'Jack and Jill' bathroom, basically babysitting his own son.

The people who loved him knew what he was capable of. So their love was tinged with caution.

Tucker was the only person in his life who'd ever looked at him with open trust.

No. Not true. One other. But not for a very long time. And he hadn't deserved that trust at all.

He would deserve his son's trust. Whatever he had to do, he would be strong and steady, calm and controlled with his boy. He would eat his gun before he'd hurt Tucker—or allow anyone else to, ever again.

And that was why he would hurt Tucker's mother again—and this time on purpose—if she ever crossed his path again. She'd disappeared right after DCFS took Tucker from her, and that was the one smart move that cunt had ever made.

~oOo~

After he washed Tucker, and himself, up, Demon let him play in the bath while he went back into the bedroom and changed the crib bedding. He gathered up the soiled pajamas and bedclothes and made a little bundle on the bathroom floor. He'd get them in the wash once Tucker was back in bed.

The lavender oil was supposed to be soothing, and Tucker was indeed calm and happy as Demon drained the tub and wrapped him up in a towel, but he was wide awake. It was the middle of the night, and Demon was opening at the bike shop in the morning. Since the club had gone outlaw again, he was doing long shifts at Virtuoso Cycles, picking up repair and maintenance jobs his brothers didn't have time for.

They were doing all they could to help him keep his nose clean. Though he'd loved the outlaw life, and he'd needed the release that kind of work had given him, he'd been frantic and furious when the club had voted to go back to it. That life had to be behind him. Now he had to focus on his kid. He had to stay out of the fray. He could not get arrested again, and he *absolutely* could not do time again.

They all understood, so now he was all but managing the bike shop. And making about half the bank his brothers were. But it was worth it, if it meant he could finally get custody and get DCFS out of their fucking lives.

Once he had Tucker in a clean diaper and pajamas, he carried him out to the kitchen. "You want some milk, Motor Man?" Warm milk seemed to make Tucker sleepy. At almost three in the morning, Demon wasn't averse to a little trickery.

Tucker nodded, and Demon got to work, taking down a small saucepan from the rack hanging over Bibi's island and pouring a little whole milk into it, all while Tucker rested on his hip. He'd come to understand why women always seemed to jut a hip out when they held a child. They were making a ledge. Demon's hips didn't work that way, so he kept his arm under his son's little bottom, and Tucker held on with his legs and arms.

When Demon turned the gas flame on under the saucepan, Tucker tensed, his blue eyes wide. "No, Tuck! Hot! Hot!" he said, his little voice emphatic. He shook a hand as if he'd just touched a hot thing and then blew hard on his fingers, his cheeks puffing out.

Demon smiled and caught those fingers in his hand and brought them to his lips for a kiss. "That's right. The stove is hot, huh? Only big people can touch it." A couple of weeks ago, Tucker had touched his fingertips to a pot on the stove. Bibi had been about a second too slow to stop him. He'd ended up with blisters on the tips of three fingers, and Demon had been terrified that Rex, or Miss Kathy, or somebody would use that as a reason to take him from Bibi and Hoosier. Rex had asked about it, but nobody had made it into a deal. Kids got hurt sometimes.

And Demon felt better that even a fantastic mom like Bibi could screw up once in awhile.

As he poured warmed milk into one of Tucker's sippy cups, he noticed a tented piece of paper on the counter—from the magnetic pad Bibi kept on the side of the fridge for her grocery list. On it, she'd written, *Had to go out. Might be away until breakfast. If so, will call. No worries, though. Love you, B.*

Demon set the paper back down and finished preparing Tucker's milk. That was a little weird, Bibi going out in the middle of the night, but not entirely unheard of. She was involved in every little thing everywhere. She was probably helping somebody out.

He chuckled. Maybe she was delivering a baby or something. With Bibi, it could be just about anything.

That thought, though, made him pause as he was handing the cup to Tucker. How pregnant was Riley? Like seven months or something, he thought. Not so far gone that Bart had stayed back from the run most of the club was on right now. Damn, Demon hoped it wasn't that.

Tucker grunted in frustration, his hand extended. "Mook!"

"Sorry, bud. Here ya go. Let's watch some TV. You want Cars?"

He shook his head. "Mins!"

Despicable Me it was. He carried his son into the family room and settled onto Bibi and Hoosier's ultra-comfortable sectional sofa. They had a big television installed over the fireplace and an elaborate home theater system that filled a built-in bookcase at one side. He got the movie going and settled back, with his son reclining against his chest, sucking lazily at his cup of warm milk. Demon pulled a throw off the back of the sectional and covered them both with it. He turned off the lamp on the table behind them.

They were alone in the house. The erratic glow of the television was the only light in the room. His son lay quietly on his lap, one hand holding his cup to his mouth, the other plucking absently at the leg of Demon's sweatpants. He smelled of lavender and baby shampoo. They both did.

Moments like this were the only times Demon ever knew genuine peace.

~oOo~

Tucker was sound asleep, his half-finished milk forgotten, less than half an hour into the movie, but Demon was in no hurry to put him back to bed. He liked this movie; it was funny and pretty cute. Way better than some of the other movies Tucker liked—

and some of the TV shows made him want to tear his eyeballs out.

But it was more than just enjoying a movie he'd seen about a hundred million times. He was warm and happy, snugged up with his son. Sure, he'd be wiped out for work, but he could just close his eyes right where he was and get a couple more hours of sleep.

He was drowsing off when he heard the grind and squeak of the automatic garage door going up. Bibi was home. The door into the garage was in the family room, so Demon stayed put, knowing he'd be one of the first things Bibi saw when she came in.

It took longer than he expected for the door to open—long enough that he was working out the logistics of laying Tucker down on the sofa without waking him so he could go out and make sure she didn't need help. But then the door opened, and Bibi came through.

She flipped the switch near the door, and the can lights over the fireplace came on, brightening up the room a little. Then she saw him and stopped in the doorway, her hand still on the knob, and just stared at him.

He lifted his hand in a little wave and smiled. His voice low, he said, "Shh. Tucker had a rough spell. He's okay now, though."

Still, Bibi just stood where she was, saying nothing—and *that* was not like her at all. She even pulled the door back toward her, almost as if she were thinking about reversing course.

"You need help with something, Mama?" he asked, keeping his voice low and steady.

Bibi sighed and then squared her shoulders, like she was about to face a firing squad or something. "No, baby. I brought a friend home, Demc."

"Okay..." He was curious, but more about Bibi acting strangely than anything else. The thought flickered briefly that maybe

Beeb was bringing home a boy toy while Hoosier was off on the run, but he shooed that nutso notion away.

She opened the door all the way and then stepped into the room.

A woman stepped in behind her, looking even more reluctant than Bibi had been. He thought it was a woman, though maybe just a girl. She was petite, not more than five-two or five-three, wearing baggy sweatpants and a baggier hoodie, and those fucking ugly Eskimo boots lots of chicks used to wear. She had dark hair, caught up in some kind of disheveled knot on the back of her head.

He hadn't seen her face, because she was staring at those butt-ugly boots.

And then she looked up. It took maybe three-quarters of one second for Demon to really see her, those fucking gorgeous eyes that had, long ago, looked up at him with perfect trust. By the time that first second was complete, his world had collapsed around him.

"Hi, Michael," she said. That beautiful, sweet voice cracked over his name. Oh, fuck. Oh, fuck. Oh, fuck, fuck, fuck, fuck, fuck.

Forgetting that his son was sleeping on his lap, Demon jumped up, remembering just in time to catch Tucker before he dropped him right on the floor. Fuck!

Tucker woke and began to cry. "No, Pa!" he wailed as Demon tried to turn him and settle him on his shoulder. "No!"

Bibi finally moved again and came to them. "I'll take him, honey. I'll rock him back to sleep. Okay?"

Tucker turned at Bibi's touch and held his arms out to her. Still staring at Faith—fucking hell, *Faith* was standing right there—Demon let his son go, and Bibi carried him, still crying, out of the room and down the hall.

And then Demon was alone in a room with Faith Fordham.

Sweet Jesus fuck. He didn't know what to do.

Maybe she didn't, either. She hadn't moved. The garage door was even still open.

"Your son is beautiful."

She spoke hesitantly, shyly, and her voice broke again. Fuck, that hurt his heart so bad. Ten years had passed, but that span of time meant nothing. *Nothing.* He felt just as raw and broken as he'd been that night they'd ripped the Los Angeles patch off his kutte and taken his home away. The only home he'd ever had.

How could that be? How could a decade just disappear? How could all that time not make things softer, easier to bear?

She closed the door and took a step toward him—and he took one backward. If she came close, if she touched him, if he touched her, time would truly reverse. He could feel it. They'd end up back where they were the last time he'd laid eyes on her—him strung up in the shop and her screaming at her father to stop, to please stop, just stop.

Faith's mother holding her shoulders and making her see. Demon trying not to lose sight of her, knowing it was the end of them.

The whole club watching it all go down.

"Michael." She took another step. He backed up again—and his calves hit the other side of the sectional. He was fucking trapped. Unless he turned tail and ran, he was trapped.

And she kept coming, closing the distance between them. Ten feet, ten years.

That was how it had always been between them—him trying to back away, knowing they were wrong, and her not letting him, knowing that he wanted what she did, knowing he wouldn't be able to resist.

But she'd been just a kid. He'd been a man. It didn't matter whether they were five years apart in age or fifty. She'd been a kid, the daughter of one of his brothers. It had been on him to do the right thing, and he hadn't.

She stood right in front of him now, her expression tortured and afraid, mirroring what he felt in his own heart. Then she put her hands on his chest, and he realized he wasn't wearing a shirt. He felt completely naked, exposed and bare. Her touch felt as intense as if she had lifted his very nerves in her hands, and his cock filled out immediately, so hard it ached. He knew it was obvious, tenting his sweatpants absurdly, but her eyes had not left his, and they still weren't touching anywhere but her hands on his chest.

"Michael."

He couldn't remember if she'd said anything more than that one word since she'd walked in—which was one more word than he'd said. There were no words he could say.

He'd been given the name Demon while he was still a Prospect, before he and Faith had crossed the point of no return, but she'd never called him anything but Michael. Since he'd last seen her, the only people who really ever called him Michael were legal types—lawyers and caseworkers and cops. He'd grown to cringe when he heard it, because it always meant some bureaucrat had his fist deep up Demon's ass.

When she said it, though—that was home. Oh, fuck.

Her hands moved, sliding softly down and around his waist, leaving his nerves thrumming in a path behind her touch.

He needed to get away. His heart was pounding so hard his vision vibrated, and the thoughts in his head were shrieking and clamoring in an indecipherable mob. He'd been right—at her touch, everything was back. Ten years were just gone. He felt exactly as he had then—confused and sorry, in pain and in love.

Losing fucking everything.

Wrong. All of it was so fucking wrong. He needed to get clear.

Instead, he grabbed her face in his hands and kissed her.

She opened to him immediately, molding her body to his, clutching him close so that his erection was pressed tightly to her belly. She whimpered, and the sound surrounded his heart and squeezed. He groaned and wrapped his arms around her, lifting her off the floor—she was so light, so little, and she felt exactly as he remembered, exactly right. His tongue explored her mouth, finding it perfectly familiar. God. *God.*

He tasted salt on their tongues.

She was crying.

So was he.

He set her back on the floor and pushed her away, and then he did what he should have done before. He turned tail and ran.

Without looking back, he went down the hall to Tucker's room. Bibi was just walking out.

She gave him a sharp look and then lifted her hand to his face and wiped his wet check. "Oh, baby," she whispered. "Oh, darlin'."

Words had not yet returned to him, so he simply looked down at her.

"He's sleepin', baby. You should get some sleep, too." She slid her hand around to the back of his neck and pulled his head down. He didn't fight her. She kissed his cheek. "I love you, Deme. Whatever happens, it'll be okay. We'll stick it out together."

He stood straight up. That wasn't how it had worked out last time. But still he said nothing.

With a reassuring pat on his bare arm, Bibi headed back toward the family room. Demon went into his son's room and closed the door. Then he locked it. He locked the door to the bathroom, too.

For a long time, he stood at the side of the crib, watching his son peacefully sleeping. He tried to make himself remember that peace he'd been feeling, watching an animated movie, snug under a blanket with his little boy. But all his mind wanted to remember was Faith. He shouldn't have kissed her. That kiss felt like another point of no return. Why the *fuck* couldn't he control himself better? Why the *fuck* was it always wrong urges that got the reins in their teeth? Why the *fuck* did he feel everything—*everything*—so fucking hard?

After a while, feeling finally the sleepiness that matched his utter, desolate exhaustion, he sat on the floor and grabbed Tucker's big stuffed dog. Using that as a pillow, he curled up at the side of the crib and tried to sleep, lost in the memory of the first time his lips had touched hers.

memory

Michael walked out into the hot sunshine of an L.A. spring afternoon. No, he was Demon now. He needed to learn to think of himself that way, though he wasn't sure how he felt about it as a name. He guessed it sounded pretty badass, though it really came from being made fun of. Nobody but club needed to know that part, though.

Could be worse—the other Prospect, who'd only been wearing a kutte for a few weeks, was already being called 'Crapper,' because he'd gotten trapped in a port-a-potty. That would be way worse.

Demon was pretty sure that guy was going to wash out, though. He was a lot older, in his thirties, probably, and he bitched a lot about the work Prospects had to do. Demon knew to just shut up and do it, whatever it was.

He'd dug a big grave in the woods a couple of nights ago and dumped three reeking, half-decomposed bodies into it. No idea who they'd been or why they'd gotten dead. He hadn't asked. Hoosier had said dig, so he'd dug.

He'd been prospecting for just over three months, and it had been the three best months of his fucking sad excuse for a life. For the first time in his whole life, he had a home—a place where he could really sleep at night, without being on guard for bad shit of one kind or another to go down on him. A place where, when he got up in the morning, people smiled and said 'hey' and fed him breakfast. Sure, he also had to bury bodies or unclog vile toilets or whatever job the patches could think up for him, but he could see that they liked him, too. He felt their affection for him. They let him in on the jokes.

And when he'd gone mental on that asshole at the party a couple of weeks ago, they'd fixed it up for him and started calling him Demon, laughing at the way his face had gone fire-engine red.

So yeah, Demon was an okay name.

But right now, he was fucked. Hoosier was in a terror of a mood about something, and Demon knew he was looking for a reason to fuck somebody up. Now he was standing in the middle of the lot with a shopping list of parts for Hoosier's pet restoration project. Big parts. Not just nuts and bolts. But the club van and the flatbed were both gone. Demon had only his little bobber. He had no idea how the fuck he was supposed to manage to bring these parts back from the salvage yard. Or why Hoosier was even trusting him with a job like this. It felt like it was preloaded for a fuckup.

Maybe he could rent a U-Haul? No way. He was tapped out. Plus, he didn't think they would rent to a twenty-one-year-old, even if he'd had the scratch.

So he just stood there, the cheerful sun beating down on his head. The gorgeous day was mocking him.

"You get stuck on a wad of gum or something?"

He knew the voice coming up behind him, and he got a hit of adrenaline. Faith—Blue's daughter. He thought about her way too fucking much, and no matter how hard he tried to avoid her, he kept finding himself crossing paths with her. She was sweet and sarcastic, and so pretty—long, dark hair; big, beautiful eyes in a color that seemed different every time he saw them. She was small and slim, with pretty little tits…FUCK. Fucking stop it!

She was a patch's daughter. She was the fucking SAA's daughter. She was sixteen years old. He was trapped between needing to stay the fuck away and needing to be nice to her. And wanting her a crazy amount of want.

He'd never really wanted anybody before. Sex was not a thing he'd thought much about until recently. In fact, it was a thing he'd tried not to think about. Usually when he thought about it, he didn't think happy thoughts.

He'd gone into the system when he was two years old, and he'd never had a private-home placement for more than a few weeks.

By the time he was seven, he had such a long list of letters attached to his file no family would come near him.

ODD—Oppositional Defiant Disorder. ADHD—Attention Deficit-Hyperactivity Disorder. OCD—Obsessive Compulsive Disorder. BPD—Borderline Personality Disorder. Bi-polar Disorder. Chronic Depression. He'd been diagnosed at some point with all of those things. He had no idea if he actually had them all—or if he even had any of them.

But nobody wanted a kid like that.

He hadn't known that at the time, of course. He'd found all that out when he'd aged out and seen his file. At the time, he'd just been a kid nobody wanted. So he'd grown up in group homes. And juvie—a few years there, too.

Not much difference between one or the other, frankly. In both places, he'd fought for his life on a pretty regular basis. In both places, somebody bigger and stronger had always held him down in one way or another. Until he'd gotten big and strong enough to resist and to win.

So sex wasn't something he was all that keen on. Once he was on his own, he'd avoided it all.

But then he'd found the club. By the time he'd applied to prospect, he understood that there were things about that life he was going to need to get right with. He didn't want to start out that way in the clubhouse, around people he knew. So he'd saved up and bought himself a whole night with a hooker.

She was pretty nice and really patient. He thought of that as the night he lost his virginity, whether that was true or not. Just about four months ago.

Since then, he'd gotten comfortable with the girls in the clubhouse. He even thought maybe he was getting decent at it, and usually he had only good thoughts now. As a Prospect, he got the leftovers, but that was okay with him. He was just trying to get used to all this without anybody knowing that was what he was trying to do.

Faith, Blue's youngest daughter, was the first girl he'd ever really wanted. And it was wrong, wrong, wrong, wrong. Like head-on-a-pike wrong.

"Michael? Are you in there?" She still called him Michael. She was already the only one who still did. He didn't correct her. He liked it.

"Yeah, sorry. What's up?" He strove to keep his voice nonchalant. "Shouldn't you be in school?"

"Minimum day." She walked around to face him. She was dressed like she usually was—jeans, brown engineer boots, and a snug t-shirt that didn't quite reach the low waistband on her jeans. So unfair. He willed his cock to behave. It ignored him. "Why are you standing in the middle of the lot? You look like your download froze."

He smiled, and she smiled right back, her eyes dancing with light and color. "Sorry. Just trying to work something out."

"What's the troub, bub?" She slid her hands into her front pockets, which pulled her jeans down even farther. Demon looked up and out over the lot, to La Cienega Boulevard.

Knowing he should blow her off and send her on her way, he said, "Hooj gave me a list for salvage, but the van's out. Flatbed, too."

Faith actually bounced. "Pik-A-Part? I love that place! We can take Dante!"

That was a terrible idea. There should have been brakes squealing in his head. Better to face Hoosier's wrath when he found out he had to wait until the van got back than to go with Blue's little girl off the compound lot and all the way to the Valley.

Demon knew that to be true. But the switch people had that made them stop before they did something stupid—his didn't work. He had the switch that told him it was stupid, and the switch that told him he *should* stop, but the switch that *would* stop him was badly broken. Sometimes, it was like his own life was playing out on a screen, and he was just sitting there, powerless, watching with his fingers splayed over his eyes.

"That'd be great—if you don't need to be anywhere."

"I'm a free agent. And Pik-A-Part is better than fucking Disneyland. Let's do it!" She threw her keys at him, and he caught them. They headed off together toward Dante.

She hadn't done much more to her car with markers—just, as far as he could tell, the side mirrors and the full rear bumper. She'd told him that she did it when the mood struck her, when she saw whatever belonged wherever it belonged. She'd had a few people sign it, he'd noticed, and then she'd drawn around the signatures to incorporate them into whatever it was she was making.

He really did think it was cool. Like something he'd do, if he had a talent like that—to just see something and then do it, to follow the impulse. That generally meant trouble for him. But Faith had talent, so her impulses became art.

His just became trash.

~oOo~

Pik-A-Part was a junkyard that let people scavenge at their own risk. You went through, driving anywhere you could get your vehicle through, and just dug into the junk. There was a vague kind of organization—Fords in one general direction, Chevys in another, bikes sort of on the side, and so on—but for the most part, you just scavenged, doing what you had to do to get the part you wanted. Sometimes, you had to dig under rickety piles of rusty metal; sometimes you had to climb on top of those piles. Sometimes the part you wanted was sitting right there on the ground like it had been set out special, just for you.

When you had what you wanted, you went back up to the front, where a Quonset hut served as office and shop, and you dickered your way to a price for your loot. The club had an account, so all Demon, wearing his kutte, would have to say was that the stuff he'd gotten was for Hoosier, and it would go out for cost.

He'd gotten everything Hoosier wanted—or he was pretty sure. Some of the parts were a little rough, but they were original stock parts, which was what Hooj was after. Everything was in Dante's bed. Now, though, Demon was busy having a heart attack because Faith was climbing through the carcass of an old Plymouth Fury, which was perched on top of a stack of old carcasses. Even with all the climbing and moving around she'd been doing, nothing had moved, so it seemed pretty stable. Still, though, if she got hurt—or worse—on his watch, well, he'd be better off crawling into one of the rusty hulls waiting for the crusher and just waiting right along with it.

She'd been running around the place for a couple of hours, acting like every pile of junk was the best thrill ride ever. She had herself a bizarre mishmash of crap she was going to put on the same account—she'd said she did that all the time, and Demon hoped that was true. He knew what she intended it for. She made things out of junk. Like sculptures, or something. Blue, Hoosier, and Fat Jack all had stuff she'd made sitting or hanging around their stations.

It was pretty cool. He didn't really see what she saw in the junk or in the sculptures she made out of it, but it was cool the way she saw things in a way he couldn't. And it was cooler the way she made what was there become what she saw.

He looked up at the mountain of junk she was on and tried to ignore her pretty ass. She was half lying in the Fury, reaching for something. She looked like somebody who was about to die in a horror movie. One of those *Final Destination* things. The thought made him woozy.

He knew if he nagged at her to be careful again, she'd do something crazy on purpose. The last time he'd said anything, she'd literally hung upside down by her knees off a length of rebar that was jutting out of a pile. He'd had to lean against Dante for a few minutes after that.

"Faith, come on. I gotta get back. Hooj is gonna have my hide." That was true—they'd been here for hours.

She looked down at him, under her arm. "You are such a pill. Okay, okay. There's a shifter knob up here. I can't get it loose. Gimme a couple more minutes to try." She grunted with the effort. "Fuck!" She kicked hard in frustration, and that time, Demon was damn sure something shook.

"Faith!"

"One...more...Hah! Got it! Got it! Look—shiny!" She turned to show him, holding the black knob—nothing special, just a plastic ball—back and out to him. Then she squealed. "Ow! Fuck, ow!"

All the blood in Demon's body fell to his feet and then charged up in a rush to his head. "Faith?"

"My hair—I'm caught in something. Fuck! Ow, ow, ow!" She dropped the shifter knob and it bounced and rolled down the pile like the catalyst in a Rube Goldberg machine.

Rube Goldberg...*Final Destination*...Demon was going to fucking puke.

"Don't move! Fucking freeze! I'm coming!" Not registering that he was about twice her size and probably only going to make everything worse, he headed up Junk Mountain. He moved quickly but as carefully as he knew how and managed to get himself into the Fury with her, half-lying face to face with her. She'd stayed quiet and still, doing as he'd said.

Her ponytail was wound around part of the rusted-out remnants of the drivetrain. He got his arms around her head and worked the strands loose as gently as he could. Her hair felt like silk.

She smelled like dirt and rust and oil. Also flowers of some kind.

She was a kid. A kid, a kid, a kid. A kid. Blue's kid.

When her hair was free, she sighed happily and then giggled. "You just rescued me. I feel like Rapunzel."

"Who's that?"

"Rapunzel? The fairy tale princess with the long, long hair? She was locked in a tower and the prince climbed her hair to rescue her? 'Rapunzel, Rapunzel, let down your hair'?"

He just stared at her, not knowing what she was talking about but not caring. Her eyes were so pretty. Today, they were mostly blue, he thought.

"You don't know Rapunzel?"

He shrugged, and her eyes got sad. He didn't like that at all. He didn't want her sad for him. That was pity, and he didn't need her pity because he didn't know a stupid fairy tale princess. Life was not a stupid fairy tale, and if she thought it was, she was just as stupid as Rapun-whoever. "You go down first. I'll follow. Be careful."

Her only answer was a nod.

When they were safely on the ground at Dante's side, they had an awkward moment when he was still feeling really pissed and defensive without being entirely sure why, and he could see that she sensed his feelings.

Then she got a goofy grin on her face and ducked to the ground. When she came back up, she had the shifter knob in her hand. "Aha! Cool!" She wiped it on her t-shirt. "See? Shiny!"

She looked so cute and proud of herself that his mood dissipated, and he laughed. Then she kissed the knob. Watching her full lips purse around that piece of plastic, Demon felt an urge that would have overpowered any inhibition, even had he had one. He slid his hands over her jaw, cradling her head, and he bent down and kissed her.

Before his lips had even reached hers, she was with him. Her hands went to his hips and her body bent backward, molding to his. It was her tongue, not his, that moved first, sweeping along his lower lip. Fuck, he'd never been so hard ever in his whole life. His body was functioning on a purely physical, elemental level, and his tongue overpowered hers and pushed into her mouth. He'd never kissed anybody like this, where he wasn't even paying any attention to what he was doing or what she was doing. All he knew was the feeling, the way his heart pounded, the hot silk of her skin in his hands, the way her body slotted against his like it belonged there.

The way he wanted so much more.

Then she pulled back—just an inch, but it was enough for sense to shoulder its way back into a corner of his head.

"Fuck. I'm sorry." He let her go.

But she grabbed his kutte. "Don't be sorry. Please don't be sorry."

He looked into her eyes and tried to see what she was thinking. He thought he could see. He thought he saw trust and desire. But she was so much better than he was. Even if she hadn't been untouchable, she was out of his reach.

"We can't…"

She sighed and looked up at the clear blue sky. "I know. I know. The story of my fucking life." Her eyes came back to his. "But that was my first kiss, so don't be sorry. If you're sorry, that ruins the memory."

"Your first…? You never…?"

"Nope. And it was *awesome*. So don't be sorry, okay?"

He smiled. "Okay." He wasn't sorry anymore. He was proud, actually. And sad.

~oOo~

When they got back to the club compound, the van was back—and so were the patches that had been on the run with it. Including Blue. By the time Demon had Dante parked and had met Faith at the back of the car to hand her back her keys, Blue was just about on them. He ignored Demon and smiled at his daughter.

"Hey, kitty cat. Where you two been?"

"We went to Pik-A-Part. Michael needed to get some stuff for Uncle Hooj, and the van was gone, so I let him use Dante. *And* I got some sweet stuff for myself, too. I put it on the account. That's okay, right?"

"How much?"

"About twenty bucks is all."

"Yeah, that's fine." He turned and shouted toward the open bays, "CRAPPER! GET OUT HERE AND HELP DEME GET THIS SHIT INSIDE."

Crapper walked out, moving a lot more slowly than Demon would have, and they two unloaded Dante and brought Hoosier's parts to his station. When they were done, Demon started to head back to say goodbye to Faith, but Fat Jack grabbed his arm hard.

"Stay put, kid. Don't make it worse."

The possibilities of badness that Jack's warning portended were infinite. So Demon swallowed and stayed put, watching Blue hug Faith and send her on her way. He watched his daughter drive away, standing in the lot until Dante was out of sight.

Then he turned and headed back to the bays, moving fast, his head and shoulders brought forward like a charging bull. Demon locked his knees and stood firm. Whatever was about to happen, he would take it.

Blue grabbed a long, heavy screwdriver from a worktable he passed and came straight at Demon with it. Still, Demon held.

When Blue reached out and grabbed him by the throat and dragged him back until he was bent backward over Fat Jack's worktable, he went, not fighting, but not making a sound, either. When Blue shoved that driver into the soft underside of his chin, almost to the point of penetration, Demon held and kept his eyes on Blue's.

"That is my little girl. If you touch a hair on her, I will cut off your dick, and I will fuck you right up the ass with it. Then I will shove it down your throat until you choke to death on it. Am I coming through here?"

Demon felt sick and dizzy and furious and scared. His face was hot, so hot, and he knew that meant he was blazing, beet red. He could sense that everyone in the bays was watching, that people had come from the clubhouse, too, and that they were all giving the scene a wide berth.

But all he did was nod. His eyes steady on Blue's, the screwdriver digging dangerously into his flesh, he lifted his head and dropped it, twice, acknowledging that yes, Blue had come through loud and clear.

He understood. Faith was not meant for the likes of him.

CHAPTER THREE

Faith hadn't slept. Maybe she'd dozed a little, drifting off into memory more than dream. But for the few hours between the moment Michael had turned and left her, again, and the moment the light in the sky became bright enough to call morning, what Faith mostly did was cry.

When Bibi had come back into the room, she hadn't said much. She'd simply hugged her and then shown her where she could sleep. Then she'd said good night, hugged her again, and left her to her spiraling emotions.

So much was so fucked up. Just all of a sudden. She thought about the morning before, waking up in her loft a couple of blocks off the Venice Beach Boardwalk, having a regular morning before a regular day. Going down to Slow Drips for a coffee and a blueberry crunch muffin, hanging out in the sunshine, doing February as only Southern California did it, then going back to the loft to work on one of her current projects.

Her life. She'd been having her life. It was pretty good, all in all. Nothing special, but hers.

Now, twenty-four hours later, all that, all those years of her pretty good life, felt like a dream, one that was breaking into pieces and blowing away as she sat up.

Though she'd grown up with Hoosier and Bibi as her second set of parents and Connor as her honorary brother, though she'd spent about as much time in their house as in her own parents' house, the bedroom she was sitting in now was alien to her. She'd never been in *this* house. She'd never been in *this* town. She'd never known *this* club. She'd never known *this* life.

In the years she'd been away, everything had changed. And yet, somehow, they'd managed to pull her back into her old life, one that didn't even exist anymore. It made no sense, and it made her feel disoriented, as if the floor under her feet were unstable, like a carnival funhouse, each room tilting a different way.

Michael was here. Michael. He'd turned away from her, left her standing alone, but he was here, and he hadn't gone far.

Michael.

She'd known he was back, of course. Bibi had never talked about him much, and Faith had never asked outright, but enough had gotten through during their occasional chats over the years to let her know that he'd been called home from exile with the Nomad charter and offered his L.A. patch back shortly after her father had been killed. She didn't know the details. But after her father was dead, and with her in San Francisco and determined never to return, she guessed the club had seen no reason to leave him out in the cold any longer.

She had indeed been determined never to return. Almost two years ago, when she'd gotten the big commission that had brought her back to Southern California, she'd felt safe coming back, because the club she'd known had died. The compound had been blown up, and the club had reformed as a new charter in a different MC entirely. They'd moved fifty miles east. There were a lot of people in those fifty miles. Faith had felt sufficiently anonymous.

And she would have been. She should have been. She *had* been. Until last night.

She smelled coffee, so she pulled her UGGs back on and went out into Hoosier and Bibi's strange house.

She found Bibi in the kitchen, and Michael's little boy sitting in a high chair at the breakfast table—that table, at least, was familiar. The boy had a bunch of Cheerios on his tray, and he was playing with them more than eating them, lining them up along the rim of the tray. Every now and then, he'd pick one up and put it in his mouth, using two fingers to pinch the oat ring and then sticking out his tongue so he could set it on the tip.

He saw her looking and froze, his eyes wide.

He really was beautiful. His eyes were like Michael's. His hair was darker, more a light, sugary brown than the pale gold that was his father's, but he was obviously his father's son.

As much as he'd been instantly, painfully familiar to her, Michael looked different from the way she remembered him. He wore the years hard; even though he was only thirty-two, lines around his eyes were noticeable. That pale hair was nearly gone—not receding, but cropped close to his skull all around. And he was much bigger than he'd been. She'd known a young man with a lean frame and wiry musculature. His physique had been beautifully cut but not necessarily intimidating. Now he was almost twice as broad and bulky. He'd been bare-chested last night, and he'd looked like a gladiator, his arms and torso brawny, with the sloped shoulders that came with hugely developed trapezius muscles.

There were ragged scars over his belly and chest—they looked old, but they were new to her.

And he had a *lot* more ink—both arms were fully sleeved and he had a large piece across his chest, all of it intricate and in full color. As he'd left her, she'd seen the word HORDE inked across his shoulders in heavy black letters. When she'd known him, he'd had only the kanji symbol for 'strength' over his heart and, after he'd earned his patch, a curving, black and grey scorpion on his left bicep. She'd seen neither last night. Of course he would have covered the scorpion, but it made her sad to think that his strength was gone, too.

She smiled at his beautiful boy. "Hi there, mister."

Bibi turned. "Mornin', honey. That's Tucker. Tuck, say hi to Miss Faith."

Tucker just stared, his tongue still out, balancing a Cheerio.

"Tuck. Are you a good boy?"

He turned to Bibi, pulling his tongue in. The Cheerio stuck to his chin. He nodded.

"Then be polite. Say hi to Miss Faith."

"Hi," he whispered, and covered his face with his hands. She did the same, covering her own face. She didn't know why; it just felt like a thing to do.

And it was a right thing. Tucker threw his hands wide and grinned, his eyes squinching up. "PEE-BOO!" he yelled and then giggled like a little maniac.

Damn, he really was adorable. Faith's heart ached, and she blinked before the burning behind her eyes could become something more.

Bibi came over then with a scrambled egg, a wedge of toast, and a half a piece of bacon on a little plate shaped like an airplane. She set it down on the tray, right on top of the Cheerio installation Tucker had been working on. "You want milk or juice, Tuck?"

"Mook, peez."

"That's Granny's good boy. Milk it is." Bibi turned to Faith. "You want some breakfast, honey? Coffee's fresh, bacon's fried, and I got plenty of eggs."

Faith picked up a piece of bacon from a plate near the range and started to pick at it. She didn't think she could face sitting at the table with this little family and having a cozy breakfast. "No, thanks. I'll just have this and coffee. I want to get to the hospital when visiting hours start." Then she asked the question that was burning itself into her brain. "Is Michael up?"

Bibi had been pouring Faith a cup of coffee. She stopped and let the pot hover for a second before she answered. "No, honey. He was up and out early this mornin'."

"Avoiding me."

"It's a lot to spring on him, Faith. You know what he's like." She put the carafe back in its spot and handed Faith the mug.

"I know what he *was* like."

"He's the same as he was—if anythin', he's worse. There's a lot of darkness in that boy. He fights it, and there's sweetness in him, too, almost a purity. But he doesn't always win. And now he really knows what kind of damage he can do when he loses control. We all know. So he runs before he loses it. You can't push Demon. Let him come to you. And then we'll see what we see."

"Does he know?"

For a few seconds, Bibi simply looked her over, giving her an evaluative consideration that Faith remembered well. "He doesn't know anythin' you said you didn't want him to know. That was a good instinct. It still is. I think knowin' more is more than he can handle. So when you do talk to him, you think about that before you start diggin' into old wounds."

Faith hated Bibi's tone. The secret they had wasn't her fault. It was an injury done to her—and to Michael—and Bibi was talking like Faith was to blame somehow. Well, fuck that.

She shoved the nearly-full mug across the counter toward Bibi and dropped the remains of the piece of bacon she'd been taking apart. "I'm going to wash up and go to the hospital. Can I use one of your bathrooms?"

Bibi barely hesitated before she answered, "Sure, baby. The bathroom across from the room you slept in. In the closet, there's new toothbrushes, deodorant, shampoo, everythin'. We're practically a hotel. Will you be comin' back and stayin' here?"

When she'd woken, she'd thought that she wanted to stay. To be here, with family, with Michael so close. But now, feeling raw and defensive—and abandoned, too, though that was dumb—she wasn't sure. She guessed that she'd have to drive back to her loft soon and pack up some things. It looked like she might have to stay in Madrone for at least a few days. She'd wait until she knew what was going on with her mother before she made that decision.

"Um, I don't know. I guess I'll work all that out after I know what's going on with Mom. And if she even wants me around."

"She does, baby. Trust me." Bibi squeezed her hand. "Let me know when you know anythin'. I'll come by the hospital this afternoon, while Tuck's at speech therapy."

"Speech therapy?" She looked at the pretty, happy little boy who was putting Cheerios on top of his eggs, placing each one carefully. "How old is he?"

"Two and a half, and he's just startin' to talk. He was slow to walk, too, but he figured that out. He didn't get a great start in life, so we're givin' him some help up the curve."

Faith had a lot of questions about this little boy and the circumstances that had Michael and Tucker living here with Bibi and Hoosier, but they were questions she wanted to ask Michael, no one else.

She hoped he'd give her the chance. He didn't need to run. He didn't have to back away, not anymore. Maybe those ten years felt like nothing, but they meant everything—or they could, if he now wanted what she wanted the way he'd once wanted what she'd wanted.

~oOo~

Her mother was awake and alert—and lucid—when Faith arrived a few minutes after visiting hours began. She was still restrained to the bed, though, and it was almost more painful to see her in restraints when her eyes were clear and looked at her with recognition.

At first, she stood in the doorway and simply looked. Her mother was turned to the window. The wild frenzy she'd been in last night was gone, and she no longer looked insane. Now, she was simply a small, aging but still pretty woman who'd been in an accident. Her broken leg was in traction. A nurse must have taken the time to brush out her blonde hair.

"Mom?"

Her mother turned at the sound of her voice, and Faith knew for sure that she was fully present and recognized her. But she didn't smile. Or have any expression at all.

"Where's Sera?"

It had been nearly ten years since Faith and her mother had spoken, and still, the first thing her mother thought about was Faith's sister. She shouldn't care. She'd left for a reason. For many reasons. She didn't even like her mother. But that still stung. "In Japan, Mom. She got transferred. Remember?"

"Of course I remember. I'm not an idiot. Why isn't she here now?"

Because Sera's career was the most important thing in her life, and she didn't like their mother all that much more than Faith did. Sera had been Margot's clear favorite, and Faith had always fallen short of her sister's mark, but being the favorite had come with its own special brand of baggage, and Sera had been happy to cast it away. There was a reason she'd gone to college on the other side of the country, and there was a reason she'd taken a job with an international company. Faith didn't even know if Sera planned to come home at all. "Japan's a long way away. I don't know if she can get here."

Margot nodded and looked back out the window.

Faith was still standing in the doorway. She didn't feel welcome enough to go farther into the room, but she didn't feel like she could leave, either. "Is there anything I can do?"

"They won't let me leave until they do a bunch of tests. They won't let me have my arms free. I don't know what happened."

"You got hit by a car."

"I know *that*. They told me, and that's exactly what I feel like. I don't know why I don't remember. I don't know why they've got me tied up. Did *you* give them permission for all this shit?"

Faith nodded. "I think that's why they want to do the tests—to figure out what happened last night." Part of her wanted to tell her mother how she'd been last night, raving and naked, but that part of her was a spiteful and hurting child, and Faith shut it down.

"Well, that's just great. You show up here out of the blue and get me practically committed. Thanks for that." She sighed. "I need some stuff from home, then. Call Bibi and ask her to put me a bag together. I know you talk to *her*."

She heard the way her mother hit the word 'her,' but she ignored it. "Bibi was here with me last night. She's coming by again today. She's taking care of Tucker, so it'll be later."

Finally, Margot looked at her daughter with something like interest. Her blue eyes had an avid sheen. "You saw that little boy? You know whose he is?"

In that moment, Faith remembered the kind of hatred she'd once felt for this woman. The way she'd felt when she'd clutched her claws into Faith's shoulders and snarled into her ear to *Watch. You watch, little slut, and see what you've done. You watch it all.* The way she'd felt a few weeks after that night, on the day her parents had done something even worse, and she'd known for a certainty that she'd leave at the first chance she had to be free of her mother, and of her father, and of that whole life.

"Yes. I know he's Michael's."

Then her mother smiled a little. It wasn't a cruel smile, but it was satisfied, and that was a cruelty of its own.

And still Faith couldn't make herself turn and get the fuck away. "I could put your bag together for you. Do you still use that little frog for the spare key?" She could get the address from Bibi; she didn't want to ask her mother for that information.

Margot shook her head. "I don't want you in my house. Call Bibi."

"Mom—"

"Go away, Faith. Go call Bibi and then just leave me alone. You know how to do that."

With nothing else she could do, Faith backed out of the room and closed the door. Bibi had been wrong. Her mother hadn't been missing her at all.

~oOo~

She left the room, but she couldn't leave the hospital. It was stupid. She should just go back to Venice Beach. She wasn't wanted here. But they were doing tests today, and those tests might explain what had happened and why the ungodly *fuck* Faith's life had been turned upside down and shaken vigorously.

So she sat in the waiting room near the nurse's station and waited. She read some old magazines. She played on her phone. She read and returned some emails, stray reminders of the pretty good life she'd had. And she stewed. She spent a lot of time stewing. When the stew got too thick, she pinched her arms.

She called Bibi and told her what Margot wanted. Bibi's answer was, "Fuck that. I'll pick you up and we'll go over to that house together. I will not be a party to this bullshit a moment longer."

Faith had agreed, if for no other reason than that she enjoyed the idea of going into her mother's private space knowing she wasn't welcome there. She might even rifle through her drawers. Maybe move some knickknacks around. Just for spite.

She'd told the nurses at the desk who she was and asked them to let her know if there was any news. Twice, she'd seen orderlies roll her mother out on her bed and down the hall toward the elevators, and twice she'd seen them roll her back. But nobody came to tell her anything. After a while, she stopped paying attention to what was happening around her. She crossed her arms and stretched out her legs and let her mind turn in on itself.

So she was surprised to hear a familiar male voice.

"Is that my girl?"

She looked up and saw Hoosier—a lot greyer, his beard a lot longer, his belly a little bigger, but still her Uncle Hooj, standing there smiling down at her.

"It *is* my girl. Oh, you are beautiful as ever. Get up here and gimme a hug." He stretched his arms out. Faith stood and let herself fall into them. Those arms were still strong and solid. She turned her face against his neck and felt his beard on her cheek. That was like home.

"You okay, baby girl?"

She shook her head.

"I know, baby, I know. It *will* be okay, though. I promise. Any news?"

Another shake. She didn't want to talk. She didn't want to say that her mother had thrown her out of her room. She just wanted to be right where she was. Wanted.

"You waitin' for news?"

She nodded.

"I got some time. Beebs'll be here, and then I'm on Tuck duty. You mind if I sit with you a while and wait, too?"

And then, again, Faith had to cry.

CHAPTER FOUR

"Michael, did you hear me? Michael? Demon?"

Demon blinked and brought his attention back to the man in front of him. Findley Bennett—even the guy's name reeked of rich asshole. Demon couldn't stand him, even though he was a hoity-toity lawyer helping him try to get custody of Tucker, and he was doing it for free.

He was doing it for free so he could turn it into some kind of dog and pony show. The guy had already been on the L.A. morning news shows talking about fathers' rights and using Demon and Tucker as an example. He wanted to bring them onto these shows with him, but he wanted to have some other asshole do some kind of 'media training' on him first, and that was really and truly not going to happen.

He knew he should be grateful, and he actually was. Sid had helped him get this guy to take his case, and he was getting a famously successful lawyer to fight for him and his boy. That was good. That was lucky, and Demon normally had the world's shittiest luck. But he could see the distrust and contempt when the guy talked to him, and he hated it.

It was worth it. Getting Tucker would be worth just about anything, but he hated it nevertheless.

That wasn't what had his attention wandering today, though. Today, all he could think about was Faith.

He'd been walking around like the undead all morning, and not just because he'd been up at first light and out of the house before anyone else was moving, hours earlier than he'd needed to be at the shop.

If he hadn't left first thing, he would probably have ended up in the room Faith had taken. And he had to get his head straight before he did anything that had to do with her. He didn't trust himself. Last night, he'd been hit by an old wave of want and need that had been overpowering long ago and had spent ten years only getting stronger, without him even realizing it. If he lost control of himself, he could hurt her. Even if she felt like he did, even if she wanted, too, he could still hurt her.

Besides, did it even matter what they wanted? He'd been no good then, and the past ten years hadn't made him better. He had seen things, done things that should never touch her. The darkness in him was darker, the wrongness more wrong.

He needed to stay away. Far away. And he needed to stop thinking about her. If he couldn't find even that much control inside himself, not even enough to focus his thoughts on what was right in front of him, then there was no way he could get near her.

Seeking control in a deep breath, Demon exhaled and made himself focus on his lawyer.

Usually, he had to ride to Findley-call-me-Finn's swanky office in downtown L.A. for meetings, but today the guy had shown up unannounced at the shop, so now they were sitting in the showroom office, Finn in his custom suit and Demon in a greasy coverall.

"Sorry. Didn't catch it, no."

Finn sighed. "It's big news, Michael." Yep, only lawyers and assholes called him Michael.

And Faith. He shook her name out of his head. Tried to, anyway.

"My investigator has a solid lead on Dakota's location," Finn went on.

That got his attention. Dakota. Tucker's mom. Demon never wanted to see her again. "I told you I don't want her found. I will kill her if I see her again. That'll probably screw up the case, don't you think?"

"And *I've* told *you* that finding her could help us. It fast-tracks your case. And if she's still the disaster she was when Tucker was removed, with all the evidence in his file of how often the first caseworker let her slide, and with your solid record for the past four or five years, that's a strong visual for your case." He smiled an oily, lawyer smile. "If you think you can hold off killing her until we win." The smile disappeared. "That's a joke, by the way."

Demon leaned forward and held out his arm. It was covered in ink, but if you looked close enough, you could still see it. So he put his arm up in Finn's face. "Do you see that, right on the inside of my elbow?"

Finn looked. "A scar, right? Yeah, I see it. Did Dakota do that?"

"No. I've had those since I was nine. Burns from the lit end of a cigar. Three of 'em, all in a neat little row." He dropped his arm. "Tucker has one like it on the bottom of his foot."

"I know. They noted it in his file when he was removed." 'They,' in that instance, was Sid. She'd gotten Tucker's case when the first caseworker, a piece of shit who'd been trading Demon's kid's safety for trips to Kota's cooze, retired. Sid had removed Tucker on her first home visit. It was how Demon and Muse—and the whole club, really—had met her.

"He didn't get that with me. Kota doesn't smoke cigars. So she let some bastard she was boning do that to my kid. You have any idea how a burn like that feels? Who the fuck knows what else my boy saw or felt with her. He wakes up screaming four or five nights a week. He's not even three. So I'm going to kill her if I ever see her again. I'm not looking to go back inside, and that sure as fuck won't help Tucker, so we're all better off if she stays the fuck away."

Finn closed the open file in front of him and sighed again. "Michael, I respect your passion. I know you love your boy. I believe one-hundred percent that he should be with you, and that you were treated unfairly at nearly every turn. But I need you to let me be your lawyer and give you counsel you'll take. You look better the worse she looks. Let's find Dakota and see what she's up to. Let's just see. If she can be useful to your case, then let's use her. If she can't, we'll leave her alone. I think you can control yourself for that, don't you?"

Demon laughed a little. Finn had no idea. The most control over himself Demon ever felt was maybe half. And that was on a good day, when everything was chill. Put him in eyeshot of the woman who'd fucked up his child, and no, he didn't think he'd be able to control himself. Especially since the cunt got off on sending him over.

He'd liked her a lot at first, and he was fairly sure she'd honestly liked him at the beginning. He didn't 'date' much at all. Usually he stuck to club girls, because that was simple. But sometimes he got lonely for more than just a fuck. He'd had somebody once, only for a brief time, but long enough to know the peace in a bond like that. So sometimes, he was lonely.

In the year or so after he'd been allowed to come back home, he'd had trouble adjusting. The club moved—and became a different club—and he'd been struggling with staying in one place after the years riding Nomad. He'd started thinking about what he'd almost had before, and he'd felt even lonelier. So when Kota came up to him at a bar and started talking, he'd been open to listening.

They'd been okay for a while. Just hanging out, steady but not really serious. It never occurred to him to put his ink on her; that wasn't what they'd been. She was a stripper, and he was fine with that. He'd gotten between her and a few overly excited customers who'd been lurking after hours, and she got to calling him her bodyguard. She'd given very enthusiastic head on those nights.

But he'd been a moron, because he hadn't known she was using, all that time. He didn't figure it out until it had taken her over completely. She'd robbed him blind. Then she'd started whoring herself out for her fixes. He'd ended it and left her to her vices.

And then she'd tried to use the club to blackmail him. She didn't know anything about the club; he never talked about that shit. But he'd opened up to her, during their good times, and told her about his childhood. Things he'd never said to anyone, not even

Faith. Secrets and shames he'd harbored. And Kota had said terrible things that night, promising to twist old pains into lies that would hurt him now, make his club, his family, see his wrongness, make him lose what he'd only just gotten back.

All to squeeze more money out of him to get her next fix. He barely remembered what had happened after that. Except he remembered her laughing in the middle of it, her mouth full of blood, and he remembered thinking that she didn't even care if she got her next fix. She'd been high on tearing him down.

In the ER that night, while he was in lockup, she'd found out she was pregnant.

She'd declined to press charges. They'd let him go, and he'd gone to see her in the hospital, to apologize for hurting her. She'd told him about the baby and said it was his. Demon didn't know why he'd just believed her, but he had. He'd brought her home to his trailer, and he'd tried to help her kick the junk. He'd tried and tried, and he'd failed and failed. But he'd stuck it out with her, finding her again and again in some flophouse, her belly getting bigger and bigger, trying to figure out how to keep her away from trouble and never coming up with the answer.

Tucker was born with his mother's habit. He'd had a rough first few weeks. But the first time that boy's eyes met his own, Demon had known for an absolute fact that he was looking at his son. And he'd known purposeful love for the first time in his life.

DCFS didn't take Tucker from her, despite the addiction she'd shared with him. They put her in an outpatient program and gave Tucker a caseworker, and they sent them home. Kota moved out of Demon's trailer right away and took his boy to live with a girlfriend.

His fight to be a father to his son had started then and still hadn't stopped.

He stared hard at his lawyer. "Go ahead and look. You better know your business, though. Keep her the fuck away from me. Don't tell me where she is. Just do your thing. But if this blows up in my kid's face, then I'll know who to blame for it."

~oOo~

Demon pulled up to Hoosier and Bibi's house later that afternoon, and he was relieved and disappointed that Faith's car wasn't around.

When he'd left that morning, he'd stopped cold on the sidewalk. She still drove Dante, and the car itself was in the same cherry condition it had been in before. But now it looked finished, completely covered from top to bottom and front to rear in art. It was beautiful, and so very Faith.

He'd had an urge to hug the fucking thing—that urge, at least, he'd been able to master. But he'd ridden off with his stomach in knots.

She was gone now, though. That was a good thing. He needed time, and if she hadn't been gone, even though he'd been as prepared as possible for her to be there, he'd have panicked—which would have led to stupidity. But he didn't know if she was gone for good or just for a while. He had no idea why she'd even been there in the first place. Maybe last night had just been a special torture for him, stirring up everything and then coming to nothing.

Inside, he found Hoosier and Tucker in the family room. Tucker was playing on the floor with his beloved wooden train set, and Hoosier was watching ESPN. Bibi wasn't around, but Demon had known that when he'd pulled up—the garage door was open, and the space for her Caddy was empty.

His gratitude and trust for Hoosier and Bibi was boundless. They were giving him the best chance he'd ever had to be a father to his son. They'd been the closest thing to parents he'd ever had. Since he was nineteen, when he'd started hanging around the clubhouse, they'd treated him almost like a kid of their own. They'd given him a home and a family.

He didn't blame Hoosier for taking it away. Demon had done that to himself.

Hoosier had kept it from being worse. He hadn't lost his patch or his life, and both of those had been on the table for a vote. He'd been exiled, not excommunicated. Not ended. And things had turned out more or less okay.

As much as he'd been torn apart to be sent away from his only home, he'd felt like he fit as a Nomad right away. Rootlessness was something he understood. He'd partnered with Muse right off, and he'd found his first actual friend. They'd been rootless together, except when one or the other of them was inside, and that had been okay.

And damn, the shit that the Nomads of their old club had been into. It was life or death business in those days, and they were up to their shoulders in it just about nonstop. Demon had found stability in the surge and release of adrenaline in a firefight, and he'd learned how to channel his darkness and violence into the work that needed doing. He'd found his calling as an enforcer. Sometimes he'd gone too far, but even so, he felt more a master of his impulses than he had before.

He'd been arrested a few times, and he'd done a couple of bids, but they were short enough. If his childhood had prepared him for nothing else, it had prepared him to survive prison. Even to thrive there.

Then, at Blue's funeral, Hoosier had asked him to come home. And Demon had humiliated himself by breaking down into tears.

So he was home. He had a home. And a son. People who loved him and wanted him. And with no outlet for the crap in his head, he was losing control of his darkness again.

Tucker looked up as Demon came into the room. "Pa! Bwain!" He held out a little blue train engine.

"*T-T-Train*, buddy. T like in Tucker." He squatted at his son's side.

"Tuh-bwain."

Demon laughed. "Close enough. Did you have fun with Gramps?"

Tucker nodded and held out a shiny new engine, this one kind of purple.

"You got a new one! Who's this?" It had a vaguely female face. All Tucker's engines had faces.

"Bwain!"

"Deme. You doin' okay?"

Demon looked up and saw Hoosier eyeing him over the back of the sectional. So Hoosier knew that Faith was in town. It made sense; Bibi would probably have told him as soon as he was back. He ruffled Tucker's hair and stood up.

"Have you been in touch with her all this time?" The words came out more sharply than he'd meant them. He didn't want to accuse Hoosier and Bibi of anything. There were probably dozens of good reasons not to tell him they knew where she was. He wasn't sure even now how much he trusted himself to know.

"Have a seat, brother." Hoosier waved at the side of the sectional, and Demon went around and sat down. "Beebs's kept up with her, yeah. Until today, I hadn't seen her since she ran."

"She's been good?"

Hoosier heaved a sigh. "Yeah. I guess she actually earns making her weird, rusty art. Remember that sh—stuff she used to make?"

That thought made Demon smile and feel a little proud. He remembered climbing around with her at the salvage yard. She'd been so cute and enthusiastic. He'd kissed her that day. It had been her first kiss ever. His, too, in a way.

He closed his eyes and counted five beats. Muse had taught him that, to focus on his heartbeat until the hurt that made red edge his vision backed off. Sometimes he needed a lot more than five beats.

"Why's she back?"

"There's something goin' on with her mom. Any more is for her to say."

Not for him, then. Of course she wouldn't have been, but there'd been a little flickering light in the back of his head that had thought maybe she'd come because she couldn't stay away.

"You mind some advice, Deme?"

He shrugged, and Hoosier took that for permission.

"It all went down bad back in the day. You fucked up bad. But you were a kid, younger than your years. I knew it. Most everybody did. Even Blue, deep down, knew you were just a kid, too. He couldn't see anything but his little girl, the one who ran around with scraped knees and ratty pigtails stealing sips from beer bottles and getting caught swiping loose parts off worktables. He'd never've admitted it, but when it all fell out, I think even he knew it was more for you than just claiming his little girl's cherry."

Demon flinched at the rawness of Hoosier's last statement. "Don't, Prez."

"I'm telling you something that might help, so listen. It don't matter what Blue thought. Not anymore. He's dead and buried. And you are no kid anymore. Neither is she. I've seen you both today, and you both look like somebody ran over your best dog. Now, you both got other good reasons to be so glum, but maybe, just maybe, ten years is long enough to beat yourself up about something that wasn't really all so bad."

His face felt hot, and he tried to count beats, but he couldn't. "Not so bad? Not so bad? Are you shitting me?" He stood up, and Hoosier did, too.

"Deme. Easy. I know it was bad then. I was there." His voice was low, and sort of rolled, and Demon was still in control enough to know he was being talked down like a wild animal.

He didn't have enough control for it to work, though. "YOU HAVE NO FUCKING IDEA!"

"NO, PA! NO!" Tucker yelled. He was standing at the corner of the sectional, his sweet little face contorted into a scowl that was both angry and afraid.

Demon deflated instantly, dropping back to the sofa. "I'm sorry, Motor Man. You okay?"

For a few seconds longer, Tucker stared at him with that fearful distrust, and Demon wanted to die. Then his little boy came around and climbed up onto his lap. "Bad noise."

"Yeah. I'm sorry." Demon kissed his son's head and looked over at his President.

Hoosier picked up where he'd left off. "I'm saying in hindsight, you were a couple of stupid kids in love. The worst thing you did wasn't to Faith. Far as I know, you didn't do anything to her but love her. What you did wrong was betray a brother. That's why the club let it go to a vote at all. But that sin was dead and buried with Blue."

"What difference does it make?"

"Boy, you are so tangled up in thinking you're fuc—messed up, you can't see when somebody's offering you a help. I'm telling you the slate's clean. Don't bother about what happened before. Everything's changed for all of us since then. You were a kid, now you're a man. Act like it. Quit pouting and figure out what you want. Maybe what you have here is a second chance. You gonna moan and sulk until it goes away, or are you gonna fucking take it?"

"Fucking take it," Tucker said, with perfect enunciation.

CHAPTER FIVE

"This is where she lives?" Faith looked out the windshield of Bibi's Cadillac, ducking her head to take in the full view of the little ranch house.

Actually, 'house' was too grand a term for the building before her. 'Shack' might have been more appropriate. It wasn't small, but it was unloved. The stucco was a faded yellow, worn bare and smooth in noticeable patches. The windows and doors were covered with pocked iron bars.

Though a large attached garage dominated the front of the building, apparently that hadn't been enough storage space. Somebody had turned the front yard into a parking lot. What little 'yard' there was had been filled in with white gravel. There was a huge, dry, concrete birdbath or fountain or something in the middle of that gravel expanse. Faith realized that she was looking at a poor man's idea of xeriscaping.

The house in L.A. that Faith and Sera had grown up in had been surrounded, front, back, and sides, by an elaborate garden. The house itself had been pretty average—a palace compared to what she was looking at now, but in itself nothing special—but the yards had been amazing. Gardening was her mother's passion, and she had a real talent for it. She had an artist's eye. It was one of the few things Faith was glad to have gotten from her.

She tried to imagine Margot Fordham living in this ugly, barren, unwelcoming hovel, and she couldn't. So she said again, "She lives *here*?"

Bibi reached over and gave Faith's hand a squeeze. "It's been hard for her since your dad passed, honey. Your dad didn't do so good settin' things up for her, I guess. I know Sera's schoolin' cost a lot, too. And your mama don't have much she can do in the way of work. Not anymore."

Faith gave an absent nod. Yeah, she guessed not. The only job her mom had ever had was porn. She'd stopped doing that when she became an old lady.

"Madrone is cheap, though, compared to L.A. She should have been able to do better just from selling the L.A. house." They'd owned that house free and clear, too, as far as Faith knew.

"I don't know. A lot's been different these past few years. I got her to move with us, to keep her close, but she pulled back a lot. From the club, mostly, but from me a little, too. So I don't really know. She'd bought this before I even knew about it."

That was unlike her mother. Bibi and Margot had been best friends since long before Faith and Sera were born. They were the kind of friends who had matching jewelry and gave each other flowery mugs that said crap like *Best Friends Make the Best Sisters* or whatever. They used to share a seat at parties, getting drunk and giggling like girls. Her mother's relationship with Bibi was one of the few signs Faith had that her mother could actually be a decent person. If she was pulling away from Bibi, then things had gotten really bad.

Faith wasn't quite sure why she cared, but she did.

She didn't say anything, but when she turned, Bibi was giving her that examining stare she had.

"I know your mama's bein' a bitch right now. She's never been an easy woman, and there's obviously somethin' even more wrong than I knew." She'd thrown Bibi out of her hospital room, too—after demanding that she go to her house and pack a bag for her. "But I am here to tell you, she loves you. She misses you. She lost you, and then she lost your dad, and now Sera's off and away and never calls. She's a lonely woman who's realizin' that a lot of things she thought were right weren't. That's a hard lesson. We all do bad shit in our lives. Sometimes we do bad shit and we think we're makin' a hard choice for right reasons. Sometimes we are. But sometimes, we find out we were just fuckin' everythin' up. When we figure that out too late to fix it, well, that wears a sore spot. I can tell you that."

"You never did anything like they did, Bibi."

They locked eyes, and then Bibi let out a long breath. "I wasn't in her shoes or your shoes then. I know why your folks did what they did. I know what your mama was afraid of, and what she thought she was doing. I know I've done things I regret as a mom, even though I was tryin' to do it right. That I am sure of. I'm sure Connor could tell you stories of all the ways I fucked him up."

Faith shook her head. There was no middle ground to be had on this point. No forgiveness. She wasn't interested.

Bibi sighed again. "Come on, honey. Let's go on in and get your mama the things she wants."

The house was a little nicer on the inside than the outside suggested. Margot was a neatnik, and everything had its place. The hardwood floors gleamed. Faith felt an awkward sense of verisimilitude, because all of the furniture was familiar to her—the same black leather, glass and chrome furniture that had always been in the house she'd grown up in. The faux zebra throw over the arm of the leather sofa was in the same place it had always been, but the house itself was foreign.

Maybe that off-kilter, foreign familiarity was the reason Faith didn't notice anything remarkable right off. Not until Bibi muttered, "What the hell?" did Faith widen her focus and really see.

All over the house, in tidy rows and columns, her mother had stuck neon-colored Post-It notes. On the back of the front door were five, written in block letters with black marker: KEYS, PHONE, PURSE, read one. SHOES, another. CHECK STOVE AND OVEN, another. IRON? yet another. FAUCETS, the last.

There was also a calendar hanging on the back of the front door, the block for each day filled with reminders, the days that had passed crossed out with black Xs.

Bibi moved into the house, and Faith followed, trying to make sense of what she was seeing.

On the glass table in front of the sofa, a row of notes reminded her mother about shows and channels and how to use the remote.

There was a whiteboard calendar on the wall over the glass-topped dining table, each block filled in with colored marker.

The refrigerator was covered with a matrix of notes, telling the dates that items had been bought and when they should be thrown out. On the cabinet above the stove were notes explaining how to use the burners, the oven, the microwave, and the timer.

On the back door, there was one note: "SLY."

Faith stared at that one for several seconds. "It this...?"

Bibi's answer was distracted. "Hmm? Oh, yeah. That nasty old bastard of a cat. He's still around. Outside, mostly. He's too mean to be closed in with people, but she moved him out here just the same."

Feeling something like excitement, Faith opened the back door and looked around. The yard here had overgrown grass and a plain, square concrete patio. It was completely bare. Not even a hibachi or a lawn chair, and no plantings at all. "Sly?" She whistled and then made the clucking sound she thought of as her cat-call. "Sly!" Nothing. She went back in. There was a pet door in the bottom of the back door, so she supposed he'd be okay. There was a set of empty bowls on the floor in the corner. She found food and filled them with food and water. While she did so, Bibi wandered off. Faith followed as quickly as she could, feeling nervous about being alone in this weird house papered in Post-Its. She still couldn't find the rhyme in what she was seeing.

In Faith's mother's bedroom, they found her bed unmade, her drawers and closet open and in disarray, Post-Its everywhere with reminders about how to do things like set the clock and where the extra blankets were.

Reminder notes confetti'd the surfaces of every room of the house. Bibi and Faith wandered through, saying nothing, their only communication an occasional shared gasp.

And then, heading down the hallway as they continued their confused tour, Bibi drew up short. The hallway walls were covered with family photos. That had been the case in the L.A. house, too, and, again, at first the familiarity blinded Faith to the difference.

There were small Post-Its on, above, or below every frame. Identifying the people in the photos. People like Margot's children. Her parents. Her best friend. Her husband. Some of the notes, especially those with photos of friends, had only a question mark.

On Faith's parents' wedding photo, there was a single Post-It with three question marks.

"What the fuck is this, Beeb?" Faith turned to see that Bibi had gone white and looked like she was going to pass out. "Hey— you need to sit down?"

Bibi shook her head. "I'm okay. But Jesus, baby. I know what this is. Sweet Jesus."

"What?"

"Hoosier's dad—you remember him at all?"

Faith had a vague recollection of an old guy at a few of their parties. She thought she remembered him being pretty grumpy. Not really a grandpa type. "I think so, yeah."

"We brought him out to be near us after Hooj's mom passed. He had…fuck, Faith. He had Alzheimer's. When it started, he forgot little shit, like losing his keys or forgettin' to close his pants, leavin' the fridge door open. Stuff we all do sometimes, but he started doing it all the time. When it really started to come on, he got all distant and belligerent. It wasn't so easy to tell at first, 'cuz he wasn't so nice a guy anyway. But I think he knew what was happenin' and didn't want people to know. It started like this, honey. It looked like this—him tryin' to remember what he kept forgettin', pullin' away from people close to him."

Faith shook her head. By the time Bibi took a breath, she was shaking her head vigorously. "No way. Mom's fifty-six. That's barely old."

That got a little bit of a smile. "It ain't old, period, baby. She's too young. God, I hope it's something else. That doctor not called yet?"

Again, Faith shook her head, pulling her phone out of her bag at the same time. "Fuck. I have a missed call and a voice mail." She listened to the message—and it was, indeed, Dr. Tomiko. "Yeah, she called. She wants to talk to me." Closing the barn door while the horse ran free, she toggled her ringer on.

"Well, let's get movin'. You mama keeps her suitcases in that room over there."

~oOo~

Though the afternoon was moving toward evening when Faith and Bibi got back to the hospital, Dr. Tomiko was standing at the nurse's station. When she saw them, she turned and stepped forward, like she'd been waiting specifically for them.

"Hi, Miss Fordham." She extended her hand, and Faith took it and gave it a halfhearted shake. The things Bibi had said while they were standing in her mother's hallway were clanging around in her head. They hadn't talked much on the drive; they'd both been preoccupied with what they'd seen and what Bibi thought it might mean.

What, Faith wondered, would it mean for her? She knew it was selfish, and maybe even coldhearted, to think about herself in this circumstance, but knowing didn't make the thoughts dissipate. Sera was thousands of miles away. Who else was there to take care of their mother if she would need taking care of? Bibi? She was taking care of Tucker. And managing the clubhouse. And all the other gazillion kinds of things she'd always been involved in, Faith was sure.

Dr. Tomiko motioned toward the empty waiting room. "Let's sit down."

"I'll just go in and sit her while you two talk," Bibi said. Faith reached out and grabbed her hand. She didn't want to be alone to hear whatever the doctor thought she needed to sit down to hear.

"She's sleeping right now," Dr. Tomiko said. "Maybe you could go have a coffee?"

"No. She can stay. She's my mom's best friend. She can hear all of it—I'd tell her anyway."

The doctor nodded. "Okay, then let's talk."

They all sat, clustered in a corner of the waiting room. Dr. Tomiko maintained perfect eye contact with Faith—as if, Faith thought, she'd had training on the way to appear compassionate and involved when giving hard news. "We did a long series of tests, last night and today. We've ruled out stroke, tumor, hydrocephalus, encephalitis or any other infection. We've ruled out drug or alcohol-related complications. Your mother shows some signs of past alcohol abuse, but my guess is that she doesn't drink currently?"

Faith shook her head before she realized that she had no idea if her mother drank currently, but she sensed that Bibi did the same at her side, agreeing. They were ruling things out, which should be a good thing, right? It didn't feel like a good thing. Infections had cures. They ran their course. A tumor could be excised. Fluid could be drained. The things the doctor wasn't ruling out—those were things that endured. That changed lives.

"Your mother had…we'll call it an episode…during the MRI. She became disoriented and very agitated. She had to be sedated in order to ensure her safety. It was a light dose of valium, just enough to calm her. But she hasn't come back from that episode yet. We had to restrain her again, and she's not clear on basic details of her current life. But she's calling for her husband—I believe you told me that he's deceased, right? Has been for some years?" Faith nodded, and the doctor nodded in response. "I'm not ready to make a diagnosis yet, though. I need some details about her behavior before last night."

Last night. It still hadn't even been twenty-four hours since she'd gotten a call from this hospital, yanked some random clothes on, and driven to Madrone. The striking absurdity of that, of how much had changed in so few hours, rendered Faith mute, nearly insensible.

But Bibi spoke up. "We just came from her house. We saw some things." She told the doctor what they'd seen at Faith's mother's house. Faith watched as the doctor listened. She began to nod. In her eyes, Faith saw somber excitement—like she was figuring out a puzzle, but the picture it was making wasn't pretty.

Then Bibi, finished with her description of the Post-Its, asked, "Is it Alzheimer's, doc?"

"No," Faith found her voice. "No. She's too young."

Dr. Tomiko turned and directed her answer to Faith. "She is a little young, yes. Normally, we see symptoms after age sixty. But that's a norm, not a rule. I've seen cases of early-onset in patients as young as thirty-four. As I said, there are more tests I'd like to do, but what you describe in her house is a classic coping strategy at the onset of progressive loss of cognition. Not all dementia is Alzheimer's, and a lot of the diagnosis is ruling out rather than ruling in. But that's the direction we're going to take our diagnostics at this point, yes."

"But why was she running around naked in the middle of the night, raving? How is that memory loss?"

"Any kind of dementia is more than just memory loss. It's loss of *cognition*—the ability to think in a connected, linear way. Add that to lapses of memory, sometimes years or decades that are just lost, and the world becomes a terrifying, alien place."

Bibi sniffed, and Faith realized she was weeping. Faith herself was too numb and dazed to feel anything but confusion.

"So now what?"

"The break in her leg is severe enough to warrant that she stay admitted for at least another five or six days. I'd like to use that time to refine my understanding and give you a definitive diagnosis if I can. I suggest you bring in another neurologist, too, for a second opinion. When she's discharged, she'll need help at least until the cast is off—maybe longer, depending on the diagnosis. There'll be some physical therapy she'll need for her leg, and some occupational therapy to help keep her as lucid as possible for as long as possible. There are meds, too, that can help. Again, this is predicated on firming up a diagnosis in the first place."

"Okay." That was all Faith said. She was having her own cognition problems at the moment and felt too exhausted to try to make sense.

It was more than merely the upheaval and emotional intensity of the past day that made her feel so suddenly fatigued. It was the looming, dawning thought that was trying very hard to make sense, was demanding to be understood—the thought that Faith, who'd run from this family ten years before, who'd left hurting and angry and lost, who had been forced, by the people she should have been most able to trust, to endure a violation that still tore her up when she contemplated it, that she would end up her mother's caretaker.

A woman who'd called her a slut and a whore, who'd said only hours before that she wasn't wanted—that woman, her mother, would become Faith's responsibility. She knew it was true. It didn't matter whether the diagnosis was definitive or not. Faith knew it was true.

She pinched her arm. Hard.

"Thank you, doc." Bibi's tone was dismissive, and the doctor caught on.

"Of course. I'll stay in touch, and you have my card if you think of other questions." She extended her hand again, and Faith stared at it for a second before she shook it.

When Dr. Tomiko was gone, Bibi put her hand on Faith's thigh. "You know what, baby? I'll take this shit in to your mama and sit with her a while. Why don't you go on back to the house? Take a hot bath and lie down."

She shook her head. "I can't. Michael's there. I can't deal with all this and that, too. And…God, I have to get out of these clothes. I've been wearing them for a whole day—and I picked them up off my floor when I put them on. No. I'm going home."

"Faith, no."

"I'll be back. I will. I need to be in my own place and get my head on right. And I need to pack a bag of my own, I guess. Give me a couple of days, and I'll be back."

Bibi just eyed her in that incisive, insightful way of hers.

"I'll be back, Beebs. I promise."

~oOo~

She had meant to get right on the freeway from the hospital and head west just as fast as traffic would allow. But instead she found herself parked on the wide concrete expanse in front of her mother's, sad, ugly house in a sad, ugly neighborhood. She didn't have a key, but she knew she'd find the spare if she wanted to. But that wasn't why she was here. She got out of Dante and went around to the back yard. Then she sat down on the slab patio and called out softly, "Sly…you here, dude?" She made her cat-call, ticking her tongue against the roof of her mouth. "Sly…Sly…Sly…"

She sat there a long time; it was full dark when she heard the deep, low growl she remembered. She smiled.

"Hey, psycho. C'mon." She held out her hand in the direction of the growl and kept it there, not moving. Finally, from the dark yard came a huge black-and-white cat, his gold eyes glinting in the light from the neighbors' yards. He came on her, crouching low, his ears back on his head. He was bigger, heavier, and missing half of his left ear now, but he was her cat.

She couldn't believe her mother had kept this cat—who liked exactly two people on the planet and thought everyone else was a bitter enemy to be destroyed.

Unless there were babies. He hated all living things except his two people—and babies. He loved babies.

Growling the whole time, Sly inched up to her. She kept her hand out and steady. When he got close enough, he nosed her fingertips, and then batted at her hand, all his claws, honed by a life outdoors, extended. He drew blood, but she didn't flinch. She'd been ready. She remembered this dance.

Then he put his head under her hand and rubbed himself on her. And then he climbed into her lap and lay down, purring. He stretched one paw out over her leg and flexed his talons of death, and then he relaxed completely.

She scratched at his ears, and he blinked up at her. He remembered her.

Faith sat on the patio of her estranged mother's strange house, reuniting with her old cat, and let memory take her away.

memory

Well, as birthdays went, this one wouldn't be landing on any best-of lists. After the last of her few friends left to the soundtrack of her parents screaming at each other, Faith stood in the back yard and kicked at a salvia plant. When she heard something crash inside, she knew Act II would be underway, soon, and she decided to blitz before she got caught in the crossfire.

She just drove around without any real destination. She could have gone to Bethany or Joelle's, but they'd just left, and they'd want to talk about her parents' fireworks finale. And that was a boring and annoying topic.

As she drove past the big community park, and saw that there was some kind of fair or carnival or something going on today. That was at least something to occupy her time, so she looked for a parking place. The park was crowded, so she had to park a few blocks down and over. But that was a time-killer, too, so it all worked out.

It wasn't much of a fair. Just some dumb rides, the kind they pulled in on flatbeds, and some food booths. And some people playing music. But then she saw a line of bikes, bikes she recognized. She couldn't remember if she'd ever known that the club was working this fair, but it was the kind of thing they did. Uncle Hoosier called stuff like this 'charm patrol'—doing nice things for the neighborhood so the neighbors didn't notice so much when they were doing things like selling drugs and guns to bangers.

She wasn't supposed to know about that stuff. There was a lot she wasn't supposed to know about. But people tended to forget she was around.

Michael's bike was one of those lined up on the street. It made sense—he was a Prospect, and Prospects got gigs like this. She kept an eye out for him while she wandered around the park.

She kept an eye out for him whenever she was around the club, but he wasn't all that easy to find. It had been almost four months since he'd kissed her. She thought about that kiss every day. Her first and still her only kiss, and it had been amazing. But she could count on her fingers the number of times they'd spoken since—and have a few fingers left over. She thought he was avoiding her.

That made sense, too, she guessed. Her father had probably threatened him. He was always scaring boys away. It was like he wanted her to die a lonely virgin.

After maybe half an hour or so, she heard the unmistakable roar of bikes rolling away. She turned and looked. All but one bike was gone. The club booth must have closed up. Or the guys had been called away for something.

But the one bike left was Michael's. She sharpened her eyes.

She saw him emptying a big trash bin near the food booths. Her heart picked up its pace as she crossed the grass in his direction. He was bent over, tying up the bag, and she came up behind him.

"Hey."

He jumped and wheeled around, his face turning red. Moving the smelly bag of garbage in front of him, holding it almost like it was a shield, he took a step back before he said, "Hey."

"Didn't mean to scare you. Just thought I'd say hi."

"You didn't—scare me, I mean."

Yeah, right. He looked totally calm, standing there holding a dripping garbage bag up in front of his chest. Sure.

Well, this just sucked. Her disgust and dejection leaked out of her in some kind of huffy noise. "Okay. Sorry to interrupt your important work there. See ya." She turned and walked off, trying to seem like she didn't care.

"Wait—Faith, hold up."

She turned to see him coming after her, still holding his stupid garbage bag. "Sorry. What are you doing here? I thought there was a party for your birthday. Oh—happy birthday."

"There was. It got called on account of my parents shouting at each other."

"That sucks. I'm sorry."

She shrugged. "It's no big. It's what they do. It's the same every time. They shout and scream, then my mom throws things. Then my dad storms out and bangs around in the garage while my mom bangs around in the kitchen. Then she thinks of something more she just has to say, and she goes out to the garage and shouts it at him and then goes back inside. Then my dad chases after her and she says more mean things. Then he shouts something like, 'One of these days, bitch, I'm going to cut that nasty tongue right out of your mouth.'"

Michael laughed—a surprised noise, almost like a cough. "Your dad likes cutting body parts off, huh?"

Faith thought that was a weird thing to say. "Nah. He'd never do it. That's usually about the end of the fight. She slaps him, and he punches a wall, and then they fuck really loud for like the whole rest of the night. I've seen that movie a hundred times. Thought I'd skip it today." She nodded at his pet garbage bag. "You're dripping. It's gross."

He looked down at it like he hadn't known it was there. "Fuck. Yeah. Gimme a minute?"

Was he going to hang out with her? Holy balls, that would brighten her birthday up. "Yeah, sure."

She waited while he took the garbage off somewhere. When he came back, he was drying his hands on a paper towel, which he tossed in the newly-emptied bin. He smiled as he walked up to her. "Want some company for a minute?"

Smiling and trying not to look like a dork about it, she nodded, and they walked down the little path between the booths.

At the other end of the park, an animal rescue group had a little setup, a ring of cages, crates, and small pens. Faith bounced a little. "Hey! Babies!" She took a couple of quick steps toward the animals, but realized that Michael had stopped those few steps back. He looked...mad, or something. "What's wrong?"

"I hate these things."

"What? Animals?"

"No. These cages, everybody poking at them, and nowhere for them to go. It sucks."

"But people adopt them and take them home. This helps them."

The noise Michael made then was pure contempt. "Right." But then he looked at her, and his expression softened. "Sorry. Ignore me." He closed the distance between them, and they did a tour of the crates and pens.

It was the end of the day, and it looked like the group had had a pretty successful adoption drive. Though they had a big sign advertising puppies and kittens, most of the animals left were grown. There was a sign hanging from their table that advertised a discount on the adoption fee for adult animals, too, but that apparently hadn't swayed many people.

Tucked back behind the table, not part of the circle of adoptable animals, was a good-size wire crate. Inside it was a big cat with long black and white fur, like a tuxedo. He was wedged tightly against a back corner of the crate, his gold eyes wide and suspicious.

Michael went around the table and squatted next to the crate. The cat made a fierce, threatening sound, a growl and a yowl both. Michael sat down on the grass. "Hey, dude."

The young woman managing the animals came over. "I'm sorry. He's not up for adoption."

Michael looked up at her, and Faith saw aggression in his eyes. His cheeks were pink. She'd noticed he got really blushy when he was upset, or just felt strongly in one way or another. He'd blushed hard when he'd kissed her, too.

"Why not?" he asked.

"He's...not well socialized. You should get away from the crate, too. When he makes that sound, he means business."

"Then why is he here?"

The woman looked a little guilty. "It's weird. He's really aggressive with people, but he loves babies. We came in today with a litter of orphaned kittens that he's been taking care of. They all found forever homes." At that, she smiled perkily.

"So he had a family this morning, and he doesn't now?" Michael's face was getting really red, and Faith felt a little worried.

Now the woman was angry. "Look. We're a no-kill shelter. Tom would have been euthanized the very second he went into any other facility. It takes three people to hold him down to even do a simple vet check. He's bloodied all of us. But he's still got a home."

"Where does he live when he's not at the park?"

"With me."

"Sleeping in your lap while you watch television?" There was a sharp, nasty sneer in Michael's voice.

"I told you, he's not well socialized."

"So you keep him penned up."

"He has a room of his own. Is there something you want?"

"I just want to sit here with him for a few minutes. That okay?"

The woman stared hard at him. Then she looked at Faith, who nodded. She had no idea what to think about any of it, but Michael wanted to sit with this apparently crazy cat, so she wasn't going to get in his way.

"Fine. Just…don't sue us if he slices you open. We don't have any money, anyway."

"Do I look like somebody who'd sue anybody, lady?"

Without another word, the woman turned and walked off toward friendlier people.

Faith sat down at Michael's side. The cat growled at her, too.

"It's okay, dude," Michael said, almost crooning the words. He put his hand flat on the side of the cage, near the cat. Immediately, a paw lashed out and left a long red seam on Michael's palm—but he didn't even flinch.

"Look at him. He's not mean. He's scared. God, I fucking hate people."

Without thinking about what she was doing, Faith put her hand on Michael's leg.

He stared down at it, his hand still flat on the cage. For maybe as long as a minute, the three of them were still and quiet. Then Michael said, "I was a foster kid."

She knew that. She'd overheard Aunt Bibi and Uncle Hooj talking about it. But that seemed a wrong thing to tell him. So she said only, "Yeah?"

"Yeah. I went in when I was two. I never got adopted or even had a family placement for very long. A couple times a year, though, they'd do this adoption fair thing. You know what that is?"

She didn't, so she shook her head. But he was still staring at her hand, so she said, "No."

"It's like this here—a bunch of foster kids get dressed up as good as they can and get taken to a park. People who are thinking about adopting go to the park and look over all the kids. If they see one they like, they take them home. It's more complicated than that, but that's basically it. A bunch of unwanted kids trying to be was wantable as they could be, a bunch of rich assholes walking around deciding which one matched their furniture the best. It fucking sucked."

Faith felt her eyes burning. She didn't know what to say or do—all of this was way heavier than she knew how to deal with. So she squeezed his leg a little. That felt silly, but she couldn't think of anything better.

He twitched under her touch and then went on with a story that wasn't yet finished. "People used to come up to me all the time. I guess I was a cute kid. I mean, I don't know. It's not like I have pictures. All I saw in the mirror was me. But people said all the time that I was…was…*beautiful*"—he flinched and almost spat out that word—"so lots of people would come up to me at those things. But I never got picked. Probably for the best."

While he'd been talking, the cat had inched closer to his hand. Michael had never moved it, even though blood was now dripping off the side of his palm from the slice the cat had made through it. Now, while they were quiet again, the cat stood and pressed his body against the side of the cage, against Michael's hand.

And started to purr like a motorboat.

Michael laughed. When the cat turned and put his head against the wire, he finally moved his hand, sliding his fingers into the cage and scratching furry black ears. Then he opened the cage and pulled the cat out.

"What are you doing?" The woman was back, but she pulled up short when she saw the cat draped over Michael's shoulder. He hissed at the woman and then turned his face toward Michael's neck.

"How much to adopt him?"

"What?"

"How much?"

The woman stood there with her mouth open, blinking. Faith's father would have said she was 'catching flies.' Then she closed her mouth and narrowed her eyes. "Take him. I'll waive the fee. You have to put him in a carrier to get him home, though, and he's not going to like that at all."

"It'll be okay. He knows I'm not gonna hurt him."

Faith didn't know how Michael thought he was going to be able to keep a cat in the clubhouse, which was where he lived. But she kept her mouth shut. It felt like something important was happening here, between Michael and this cat, and between Michael and her.

He was right about the carrier. The cat went from Michael's arms into the cardboard box without a fuss. And then they walked back down through the park.

He walked her to Dante, cradling the carrier at his chest, talking into the air holes.

"Tom is a stupid name for a cat. They didn't even care enough to give him a good name."

She smiled. There was a good chance that today her crush on Michael was turning into something more than that—which sucked extra hard, since nothing was going to happen as long as her father had anything to say about anything. "So give him a better name. What do you like better?"

Michael peered into the holes. Faith couldn't imagine he could see much in that dark space, but it seemed like he could. "He looks like that cartoon cat. The one who's always chasing Tweety?"

"Sylvester? Yeah, he looks just like him. But I think he's tougher than that. More like Sylvester Stallone."

He turned to her and grinned. "Sly Stallone. Yeah. That's his name."

When they got to Dante, Michael handed her the box full of cat. "Happy birthday."

She stared at him. "What?"

"He's for you. Happy birthday."

"You're giving me a free, feral cat for my birthday?" She'd meant it as a joke, but she was sorry she'd said it, because he blushed, and hurt went through his eyes. He'd really thrown her, though. She didn't think she could go home with a cat any more than he could. Especially not a man-eating beast.

"He'll like you. I know." He set the box in Dante's bed, then opened the top. Lifting Faith's hand, he put it in the box with Sly—who immediately swiped at her, drawing blood.

But then he bumped their joined hands and purred.

"See?" Michael closed the top of the box, and then he noticed that her hand was bleeding. "Oh, damn. Sorry."

He lifted her hand again, and this time he took it all the way to his lips and kissed the new wound. Faith's heart raced.

And then he held her face in his hands like he'd done before, and he kissed her, and she was fairly certain she was going to pass out.

This time, she was determined not to pull away. The first time, she'd been overwhelmed and not sure how to kiss and breathe at the same time. This time, she'd just go ahead and pass out if she ran out of air, but she was not going to pull away, not ever.

His lips felt so fantastic. He needed to shave, too—there was bristle all around his mouth, like sandpaper. He was so blond she hadn't noticed the scruff until it was rubbing against her skin. But oh, she liked it. She liked the way it hurt a little. And she loved the way his tongue moved inside her mouth, soft but greedy, and the way his hands were tense around her face. If everybody kissed like this, Faith couldn't understand why people weren't doing it all day every day. Because this was the best thing ever.

Then one hand left her face, and she almost whined, but she was afraid to make any noise that might spook him and make him stop. She focused on their lips and tongues, on trying to learn what he was doing so she could do it, too.

His hand was on her waist. Moving up under her shirt. Oh, shit, that felt good, just his hand on the skin over her ribs. Oh, shit. She couldn't stop a little whimper.

He groaned in response and then turned them, pushing her back against her car. And then—oh shit oh shit—his hand was on her boob. Over the bra, but still. No one had ever touched her there. The nerves in her boob felt carbonated, billions of bubbles popping under her skin. She wanted him to move her bra. More than anything else in this life, she wanted him to get that stupid thing out of their way. She wanted his hot skin on hers.

Oh, she wanted that so bad! She'd thought she'd felt horny before. She'd done some experimenting. She'd gotten one of the candles her mom kept stocked for the dining room centerpiece, and she'd…explored…a little and made herself feel pretty good. But she'd never felt anything like what she was feeling right now. If he threw her down on the sidewalk and just fucked her, she wouldn't stop him. In fact, she'd cheer.

He groaned again, louder this time, and she realized she was moving, rocking her hips against him. She could feel that he wanted her. What she felt was big and scary, and she wanted that, too.

He was shaking. His whole body was shaking. His hand on her boob was shaking, even as his thumb moved back and forth over her nipple, through her stupid bra which she was throwing away as soon as she got home, throwing all her bras away.

Then his fingers hooked into the top of the cup and started to pull, and she was so thrilled, so relieved, that she had to say something. She broke away from his mouth and gasped. "Yes! Oh please, yes!"

He jumped away from her so far and so fast, she might as well have had a cattle prod.

For maybe two seconds, he stared at her, his face red and his blue eyes vivid with what looked like bewilderment.

And then he ran. He turned and ran down the sidewalk, back toward the park.

She stood there, gasping, her top askew. She heard a strange sound and turned to see the box moving a little. Oh, right. She had a birthday cat. A crazy cat from a crazy guy.

Instead of crying or screaming or otherwise pitching a fit, though she really wanted to, she straightened herself out, caught her breath, picked up her new cat, set him on the passenger seat, and drove home.

Maybe the fight she was going to get from her mother about her new cat would take her mind off what had just happened.

Probably not.

CHAPTER SIX

Demon woke and had no idea where he was at first. Hell, that sense of displacement was so strong he had no idea *when* he was. He sat up and reached for his piece.

A piece he no longer carried with him everywhere as a matter of course. Because he hadn't been a Nomad for years.

Sitting up on the side of the bed, life came back to him. He was in the clubhouse dorm. Okay. Okay.

All the single patches had rooms in the dorm, a place they could take the girls. Or more than that—Connor, Lakota, and P.B. all lived at the clubhouse. Demon had, too, until he'd hooked up with Dakota. She hadn't like it here.

Demon's room hadn't been getting much use of late. Not at all since Tucker had been placed with the Elliotts. His attention was on his kid, not his dick.

He was there now because he'd gone for a ride after he'd put Tucker to bed the night before, and he hadn't been able to face the idea that Faith would be in Bibi and Hoosier's house when he got back.

Hoosier thought he had a second chance—that *they* had a second chance. But for what? They'd only ever been what could possibly be construed as 'together' for a few weeks, and she'd been just a kid. Hoosier had said he'd been just a kid, too, and maybe that was right. He'd known then that, for all the things he'd experienced growing up, his experiences hadn't been like those of normal kids. He'd been old in ways they were not, but he'd missed the things kids weren't supposed to miss.

He'd felt dumb a lot of the time, not catching jokes and references that people made. Maybe that had made him young. Maybe that was why he'd been so drawn to a teenage girl in the first place. She was so much more normal than he was, so strong and centered. Almost like she'd been the older one. But she was also a little weird, in a way he understood. He hadn't felt like a wrong piece in a puzzle when he was around her.

But that had been ten years ago. Ten long, important years, full of a lot of life. The things he'd done in those years hadn't made him any more normal. He didn't know what her life had been like, but it sounded like it had been good. She was making her art things. That was good. She was good in the life she had. It was probably better for the past to stay where it was, then.

And yet—when he'd seen her, he'd felt every single feeling he'd ever had for her, all at once, and in the same intensity they had ever had. No—stronger. He still loved her. He didn't think he could deal with knowing for a fact that they couldn't have a second chance. He couldn't deal with learning that she hadn't kept her feelings simmering the way he had. Even though he'd never thought to see her again, now that he had, everything in his head and heart was in turmoil, and he could feel the strands of his tenuous control snapping under the strain.

So he hadn't gone back to the Elliotts'.

He could have stayed in his trailer, but he barely went into that dump anymore. He kept the rent and utilities up, just to have an address that wasn't the clubhouse or somebody else's house, but that tin can was depressing. He'd lived with the Elliotts as long as Tucker had. That was where his family was.

So he'd come to the clubhouse. And he'd sat at the bar for a while with some of his brothers, drinking too much. He wasn't hung over—for whatever reason, his body didn't do hangovers, not physically—but there were fuzzy spaces in his memory, so he knew he'd gotten pretty fucking drunk.

Demon didn't, as a rule, get drunk. He didn't do drugs at all. He drank, but he tried hard not to cross beyond the buzzed zone. A guy like him, with a faulty switch on his impulses even when he was sober, had no business putting things in his body that encouraged impulsive behavior. But a biker couldn't really be a teetotaler, so he drank with his brothers and tried to pay attention.

Last night, he'd missed the sign, that one drink that was the last chance to slow down. He looked at his hands—they were uninjured. Well, good. Then he hadn't started a brawl.

But when he got up, he dislodged a purple thong from a wad under his pillow. Fuck. Then that part of his memory revived, and he remembered that he'd brought Coco back here last night. He looked frantically around the room but saw no other signs that he'd had a guest. Club girls knew to get moving when the fun was over, so she would have left, probably when he passed out. Feeling a chemical surge of panic in his blood, he ran to his little closet of a bathroom and checked the wastebasket.

There were two used condoms and their wrappers in the bottom. Demon leaned his hands on the sink and blew out his relief. The club had all the girls tested regularly for creeping crap, but Demon had himself an object lesson for forgetting about birth control.

He loved his boy with everything he had in him, but Tucker had an epically shitty mother and had had an epically shitty start in life, and that was Demon's fault. Getting carried away. Faulty switch.

Just faulty in general.

Since he was already naked and standing in the bathroom, he took a shower. He always felt better after a shower, like his bad feelings sloughed off in the spray of scalding water.

When he went out to the Hall, it was still early. But it looked like a Prospect had made a doughnut run, and there was fresh coffee. One of the great things about living at the clubhouse—there was always food and drink, right there waiting.

He was surprised to see Muse sitting at the bar so early. Muse didn't work in the shop. For his on-the-books job, he worked with the entertainment industry, managing the club's bike rental business and doing technical advising on movie and television sets. Several of the SoCal Horde worked with Hollywood, as TAs or stunt riders. A couple of them, Muse included, had even been in a movie scene once or twice. The Night Horde had a little fame, and a couple of their old ladies were famous, too.

Demon thought it was a little weird, all their connections to famous people, but it made some sense, too. They were in SoCal, after all. When Hollywood wanted badass bikers and 'authenticity,' they came waving stacks of cash. Plus, Virtuoso Cycles was widely considered the best custom bike shop in California, and they had a couple of wizard builders, so there were Hollywood types, the kind who considered themselves 'edgy,' around pretty often, commissioning builds or getting bling installed on their stock bikes. Or just getting maintenance done—none of those assholes could even change their own fucking oil.

Muse, though, wasn't usually in this early, unless he was taking bikes to a filming location somewhere. He'd been doing a lot less of that, leaving it more and more to Fargo, his assistant and one of the current batch of Prospects, because Muse was working the outlaw side, and that was really his main job.

Like Demon, Muse was an enforcer. But Muse still actually did that work. Demon was staying clean. So far, he'd been able to stay clear of their work with La Zorra, a chick cartel kingpin—or was it queenpin?—who was becoming a major player in the border drug trade.

He knew it was just a matter of time before his hands would be dirty, too. He hoped that he'd have custody of Tucker before that happened.

"Morning, brother."

Muse turned and raised his eyebrows. "Deme. You good? Saw your bike—there a problem at Hooj's? Tucker okay?"

Before Demon could answer, Muse's big, black German Shepherd, Cliff, trotted over. Muse brought him to hang at the clubhouse sometimes—usually when he was feeling guilty that he hadn't been able to spend time with him for a while.

Demon squatted down and gave his buddy some love. "Yeah. We're good. Just needed...I don't know. But I'm okay." He let Cliff lick his face, then ruffled his ears and stood up.

Muse's expression was skeptical. "Somethin' up?"

Demon considered Muse his best friend. Muse had a few stories about the foster care system himself, and he probably knew more than anybody else about Demon's childhood—not everything, but more. When Demon had been exiled to the Nomads, Muse, about a decade older and more experienced, had stepped in and helped him work out how to be homeless again. So he felt a real, deep, solid bond between them. But Demon had never talked about Faith with him or anybody who hadn't been around and known already. He didn't know what Muse might have heard over the grapevine—probably at least that he'd fucked a brother's daughter—but he hadn't ever offered anything up, and Muse, a tightlipped motherfucker anyway, had never asked.

So Demon wasn't going to start now.

"Nah. I'm good. You're here early. Got a movie gig?"

He sighed and shook his head. "Diaz and J.R. got caught up in some shit with the Rats. I'm waitin' on Connor—we're meeting them and Bart and Ronin for some payback. Figure we'll hit 'em early, with their pants down."

"They whole? What kind of shit?"

"Ran 'em off the road. Bikes're scraped up a little. Them, too, but they're good."

The Dirty Rats were another MC, much bigger than the Horde, with lots of charters—and a really vile, and well-earned, reputation. They had never been rivals before, but the Horde had put down half a charter's worth of the bastards during a cartel fight, and now the Rats were looking for payback. No big, organized offensive, just shit like this—running guys off the road, ambushing them outside a bar, catching them off their guard.

Since the Rats weren't known for their decorum or subtlety, it seemed like they were trying to stay off somebody's radar. Otherwise, they'd've just come in for a retaliation hit. The Horde had ended their guys months ago, and all they'd faced from the Rats since was penny-ante shit like this.

Which probably meant something big was brewing somewhere.

Part of Demon—the largest part—wanted to offer his help. He wanted to be outlaw. He liked putting hurt on assholes. He liked the charge and the focus of working outside the bleeding edge of society. There was calm in it that he didn't get any other way. And he deeply hated that two of his brothers had been attacked, and he was going to sit here at the shop screwing parts on bikes while his family took care of the problem.

There wasn't much he could say. He wasn't part of what was going on. It was right—he needed to do what he had to do to make his best case for custody of Tucker, and that meant staying as clean as he could. But it was wrong, too. So he changed the subject, sort of. "You got your truck? You brought Cliff. You're not riding out today?"

"I'll take the Sportster. It's still here from when I thought I was gonna have to sell it. The Knuckle's running rough lately, and anyway, I didn't want to leave Cliff at home. Sid's in Orange County for a couple days."

"Problem?"

"Nah. Her mom's winning some award, and there's some kinda formal ceremony. Not my scene."

Demon chuckled a little. Several of the SoCal Horde who'd taken old ladies had ended up with rich chicks. Bart was married to a famous actress. Diaz to a supermodel. Now Muse had marked a girl whose mom was a fancy lawyer like Findley-call-me-Finn Bennett and lived in a fucking mansion. Not the kind of women people thought of as the type to want a biker.

But people tended to resist type, Demon thought. Good people did, anyway. It wasn't about type. It was about being understood.

It was about finding someone you fit with, someone whose puzzle matched your own.

Demon closed his eyes and thought about Faith. For all the ways he knew they'd been wrong, in that way they'd been right.

Maybe they could still be. He needed to get straight enough in his head to talk to her. Tonight. Tonight, he'd talk to her. He would. He could.

But for now, he turned back to Muse.

"Wish I could help today."

"No question, brother." Muse put his hand on Demon's shoulder. It was a gesture, a touch, meant to share strength, to calm Demon's unsettled soul. He knew it, and he appreciated it. He always had. "It's right you stay back. You don't need trouble you can avoid, not right now. I told you we'd do all we can to keep you clear."

~oOo~

Just before noon, with the guys still out on their payback run, Demon was working in the shop, tricking out a Wide Glide. Trick was there, starting a new custom build, and P.B. was doing a repair job. Jesse was working the showroom. Nolan and Double A, Missouri members on loan from the mother charter, were helping out on a couple of bike maintenance jobs. Just a regular day, though they were all on alert in case they got a call for backup.

The intercom whined and went live. "Guys!" Jesse said into the room. "Bibi brought lunch—from The Bunkhouse!" The Bunkhouse was the best steakhouse in town. Usually, they sent a Prospect out at lunch for fast food.

"Awesome!" P.B. crowed and set down his tools. Trick just rolled his eyes and kept working. He was a vegetarian or a vegan or one of those plant-eater types.

Then Bibi's voice came over the 'com. "We brought you a big salad, Trick. And Tuck's lookin' for you, Deme. We're settin' up in the Hall."

All the mechanics were grinning when they came through from the shop to the clubhouse. Bibi had set up a family-style meal, pushing some of the small tables together. Cliff was walking around the table, his tail wagging, his nose in the air, smelling steak.

A meal like this in the middle of the day was unusual, especially with half the club out, but Hoosier was in the Hall, too, and he didn't seem concerned.

"Any word on the job today, Prez?" Demon asked, picking Tucker up and hugging him.

"Yeah. They're whole and clear, on their way back. Stirred up some sh—trouble, just like they wanted. We'll see where it goes. I want to bring this sh—thing to a head."

Bibi came over to Demon and Tucker. "Show your pa what you learned today, Tuck."

Demon smiled at his boy. "You got something new, buddy?"

Tucker nodded, then dropped his head to his father's shoulder.

"Don't be shy, Tuckster. Tell your pa." Bibi grabbed his foot and gave it a shake.

Lifting his head and looking at Demon with serious eyes, Tucker said, "Lub you, Pa."

"Holy shit," Demon whispered. Tucker had never said those words before.

"Shit," Tucker agreed solemnly.

Laughing, Demon hugged his son. "I love you, too, Motor Man. I love you so much."

"Lub you."

His face felt hot, but not in the way it usually did. He held his son close and felt good and right. He felt strong. He looked down at Bibi.

"Thanks for last night."

"No worries, baby. You needed some time alone, and you know I've got Tuck."

"Thanks."

"Did it help?"

"Yeah. I'm gonna talk to her tonight. I think I can be cool about it now."

Bibi went a little pale. "Deme, that's not gonna work. She's not there."

Just like that, everything good Demon had been feeling withered away and left acid and bile in its place. "What? Where is she?"

"She went home—"

Before she could finish, Demon yelled "FUCK!" and Tucker flinched and began to cry. Grasping the last threads of control he could, he handed his son to Bibi and stormed toward the dorm before he lost any more of his shit in front of his kid.

Before he could get to the hallway, Bibi's hand was on his arm. He spun and yanked his arm away. Bibi—without Tucker—jumped back, flinching, and then Hoosier was between them. "You take a breath right now, boy. You get yourself under control."

"FUCK! FUCK!" His mind rioted. She'd left! She was gone! She'd shown up just to fuck him up and then was gone. Fuck!

Hoosier, though smaller than Demon, didn't hesitate. He grabbed him by the kutte and shoved him toward his office. Vaguely, Demon heard Cliff barking in the Hall.

All Demon could think about was getting those hands off him. He fought back, punching his President in the face, knocking him down.

Then the hallway was full of men, yanking Demon back. He fought hard, trying to get free, thinking only about getting away. Away. Back on his feet, Hoosier punched him in the gut twice while P.B. and Trick held him, and that knocked the wind and the fire out of him.

In front of his kid, he'd pulled that shit. He could hear him still crying.

"Sit him on my couch. Christ on a crutch."

When Demon was on the couch and alone in the office with Hoosier and Bibi, Hoosier pulled up his desk chair. Bibi stayed near the door.

"I'm sorry. I wouldn't've…I don't think…I'm sorry."

Bibi answered. "It's okay, baby. I know. But you didn't let me finish. She only went to pack herself a bag and get some things settled at home. She'll be back tomorrow."

That should have been good news, but Demon frowned. Tomorrow? How could she get all that done in a day? Why hadn't she had a bag in the first place? It didn't make sense. He didn't know where she lived, but it had to be far away. Out of his reach. She'd had Dante—she'd driven. So…"Where's 'home'?"

Bibi didn't answer right away, so he looked at Hoosier. "Where does she live?"

"You keep a lid on, Dcmc. I'm not fuckin' around here."

Words like that only made him more agitated. They expected him to be pissed. "*Where?*"

"Venice Beach," Bibi said.

For a few seconds, Demon's mind went blank, full of white noise. She was in L.A.? All this time, she'd been fifty miles away? He'd imagined her in New York or London or the fucking Yukon. Mars, maybe. Far away, out of his reach. But she'd been in his back yard. She'd known where he was. She'd been *close*. And she hadn't sought him out. Even though her father was gone.

"You knew where she was. All this time?"

Bibi took a couple of steps closer. "She's only been close again for a year and a half or so."

"But she knew where *I* was."

"Yeah, she did."

"She doesn't want to know me."

"She's scared, Deme. Just like you."

"*Like* me, or *of* me?"

Hoosier answered that. "Stop it, boy. I'm sick to shit of this drama. You're not some kind of wild animal. Did you ever hurt her?" Demon opened his mouth to say that yes, getting near her at all had hurt her, but Hoosier waved his hand abruptly. "I'm not talking about all the painful love bullshit. Did your hands hurt her body? Ever? Did you ever lose control around her?"

Not in the way Hoosier was asking, but yes. Every time he was with her, he lost control around her. Demon looked down at his hands in his lap and remembered when there'd been just no more control to be had.

memory

When a new member got his patch, his brothers set out to get him as drunk as they possibly could. Demon was a lightweight, relatively speaking, so they hadn't had to work very hard.

He didn't really like being drunk. It made him feel like everything around him was out of time, like it was a parallel universe where everything was almost but not quite right, and time was just slightly out of sync. It confused him; he didn't totally understand what people were saying or doing.

Like the way his brothers had all been laughing when a couple of girls pulled him out of his pants and started taking turns blowing him in the Hall. Was that a joke? At his expense? He didn't like being laughed at. And he sure as fuck didn't like everybody watching that shit. Some guys didn't mind getting off in the middle of everything, but Demon didn't like to see it, and he damn sure didn't like to do it.

Which was why he'd been thrown out of his own patch party, he guessed. Or, at least, told to 'go outside and cool the fuck off.'

He was just as glad. That had sucked. He'd never had a party in his honor before, and he'd hated it, everybody paying attention to him, fucking with him, like they were trying to make him lose control. Well, mission accomplished.

So, feeling unsteady but capable of walking, he went past the picnic benches, through the lot, and right out of the compound. He didn't know where he was going, but he went anyway.

He'd walked for a while, deep inside his head, trying to quiet the chaos that too much whiskey had only made louder, when a horn honked on the street at his side. He jumped and stopped, preparing to tell the asshole driver to shove his horn up his ass and to offer to help that happen.

But he was looking at Dante.

Faith leaned over and rolled down the passenger window. "What're you doing?"

"Walking."

"To my house?"

"What?"

She pointed up ahead. "This is my street. You're walking to my house. At twelve-thirty at night. If you're looking for my dad, he's at your party."

"What?" He didn't feel as drunk as he had when he'd left the clubhouse, but nothing was making sense yet.

She pulled to the curb and parked. Standing on the sidewalk, confused as hell, Demon watched her get out and walk up to him. "Are you okay? Did you walk all this way?"

"All what way?"

"I live about seven miles from the clubhouse. Seven miles through not the best parts of town. You know that. Did you walk from there?"

"I guess." She obviously thought that was important, but he didn't know why. So he changed the subject. "How's Sly?"

Cocking her head, she grinned. "He's good. I'm not trying to keep him inside anymore. He hates my folks. He's happier having the run of the neighborhood, I think. He comes in and sleeps with me almost every night, though."

"Lucky cat."

Faith gave him a surprised look. She stepped up to him and put her hands on his chest. That felt fucking awesome, even through his kutte, and he put his hands over hers. That felt even better.

"Do you want a ride back to the clubhouse?"

No, he absolutely did not want to go back to the clubhouse and get laughed at again. Or looked at weird. Or yelled at for breaking a table. He didn't even have his patch sewn on yet, and he was already in trouble. Fuck.

"No."

"What do you want to do, then?"

He knew exactly what he wanted to do. More than a year, he'd wanted her. He tried to stay away, but she kept showing up in front of him, talking to him, being beautiful and sweet. Since her birthday, he'd managed to keep from being alone with her. But every time he saw her, he wanted her. It was getting harder, not easier.

He was tired of fighting it all the time. So he kissed her. As soon as he did, he knew his fight was lost.

She kissed him back, moving her tongue with his, curling her fists around his kutte. He knew he wouldn't stop this time. There was too much in his head, too much whiskey still in his snoot, too much needing to feel okay. The part of him that knew he should stop was almost inaudible.

Almost. He pulled back. "You have to stop me," he murmured on her lips. "I can't stop. You have to do it."

"I don't want to stop. I want to be with you. I want it so bad." She looped her arms around his neck, and he lifted her off the ground, clutching her close. They stood like that on the sidewalk, kissing deeply, Demon thinking of nothing at all anymore except his need, feeling her body touching his all the way to her feet. She felt right there. She fit with him.

She pulled back from their kiss and looked at him, panting, her lips glistening and her eyes sparkling in the streetlights. "We need to go someplace. Will you ride if I drive?"

He nodded and covered her mouth with his again.

~oOo~

Faith didn't drive far, just about ten minutes, to an empty parking lot on a bluff overlooking the coast. They didn't talk on the way; Demon looked out the passenger window and watched the passing lights, trying to think and make a right choice, but knowing full well that that boat had sailed. He wasn't really drunk anymore. He was just tired of fighting his nature.

She killed the engine and leaned toward him immediately, shifting on the bench seat so that she was on her knees at his side. She took his face in her hands, the way he did when he kissed her. When she bent her head to his, he flinched back a fraction of an inch.

"Stop me. Please stop me."

"No," she whispered. "I don't want to stop. I think I'm in love with you."

Demon didn't know how that could be true, but he didn't care. Hearing this girl say those words sent a surge of powerful need through his blood, his muscles. He was done running. Taking over the kiss, demanding that it be more, he grabbed her, pulling her onto him. Then he rolled and laid her out on the seat and covered her with his body. Her legs came up and circled his hips, and he could feel her heat grinding against his, heedless of the layers of denim between them.

Groaning, feeling desperate and frantic, and fearful, too, he pushed her sweater up, and her bra, and covered her beautiful breast with his hand. She cried out an encouragement, a plea, and her own hands moved between them and worked the buckle on his belt.

He didn't stop. He couldn't.

~oOo~

You asshole. You bastard. On the seat of her car. In a parking lot. It was her first time, you piece of shit.

The thoughts and their loathing besieged him while his body still shook with the aftershocks of his finish, while she was staring up at him, her eyes wide and wet, her hands on his shoulders, digging into the hoodie he still wore.

He sat back in a rush and felt the cooling, wet stick of semen on his belly. He looked at her, still lying on her back, her legs splayed, one bare and the other still in her jeans, and saw the wet on her belly, too, glimmering in the parking lot lights. He'd come all over her. Because he hadn't been able to control himself enough to put a condom on. He'd barely been able to pull out. Jesus. Aw, Jesus hell.

She was noticing her sticky belly and looking for something to wipe up with. He yanked his hoodie over his head and handed it to her. It was February and cold for L.A., but his t-shirt would have to do. He deserved to be cold.

"I'm sorry. I'm sorry. God, *God*, I'm sorry." He opened the door and got the fuck out of the car, leaving his kutte behind, not even bothering to put his stupid dick away.

"Michael! Michael, please! Please!"

At the plaintive sound of her voice, he pulled up short. What— he was going to top off the worst thing he'd ever done by leaving her alone, covered in his scum? Fuck, he was worthless. Despairing, he raked his hands through his hair and over his face. He could smell her on his fingers. The image that scent evoked made him hurt with need and guilt.

He closed his jeans. Before he could open the door and get back in, though, she was out and running around Dante. She was crying and furious, and his face felt so fucking hot. Look how he'd hurt her. He couldn't see that, deal with that, so he dropped his eyes and stared at the gravel.

"You're ruining it! You jerk! You pussy! Don't ruin this! Fuck! Fuck you! Fuck!" She shoved at him, sobbing. When he didn't react, she shoved at him again.

Then she just grabbed hold of his t-shirt and shook it.

Not knowing what else to do, and feeling like a wart on the ass of a maggot, he put his arms around her and pulled her close. "I'm sorry. I didn't mean it, any of it. I'm sorry."

"Stop it! Shut up!" she cried, her face wetting his chest. "Don't be sorry. I told you. It ruins everything."

He *was* sorry, but he was making it worse by saying so. He thought of something he could say. "I'm sorry for making you cry."

She was quiet for a moment, settling down. "Okay. You can be sorry for that."

That made him smile, and he kissed the top of her head. "What we did was okay?"

Her face moved softly on his chest as she nodded. "I liked it a lot. It was even better than I thought it would be."

"I didn't hurt you?"

"Uh-uh." She leaned back. "I just feel a little…stretched, maybe?"

The relief he felt to know that he hadn't hurt her weakened his knees. But it didn't mean that what they'd done was right. He'd had his patch a matter of hours, and he'd just fucked the club SAA's underage daughter. He'd taken her virginity, in fact. There would be a huge price for that. There should be.

"I should get you home."

She grinned and shook her head. "I drove, remember? We go when I say so. Right now, I want to sit on the car and watch the ocean." Her eyes narrowed. "Please don't puss out."

He nodded, and they went and sat on the hood of her car. Demon put his arm around her and held her close. It felt good to take care of her, to keep her warm, to tuck her small body next to his as if he could keep her safe.

"Can I ask you something, Michael?" She didn't look at him, just stared out at the black night and water below.

"Yeah." He watched her profile.

"Why do you run?"

"What?"

"You kiss me like you do. You look at me sometimes like I'm dipped in chocolate. You gave me a cat. We just did what we did, and I felt like you liked it. Like you like *me*."

"I did. I do." More than that, he thought. But he didn't say it.

"Then why do you run?"

"You're just a kid." It was the best reason he had.

She scoffed. "Please. Maybe—*maybe*—that was true when we met. But now I'm seventeen and almost seven months. Connor boinked my friend Bethany a couple of weeks ago, and she turned eighteen last month. Nobody had palpitations about that. Does some magical fairy come to girls' houses on their eighteenth birthday and make their twats ripe or something?"

Appalled and charmed by her take on the matter, Demon laughed. But his humor didn't last long. "Your father…he'll—"

"I know, I know." She heaved a big sigh. "God, my life *sucks*."

That pissed him off, and he took his arm from her shoulders. The life she had—what he would have given to have had even a piece of a life like that. She was surrounded by people who loved her. The way everybody in the clubhouse doted on her—and God, the way Blue loved her and she loved him? Sometimes, he'd watch them, Faith smiling at her father, her father teasing her gently, calling her kitty cat, and his stomach would cramp. Was it envy he felt? No. There was hostility in envy that Demon didn't feel toward Faith.

What he felt when he saw the way she was loved, and the way she was so comfortable and assured in that love, was just...lack.

"That's fucked up. Your life doesn't suck at all. You have a great life."

Instead of feeling guilty, she got pissed right back. "What do you know about it?"

"I know you have a mom and dad who love you, and a house with your own room, and a car of your own, and you do pretty much what you want and have pretty much what you want. I know that much. Trust me—that isn't a life that sucks."

Her anger evaporated. "Okay. It's not always so great, though."

He couldn't stay mad, either. Not at her. "I know. Sorry I jumped down your throat. I'm just saying—could be worse."

"Yeah. It makes me sad that yours was."

He shrugged and put his arm back around her. "What do we do now?"

"You're not running?"

It was too late to run. "No. But Blue is going to take me apart when I tell him. Even if he doesn't kill me, I'll probably lose my patch." He tried to laugh, but the sound that came out was something different. "I don't even have the thing sewn on yet."

"Don't tell him. Not yet."

"You want to wait?" That was the wisest course. It made him feel sick, though, now, after he'd given in and knew what it was like to love her. He wasn't sure he could go back to avoiding her.

But she shook her head. "No. I don't want to wait. I just don't want to say anything."

"You want to sneak? To lie?" Demon was well acquainted with sneaking and lying—it was how he'd survived a lot of things he'd had to survive—but he didn't want to start his life in the club that way.

"Just until I'm eighteen. He'll still be pissed then, but there'll be less he can do about it. I don't want you to get hurt—and I don't want you to lose your patch. I know what it means. But I don't want to not see you. If you want to be with me, then I want to be with you. I don't want to wait. We'll just have to be careful for a little while."

"Why? I'm no good. Why do you want this?"

Her smile was the sweetest thing he'd ever seen. "I told you. Because I love you, stupid. You *are* good, and I'm in love with you."

He believed her. He'd do anything for her.

Even betray a brother.

CHAPTER SEVEN

Faith had felt better once she got back home. Not really thinking it through, just knowing she couldn't leave him behind again, she'd brought Sly back with her. He'd ridden contently most of the way, curled on her lap, bumping his head on her arm when he'd wanted to be stroked.

He'd been slow and suspicious when she'd set him down on the worn wood floor of her loft, but it was a big, wide-open space with wide, long windows lining two whole walls, so he'd slunk around a while and then found a sill to camp on. She'd run out to the all-night market a couple of blocks down and brought back cat food. He'd dined in mismatched china bowls. All of her dishes were oddball flea market finds. She liked to make mismatched things match.

In the morning, she'd woken with her old cat curled up on her pillow with her, purring, his furry paw on her head, flexing his claws into her ear in a gentle, contented rhythm. She'd lain still and enjoyed that as long as she could.

Just having a shower with her own stuff and putting actual clothes on, her jewelry, doing her hair and makeup—just that made her feel more in control of herself, if not of the new circumstances of her life. Going to Madrone in the middle of the night in ratty sweats had been like going to battle without armor.

Now, though, she was back in the world she knew, out in her life, taking care of her business, and she felt strong again. Protected. A niggling thought had crept in the back door to suggest that she didn't have to return to Madrone, that her mother's problems were not her problems, that whatever she and Michael had had was old news and should stay that way, that she could just pretend the past couple of days had never happened and return to her regularly scheduled programming.

But that was impossible, too. She couldn't know what was going on and stay away. Her mother was cold and could be cruel, and

Faith wasn't sure she deserved her love. But she couldn't leave that mess to Bibi. Bibi couldn't do everything.

And now that she'd seen Michael, she had to know.

So, dressed in one of her favorite outfits, wearing her very favorite studded combat boots, looking hot and feeling strong, Faith began to take the steps that would, if necessary, close up the life she'd built for herself, by herself, so she could go home to a place she'd never lived and take care of a mother who didn't want her.

She'd gone down to Slow Drips with her tablet to send and answer emails and try to make a couple of quick appointments. With that sort of boring, administrative work, she'd learned that she focused better away from home. She was more focused on the work she did at home, then, too, if it wasn't tainted by the gloom of business.

At home, she made her art—that was why she had the loft. She had a whole floor of an old warehouse that was in the middle of being refurbished into condos. Hers was still, for the most part, a warehouse, with some rudimentary refits for a kitchen and a bathroom. It was a rental, and she knew damn well she wouldn't be able to afford to buy one of the condos when they got around to renovating her unit. But until then, she was getting a great rate and her landlord was pretty chill about her doing heavy-duty welding at home.

How she would manage to keep making art if she had to move to Madrone long-term, she didn't know. She had a couple of commissions, one of them huge. She would have to work that out. Somehow.

After she finished her emails and got back confirmations on two appointments, she packed up and ran some errands, walking around her neighborhood for as many of them as she could.

Venice Beach was both an L.A. neighborhood and its own unique little place. It was different from just about everywhere Faith had ever been, and she'd been to some interesting places. She'd traveled quite a bit, and she'd lived in the Haight in San

Francisco for about eight years. But when she'd lived there, the Haight was becoming gentrified, full of gajillion-dollar Victorians and lofts. There had still been signs of its Flower Power heyday, but they were more museum pieces than neighborhood landmarks.

The same thing was happening to Venice—hence the precarious future of her awesomely rugged apartment—but more slowly, she thought, with more resistance from the locals. And the boardwalk continued to be a cornucopia of freakiness. She loved it.

What she knew of Madrone did not inspire in her any confidence that she could be happy in a life there, even without the specter of taking care of Margot. Faith pretty much thought the whole Inland Empire was an armpit. She didn't understand why the club had moved out of the eclectic bustle of L.A. to some rinky-dink subdivision town.

Madrone was pretty, sitting between the San Gabriel and San Bernardino Mountains, but it was pretty in a doctor's-office-waiting-room-print sort of way. Faith liked this kind of pretty. Venice Beach was pretty in an ugly way. Nothing matched, but everything belonged together. Like her sculptures. Like her.

~oOo~

She had a late lunch meeting with the director of the park that had commissioned the big piece she was making: a twenty-foot-long snake that would sit at the entrance to the new children's area and be suitable for climbing. She was working in four five-foot segments, and had most of the third segment finished.

It had been a nightmare to navigate the logistics of merging her style of art—using scavenged and salvaged metal parts—with the safety needs of what amounted to a big jungle gym. Rusty engine parts were sharp. Also rusty. Not so great on little hands and knees. But the park board loved the idea of recycled art and had been so taken with a piece she'd had installed in the courtyard of the Children's Hospital—two children flying a kite, one of them in a wheelchair—that they'd offered her the commission without even opening it up for applications. She would never have applied to a playground project.

She'd worked it out, but it took longer, because she had to file and seal the segments once they were created. She'd already asked for one extension. Now she'd had to ask for another. And she'd lied when she'd told the director that she needed only three more months.

There was no telling, at this point, whether she could finish it at all.

But she put that doubt out of her head and drove back home. Things would work out, one way or another. It was a pretty fair bet that whatever happened with the snake, the result wouldn't kill her. That was true for her mother, too. Probably. So she'd just keep on keeping on.

With that mentality, she parked Dante in her space in the garage under her building, gathered up her few purchases, and headed to the door that led into the back stairwell of the building. There was an elevator, but it hadn't worked while she'd lived here, a victim of the construction happening on other floors.

The back door was locked. That was true almost half the time, but Faith's landlord had never gotten around to getting her a key for this door. So she huffed a sigh, shifted her canvas bags around to a more long-term hold, and walked through the garage street entrance and around the block to the front door.

Born to a biker and raised in an MC, Faith always noticed the motorcycles around her. She had strong opinions on just about every make, model, and iteration. She didn't ride herself—her father would never teach her, and after she'd left home it hadn't been a priority to learn—but the interest and knowledge was deeply ingrained, like it was coded into her genetics.

So she noticed the mammoth Harley V-Rod Muscle, a gorgeous, highly customized model, solid matte black with a big, fat rear tire, at least a 300, maybe even a 330. The thing looked like it had been ridden straight up from the fires of hell.

No matter what had happened with her family, she was a biker's daughter. Faith felt a thrill just looking at that beautiful bike, a thrill so sharp it honestly made her a little wet.

Then she saw the art on the tank. *Night Horde SoCal*. A horse skeleton with a flaming mane and tail. And in script below: *"Demon."*

She stared at that tank and then turned and stared at the door into her building. Was he in there? For a long, breathless moment, she stood on the sidewalk, holding her bags, letting people pass by her, and stared.

Finally, she went in.

He was sitting on the floor outside her door, leaning against the wall, one leg stretched out before him, the other bent up at the knee, his arm resting on it. She had the whole top floor, so there wasn't really a corridor. More like a landing. He stood when he saw her coming up the last flight of stairs.

"Michael?"

His eyes caught and held hers as she climbed, but he said nothing until she reached the landing and was standing in front of him.

"You were right here. *Right here*." His voice was deep and quiet, beautiful, but soft with hurt. They were the first words he'd said to her since that night ten years ago, and they hurt her to hear.

She nodded.

"Why?"

She knew what he was asking—why had she stayed away, knowing they were so close? Because there were things—there was one thing, a big thing—he didn't know. Because she'd been afraid she'd hurt him more if she'd sought him out. Because she couldn't get so close to her mother. Because she didn't know if he'd still want her.

"I don't know. Afraid, I guess."

"Of me?"

"No, Michael. Never of you. Of…it. Us. What happened. I don't know."

"Are you still afraid?"

Again, she nodded. She was still afraid.

"Me, too." He laughed and smiled sadly—even sad, his was the most beautiful smile. It made the intensity and distrust that seemed a feature of his face disappear and left behind kindness and…well, faith, though Faith felt corny to think it.

"Will you come inside? Will you talk to me?"

Michael nodded and held out his hands for her bags. After she passed them over, she unlocked her door and let him into her life.

As they came in, and Michael went to her table and set her bags down, Sly jumped down from his newly-designated favorite sill and meowed a threat. He came forward carefully, his body skimming the floor, his ears back.

"Holy shit," Michael muttered. "Is that…that's…"

"Yeah. He was at my mom's."

Michael turned to her. "You didn't have him with you all this time?"

She shook her head. "Long story. My mom kept him."

Giving her something like a scowl, Michael squatted and held out his hand to the cat. "Hey, dude."

Sly slunk forward, growling all the way. He sniffed Michael's fingers and swatted at his hand. It was his greeting ritual, and a test. Not many people passed. As far as Faith knew, the only people who had were in this room right now.

The trick was to be steady. Not to flinch, not to run. Sly bumped Michael's hand and came forward, relaxing. Michael picked him up and held him snugly.

He scratched Sly's truncated ear. "He looks a little rough."

"He always was a scrapper. But he doesn't like being cooped up in the house. He probably took on the whole neighborhood." They were talking like normal, like friends. As if the past ten years hadn't happened. It felt weird. And right, too.

"Are you keeping him here now?"

Faith didn't know the answer to that. She didn't know if she was keeping *her* here. It depended on her mother. And on Michael. And on more things than she could sort out at one time. She took a deep breath and let it out slowly. "Michael. What are we…?" She'd meant to finish the question with the word 'doing,' but it wouldn't come. But it sounded right as it was: *what are we*. That was really the question, wasn't it?

He put Sly down, and the cat sauntered off, content, toward his fancy china bowls, already the master of this place.

Michael took the three steps that put them face to face. "I can't talk, not about…before. I thought I could. That's why I'm here, I think. But I can't. I don't know what to say. There's too much."

Faith looked up at him. He was so strong and broad, so beautiful. His fair hair and beard were close-cropped, not shaved. She missed the smooth cheeks and shaggy mess of pale hair he'd had. The scruff over his head and face now made him look older. Wearier. But he was still so very beautiful. His deep blue eyes were intent, locked on hers.

"Then what do you want, Michael?"

He looked at the floor between them, and Faith got the sense that he was steeling himself. Then he met her eyes again. "You. I want you. We were wrong before, but maybe we can be right now. I love you, Faith. I never stopped. I don't know how you feel, but—"

She put her hand on his mouth to dam up his words. "I love you, stupid. I never stopped, either."

His expression showed the perfect relief that Faith felt herself. He put his hands around her face and murmured, "I won't stop. I'll never stop." Then he kissed her, and she leaned in, curving her body to fit with his, moving her tongue with his, holding his head in her hands as he held hers.

Kissing Michael, even after all this time, was perfectly familiar. They understood each other's bodies, even though they hadn't had long to be together, and they hadn't been together in a long time. But he kissed differently now, too. He was more confident—but maybe that was simply a feature of their age. He was thirty-two; she was twenty-seven. They both had more experience. And whatever they might have now, next, it wouldn't be something they had to keep in the shadows. They needn't feel guilt or apprehension now.

What had happened before couldn't happen now. They were safe now.

That realization, and the way it swept her fear right off the edge of her consciousness, sent a fire through Faith's blood. She grasped Michael more tightly, pulling herself up on him, getting as close as she could. She wrapped her arms around his head, and he groaned and moved his hands to her waist, enclosing her in his arms and standing up straight, lifting her off the floor.

He walked across the room, straight to her bed as if he'd known where it was. When he laid her down on it, his knee on the mattress between her legs, Faith felt a brief flash of memory that, irrationally, brought her fear back.

They'd only ever been on a bed together one time before. The last time. When they'd made at least one terrible mistake.

As that memory dragged its claws over her heart, Faith pulled back with a gasp. She opened her eyes and found Michael looking down at her, his face flushed, his eyes worried. "Faith?"

She shoved the past away. They were safe. "I love you," she said, to have a reason for having pulled away.

"I love you." He smiled, and she believed they were safe.

They were both still fully dressed, and that would not do at all. She shrugged out of her leather jacket and pulled her long t-shirt over her head. Michael stayed where he was, looming over her, and watched, his eyes vivid with lust.

She went for her bra, but he put his hand on her chest, splayed so that his thumb and fingers hooked over her collarbones, and held her down. Kneeling, his legs framing one of hers, he hooked the fingers of both hands into the straps of her bra, then slid them down and into the cups until the backs of his fingers brushed her nipples. The touch made her muscles go tight and hard, and she arched up as high as she could, wanting more, wanting him to make her feel everything. A decade's worth of everything.

His hands went back up the straps to her shoulders and then pulled the stretchy satin down her arms, pulling until the cups folded down, too. And then he bent down and took a desperate nipple into his mouth.

"Oh, fuck, oh fuck," she breathed, needing to make an utterance but trying to be quiet. Michael had always been quiet when they were like this, silent except for anguished groans when he finished. He'd seemed distracted, almost disturbed, by the sounds she'd made. He'd been her first, and their short time together had built in her a shyness about making noise during sex—but her natural inclination was to vocalize. To this day, she fought those two impulses always.

This time, instead of flinching or even pausing in his attention to her breast, he answered her quiet words with a low groan, and the hand he wasn't propping himself up with slid down, over her belly, and into her leggings.

Just as his fingers pushed over her pubic bone, he lifted his head abruptly and stared down at her, his fingers moving over her mound, into her folds, exploring. It felt good, so fucking good, and she could feel him feel how wet she was. He was surprised, though, and when his fingers returned to the bare skin over the bone and brushed back and forth, she understood. Feeling breathless and a little shy, she smiled. "I've been doing that a while. Everything feels more intense shaved."

Before, she'd been pretty natural, just shaving what showed around her bathing suit and trimming the rest. He returned to her folds and let his fingers move lightly over the bare, delicate skin. His touch made her twitch and gasp.

"So good," she whispered.

Still without a word, he took his hand away and leaned back. He took hold of her waistband with both hands and pulled, and she lifted her hips to help him.

He pulled her pants and underwear together down her legs, until he got to the boots she was still wearing. Then he stopped and, smiling down at her, lifted her feet onto his thighs and started unlacing her boots. He was yet completely dressed, boots and kutte and everything, but she didn't protest at all when he pulled her boots off and then rid her of her lace-up leggings and her underwear. All she was wearing now was a bra, scrunched up under her breasts. She reached under her back and unhooked it, then tossed it carelessly away.

Now, she was totally bare, and he was staring down at her like she was an exotic delicacy.

He pulled her to the edge of the bed, knelt on the floor, and fed on her as if she were.

And oh, fuck, he was good at it—better than she remembered. He lifted her legs onto his shoulders and then moved his hands to her breasts so he could pluck and tweak both nipples in time to the rhythm of his lips and tongue.

He went down on her like there was nowhere in the world he'd rather be, and she could think of few places she'd rather have him. The scruff on his face, the buds on his tongue, the heat of his breath, the rough skin of his fingers exciting her excitable nipples—it all made a symphony of sensation that Faith could barely contain.

She wasn't a prude. She had not been celibate during the past decade, not by any stretch. She enjoyed sex and hadn't required an emotional connection to enjoy a physical one. But this—he'd been her first and in many ways, both emotional and physical, her best lover. He was better now. It was all better now. It was so good.

So good. So good, Oh, fuck, so good. She pulled her knees up and grabbed his head, holding him to her as she came, curling up around him, trying to be quiet but failing.

He stayed on her, his tongue flicking at her clit until she couldn't take the intensity for another second. When she pushed his head back, he stood and began, at last, ridding himself of his clothes.

Except for his kutte, which he hooked on the corner post at the foot of her bed, he dropped his clothes wherever they happened to fall.

Damn. He was gorgeous. The same man she loved, but dramatically different, too. He was massive, the muscles on his arms, torso, legs, everywhere, deeply cut. He knelt again on the bed and leaned over her. Then he twitched and sat back, reaching to the floor. Faith didn't understand at first, but he'd picked his jeans up and was fishing in the pocket.

She made a call. She hoped it was the right call. But she knew he'd tell her if it wasn't safe. "Michael."

He stopped and cocked his head. She hadn't understood before why he was so quiet during sex, and she still didn't. It was just who he was. She loved his silence for that, if nothing else. She loved knowing that about him, feeling the hominess in that familiar silence now. She stretched out her arm and showed him a small scar. "I have an implant. You don't need that."

She'd used an implant for most of the past decade. Michael hadn't been very good at getting a condom on right from the beginning, and sometimes not at all, though he always pulled out. And she hadn't been good at stopping him. She'd learned it was better not to have to think about it in the heat of the moment. Because sometimes the moment got too hot to think.

He stared at her for a few seconds, then dropped his jeans. And then he was on top of her, his weight so much more than she remembered. He pulled her leg up to his hip, holding himself with his other hand, guiding himself into her.

He filled her, huge and hot. She felt full in more than just her body. She felt complete. She bent her head back as he pushed deep, unable to stop her cry. "Oh God, Michael!"

When he didn't move, Faith settled back on the mattress and opened her eyes. He was staring down at her, pain riding his features hard. His cheeks were red. She didn't understand. "Michael?"

His head fell, sagging from his shoulders. "I…can't. I can't."

The fear she thought she'd swept away came back and leaned in. "You can't what?"

He shook his head.

Oh, no. This was not all going to fall apart while he was inside her. She lifted his head in her hands and made him face her. His eyes glistened. "You can't what?"

The pain in his expression deepened, but he didn't answer. He wasn't going to tell her. But she wasn't going to let him go. She knew one thing he couldn't do: resist. She flexed her hips, drawing him into her as deeply as she could. His groan overwhelmed her own gasp, and he pleaded, "Faith, I…"

She flexed her hips again. And again. "Shut up, Michael. Shut up and fuck me." Pulling his head down, she lifted up to meet him, and she kissed him hard, demanding that he finish what they'd started. With a sound of defeat, he did.

At first, he was gentle and slow, careful, like he was still fighting the demon that had come between them, whatever it was. They kept their mouths joined, kissing as he moved inside her and she moved with him.

But then her pleasure kicked into high gear and she began to move to her own rhythm, chasing the ecstasy she knew was headed her way. He sped up, too, keeping up with her. She knew the moment when he lost control—and she thought she knew, too, what he'd meant when he'd said *I can't*—because he made a sound that could only be called a growl and sat back on his heels, yanking her hips up with him. And then he fucked her harder than she'd ever been fucked before, far harder than he'd ever fucked her, so hard and so fast that she felt jackhammered, and her grunts and cries were broken and syncopated by her bouncing body.

He'd been intense before, but this ferocity shocked her. Yet it didn't hurt her. She came hard then, and in a totally new way, one she couldn't describe, like he'd found another spot in her body that could stimulate to climax, something even deeper than a g-spot. Her juices let down in a rush just as he came, groaning as if his release were torture, his fingers digging deeply into her hips, his head thrown back, the muscles and veins in his neck and shoulders bunched and swollen, his skin flushed dark red all the way to his pecs.

When Michael relaxed, he did so completely, collapsing onto her in a heap. Faith wrapped her arms around him and held him, feeling his body shaking. This big, tormented man was so different from the smaller, tormented boy she'd known, but so alike, too, wanting so much to be good, trying so hard, and so much in need, that she felt like she was falling in love all over again.

Slowly, their breathing returned to normal, and he lifted away and looked down at her. "Did I hurt…I'm s—"

She put her hand over his mouth. "Don't you dare. I'm not hurt. I love you. I loved that. There is nothing here at all to feel bad about. We're safe now. We're good."

Nodding, he kissed her hand. "Okay. Okay. We're good. Okay."

He dropped his head and tucked his face against her neck, and she held him.

CHAPTER EIGHT

Demon woke on his back, with Sly curled between his knees and Faith leaning over him, running her hands over his chest, making soft swirls and waves of sensation over and over.

He had Faith in his arms.

In his head and his body, he was quiet. He could have wept for the ease he felt, alien to him in its comfort.

Seeing him awake, she smiled down at him and put her hand over his heart. "It's still there."

He smiled and combed his hand through her beautiful, dark hair, messy now from their sex. "My heart? Yeah. Waiting for you."

That made her smile grow, but she shook her head and traced one finger over his skin. "No. Your ink. The one I knew. The kanji. I thought you'd covered it up, like your old club ink, but it's still in here. Just…tangled up in the rest of the ink now."

The symbol for strength. He'd gotten it shortly after he'd aged out of foster care. He'd been homeless at the time, but he'd managed to squirrel away the cash for a cheap tat. It had felt important—crucial—to him, at eighteen, to get that ink. Back then sixty bucks had been a whole lot of money. He'd skipped food and shelter to save it. But that kanji had meant everything to him. It seemed stupid now.

Less stupid in this moment, though, with Faith tracing her fingertip over that old ink.

Her hand moved over his chest and traced a scar across his ribs, and another high on his belly. "What happened here?"

Demon put his hand over hers. "Life. Not important." Not even to Faith would he talk about the club, past or present.

She met his eyes. "Club stuff, huh?"

He shrugged. "Got into some scrapes."

"What was it like, being a Nomad?"

Feeling some of his peace ebbing away, he sat up against her headboard. "I don't want to talk about that. I just want…I want…" He was afraid to say. Everything he'd wanted had been lost to him—Faith, his home, his son. But he'd gotten a chance to have it all back—his home, his son, and now, maybe, Faith. The thought that he had traveled that full circle should have brought an even deeper sense of peace, maybe even happiness. But instead, Demon felt a creeping certainty that it was indeed a circle he was on, that he would lose it all again.

"What do you want, Michael?"

"I don't want to talk."

She stared down at him, her smile gone, but her expression neither angry nor sad. Curious, maybe. Interested. Her eyes were so beautiful, expressive and changeable, almost every color they could be.

Bending toward him, she brushed her lips over his and murmured, "What do you want?"

He cupped her face in his hand. "I want to love you."

Smiling then, she pressed her lips to his mouth, then his cheek, his jaw, his neck, his shoulder. He took a deep breath and let himself focus on nothing but her loving touch. His cock was full and aching, but he stayed calm and tried to simply feel, to let it happen.

Then she worked her way down his arm, pausing at his elbow to kiss the scars there. She knew what that was, and he tensed. But before he could pull away, before even his chaotic head could try to fuck the moment up, she rolled against him, putting her back against his side as she continued kissing all the way to his hand.

When she began to suck his fingers into her mouth, one at a time, he turned toward her, upsetting Sly, who hissed halfheartedly and then hopped to the floor.

Her nude body was nestled against his as she sucked on his fingers, and he rocked his hips, letting his cock slide against her pretty ass. Sweet Christ, how she felt. With Faith it was more than sex, far more than fucking. It was overwhelmingly physical, and yet that was hardly even the point. Maybe that was what love was, when the physical act was an extension of the connection, not the connection itself. He could have simply lain on this bed in this weird room for his entire life, with Faith in his arms, and done no more than that, and it would have been more erotic and fulfilling than the most athletic sex he'd ever had.

Which wasn't to say that his physical need wasn't riding him hard, as he rocked their bodies together and she sucked his thumb as if it were his cock and then moved to his other hand. Looking over her shoulder, he was transfixed by the sight.

She'd never had him in her mouth; he hadn't wanted to abase her in that way. They hadn't even had sex in the position they were nearly in now. She had sucked just now on more fingers than he'd need to count the days or nights they'd been physical together before. It had all been new for her, and he hadn't wanted her to feel like a whore. In those days, with his own weird feelings and beliefs, blow jobs and sex from behind were degradations.

Experience and distance had tempered those oddities in his perception. He hated to admit it, hated to even think it at this moment, but Kota had helped him in that way, too. She had been wild and entirely uninhibited, and she had demanded things of him that he, trying to be someone who could be a partner, had tried to give her. His aversions had abated.

He shoved that bitch out of his head. He wanted no good memories of her. She had tainted all of them. And he was here now with Faith, who deserved all of him, every atom, every thought in his head.

Then she turned her head to kiss his bicep, and she got every single thought. The movement had shifted her thick hair, baring some of her neck. He lifted his hand and brushed it fully away. Behind her ear, about the size of a quarter, was her only ink.

The kanji for strength.

Immediately, entirely, overcome, he laid his head against her, his forehead on that symbol.

She started to turn her head, but stopped and took a breath. "Oh," she said on the exhale. Then she lifted his hand back to her lips and kissed his knuckles. "I never stopped loving you, Michael. Not for a minute."

He couldn't answer. He had no words. All he could do was hold her to him, curl his body around hers, and keep her close.

They were quiet like that for a long time. Demon was submerged in an ocean of love and fear. To have her, now to really have her. There was a future he could almost see, one in which he and Faith and Tucker, and Sly, too, and all the kittens Sly could love, all made a family together. In a house like Bibi and Hoosier's, maybe. With a yard and a swing set. And a grill. Faith could have her weird sculptures everywhere. He'd build out a garage for her art and his bikes. They could be happy. They could be real. And strong. Tucker could grow up the way a boy should grow up.

But he was afraid, terrified, to let that picture develop in his head. Even if he were given a chance for all of it, it wouldn't happen. Because he wasn't that man, the man who could be strong and stable for a family. He knew it. He'd scared his boy twice in the past two days, blowing up in front of him. He would never hurt Tucker, he knew it in his bones, like he knew he'd never hurt Faith, and like he knew that the same did not apply to anyone else on the planet who ended up in his way at the wrong time. He'd never lash out at his boy, he'd never lash out at his love, but he could scare them. He could lose their faith. He would. He had.

At that moment, gripped by that certainty, he almost ran. His body tensed, ready, and he started to pull his hand from Faith's hold. But, as if she sensed his turmoil, she took that hand and put it over her breast, and then lifted her arm over her head, making her breast tauten against his palm, the nipple growing hard. She put her hand on his head. "Michael…just love me. Don't worry so much. Just love me."

With his eyes closed and his head on her shoulder, he moved his hand, feeling her body respond to his touch. She was so beautiful, sleek and firm. Her ass moved against him, restoring his cock to fullness right away.

He shifted so that the arm under her could take possession of her breast, freeing up his other hand to slide down and between her legs and find her wet, ready heat. She was shaved, her skin smooth and velvety. That had thrown him, at first, last night. What he knew of Faith had been etched into his brain a decade before. There was still so much that was the same that it took a moment for him to accept the differences, to reconcile the present with the past, the reality with the memory.

She moaned quietly and lifted her leg up, setting it back on his hip, opening herself wide to him.

"You want it like this?" he asked, keeping his voice low. The years had tempered his reservations, not eradicated them.

Her body already writhing in time with the movements of his hands, she nodded. "Yes. Oh, yes."

Shifting their bodies, he slid into her. Earlier, as soon as he'd been inside her, the urge to completely give himself over, to take everything he'd wanted for so long, to *have* her, had been absolutely consuming. He'd been sure, *sure*, he was going to go too hard, be too much for her. He'd known he hadn't been capable of keeping himself in check. But she'd refused to let him go.

And he *had* lost control. But she'd gone with him. He hadn't been too much.

This time, he felt calmer, and he even had the luxury to really feel the perfection of their physical connection. He'd been fighting everything so hard before that he'd been locked in his head, resenting his body's demands. Now, he could feel her, the way he still knew her, the way she molded to him like she was meant for him, inside and out.

He realized that this was the first time, in all the time he'd known her, that he was free to just enjoy her, without guilt, without fighting his nature. He shoved his fear of the future aside as hard as he could. In this present, they could be perfect.

He sped up, moving his hand again between her legs, finding her clit and listening to her responses to understand what she wanted of him. Though noisy sex, grunting like animals, made him uncomfortable, stirring up skittering thoughts and memories, he liked Faith's quiet, almost shy gasps and whispers. Barely using words, she was telling him what she wanted, that she liked what he was doing. She knew now what she wanted in a way she hadn't known before. He wanted to give her that.

Her hand moved down from his head and slid between her legs, where his hand, and his cock, both moved with increasing intent. She touched herself with him, and she touched him, sliding her fingers around his cock as he thrust into her.

That felt...holy *fuck*, that felt amazing.

"Oh fuck," he muttered and then clenched his teeth together to keep his mouth shut.

Looking over her shoulder, she said, "Michael, I like that. Talk to me."

He shook his head against her shoulder.

"Okay," she whispered and then rolled onto her stomach. Demon followed her, putting more of his weight on her as he thrust harder, losing his ability to hold back. With Faith's hand, his hand, and his cock between her legs, and her tight, swollen nipple between his fingers, he thought the climax that was coming for him would run him over.

And then her body clenched and spasmed, and she began to bounce her hips as she milked him. She didn't cry out, except for a strangled noise in the back of her throat.

He came before she was finished, hating the rutting-beast noise that was forced out of his mouth as his body tensed and he filled her. He kept up his pace until she could complete, too.

When it was over, he lay down with her, turning her to her side so he could stay off of her but still inside her.

"Faith…"

"Don't apologize," she sighed, patting his hand where it rested on her belly. "Don't even try. That was fantastic."

Lifting onto his elbow, he kissed her cheek. "I wasn't gonna. I was just gonna say I love you."

She grinned. "Okay. You can say that."

"I love you."

~oOo~

"Am I an asshole if I ask what this is supposed to be?" Demon stared at the tubular hunk of metal. He could make out all sort of things he recognized in it, but he had no idea what they made together. Not what they had been manufactured to make, that was for sure.

"It's a snake."

He turned and gave her a look. She was giving him shit. No way that was a snake. "Seriously."

"Yeah." She walked over. "Well, this is a part of a thing that will be a snake. It's so big, I have to make it in segments. I'll weld the segments together on site."

It was almost as tall as he was and as wide as his arm span. "How're you getting it out of here?"

When she put her hand on his arm, in a comfortable, casual touch to direct his attention, heat like fire emanated from that point through his body. He stared down at her hand, and she ducked her head to catch his eyes. Nodding toward a big...thing hanging on a brick wall, she asked, "You see that tapestry?"

It looked like a rug of some sort. A raggedy rug. "Yeah."

"There's a loading door behind it, and there's a rig outside that comes up to this floor. It's how I got pretty much everything up here—and how I get my work out. I have a storage space for the finished pieces."

He looked around her apartment, if that was what it was. It a big room with a rough, wood floor that looked like it had been painted about fifty times, all different colors, none of them recently. The walls were brick, except for the drywall bathroom that had been erected in the middle of one brick wall, serving as a kind of room divider, he guessed. The ceiling was bare beams, probably iron, considering how old everything looked, and about twenty feet up. Two walls were lined with tall windows that looked out over the streets.

By way of furniture, she had a couch and a couple of low, sloping chairs and a big, square coffee table, all arranged on another raggedy rug, this one on the floor. On another ugly rug, a massive old armoire stood against a wall near her iron bed. An old steamer trunk was at the foot. A tall stack of big books, art books, Demon thought, served as a nightstand. And a Fifties-style Formica table and four vinyl chairs were arranged near the door and what passed for her kitchen.

What passed for her kitchen was a row of white cabinets topped with butcher block, with a sink in the middle and three rows of shelves above. An ancient range and refrigerator bookended the cabinets.

For décor, she had that big rug, or tapestry, hanging on the wall, a whole bunch of unframed canvases in all different kinds of styles, and about ten floor lamps scattered everywhere. And lots of her own art, from small pieces that stood on tables to freestanding pieces.

Also, her clothes. They were draped over the open doors of the armoire, on top of the steamer trunk, scattered around a full, wicker laundry hamper. Faith was kind of a slob. He remembered the day he'd seen her bedroom at her parents' house. And, though it was a somber memory, a painful one, he smiled. She'd been a slob then, too.

All of that took up about half, maybe two-thirds, of the space. The rest of the room, where they were currently standing, looked like the bike shop, with industrial lights, a welding rig, big bins full of metal salvage, and a massive workbench that Demon coveted a little. This area was perfectly orderly and organized.

"You really do make a living with this? Digging around junkyards?" She'd loved that. He was happy to think that she'd been able to do what she loved for work. He had that a little, too.

"Yeah. It's more than playing in junkyards. It's hard work, especially when people tell me what they want and I try to make it happen. That kind of sucks. I'm much better when I just do what I want without thinking about making anybody but me happy. But being what people call 'edgy' doesn't really pay the bills, so I try to balance it all out. I'll make a piece like this snake, which is not my thing but will keep me in whiskey and HoHos for a year, and when I want to tear my face off in frustration, I stop for a while and work on something like that over there."

She nodded toward a piece in the corner, a freestanding sculpture that looked like a nude woman, her long hair made of chains. Her head was thrown back and her arms were outstretched but obviously incomplete: one stopped at the wrist, the other barely past the shoulder. Like everything else he'd ever seen of hers, it was made of parts: sprockets, nuts, bolts, gears, pistons, just about every kind of gizmo he could name.

As he got closer, he noticed that the woman's mouth was open, like she was screaming. Then he noticed that there was a hole in her chest, and the area around it had been made to look as though her ribs had burst outward, as though her heart had been ripped out.

"Jesus," he muttered. Then he darted a guilty look at Faith. "Sorry."

She was smiling. "Don't be. It's not supposed to give you fuzzy feelings. She's in pain."

He peered more closely at the woman's chest. She had nipples. Somehow, that detail made the woman seem more exposed and vulnerable and made the sculpture more upsetting. He blinked and took a step back.

He didn't like it. It made him feel unhappy and powerless. But he wasn't about to tell Faith that. So he said something he thought was probably true. "It's really good."

Her laugh told him that she knew what he was feeling and why he'd given her the empty compliment he had. "Thanks. It's not everybody's taste, I know. It's not really about taste, I guess. Just expression."

Looking back at the sculpture, he asked, "And this is what you want to express? You said you make something like this for yourself?" That thought made Demon feel even worse. Faith should have a life that gave her nothing but happy thoughts.

"Yeah." The sound of that simple word was surprisingly close, and he turned to see that she had come right up to him. She was smiling up at him, her eyes understanding, like she wanted him to know it was okay he didn't like her art. He still felt bad about that, though.

He put his hand on her waist. When they'd gotten out of bed, she'd pulled her weird t-shirt back on. It was sleeveless and almost as long as a dress, black with a big white skull on the front. But the skull was made of flowers. She really liked things to be made out of parts of things they weren't.

He'd been surprised by the way she'd been dressed when she'd come up to her door. The Faith he'd known had been a jeans-and-t-shirts girl, sweaters and hoodies in the winter, the same pair of scuffed-up engineer boots no matter what. In Madrone, she'd been wearing baggy sweats. The Faith who'd come up those stairs, though, had been dressed all in black, in that t-shirt, a leather biker jacket, and the kind of tight, stretchy pants that women called leggings—but these had laced up the front, showing a swath of her legs all the way to the bottom of that shirt.

And her boots—like combat boots but covered in metal studs. Her makeup was dark, too. She was almost punk. Or Goth. One of those. She looked good, really good. Gorgeous. Just different, in a way that disquieted him. Like she was dressed for battle.

It was like her art, he thought. He didn't like to think that she was angry or defensive. Faith at seventeen had been open and confident. She'd been happy, despite her frustrations with her life. If she wasn't now, Demon felt pretty sure it was because of him.

"What are we gonna do, Faith?" he asked, because he couldn't say those thoughts, and he'd been quietly staring down at her for too long, and creases had formed on her brow.

She slid her arms around his waist and rested her head on his chest. "Be together."

"How?" He kissed the top of her head.

"Do you know why I was in Madrone?"

"Hooj said something was going on with your mom."

"Yeah. She's in the hospital. She had some kind of episode and got hit by a car."

"Fuck!" He leaned back and tilted her head up to look at him. "She okay?"

Margot Fordham was someone who'd remained on the edges of his life. She'd moved to Madrone with the club, and she made occasional appearances at the clubhouse or at Hoosier and Bibi's, or at Bart and Riley's. He did all he could to avoid her. His sentiment toward Faith's mother would have been hate if his own guilt would have cleared enough of a path for it to get through, but he didn't exactly wish her ill. Not exactly.

"They think she has Alzheimer's. I think it's pretty bad already. She didn't tell anybody she was having trouble."

"Jesus, Faith." The woman he knew was vibrant and put together. He didn't think of her as old, certainly not old enough for that. He thought of the burden that could mean for Faith, and his arm tightened around her waist.

"Yeah. I don't think Sera's going to come home at all. I'm going to have to take care of her. I was struggling with all that, leaving this life to take care of her when she doesn't even like me. But if I have you, I think it'll be okay. If we're good, I can work the rest out."

Demon's heart felt tight. "What are you saying?"

She looked up at him. "I came home to figure out what to do. I think I know. I'm going to pack up some things and go back to Madrone. I'll take care of my mom. And I'll have you. I'll really have you."

He lifted her off her feet and held her close, the way he always had, and she fitted against him the way she always had. "Yeah, you will."

CHAPTER NINE

Faith stared at the thick stack of pamphlets Dr. Tomiko had handed to her, one by one, as she'd talked. Information about the medications she'd prescribed. Information about occupational and physical therapy regimens and programs. Information about how to make a home safe. About in-home nursing and assistance. About adult daycare programs. And long-term residential programs.

The doctor had sat with Faith and Bibi for a long time, describing the diagnosis and prognosis with conscientious care. She'd answered Bibi's questions. Faith hadn't had any; she was too dazed, even though she'd expected the diagnosis, to think of any question except one: *Why?*

Stage Four Alzheimer's. There were only seven stages. Her mother had likely been declining, and compensating, for years. Maybe since Faith's father had been killed. Not even Bibi had known.

How could Bibi not have known? Faith turned to her mother's best friend. "You saw nothing before now?" She tried to keep accusation out of her voice because she didn't feel accusatory. Curious, but not accusatory.

But Bibi's eyes narrowed a little. "It's been different for us the past few years. Since Blue died, and everythin' changed for the club right after. You were gone, and she lost Blue, and Sera went off to New York. It was a lot of loss for your mama in just a few years. She pulled back. We didn't see each other as often, and when we got together, there was just somethin' in our way. Not keepin' us apart, just not lettin' us as close. She wouldn't talk it out, and I thought she was mad about the club. I guess, thinkin' about it now, after hearin' all this, maybe there was shit I missed. Shit I thought was nothin', just Margot bein' pissy, or distracted, or I don't know. Maybe it was signs that she needed help." Bibi dropped her head into her hands and sobbed, "Hell, Faithy. You're right. How didn't I know?"

Faith put her arms around Bibi. "It's okay. I didn't mean to sound like I blame you for anything. I just can't get my brain around all this."

Bibi sniffed and sat up, wiping her tears away, careful not to smudge her mascara. "Okay, darlin'. How do we handle this? We need a plan."

"This is for me to handle, Bibi. You do enough. I'll…I guess I'll move into Mom's house." The thought of living in that dreary box with a woman who was losing her mind made Faith's stomach hurt, but she didn't see another choice. She'd convert the garage into a studio, maybe. That could work. She'd contact the home nursing service and get some help. That could work.

Bibi grabbed Faith's chin and gave it a shake. "Don't you be a martyr, Faith Anne. This is family. Margot and you are family. You are not in this alone. We take care of each other. So, we'll make a plan."

Liking the thought of having a support system, one she knew and understood, people who knew her mother and could understand Faith's worries and frustrations, Faith swallowed back the lump in her throat and nodded. "Okay. Thank you."

"Don't you thank me for doin' what I should do, baby. I love you. You're back home now. We'll make your mama's life as good as we can. We're gonna make it through this and be okay. Okay?"

She nodded again. She even believed Bibi. Because she wasn't alone. She had her family, and she had Michael, too. With Michael, she could almost imagine a future in which living in Madrone was her best-case scenario.

"We should go in and see her." Bibi's voice didn't project a lot of enthusiasm for that idea. Faith's mother was lucid today and had talked to Dr. Tomiko already. There was approximately zero chance that she would be glad to have visitors. And, Faith thought, even less chance that she would be glad to hear the plan.

"Yeah. Together."

Bibi stood and held her hand out to Faith. "You know it, darlin'. Together is how we go."

Margot was lying with her eyes closed when they came into her room. What Faith noticed next was that the arrangement of flowers she'd picked up that morning from the gift shop downstairs—nothing fancy, just a dozen daffodils in a green glass vase, but daffodils were her mother's favorite flower—were gone. It had been a random impulse to buy them, a half-considered attempt to start a détente, but Faith was still hurt that they had been discarded already. When she moved toward the chair nearest the bed, she saw a small wedge of broken green glass on the floor next to the bedside table. She had an image of her mother, no longer restrained, sweeping the flowers off the table.

That hurt more.

But she shook it off, and she and Bibi sat side by side.

Margot sighed. "What do you want?" she asked, without opening her eyes.

Bibi answered. "Dr. Tomiko talked to Faith and me. I'm so sorry, baby."

"Not your problem. Or hers, either." She hadn't yet opened her eyes.

"Mom, I'm here."

"I know. I don't know why."

Bibi reached over and squeezed Faith's hand, and then she did something that Faith would cherish until she died. She stood up and leaned over the bed, getting right in her mother's face. "You listen here, Margot. This is me. I know you. We have been friends for almost forty years, and I know everything there is to know about you. I know what you hate, what you love, what you *regret*. I know what you're afraid of. So you can lie there and be a cold bitch all you want. But you are losin' your mind, baby, honest and true. Bein' a bitch ain't gonna change that truth. You have this one chance to settle things up before it really leaves you. I love you too much to let you fuck that up. So here's how it's gonna be. Faith, because she is the good girl you raised, is here to move in with you and help you. I'm not sure you deserve that, but you're gettin' it. Hooj and me, and Connor, and the whole club family, we are here to help you."

Now she opened her eyes. Faith, still seated at the side of the bed, couldn't see into those eyes, but she could see the rage on her mother's face as she glared at Bibi. "Help me? You mean watch me drool and piss myself. I don't think so. I don't need help to do that. I damn sure don't need hers."

Bibi smiled and brushed her friend's blonde hair back. Margot knocked her hand away. "That's a good show, baby. But I know you know you need Faith's help. I also know you don't think you *deserve* it. Good thing no one here gives a damn what you think."

"What about…where's…" Margot stopped, and everything about her attitude changed with a blink. Her expression went slack and then became worried. "Where's…the other one?"

Tears pricked at Faith's eyes when she realized what her mother had forgotten. Her welling eyes met Bibi's—she was just as saddened.

"Sera, Mom. You want to know where Sera is?"

For the first time since she'd come into the room, Faith had her mother's attention. Margot turned and looked at her, without recognition, her brow furrowed. "Sera? No, that's not right. My daughter."

Daughter, in the singular. "Serenity?" Faith guessed, using her sister's full name.

Her mother smiled, relieved. "Yes! What about Serenity? Is she here? Who's picking her up? I need to call Blue."

Dr. Tomiko had said that stress could trigger lapses. Faith hadn't expected it to happen so abruptly, in the middle of a sentence like that.

Looking plenty stressed herself, Bibi patted Faith's mother's hand. "I'll handle it, baby. You just rest."

"Thanks, Bibi. I don't know what I do without you. This damn leg is really cramping my style." She patted her cast absently and closed her eyes.

Bibi smiled down at Faith, her mouth trembling. "C'mon, honey. Let's start working all this out."

~oOo~

Bibi and Faith sat in the hospital cafeteria for a couple of hours and pored over the pamphlets the doctor had provided. Then they both had whipped out notepads—Faith's on her phone, and Bibi's a little spiral-bound journal from her purse—and divided up the tasks. They had a few days before Margot would be released. In that time, they'd have to get a lot of things set up for a new life.

The first item on Faith's to-do list was to call her sister. So, after Bibi left to head home and take over Tucker so Michael could go to the clubhouse for their Keep meeting, Faith sat in the cafeteria, which was starting to fill up with dinner-seekers, and dialed her sister's number.

She expected to leave a voicemail, but Sera answered. "Faith? Hey, what's up?"

Faith and Sera got along, but they had never been the kind of sisters who were good friends. They were much too different in personality and interest for that. They were so different that they had barely competed. They hadn't even had much of a rivalry about their parents' affections. Their mother had preferred Sera, and their father had preferred Faith, and everybody had just sort of accepted that as the way it was supposed to be. Until Sera, three years older, left home. That was when things had gotten really dicey between Faith and Margot.

When Faith left home, she and Sera began keeping up a casual correspondence, talking maybe four or six times a year. As far as Faith knew, her sister had never told their parents where she could be reached. They had that much trust between them, anyway. And after they'd both gotten out on their own, Faith had come to know that Sera's feelings toward Margot were less than completely devoted. Their mother's demanding kind of love had been its own burden. Until the end, Faith had had the better deal. She and their father had been legitimately close. They'd understood each other.

Faith would never say it to her sister, because there was nothing productive in the observation, but she thought the same was true between her mother and sister. Though that relationship had been fractious, Sera was, in fact, quite a lot like their mother, despite being an up-and-coming international finance executive instead of a retired porn star—and, in general, a much nicer person.

"I have a diagnosis. It's Alzheimer's."

"Fuck," her executive sister muttered. "How advanced?"

"Stage Four, which is the first stage of real impairment, if I understand everything right. Her doctor talked to me and Bibi for a long time. It's a lot of information."

"I've done some research, too, and that's how I understand it. What about her leg?"

"It's setting well. They'll release her after the weekend. Sera, I need you to come home. I need help with this." Faith knew when she said it what Sera's answer would be. It had to be said, but she and Bibi had started planning with the understanding that Sera would not be around.

"I can't, sis. You know I can't. I can't just walk away from this job, and I *asked* for this transfer. I can't even take time off right now. I'm working on a huge project, and I'm closing on a house, and things are just crazy here." She paused, and Faith could almost literally hear her dragging the next words out. "But I can cover the cost of a facility. I did a little looking online already. There's an excellent place right there in Madrone. The San Gabriel Rehabilitation and Care Center. They have a wing specifically for patients with dementia. It's first-rate."

That, Faith had not been expecting. "Sera, she's still lucid sometimes—maybe even most of the time. We can't put her in a place like that while she's still Mom. It'll kill her."

"And you care because…"

"Fuck you, Serenity. You're the one she asks for, you know. She doesn't even want me here."

"Then leave. Let her deal with this on her own. Don't play the martyr with me, Faith. You bailed on the family a long time ago, and I don't blame you. Maybe I don't miss her much, either, but don't think you can slide in now and make me feel like I'm not pulling my weight. Mom made her bed. With both of us. I have a life, and I'm not giving it up. If you decide to be there, then that's your call. I won't hold it against you if you go back to Venice Beach and weld trash together."

Angry and hurt, Faith just wanted off the call. "Fine. I'll call you if we need money."

"Do that—really, sis. Do that. I'll help that way. And I can help a lot."

"Great. Bye."

"Faith, wait. What I said was bitchy, but really think about keeping your life. We owe her nothing."

"It's not about owing, Sera. It's about…I don't even know. But I can't know that this is happening and just go on like I don't."

Sera sighed. "Okay. Then do what you need to do. Send me the bills."

~oOo~

That night, Faith went to the Night Horde SoCal clubhouse for the first time. Feeling raw and edgy after dealing with her mother's news and talking to her sister, she wasn't much in the mood for a party at all, much less a party at an MC she didn't even know. She wanted quiet. She wanted to curl up in Michael's arms and tell him about everything, so she could sort it all out and let him make her feel better.

They had taken Sly back to her mother's house and then spent the night together, in his room at Bibi and Hoosier's. They were both up and dressed before Tucker was awake, so they hadn't had anything to explain yet to that little guy. Faith wasn't sure how things would go for them now. She would have to move in with her mom. Michael couldn't very well move there with her, even if not for Tucker. Margot and Michael would make even worse roommates than Faith and Margot would be.

They were finally together, and still her family was between them. Faith was frustrated and trying not to despair. So she wasn't in a great mood when she parked Dante and went through the front door of the clubhouse. It was Friday night. Michael needed to be at the clubhouse, and he wanted to be with her. So here she was.

She was struck at once by the same sort of familiar dislocation she'd felt again and again in Madrone—that sense of a home she'd never seen before. The main room—this club called it the Hall, because the mother charter had some kind of Viking thing going on—looked, smelled, and sounded like a biker club: dark walls, low ceiling, battered furniture, a big bar with lots of booze, a big television. A pool table, pinball and video games. A stripper pole. Posters of nearly-naked women, beer and bike signs, bulletin boards full of snapshots of men on bikes and women on men on bikes. The smell was smoke, old beer, and man, with just a slight overtone of cheap perfume. The music was loud. All of the men in the room were clad in denim and leather, and most of the women were barely clad at all. It was home.

But the dark colors were different. The battered furniture was different. Most of the men and women were different. The big sign on the wall near double doors that led, she assumed, into the chapel—or, no, they called it the Keep—was different, a horse with a flaming mane.

The only old lady she knew was Bibi, but Bibi was home with Tucker. In fact, as Faith scanned the room, she didn't think there were any old ladies present. You could always tell an old lady from a passaround. Their posture and attitude was totally different. And they covered up more. They weren't nuns, but they were the exact opposite of available, and thus not putting their offerings on display.

No. At this party, she was the only woman in the room who wasn't pussy on tap. That completely sucked. She would not be staying.

But she would stay long enough to say hello to the men she did know. She saw Hoosier and Connor. And—oh wow, was that Sherlock? He'd been a Prospect when she'd left. He was a good guy. Kind of a dweeb, for a biker. But he'd filled out and looked good.

No sign of Michael. That also sucked. Squaring her shoulders, she made a beeline for Hoosier and Connor. Hoosier gave her a hug and a kiss on the cheek, and then Connor grabbed her, and his face split into a huge grin. That sucked a lot less.

"Well, hot damn. Bambi!" He wrapped her up in his big arms and squeezed her so hard her back cracked. Then he set her down. "Look at you, all growed up." He looked her over, raising his eyebrow at her black leather pants and spiky, strappy shoes. She'd dressed for the event she was attending—like an old lady, though, whether she was one or not, not like a club whore. "Got a Joan Jett thing goin' on. I like it. It's hot."

She grinned and punched him in his gut—which was rock hard and kind of hurt her hand. "I see you're still a butthead, and totally gross. I'm basically your sister. So yuck. Also, call me Bambi again, and I'll take your berries."

He shrugged broadly, lifting his hands up, "What can I do about it? You got those big doe eyes."

"Bambi is a boy, moron," she laughed. It felt good to be with Connor exactly like she'd always been, like she'd been gone a week and not a decade.

Connor laughed, too, and picked her up again in a crushing hug. "I missed you, Bambi girl. I'm glad you're home."

When he set her down again, Michael was standing there, his cheeks blotching red. The way he eyed Connor, Faith knew right away that he was jealous. He'd been jealous of Connor in their time before, too. He hadn't liked the easy, affectionately physical way she'd been with Hoosier and Bibi's son, and he hadn't liked that there'd been nothing at all he could say or do, no sign he could give to claim her.

He hadn't needed to claim her. Connor was older, a couple of years older than Michael, and Faith had grown up knowing him like a brother. She could see that he was good looking, but the thought of him that way was just…ugh. She'd tried to convince Michael of that then, but they hadn't had enough time together for her to get all the way through.

Of course, now Connor knew what had been between Faith and Michael then, and apparently knew what was between them now. So in response to Michael's look, he grinned and raised his hands in affable surrender. "Easy, Deme. Just sayin' hi."

Faith put her arms around Michael's waist. "Hey. I missed you."

He cupped her face in his hands and kissed her, and she relaxed against him and let him take it deep. Right there in the clubhouse.

That felt fucking fantastic. It nearly erased all the chaos in her head from everything that had happened earlier in the day. They were standing in the middle of his clubhouse, and he was claiming her.

The thought that she could have everything—she could have her art and her family and her love—took hold. If the price for all that was her mother's care, then so be it. It would work out. It would. She could feel it.

He pulled away and smiled down at her. "I want you to meet somebody." Taking her hand, he led her to a patch standing near the pool table, holding a cue in one hand and a beer in the other. He was considerably older than Michael, in his forties somewhere, she guessed, with greying hair and a full, greying beard. He was handsome, with blue eyes in a bright, piercing hue. "Muse. This is Faith, my...my old lady." He looked down at her as if for confirmation, or to make sure she wasn't angry.

She wasn't even the tiniest bit angry. She smiled back and squeezed his hand.

Muse smiled, switched his cue to rest in the crook of his other arm, and shook her hand. "Good to see you," he said. And that was all. He was up at the table, so he poured his beer down his throat and set the empty on a little round table near a support pole.

Faith looked at the table, watched Muse set up his shot. "Not the two?" she asked without thinking. Michael chuckled at her side, and Muse looked back at her, still bent over the table.

"Pardon?"

"Go for the two, you can get the four, too. If you bank it right, you can fuck up the fourteen for your buddy with the dreads."

Muse's eyebrows went way up. The guy with the dreads stepped forward and held out his hand. "I'm Trick, sweetheart. And if we get consultants, then I'm going to need a time out to find one of my own."

"Sorry," she muttered and shook his hand.

"I guess you play," Muse said, standing up without taking his shot.

Michael chuckled again. "She plays."

Faith scowled at him, but she'd brought it on herself. She'd felt more comfortable than she'd realized in this room, and she'd forgotten for a minute that this wasn't her clubhouse. "I used to play. I haven't in a long time. I'll shut up and watch."

Nodding, Muse went back to his shot, setting up this time to go for the two. He took and made the shot and held up his fist toward Faith. She bumped it, grinning. She was glad she was here. It did feel like home.

Michael took her around and introduced her to any of the patches who weren't busy doing things he didn't want to interrupt. She met Bart, and Lakota, J.R., Ronin, and Diaz. She was reacquainted with Sherlock. There were a few others, but they were busy. Faith figured she'd meet them eventually. They'd have to come up for air.

After a while, he took her to the side of the room and sat down in a big, old leather armchair. He pulled her onto his lap. "Tell me about your mom," he said. In his arms, in the midst the chaotic revelry of a Friday night clubhouse party, Faith put her head on Michael's shoulder, her mouth near his ear, and told him. He held her and let her talk.

They were still sitting like that when Michael became suddenly rigid with tension, and Faith realized that the noise in the room had changed—the talking was fading out, leaving only the blaring sound system. As he set Faith on her feet and stood up, pushing her behind him, somebody turned off the sound system, too. And then the Hall was nearly silent.

She could hear Hoosier, though. He was saying, "Go on. You know this is no place for you."

Then Michael stepped forward, and Faith was able to see around him. A woman had the attention of literally every person in the room. There were men on couches with their dicks out who were pushing girls away and standing up like they were facing an enemy.

She was small. Not short, but frail. Skinnier than was healthy. Her long hair was like straw, and a red dye job had grown out, showing several inches of brown. She looked sick, with blotchy skin and dark circles under her eyes.

Michael was walking toward her. As he moved, Faith realized who she was. Tucker's mom. She couldn't remember her name, though.

"You need to get out of here, Kota. I swear to God. You need to go right the fuck now." Michael's voice was low and heavy with menace. If those words in that voice had been directed at Faith, she would have turned and gone immediately.

But the woman—Kota—laughed. "What are you gonna do about it? Kill me? All these *heroes* are gonna let you kill a woman? Fuck you, Deme. I want Tucker. You got some guy sniffin' around me. You think you can hunt me down? Scare me? No. I'll hunt *you* down. I got me a lawyer, too. I'm gonna get Tucker back. You watch. I got lots of shit I can use on you."

There was movement around Michael and Kota, and Faith's eyes were drawn to the sidelines. Muse gestured at Hoosier, who shook his head, then nodded at Sherlock and Bart. Those two left, and Muse walked over to Michael and put his hand on his shoulder.

When Kota saw that, her expression became villainous. She smiled a smile that chilled Faith's heart.

"Aww. Ain't that the sweetest thing? You take Muse's cock, baby?" At that, Connor reached for her, but she knocked his hand away and ducked out of his reach. She went on, speaking faster and louder, like she knew they would try to shut her up. "You like it deep? He give you a good pounding? I bet he does. I bet you bend over for all these guys. Your *brothers*. You like it, baby. I know you do. Hard and deep. Just like when you were a kid."

The sound Michael made was inhuman, unearthly, unadulterated fury and agony. He flew at Kota and took her to the floor. The chaos then was too much for Faith to make sense of. All she saw was Michael's arms flying almost too quickly to discern, and blood spraying.

After a long, long minute, his brothers tried to pull him back, but he threw them off again and again.

Finally, they got him off of her, four men struggling and at last succeeding. He was stippled and striped with blood and gore. But Kota was alive and conscious. And she was laughing. Through a broken horror of a face, in a voice that was hoarse and choked, she laughed. And then she said, "See if you get him now, asshole." And laughed all the harder.

Michael roared in anguish and tore himself free from his brothers. But he didn't go for Kota again. He turned toward the back, toward Faith, and then froze, his face, his whole head, a dark, sinister red, and she could see it dawning on him at the moment that she had seen it all. He roared again and ran toward the door to the back. Faith tried to stop him, but he pushed her away, so hard that she lost her feet and landed on the concrete floor.

He saw what he'd done, and she saw the complete desolation in his eyes. She knew that look. And then he was gone.

The woman who'd torn everything apart was still laughing.

Muse kicked her in the head and shut her up.

Faith sat on the floor, sobbing, terrified and heartbroken, remembering the last time she'd seen that look in Michael's beautiful eyes.

memory

Faith sank the ten and the thirteen into the side and corner pockets and then turned and, giggling, smirked at Connor. Her father held up his hand, and they slapped a high five.

"You know," Connor grumbled, "it's a lot less cool when you look so fucking pleased with yourself. Fast Eddie would never have giggled."

"I don't know who that is. And you're just pissed that a girl is kicking your ass. Troglodyte."

"Blue! She doesn't know Fast Eddie?" Connor turned to Faith. "*The Hustler*. Paul Newman. Coolest pool player ever. And I'm letting you win, because I am a gentleman. What's a troglodyte?"

"You are, butthead." She lined up her next shot and felt a gentle nudge of her foot on the floor. Looking down, she saw her father's scuffed cowboy boot pushing her foot toward the proper position under the cue. She grimaced. Connor was distracting her.

She stood up to reset her stance, and she decided to show him just how good she was. Her daddy had taught her well, but he didn't let her play at the clubhouse often; he didn't like her bending over the table here. They had a table in their garage at home.

She set up a double bank shot and spared a glance up to see Connor frowning at the table, trying to figure out what she was doing. Cool.

Except she missed. She was thinking about Connor more than the game. He crowed with glee and then pushed her back to set up his own shot. Faith stepped over to her dad, who handed over her bottle of Coke.

"Showin' off is the express to trouble, kitty. You know that."

"I know. He's so cocky, though."

"What d'you think you are?"

Faith turned to her father, who was giving her a smugly wise look. "I'm not cocky."

He laughed. "Whatever you say, darlin'." He took a drink of his beer, and when he put the bottle back at his side, his smile was gone. "I'm not so sure about tonight. You don't have any other friends you can ask?"

She shook her head. Hoosier, Fat Jack, Blue, and Dusty were riding to Nevada in a couple of hours for a whole-club officer meeting. They'd be gone until tomorrow night. This run had coincided with Bibi and Margot's annual girls' week at a Palm Springs spa.

There were no other old ladies in the club. With a lie, making up reasons that Bethany and Joelle couldn't have her over, and insisting that, since she was only a few months away from her eighteenth birthday, it was ridiculous to think she needed a minder, Faith had convinced her parents to let her spend the night alone in the house.

She wouldn't be alone, but Blue didn't ever, ever need to know that. Never in her life had she been so excited for her father to go on a run. A whole night with Michael. In a house. In her bed. It wasn't just Connor distracting her from the pool table.

Her father sighed and draped his arm over her shoulders. He grinned down at her. "No wild party—or just try not to have Joe Law on my porch, okay?"

That was a joke, so she laughed. He knew she didn't have enough friends for even a mellow party, especially if, as he thought, Bethany and Joelle were otherwise occupied. "I'll make sure to pay off the neighbors."

"That's Daddy's girl." He pinched her chin. "For real, though, kitty cat. You lock up. And I'm gonna send the Prospect by to check in. And you keep in touch. You hear?"

She rolled her eyes. "Daddy! I'm not a kid!"

"You are my baby girl. Always will be. And I want you safe."

"Fine." With a sudden, devilish inspiration, she looked up at her father and smirked. "Maybe I'll invite Sherlock in for a nightcap."

Blue didn't see that humor in that, and Faith realized that it was really goddamn stupid to joke around so near the truth. His dark eyes narrowed. "Make another joke like that, and I'll hire you a babysitter right now."

"Sorry. Everything'll be okay, Daddy. Promise."

He looked down at her for another second or two, then kissed her cheek and hugged her. "I know. I trust you, kitty. You're my girl."

"Hey, Bambi. You should take a look at what you're missing."

At Connor's snide tone, Faith turned back to the table she'd been ignoring. He'd run it. His solids were gone, and he was setting up the eight ball.

"I'm not scared. You're gonna scratch."

"Cocky little shit," he muttered and took his shot. He didn't scratch. In his celebratory delight, he caught her up and lifted her off the ground. "Don't cry, Bambi. Better luck next time."

She stuck her tongue out, and he put her down, still laughing.

Feeling the back of her neck prickle like she was being watched, she looked over the table and across the room. Michael was staring at her, his cheeks red and blotchy, the way they got when he was mad—or getting there, anyway. When he was really mad, he got a lot more than blotchy. He was jealous. She couldn't figure out how to make him not be.

Also, she kind of liked it.

~oOo~

Michael came to her house that night long past dark. She opened the back door and found him squatting on the patio, letting Sly rub his hand. The cat was purring so loudly he sounded like he had mechanical parts.

Looking up at her, Michael grinned. "Hey."

Faith's heart thudded heavily in her chest. A whole night in his arms. No screwing in Dante. It was going to be the best night of her life. "Hey." She realized she hadn't heard his bike come up the drive. "Where's your bike? We should put it in the garage. My dad has Sherlock checking on me."

"He said. I parked a couple streets over." Standing, he came to her and put his hand on her cheek. "You sure this is a good idea?"

"The house is ours tonight. I want to have a normal night with you and feel what it's like to be totally naked and sleep together. It's a perfect idea."

"Okay. I want that, too. I love you." Smiling, he brought his other hand up to her face. Holding her the way he so often did, he bent down and kissed her.

~oOo~

"Do you have any clothes in your drawers?"

"Hmm?" Feeling happy and cozy, settled on Michael's chest, tracing her finger along the tattoo over his heart, Faith left her eyes at half-mast. She'd been right. The night before had been the best night ever. To be comfortable and to be able to go slow and feel each other—it was almost like last night was their real first time. Times—plural. She smiled.

They'd only had one weird moment, when she'd tried to go down on him. Of course, she'd never done anything like it before, but she'd wanted to try. His reaction had been nearly violent, shoving her away. She'd thought at first he didn't want her to do it because he didn't think she'd be any good. But it had seemed more like something was going on with him.

He wouldn't talk about it, though, and she didn't push. She wanted everything to be good and happy while they had this chance. They'd gotten past that awkward spell and kept on with their good and happy night.

"There's clothes all over the place. What's in your drawers?"

"More clothes." She waved lazily around her room. "That's the stuff I wear most. No point putting it away if I'm just gonna put it on again in a couple of days."

He bent his head so he could see her face on his chest. "You're a slob."

Her mother said that all the time, so Faith gave Michael the same answer. "No. I'm *efficient*."

Laughing, he kissed her forehead. God, she loved this peaceful relaxation. She didn't want it to end.

"What's this mean?" She traced the Japanese character on his chest again.

"It's kanji. It means strength—I think like the perseverance kind of strength, not like muscles. I hope that's what it means, anyway."

"I like it. I like your muscles, too, though." She moved her hand down and caressed the ridges of his belly and then over to one of the really amazing muscles that slanted over his hips. As she touched him, his cock filled out and raised the covers.

She wanted this to be her life every single day.

But he groaned and grabbed her hand. "I gotta get going, babe. I was supposed to be on shift at the shop almost two hours ago. They're gonna start looking for me."

He'd never called her 'babe' before. She liked it. "Can't you just bail for the day? I don't want this to be over."

"I don't, either. But we can't have people wondering where I am. Not with Blue and your mom both gone."

He was calmer than he usually was, by far, but Faith knew he had a clear, short limit to how much control he had. Especially when it was something he really wanted. So she raised up and kissed him, sliding her leg between his. After a few seconds, he grunted and rolled over on top of her.

But then he lifted his mouth away. "We have to stop. You have to let me stop. I have to go. And we're out of condoms."

Reaching between them, she put her hand around him, running her thumb over his tip. The first time she'd touched him, she'd been surprised by how velvety the skin was there. He shivered and tensed at her touch.

"You could pull out. Like you do sometimes." She spread her legs, settling him fully between them.

"God, Faith. I can't…you know I can't…" He was shaking with the effort to resist. It gave her a sense of power that she liked. She didn't understand it, but it was erotic in some way. Still holding him, she flexed her hips.

And he gave up.

~oOo~

Michael was still resting on her, panting, and she still had her arms and legs wrapped around him when Faith heard the sharp click of a gun being cocked.

He heard it, too; his body became iron.

"Oh, Demon. The trouble you're in. You get off my daughter right now. You move slow, or I will give her a brain facial. Trust me, I know what I'm doing with this thing."

Faith's mother was home. She couldn't be—she wasn't supposed to be home until after dinner! Like six hours from now, at the earliest! They always stopped at a restaurant for steak and lobster as the grand finale.

Michael lifted his head and looked down at her, and Faith saw an abyss of sorrow in his eyes. *I'm sorry*, he mouthed.

But it wasn't his fault. It was hers. If she'd let him leave when he'd wanted to, he'd have been on his way to the shop right now. If she'd let him leave even earlier, when he'd wanted to be on time for work, he'd have been up to his elbows in bike parts by now. This was her, not him.

She shook her head, trying to say that when her tongue wouldn't work to make words.

"Move now, Demon. Right now."

He got up, slowly, carefully, sparing a chance to brush her cheek with his finger. Then he stood up and turned from her, facing her mother, unaware of, or unconcerned by, his nakedness. "Margot, I—"

"Shut up. You got nothing I want to hear." She looked him up and down. "Holy hell. No condom? Are you shitting me?" Her eyes moved to Faith and locked on her belly, which was still sticky with his semen. "Look at you. Covered in come like the whore you are."

Michael took a long stride toward Margot. "Don't call her that."

She tightened her aim again, right on his chest. "I told you to shut up. Your *whore* there is definitely not a concern of yours anymore. She is my problem. You, on the other hand, are not my problem. You are Blue's problem. I think you'd be smarter to think about that. Get your goddamn clothes on and get out of my house."

As he grabbed his jeans, he turned and looked down at Faith, who was still so stunned and afraid that she hadn't moved at all. He pulled the cover over her bare body. "I love you," he said, clearly and without hesitation. "I love you."

Before she could answer, the air in the room broke apart with explosive noise, and Faith reflexively curled into a ball.

Her mother had fired the gun into the ceiling.

"Next one goes into your head. Get out. Dress in the yard."

Michael grabbed his clothes and left. Margot followed him out, her little Smith & Wesson apparently trained on him the whole way.

When Faith was alone in her room, still too much in shock to think clearly or feel fully, she got up and cleaned herself up. She was closing her jeans when her mother came back and stood in the doorway, her arms crossed under her augmented chest. She looked angry, but surprisingly calm. When Faith thought about this moment later, she would decide that there was a hint of satisfaction in her anger.

"Do you have any fucking idea what you've done to that boy? What your father will do? And the club? You probably killed him, you little slut. How long have you been fucking him?"

Faith didn't answer. She was too busy grappling with the reality of the consequences they'd—*she'd*—set in motion. It was her fault. Hers. He'd tried to avoid her. She'd sought him out, again and again. Even now, today, he'd tried to leave, and she'd pulled him back. This was her fault. Whatever happened next, she had done it.

She wrapped her arms around herself and pinched at the skin above her elbows.

No. Her father loved her. She would talk to him, make him understand that she loved Michael, that he loved her. She would make him see, and they wouldn't have to hide anymore.

It would be okay.

~oOo~

Her father did not understand. It was not okay.

Her mother had been right. He had put Michael's life on the table, but he'd lost that vote. Then he had demanded his patch. He'd lost that vote, too, but with only one vote against him. Faith didn't know whose, but she thought it might have been Hoosier, because Blue was almost as angry at the President as he was at Michael.

They were sending Michael away. The vote that had passed was to send him to the Nomads. He was leaving.

But not before Blue was granted his right to vengeance.

And now Faith was standing in the bike shop, late at night, her mother's hands gripping her shoulders, her long, manicured nails digging like claws into her skin. The whole club—all the patches, and Bibi, Margot, and Faith, too—were arrayed around the large, industrial space in something like a circle. In the middle stood Michael, shirtless, strung between two support poles, his arms splayed and chained high above his head, but his feet on the ground.

Thus exposed and unable to defend himself, Michael kept his feet for a long time while Blue, with both hands wrapped with lengths of chain, beat him. He punched and punched, and when his arms grew tired, he unwrapped the chains from his hands and used one length as a whip. He beat him until Michael finally lost consciousness, his legs sagging.

Until then, he kept his eyes on Faith. Even when Blue shouted at him to quit looking at her, even when the blows landed on his face, he came right back to her. He blinked blood away to see her. He made no sound but that forced out by the expulsion of his breath on impact of each body blow, and he looked at her.

She wanted to look at him, too, to hold his eyes with her own, but he was so hurt. Her father, her *daddy*, was hurting him so much, and she couldn't bear it. So she tried to look away, but her mother wouldn't let her. She whispered in her ear to watch what she'd done, to see it. And she watched.

"Daddy, stop! Please stop! Daddy, please! Don't hurt him! Stop!"

She screamed and screamed, but her father ignored her. Until Michael was unconscious, and Fat Jack finally stepped up and put his hand on Blue's cocked arm.

"Enough, brother. You lost the vote to end him. You need to stop before you do."

The room then was quiet. All the men were somber. Blue dropped the chain and turned to face Margot and Faith. He was spattered with Michael's blood. He looked at Faith first, his eyes sad.

"Daddy…" Faith wailed.

He looked away, to her mother. "Get her the fuck out of here. I don't want her back here ever again."

Then he stalked away toward the clubhouse.

Faith tried to go to Michael, but Margot yanked her back. "Don't be stupid. You've done enough. You are never seeing Demon again. You come with me right now."

Dusty and Hoosier were taking Michael down. The last thing Faith saw before her mother dragged her out of the building was his body landing on the floor in a lifeless heap.

CHAPTER TEN

Demon rode and rode, Kota's blood drying on his skin. As long as he was moving, he could focus on his bike eating up the asphalt under him, the way his headlight made the reflective stripes flash and glow. He could watch that, and feel the wind, and not think. He couldn't think. The thoughts in his head would kill him.

He rode until there was nothing around him but California desert: rocks, scrub, hard-packed soil, and the sparse, spiny trees known as Joshua trees. One of the homes he'd been in as a kid—not the worst one, by a long shot—had been run by a church. He knew who Joshua was in the Bible. The tree was supposed to have been named after him because it looked like Joshua raising his arms in prayer. Demon didn't see it. Diaz had once told him that he'd been taught the tree was called a desert dagger. He liked that name better.

Whatever anybody called them, Demon liked the trees. They were ugly and lonely, and they grew where things didn't.

There was a spot he knew, not far off the road, where a loose group of those trees clustered around a big, flat rock. He'd found the place years ago, shortly after he'd come back home, when he'd pulled off the road to take a piss and had seen the sun setting, silhouetting the trees and the rock in fire. Sitting on the rock had made him feel calm.

When he'd been struggling to find a tether after years of being the psycho Nomad who got called in to tear shit up, he'd come out here, after a long, silent ride, and just sit where no one could provoke him, no one could hurt him, and he couldn't hurt anyone. He'd sit on the rock, look out at the horizon through the spindly foliage, and wait until he was calm, however long that took.

He hadn't headed toward that rock on this night with any sense of doing so. He'd just ridden, seeking solitude, striving for distance, trying to get far away from people he loved before he could do any more damage, before he could see them finally know him for what he really was, before he could see the love they had change to disgust.

Faith had been there. Oh, fuck. Faith had seen it all.

When he dismounted, he took his Glock out of his saddlebag. It was a risk, carrying an unregistered weapon when he was trying to stay clean, but with Dora Vega and her Águilas cartel stomping on the Castillos, and the Dirty Rats gunning for the Horde, the risk was greater lately to be unarmed.

Not that he thought anybody would come up on him tonight, in the dark desert. That wasn't why he had his Glock.

He walked through the desert daggers and climbed onto the rock, facing west, even though the sun had set long ago. He set his gun on his lap and stared into the night. And then he thought.

It was a clear, late-winter night, with a bright half-moon, and he was far enough from the massive glow of SoCal civilization that the stars even made it through. The sky was huge and the horizon far. In a place like this, miles from any other soul, Demon could almost believe that his own soul wasn't a ruin.

But it was. He was a ruin. Everything in his life was a ruin. Only yesterday—even earlier on this day, in fact—he'd been letting himself think that he could have what he wanted. Now, it was all gone. Kota had exposed his worst secret. But more than that, he'd let Faith see him become the animal that lurked inside him.

And he'd lost Tucker. What he'd done to Kota before had kept him from his son. He'd never get custody now. They'd probably even take him from Hoosier and Bibi. Unless he wasn't around. If he wasn't around, maybe Hoosier and Bibi could keep him. Demon trusted them with everything. Tucker would grow up happy with them. He couldn't doom his son to repeat his own childhood.

That childhood was clamoring to be remembered now in ways Demon never allowed. He kept all of it as far back as he could, locked up. But he knew that his problems, the way he couldn't keep control, the way he couldn't stop even when he knew he should, the weird ways he saw things, all of that was his old shit leaking out the sides of the box he tried to keep locked.

In sixteen years as a ward of the state, Michael, the boy that Demon had been, had been used like that in four different placements. He'd been five and in a family placement the first time. The man had used his hands, his fingers. He had also taught Michael how to give a blowjob.

That placement had only lasted a couple of months. Though the man had told him never to tell about their secret 'fun,' when Michael got expelled from kindergarten for beating up another boy, he'd told the woman what was happening. She'd slapped him hard and sent him back to the state. He didn't tell anybody else. He hadn't wanted to get hit again.

When he was seven, he lived in a small group home, run by a husband and wife. The woman worked the night shift. That man had liked to be jacked off while he watched television. He'd sat with his arm around Michael and curled his fingers in his hair, moaning and whispering how beautiful he was.

The man who'd scarred him with a cigar had been a supervisor at an institutional group home. Michael was there three years, from nine to twelve. By the time he left that placement, on his way to his first stint in juvie, he'd been taught just about all of it. That man had liked to put the boys on each other and watch. Boys who got hard got to be tops. Boys who didn't…Michael never did.

His first stint in juvie, a guard took a shine to him.

By the time he got out, when he was thirteen, no one was ever going to touch him again and live.

Which was why he'd done a second stint in juvie and aged out of the system behind bars. But no one touched him anymore.

It had taken him all those years to grow strong enough in body and spirit to stop it. Resistance had meant more pain and fear and loss—beatings and shame, dislocation and deprivation. When he was so small, that fear had been greater than the fear of what had been done. More than that, after a while, he had begun to understand the things that had happened as simply his life. He'd never accepted it, but he had come to expect it.

When Demon remembered his childhood, that resignation was his greatest shame. That he had let those things happen. That so many years had passed before he'd really fought back.

He would eat the gun in his lap before he'd risk a fate like his for his son. It wasn't even a question. If being gone kept Tucker with Bibi and Hoosier, then it was easy.

But he didn't know if it would. So he stared at his gun and did nothing.

~oOo~

He saw the motorcycle coming up the empty road long before he could hear that it was Muse. He sat and watched him ride up, a beacon of white light on a black road. He pulled off at almost the same spot Demon had. He wasn't surprised. Muse had found him here before, and Demon knew that either Bart or Sherlock could track him with the GPS in his phone.

He'd been half expecting Muse to show up. Only half; the other half thought they might just let him disappear.

So he sat where he was and watched Muse dismount and climb up on his rock. They were sitting side by side before a word had been exchanged between them.

"She's dead, Deme."

Demon hung his head. He still thought the club would help him cover it up, but he'd killed a woman, someone innocent in club business, and he'd done it in the clubhouse. Best case, he thought, they'd send him away again. Away from Tucker, away from Faith, away from his home. He stared at his gun.

"You didn't do it. I did. Hooj's call. She was already loaded up to her eyeballs with shit. I filled her up the rest of the way and dumped her in an alley in San Bernardino. It's gonna look like a junkie whore turned a bad trick while she was high off her ass. Nobody's gonna give half a shit about it. You're clear of it, Deme. You're clear of her. You and your boy. She can't fuck you up again."

Without yet lifting his head, Demon began to cry, and Muse put his arm over his shoulders and let him.

After a minute, as Demon choked off his tears, Muse asked, "You plannin' on huntin' coyotes out here?"

Demon turned and looked a question at him. Muse nodded at the gun in his lap.

"What's that about?"

He shrugged. He didn't know how to say everything in his head, or even if he should say it. What he said was, "I'm not gay. What Kota said—I'm not gay."

"Didn't think you were."

They were both quiet for a spell, and Demon knew that Muse would let it drop right there. Maybe the whole club would. But it would lie there, in the middle of everything everybody knew or thought they knew about him. He didn't know how to make that not true, and it was choking him now, all the memories loose and screaming in his head, grabbing at him, pulling him into shadow.

He had to get them out, but he couldn't let them be said. He tried to think if there was anything he could say.

"Kota came up in the system, too. She ran when she was fifteen, but she went in before she was a year old. I think maybe that was why I thought I could be close to her. We weren't good long, but when we were, we talked about it. She told me about the shit that happened to her. And I told her about the shit that happened to me. Never told anybody else, not *anybody*. I was stupid to trust her. But she lied, tonight. She lied. The shit that happened to me—I didn't like it. Not ever. It hurt, and it made me sick. It scared me and made me mad. It fucked me up so bad. It hurt. I hated it. I hated all of it. I'm not gay."

"I know you're not, brother." Muse's voice was tight. "But what you're saying—what happened to you wasn't about that. You were a kid. It was abuse, not sex. You were tortured." Muse looked out at the horizon. "And I'll tell you something else. I knew already. I was in the system a little, too, remember. Nothing like you. But I saw what it could be when it was wrong. And I see how you are. It's not a tough puzzle to put together, Deme."

That thought had never occurred to him—that those scars were visible, that everyone in his life had already known his shame. "Do you think anybody else…"

"Maybe."

"FUCK!" he shouted into the desert. "FUCK!" Throwing his hands onto his head, he began to rock, trying to keep himself contained inside his skull. "FUCK!" His gun slid off his lap and clattered to the rock, then slid off the rock and landed on the ground.

Muse's hand locked hard on the back of his neck. "Deme. Five beats."

He heard, but he couldn't. He shook his head.

"Yes. Make it ten. C'mon, brother. One…two…three…" As he counted, his voice low and calm, he steadily increased the pressure of his hand on Demon's neck. "Four…five…six…"

When he got to ten, he was holding Demon down hard, keeping him from rocking. He didn't ease up. In the same calm voice, he said, "It's not a bad thing, my brother. We all love you for who you are. No secrets. No shame. That's family. Trouble is as much the glue as love."

Demon shook his head.

"Yes, Deme. Yes. It don't matter. We know who you are, however you got there."

"Faith…"

Muse's hand eased up a little, became support instead of restraint. "Well, she don't remember me, and I barely remember her. She was just a little thing way back when I went Nomad. I know you two have a past, and I know it's not all pretty. But the woman I saw tonight—she's upset, but it's worry for you she's feeling. She wants you to come back." He shook Demon a little. "You got a family, brother. They're waiting for you. Let's go home."

More scared than he'd been since he was a boy, Demon nodded.

When they got down off the rock, Muse picked up the Glock and slid it into the back of his jeans.

~oOo~

When they walked back into the clubhouse, the Hall was quiet. The passarounds and hangarounds were gone. Demon didn't see any women at all. Faith wasn't there. But all his brothers were. Every one of them. Muse led him to the bar, where Bart, Jesse, Lakota, and Connor were sitting. They sat down, too.

Bart slapped Demon on the back. "Beer or Jack, brother?"

"Beer is good." He needed a beer. Just one. It was more than the drink. It was sitting here with his brothers.

Bart looked at Fargo, the Prospect behind the bar, and the kid nodded and reached into the cooler. When Demon had his bottle, his brothers lifted theirs at him, and they all drank.

That was all.

Hoosier walked up behind him and dropped a hand on his shoulder. "How you doin', brother?"

He turned and faced him. "I don't know, Prez. Where's Faith?"

"I had Peaches take her to Bibi. She needed a woman's touch. She'll be glad to see you, I can tell you that."

He nodded. "What Kota said—"

His President cut him off. "No need. You got no troubles here. You understand? It's all good here."

"Thank you."

"Nothing to thank, son. Finish your beer. Then go see to your lady." With a wry smile, nodded at Demon's hands. "Might wash up first, though."

Demon examined his hands. They were still crusty with Kota's blood.

Weary from the way his emotions had been buffeting his head for hours, Demon thought he might break down. It was Hoosier who'd broken the news to him of his sentence ten years ago, sitting him down and easing him into it. It was Hoosier who'd then led him to the shop to face Blue, giving his shoulder a reassuring squeeze before he let go.

It was Hoosier who'd brought Muse in to teach Demon the Nomad ropes when he was healed enough to ride out.

It was Hoosier who'd welcomed him home after Blue was dead.

He trusted his President implicitly. He understood in this moment something he didn't think he'd ever fully realized. Hoosier was more than a man who was like a father to him. He *was* a father. The only one Demon had ever had.

And Muse was a brother in ways that transcended the patch they both shared.

Tipping back his beer, Demon swallowed down the rocks that seemed to have filled his throat, and he remembered.

memory

They hadn't taken his patch, so he was still their brother. They set him up in his room in the clubhouse and put the P.O.T.s on nursing him back to health. Some of his brothers even stopped by to check in on him. Not many, and not for long. Blue was still on a rampage, so for the most part, they left Demon on his own. Only Hoosier made a regular appearance.

It was a week before he was strong enough to ride—and then only just. But he was ready to go. Knowing that the family he'd lost was everywhere around him had been hard to bear. Knowing that the love he'd lost was close but not allowed anywhere near him, knowing that he had fucked up her family and the way her father saw her, remembering the fear and sadness in her eyes in the shop, the pity and guilt—that was just too much. He had to get away. Maybe when he was away, he'd be able to lock it all up with the rest of his horrors.

So he was sitting on the edge of the bed, lacing up his military-surplus combat boots, the pack holding everything he owned but the bike he'd ride out on leaning against the wall near the door.

After two sharp raps on the door, it opened, and Hoosier came in. He was holding a kutte. Demon assumed it was his own. They'd taken it in the shop, when they'd stripped him to his skin from the waist up, and they'd torn the *Los Angeles* patch off the front and the *California* bottom rocker off the back right there. Now, Hoosier set it on the bed at Demon's side, showing a new patch that read *Nomads*. He knew the bottom rocker would read the same. They were brand new, but they wouldn't stand out much; he'd hadn't even had his patch two months.

He was damn lucky he still had it. He hoped he'd feel that luck someday.

"Muse is ready to ride. How 'bout you?" Hoosier closed the door and took a couple of steps to lean against the cheap bureau. "You good?"

Demon had met Muse a couple of times, but he'd been a Prospect, and Muse had paid him no mind at all. He didn't have a read on the man who was going to ride with him, and he had no idea what he knew about why Demon was joining the Nomad charter, or what he thought about what he knew.

Nomads didn't always ride with a partner, but it wasn't unheard of. Demon was glad that he would, even if his partner was a stranger. He thought he'd just spin out into space if he were left completely on his own.

"Yeah, Prez. I'm ready." He dropped his head and swallowed hard, and then he looked Hoosier in the eye. "I'm sorry."

"Yeah, you've said. At some point, Deme, that's just words." Hoosier considered him a moment before he spoke again. "There's no send-off out there. You understand? You're still one of us, but you fucked up. Right now, you need to get some distance and give your brothers time to remember that patch on your back. When Blue settles down, everything will. Meantime, you get some miles on your tires and some grit in your teeth. You learn to be a brother. Let it show that you deserve that patch. Look to Muse. He's steady."

"Understood." He stood, picked up his kutte, and slid it over his shoulders. Hoosier handed him his pack, and Demon took it, staving off a grimace at the way the weight pulled his mending ribs. Then he followed his former President out into the main room of the clubhouse.

No one was there. None of the men who sat at the table he'd patched in with, none of the brothers he'd lived with, worked with, partied with. Only Muse, leaning on the bar. As Hoosier and Demon came into the room, he stood up straight and took a step toward them, his hand coming out.

"Demon. Hey, brother."

Demon clasped hands with his new partner. "Hey."

"Ready to ride?"

"Always." Demon turned and held out his hand to Hoosier. "Thank you, Prez. For everything."

Hoosier grabbed his hand and gave it a shake hard enough to make his body ache. "Good luck, brother."

~oOo~

Muse slid into the booth. "I'm guessing the redhead has our table?"

"What?" Demon looked up from the menu. He didn't even know why he checked the menu. They were at yet another location of a big chain of truck stops, and he got the Hot-n-Spicy Burger at every one.

"Passed her up by the register when I came in. She's got the big googly eyes for you, brother. I figure she'd ice anybody got in her way between here and there."

Demon looked over and scanned for a redheaded waitress. Yep. Behind the counter, near the register, staring at him. When their eyes met, she grinned, blushed and turned away. She was cute, but no.

He looked back at his brother and shrugged. "I guess so. Didn't pay that much attention."

"Shame." Muse dumped a creamer into his coffee. "Got a ten-spot says she'd blow you in the john before we ride out." His grin was ironic. After six months on the road together, he knew Demon wouldn't take that bet.

Demon suppressed a shudder. "We're three hours out of Corpus Christi. I'll take my pussy on tap, thanks." P.O.T.s were all he'd touch—and not always even that. Some of the charters they'd worked at, or just rested their heads at, were rougher than others. He'd gotten to the point where he thought he could tell if the passarounds were there because they wanted to be. Those girls, he'd spend some time with. In a couple of the clubhouses, though, the girls looked used up and jumpy. They had marks on them—bruising and tracks. He could barely stand to stay there and pretend to drink.

He'd known even before he'd started hanging around the L.A. clubhouse that the club as a whole was into some dark shit. They had a fearsome reputation. Yet L.A. had been fairly mainstream outlaw, and they'd been working with the public, too. Demon had pulled his gun only twice since he'd had a kutte, Prospect or otherwise. Club life had been pretty calm. Now, though, he was getting an advanced education in how dark the club could get.

And how the Nomads were expected to be the darkest of all.

The redhead came over and took their order. When she left, lingering as she took the menu from Demon's hand, Muse chuckled. "Damn shame."

He rubbed his hands over his newly-cropped head and changed the subject. "You reach Carrie? She good?"

Muse had stayed out by the bikes to call his sister, who'd left a couple of messages. "Yeah. I just pissed her off, but she's good. I'm gonna need a swing through L.A. again soon, though." He gave Demon a long look. "You think you're up for that?"

Demon was shaking his head before Muse had finished the question. He wasn't sure he'd ever go back to L.A., unless he was ordered there. It was only in the past month or so that he'd stopped waking up every night in a cold sweat, hard and afraid, feeling Faith under him and her mother behind him. "No. But it's cool. I'll call Zed and see if anybody's got a quick job somewhere. We can hook up again after."

"You know, you could take some time. We been riding hard more than six months now. You could sit your ass in Vegas or something."

"I'm good. I'll call Zed. Just let me know when you want to take off."

"Okay, brother. Let's finish this job, and then I'll go." He squirted ketchup onto his fries. "This intel better be good. I want this motherfucker. Sick to shit of chasing him around."

~oOo~

The intel was good. Muse and Demon sat in a rental van at the back of a motel parking lot in Laredo, Texas, and watched their target, Ernie Jennings, pull bags of takeout from the back seat of mid-range Toyota sedan—also a rental.

"That's a lot of food for one guy," Demon observed. "He's skinny, too. You think he's got company?"

"Fuck," Muse grumbled by way of response. "I want this fucker, Deme. Four weeks we've been looking. He's always one step up. I don't give a fuck if he's got company. We'll just dig a bigger hole."

Muse had been dogged about this job, and Demon understood it. They were after a rat, a guy who'd given up information to enemies of the club's Billings, Montana charter. Muse was closer to that charter than to any other besides L.A., which had been his home base, just like Demon. The information in question had gotten three brothers killed.

Demon wanted the guy, too, but he didn't want to take innocents down. Before he'd gone Nomad, he'd killed one man: just before his fifteenth birthday, he'd beaten a man to death. In six months with Muse, he'd killed three more. Between the two of them, that tally more than doubled.

He liked it. Not his first killing; that one had been rage and a mania of years of bottled-up self-defense, and he barely remembered it. But what he'd done with Muse, killing in cold blood, meting out justice or vengeance, he liked that. It made him calm, it made his head quiet, made him feel more in control, and that scared him. Maybe there was a serial killer lurking inside him amongst his demons. Killing innocents was a line he couldn't cross.

"What if it's a woman?"

Muse laughed. "You don't run out and buy takeout for a whore, brother. He's not married, and he's been running solo all this time, so I don't see it being a girlfriend, either. It's probably a contact. Laredo is a border town. Must be seven, eight major transport companies right here on the Rio Grande, most of 'em dirty. My money's on him sitting in there waiting for a contact to bring him papers and a seat in the back of a truck. We get him now, or he crosses the border and is out of our reach."

"If that's true, couldn't K.T. call Sam, ask for the Perros to handle it?" This was a Billings job. Demon thought it made sense for the Billings President to call the President of the mother charter, who had a close relationship with the leader of the cartel most of the club worked with, and seek help on the Mexico side.

Muse shook his head. "This is not a job you subcontract, Deme. This is club payback. I want him. He's not walking out of that room again." He pulled out his gun and checked the magazine, then screwed a suppressor into the barrel. "We'll give him a few minutes, see if he gets company. But we go either way."

"Okay, Muse. We go."

~oOo~

It wasn't a woman. Or a contact. It was a boy.

A small, scared boy about ten years old, wearing nothing but a pair of Fruit of the Looms. He had dark, sticky traces of duct tape on his wrists and ankles, and a rectangle of patchy red skin over his mouth. Jennings must have bound and gagged him so he could go out and run his errands.

Those were details Demon thought about later. In the moment, he barely thought at all. He saw the boy, sitting at the little table in the corner with cartons of Chinese food spread out in front of him. He saw Jennings, also in nothing but his underwear, showing the concave chest and pallid paunch that skinny men sometimes got when their dissolute lives reached the fifty-year mark. Demon saw all that, and he didn't even bother to think.

When Muse managed to pull him off of Jennings and throw him against a wall, Demon saw the boy, curled up tightly on the chair he'd been on, staring at Demon as though he were, in fact, a demon. It was him the boy was most afraid of.

He scrambled to his feet and tried to get out. He had to get out. But Muse flung himself between Demon and the door. "I need your help here, brother. You can't run. You have to chill."

But he couldn't. He couldn't look at that boy. He couldn't be in this room. Grabbing Muse by the shirt, he tried to pull him away from the door. But Muse was bigger and stronger than he was. Demon had been trying to bulk up, but he was still fairly lean. Muse grabbed his shoulders. "Chill, brother, chill! Take a breath."

Demon shook his head. He couldn't breathe.

"Yes. You're gonna get us both locked up. Texas prison's no fun. Trust me on that. Take a fucking breath."

He tried, but his entire body was on lockdown.

"Try this. Listen to your heartbeat. I bet it's loud. You hear it?"

Demon couldn't answer, but Muse went on anyway.

"Count, but slow. Try to make your heartbeat match. One…two…three…four…five…"

By Muse's count of five, Demon could think. He was agitated but back driving his body again. He relaxed, and then Muse did, too.

Before Muse let go, he asked, "We good?"

"Yeah. I'm here."

"Good. We got us a mess to handle."

"We can't—not a kid. Please."

"No, brother. Not a kid. Do me a favor. Wash yourself up and go get the van, back it up close. I'll fix it with the boy. We'll get him home."

~oOo~

Much later that night, Demon sat at the bar in the Corpus Christi clubhouse. He was achy from killing a man with his bare hands and then digging his grave in rock-solid Texas dirt, and he was on edge, waiting for Muse to want to talk about what had gone down.

When Muse came out from the back and sent off, with a swat on her ass, the girl he'd taken back there, Demon felt sure he'd come over and want to talk. And he did come over.

"Cuervo. Silver," he barked at the Prospect behind the bar as he sat next to Demon. "You're not partaking, Deme? Meat's pretty fresh here."

"Nah." He could not have been less interested, not after the night they'd had. His own mouth betrayed him, and he started the conversation himself. "What was that kid doing there?" He knew the boy had been stolen from the street, but it didn't make sense. "Why would he take a kid like that when he was on the run?"

"We'd know if I'd had a chance to grill him first. We'd know other shit, too. Important shit."

"Sorry."

Muse shrugged. "Can't be undone. No use getting tangled up in it. I called Gizmo. He said there was some perv shit on Jenning's hard drive, but he didn't know about more than that. My bet is the stress got to him, and he was looking to ease it."

"If that kid decides not to go with the story you gave him, he'll take us both down."

"Yep. But like you said, we weren't gonna kill a kid. We saved him, Deme. Gave him back to his mom. We're heroes to them. They won't sell us out."

"Okay." Demon finished his beer and waved the empty at the Prospect. "Cuervo this time." Tonight, he wanted to get drunk.

"You want to tell me what that was tonight, brother?"

Demon had known the question would come. He'd fucking invited it. But he shook his head.

"Fair enough." Muse swallowed down his tequila and tapped the glass on the bar for a refill.

CHAPTER ELEVEN

"PA! PA! PA! NO! PA! PAAAAA!"

"Tuck, c'mon, honey. Pa's not here. I got ya. Shhh. Shhhhh."

"NO! PA!"

Faith got up from the sofa, where she must have finally fallen asleep, and went down the hall, following the sound of Tucker's wails and screams. She stopped in the open doorway of his room and saw Bibi struggling to hold the hysterical toddler.

"Can I help? Is he hurt?"

At her voice, Tucker looked over. Whatever he saw when he saw her, it wasn't what he'd wanted to see, and he increased his struggles. Obviously frazzled, Bibi snapped, "I got it, Faith. Just go!" Tucker screamed, responding to the edge in her voice.

Chastened, Faith turned and went back down the hall. She stopped in the kitchen for a glass of water, then went back to sit on the sectional in the family room and continue her vigil. Tucker wasn't the only one who wanted his pa to be home.

She heard the bath running in the bathroom between Tucker's room and Michael's. She'd spent the previous night in that room with Michael, feeling happy and loved. But now she was alone, waiting and worried.

It had been hours since Peaches had brought her back to Hoosier and Bibi's. Bibi had been there for her, sitting with her, ready to talk, but Faith hadn't been able to talk much at all, other than to try to describe what she seen, how she felt. Sense was beyond her.

There was just too fucking much going on—her mother, her life, Michael, his son, his past, her past, their past, everything they'd lost, everything they might be able to have, everything getting in the way. The past crashing into the present and maybe leaving nothing but wreckage.

What that woman had said—it was true. Some of it was true, enough to make Michael so upset. *When he was a kid*, she'd said. He'd been abused, then. She'd had no idea. She'd known he'd grown up in foster care, and that his life had been hard, but she'd never had details, and it had never really occurred to her to wonder. She'd had, she supposed, a middle-class teenager's idea of what foster care meant. She'd thought he'd grown up poor and unloved, and that was heartbreaking enough.

But it was more. Sitting in Hoosier and Bibi's family room, the images and sounds of the scene in the clubhouse careening in her brain, she understood that she should have known, that the things about Michael she'd thought seemed unusual were signs of his torment. But then, before, she hadn't had the experience to see it.

She *had* been a kid, though she'd always insisted that that wasn't true.

Tonight, she'd seen deeper into him than she ever had before, and the sight made her heart sore. It scared and confused her, too. She'd known he could be violent. It was one of the things her father had shouted at her, that Michael—Demon—was a 'psycho.' She'd never really seen evidence of it herself until tonight, though. She could still hear the crunch of bone, the wet sound of blood spattering, and the way the crunch and spatter softened into something else after a while.

The way the men in the Hall had stood back for a long time and just let him hit that woman.

The way she'd laughed.

His bloody face racked with regret, and the swirling miasma of rage, guilt, and fear in his eyes when he'd seen Faith watching.

The way he'd run. The way he always ran.

Possibly worse than any of that—Faith was jealous. She hated it, but it was there. That woman, that sick, cruel, pathetic woman, had had a child with Michael. Tucker, and through him Michael, would always be hers in a way Faith couldn't touch.

She hated that it was true, and she hated the way it hurt.

Bibi came out of the bathroom, holding a much calmer Tucker in her arms. When she took him into the kitchen, Faith got up and went there, too.

With his head on Bibi's shoulder, Tucker eyed Faith, but not with fear or suspicion. Just interest. Whatever had made him so upset, the storm had passed.

"Hey, buddy."

He held out a small, green rubber frog.

"Is that for me?" She reached out to take it, but he pulled his hand back. A little smile lifted the corners of his mouth, though.

Faith laughed gently. "You're a little stinker."

"A stinker who needs more sleep. Let's get your milk, Tuck." Bibi looked at Faith. "He gets night terrors. There's a routine to settle him back down—a bath, some warm milk, and a story. Deme lets him watch television instead of a story sometimes."

It sounded like Bibi was giving Faith instructions for future need, and that abraded her sore heart. After tonight, she felt like the little bit of new foundation she had started to build in Madrone might just have been broken apart.

And that jealousy was there. She hated that woman—for what she'd done to Michael, for what she must have done to this helpless little boy, for the way that she could claim them both despite it all. She wished Michael had killed her.

But she'd been alive, flopped on a chair with an ice pack held to her face, when Hoosier had sent Faith here.

"Does he love her?"

Setting a small pot of milk on the stovetop, Bibi turned and gave Faith a sharp look. "No, baby."

"Did he ever?"

Bibi sighed. "I honestly don't know. She's a hard woman. I guess she's had a life to make her that way, but knowin' that don't make her easier to be around. Deme's so sweet and quiet with women, I don't know what he saw in her." She laughed and shook her head. "That ain't true. I do know. She looks like you."

Faith was offended to the point of outrage. That skanky, spotty, bad-dye-job, grey-toothed junkie bitch looked like her?

Before she could find breath to express her affront, Bibi laughed again and waved her free hand, dismissing the vitriol Faith had been trying to gather up. "Easy, honey. I don't know what she looks like now, but I can guess it ain't good. The last time I saw her, she looked rough. Not like you. When Deme met her, though, she was pretty. Long, dark, shiny hair and big, light eyes. And that small frame. Like you."

Bibi shifted Tucker to her other hip, and, with a grunt, he protested being moved. Then he reached out both his hands and leaned toward Faith.

She looked at Bibi, who stepped closer. And then she took Michael's son into her arms. He was much lighter than she expected him to be. And much heavier on her heart. He smelled of lavender.

He held up his frog. "Vog."

"Frog, I see. Pretty cool." Faith had no idea how to talk to a child. None of the wacky people who had populated her life before, in San Francisco, or now, in Venice, had children. She saw Bibi watching and said, "He's littler than I expected."

"Small for his age. Behind in everything, so far. But he's catching up. She was using when she had him. He was born addicted."

"Jesus."

Bibi poured warm milk into a little blue plastic cup and then sealed it up with a rubbery lid. "You ready for a story, baby?"

"Mins." Tucker took the cup and stuck it in his mouth, holding the frog against the side.

"No movie tonight, Tuck. Granny needs to go back to bed, and so do you." She took Tucker from Faith. "They won't let him run far, honey. He'll come back, you wait and see. While you wait, you sort things through. Nobody's got baggage like Deme's got baggage. Make sure you're ready to help him carry it. But don't add more. Say good night to Miss Faith, Tuck."

"Ni-bye," he said and laid his head on Bibi's shoulder.

"Night, handsome," Faith said, and then Bibi took him out of the kitchen and back down the hall to his room.

Faith went back to the sofa and waited.

~oOo~

It was only another hour before she heard the low roar of slow-moving bikes coming up on the house. More than one, but not many. Hoosier and Michael, probably. She stood up and, without thinking about it, primped a little, combing her fingers through her hair and smoothing her top. She was still dressed in the top and leather pants she'd worn to the clubhouse. She'd ditched the punk heels, however.

Though she was in the family room and watching the garage door, they came in the front. She turned and ran in that direction like she was expecting a romantic reunion or something. Realizing that she had no idea what to expect from Michael—or Hoosier, for that matter—she stopped in the middle of the main hallway.

Hoosier was just coming in, with Michael right behind. Her father's best friend, her Uncle Hooj, came up to her and gave her a quick hug and a reassuring smile. "I'm gonna head to bed. I'll see you in the morning." He looked back at Michael, who nodded. Then he headed down the hall, deeper into the house.

And Faith and Michael were alone in the hallway, facing each other. He had washed the blood away. Faith was glad; that had scared her.

"Michael."

He took a step backward, toward the door, and she thought he was going to run again. But he stopped after that single step. "I...need to check in on Tucker."

"Of course. But, Michael—please, please talk to me after."

He took a deep breath and looked past her, into the dark house, away from her eyes. "I don't think I can."

"Do you love me?"

His eyes moved immediately back to hers. "God, yes. Faith, I've only ever loved you."

"Then try."

They stared at each other, and then finally he nodded.

~oOo~

He stayed in Tucker's room for almost half an hour. Faith sat and waited, staring at the photographs on the tables and walls of the room. Photos of Hoosier, Bibi and Connor. Of her parents and Hoosier and Bibi. Of the club she'd known and this new one she didn't know. Family times she hadn't been part of.

Then he came into the family room and stood behind the sectional. She looked up at him, and he winced.

"I scared you."

"No." That was a lie, but she couldn't say the truth.

He knew it anyway. "It's still on your face, Faith. You're afraid of me."

"Michael, no. I've never been afraid of you." Until tonight, that had been true.

He was on the same wavelength. "That was true. I never saw it on you before. But now you are."

"It's not fear. It's confusion." As Faith said it, she recognized that that was the real truth. "There's a lot I don't understand. Or only half understand. But I want to. I love you." She patted the sofa next to her. "Sit with me, Michael."

He ignored her request. "Why don't you call me Demon?"

"What?" The question threw her. She had always called him Michael. He simply wasn't Demon. That name sounded odd to her, despite the hundreds of times she'd heard him called it. "I guess...I met you as Michael. You've always been Michael to me."

"Hoosier and Bibi and Connor met me before I was Demon. They don't call me Michael. You're the only one who does. Michael is the kid I was. Demon is who I am. What you saw tonight—that's who I am. That's what's inside me."

"That's not true."

"It is. What I did to Kota—it's not the first time I hurt her like that. A big reason I'm having to fight so hard for Tucker is because I hurt her like that when she was pregnant with him."

Whatever she'd been about to say died in the back of her throat.

After a few silent beats between them, his mouth twisted into a sad, lonely smile. "That's who I am. Now you know."

"Why?" She felt like she had Tucker's frog lodged in her throat.

"Why did I hurt her? Is there a good reason? She was a woman and half my size."

His use of the past tense didn't escape her notice. "Was?"

"She's dead."

"Oh, fuck, Michael." She wasn't an idiot or a naïf. She'd grown up in the family of a notorious outlaw MC. She knew that most of the men in her life had killed, and more than once. Her own father had been the club's Sergeant at Arms, and he'd been an enforcer before that, so it stood to reason that his hit list was long. Bibi had told her that Michael was also an enforcer; that meant that he'd killed more than most.

She also knew that women in and around the life didn't always have such a great ride. But it had been different here. Hoosier's charter had always had a good rep in its local community and in the club at large. He didn't like innocents getting caught up in their crap, and he had a hard limit to what kind of treatment of women was acceptable. Beating an innocent woman to death was far beyond his hard limit. Michael would face club consequences for that.

But was she innocent? She hadn't seemed like it to Faith. Not long ago, she'd been wishing Michael had killed her. Well, wish granted.

He started to speak and then stopped. When he started again, he said, "I'm gonna go to bed. I love you, but I was wrong. We can't be right, not even now. I can't ever be right."

Without another word, without giving her sore, rattled head a chance to process what the hell was happening, he turned and headed toward his room.

Faith didn't know long she'd continued to sit on the sectional in Hoosier and Bibi's comfortable family room in their big, comfortable California ranch home. At some point, she realized she was sitting there with her mouth open; the sound of it snapping shut shook her from her mindless fugue.

No. Just no.

She got up and went to Michael's door. Raising her hand to knock, she decided against it and just opened the door.

He was standing naked next to the bureau, a pair of dark sweatpants in his hands. He'd frozen when she'd opened the door, and before he could move or say anything, Faith said, "You didn't answer my question."

Pulling his pants on, he asked, "What question?"

"Why did you hurt her the first time? Did you know she was pregnant?"

"No, I didn't. But does it matter?" He rubbed his hands over his head. He was a study in contrasts—big and muscular, his muscles flexing with the movement of his arms, but still lost and vulnerable. Faith wanted to hold him, but she stayed where she was, in the open door, her hand on the doorknob.

"Yes. To me, it does."

After a long, slow breath, Michael answered, "Same thing. She threatened to do what she did tonight. I lost my shit the same way. I didn't mean it. I just…couldn't stop."

"You mean what she said. That was true."

He didn't look away. "No. But yeah. She twisted the truth up in lies so it would hurt me as much as it could. What she said about when I was a kid—that was true. Saying I liked it was a lie."

Then she hadn't been remotely innocent. She had dug into Demon's deepest wound, and she'd done it with glee. If she'd known Michael enough to know such a secret, then she knew the limits of his control, just like Faith did.

Faith closed the door and stepped into the room. True to form, Michael took the same number of steps backward, so she stopped.

"Quit moving away from me, Michael. Just quit it." Her voice was quiet; sadness had sapped the volume from it. "I love you." She took another step, and he held.

"I never want to hurt you."

"I'm not afraid of you, Michael. You're not a demon. You're a man—a scarred man with a beautiful heart. I love you. We *can* be right. We already are."

He stayed still and let her close the distance between them. When she put her hands on his chest, he closed his eyes. "I don't know why you would give me this chance."

"Because you deserve it. I think you're owed a lifetime of chances." She leaned in and kissed his chest. "I'm so sorry for what your life was."

That was a wrong thing to say; he stiffened, but he didn't pull away. "I don't want that—pity." He spat out the last word as if it had a foul taste.

"I don't pity you. I pity the boy who went through that. And I understand the man he became a little better now."

In Faith's head were still questions about Tucker's mom and how Michael had ended up with her, how someone like that had come to know his secret pain, but she didn't let them get as far as her tongue. Her jealousy was stupid, and talking more about the woman who'd torn him up so much, and whom he'd killed for it, would only cause him more pain.

Finally, Michael touched her. He lifted his hands and cupped her face. She smiled at the familiar sense of his love in that touch. She thought he was going to kiss her, and he licked his lips as if preparing to do so. But then he said, "It wasn't me who killed her."

"What?" She frowned, trying to make room for that new bit of information. Then it clicked. If it wasn't him, then it was a club call. Though she'd once watched Michael suffer at the hands of club justice, it was something Faith understood. Any reservations that might have been caught in the cracks of her mind were washed away, and she smiled. "She wasn't an innocent, Michael. If I know that, you have to."

He shrugged. "I do. But what I did—there's no way she could fight back against me. I was bigger and stronger. She was an evil cunt, but it doesn't excuse what I did."

And with that, Faith understood. Tucker's mother was small and, he thought, powerless to defend herself. Like he had been. Exactly what his childhood had been like, Faith didn't know, and she didn't know if he'd ever tell her, or if she'd ever ask. But now she knew he'd been abused when he couldn't protect himself. It tore him up to hurt somebody smaller and weaker than he was, even somebody who was hurting him and laughing about it.

She'd always known that he would never hurt her. Even after what she'd seen tonight, most of her turmoil had been trying to reconcile that gruesome show with the gentle man she knew, grappling with the thought that the years had changed him so much. But now, in this moment, as she dropped her hands from his chest, sliding over the firm sculpts of his torso and belly and then around his waist, she regained her equilibrium. She was safe. She loved him. He loved her. Now, at this time, in this present, they made each other safe.

"I know I'm safe with you, Michael. And you're safe with me."

He blinked. Then, at long last, he bent his head and kissed her.

CHAPTER TWELVE

The grunting was almost the worst of it. And the talking, the things the guard said. "Give it to me, oh yeah. Yeah. Pretty boy. Yeah." Michael gripped the edge of the rickety metal desk that shook under him, and he waited for it to be over, trying not to hear, trying not to smell. Trying not to feel. As always, a wide, fat hand slapped him hard on the side of the head when it was over.

Demon bolted upright, taking in a huge swallow of air and holding the side of his head. He recognized the dream for what it was as soon as he was awake, and he started counting heartbeats, trying to come down, as he oriented himself back into his room at Hoosier and Bibi's.

He hadn't had that dream, or any of them, for a long time. Years. But the box in his head had been opened last night. All those torments loose and dancing.

"Michael?"

He ducked away from the sound of Faith's voice behind him, as if it had been a touch. "I'm okay."

"You're not."

"Just a dream."

"Michael." She touched him then, laid her hand lightly on his back. He couldn't deal. Barely managing not to flinch away, he threw the covers back and got out of bed.

"I need the bathroom." He turned and headed toward the door at the side of the room, catching in the corner of his eye the image of Faith, in one of his t-shirts, sitting in his bed.

What he'd wanted for years was coming true. He had Faith. She was his. Even knowing who he was, she was his. And he was leaving her alone in his bed. Moving away from her again.

He went into the bathroom and closed the door. Then he walked through, into Tucker's room, and closed that door, too. Pulling up the big stuffed dog to use as a pillow, he lay down on the floor next to his sleeping son's crib.

~oOo~

"What about this one?"

"MOOOO!"

"That's right, buddy. Cows go 'moo.' Can you say 'cow'?"

"MOOOO!" Tucker pursed his lips and sat up straight on Demon's lap, really getting into the word. Demon laughed and kissed the back of his head. This morning, having breakfast and playing with his boy, he felt almost normal. As long as he didn't think about who was sleeping in his bed.

"You're a good moo-er, Tuck." He turned the page. "How about this one?"

"Fay!"

It was a picture of a sheep, and 'fay' wasn't even close, so Demon looked at his son, preparing to correct him. But Tucker wasn't looking at the book. Faith was in the room, leaning against the wall at the point where the family room led into the kitchen. Tucker was greeting her.

"Hey, buddy," she said, but she didn't move. "Where's Bibi?"

"She went to see your mom."

Faith nodded. She was still wearing his t-shirt, swimming in it, and she'd put her leather pants back on. When he'd first seen her last night at the clubhouse, before everything went to shit, he'd taken a moment just to look at her—still marveling at the ways she could be so different and so familiar at the same time. She'd been wearing those black leather pants, fitting like a second skin, a black lace top, and high-heeled shoes with straps covered in studs. She was gorgeous. And then he'd seen that Connor had hugged her in that full-body way he'd always hugged her, and Demon's face had gotten hot.

He knew they'd been practically brother and sister—or, at least, he knew that was what they said. But he also knew Connor, who chased pussy like the resource was running low. It was hard not to feel hostile when he saw a horndog like that lifting Faith off the ground. Or anybody, for that matter. That was for Demon, no one else.

He met Faith's eyes. She looked like she hadn't gotten that much sleep, even though it was after ten in the morning.

"You want me to go? I can stay at my mom's. I have to move in there when she comes home, anyway, and there's stuff I need to do."

He set his son off his lap. "Tuck, you want to play with trains?"

"Ook!" Tucker pushed the book at him. He wanted to finish the story. Demon was torn. He had to make Faith feel better. He'd been a monster last night, and then a jerk. But now, in the bright sun of a Saturday morning, things were maybe not so bleak. Maybe. But he didn't know if he could say the things he'd need to say to help Faith understand him. He had to lock that box back up, or it would swallow him whole.

And he didn't want to put his son off, either. In the past week, he hadn't been paying Tucker the attention he needed. He'd been leaning on Bibi even more than usual.

"It's okay," Faith said, in the same lackluster tone. "I get it."

"No, you don't!" Tucker and Faith both frowned at Demon's sharp tone, and he took a breath. "I don't want you to go. Please don't go." Looking at the book still on his lap, he had an idea. "Let's take Tucker out."

Her surprise was as clear on her face as her fear had been last night. "What?"

"Let's go out—the three of us."

She smiled, but her forehead creased. "How? Dante doesn't have a back seat."

"I have a truck, too. Extended cab. I've been a dad a while, Faith. I don't strap him on the back of my bike."

That made her chuckle quietly. "Okay. I'd like that. Where?"

"I know a place. Hey, Tuck. Want to go someplace fun to play?"

Tucker clapped his hands. "Yeah! Pway!"

~oOo~

Demon parked his truck along the side of the barn. Tucker was already excited, having screamed *MOOO!* at every cow they'd passed on the road.

Faith was simply smiling at him, bemused.

Demon had enjoyed the ride tremendously. His old truck had a bench front seat, and he'd pulled Faith over to sit right at his side. He'd driven with his arm over her shoulders, like they had in the time before. Her touch made him feel quiet. He wondered whether that might have been true last night, too, whether she could have calmed him after the dream if he hadn't run away so quickly.

He had to learn to hold. In most parts of his life, it would never occur to him to run. In club business or facing club justice, he never thought to run. He'd done time rather than run. He'd bled rather than run.

There was only one particular exception, when he'd made an already frightened little boy afraid of him.

But with Faith, running seemed always to be his first impulse. No—his second. His first impulse, to pull her to him so tightly she became part of him, was the thing that scared him almost more than anything else. It was so strong. It felt like it would hurt her if he let it loose, like his very love would hurt her. Like the beast inside him wanted her as badly as he did.

But then, when he touched her, when she touched him, she made him quiet. The paradox was fucking with his head. Obviously.

His arm still around her, Demon looked into the rearview mirror at his son. "Okay, Motor Man. You want to pet a cow?"

"MOOO!" he shouted from his car seat.

Laughing, Demon got out, put his kutte on, and helped Faith down. Then he went around and released Tucker.

As they came around the back of his Ford, Demon holding Tucker's hand, Tucker lifted his free hand to Faith, and she took it. They walked that way toward an older, heavyset black man in dusty jeans and a Caterpillar cap.

Malachi Jerrolds, J.R.'s father, ran this cattle ranch about fifty miles east of Madrone. In addition to a large Angus herd that supported his family, he kept a small herd of Holsteins and a flock of chickens for a side business selling raw milk and free-range eggs at the farmer's markets. He also had goats for foliage control. The place was practically heaven on earth for Tucker. Demon should have thought of it before.

Demon held out his hand. "Malachi."

"Demon. How you doin', son?"

"I'm good. This is my old lady, Faith." The words 'old lady' gave him a thrill of happiness and pride and fear. He could see that she liked to hear him say them.

"Good to meet ya."

Faith shook his hand. "And you. Thanks for this."

"You bet. And this's gotta be Tucker, then." Malachi squatted down to Tucker's level and held out his hand. "Hey, there, young man."

Tucker ducked behind Demon's leg, so Demon squatted, too, and Tucker hid his face behind his kutte. "Buddy, Mr. Jerrolds is a friend of Pa's. He's gonna let you pet his cows and goats. Can you be nice and say hi?"

"Hi," Tucker whispered, peeking out from the kutte.

Malachi reached out and patted Tucker's back. "Good to know you, son." He stood. "C'mon. The girls are all inside. Melissa is milking—maybe Tucker can give it a try."

He led them into the barn. When Tucker got a load of the array of black and white cows looking over their stalls at him, he froze, his blue eyes huge and his mouth wide open.

Demon felt a prickle behind his eyes. He'd made his boy happy. Really happy. Maybe this made up a little for scaring him with his temper lately.

He looked at Faith, who was smiling down at Tucker. He'd made her happy, too, but there was something else behind her smile, something that darkened her expression a shade or two. Demon figured that was his fault, and he wanted to make it up to her.

~oOo~

"You want me to take him?"

Faith shook her head and answered him quietly. "No. I like it." Tucker was sound asleep on her shoulder. He'd made it about halfway through his Happy Meal before he'd gotten grumpy and whiny. Demon had been surprised that Faith had picked him up and held him in her arms, but Tucker had been perfectly content with that and had fallen quickly asleep.

His little butt was still brown with dust. He had had a blast at the Jerrolds' farm. He'd petted all the cows and the goats. He'd 'milked' one very patient old girl, and he'd fed the chickens. He'd helped gather eggs. And there had been a derelict old John Deere tractor rusting out behind the barn. Both Faith and Tucker had enjoyed climbing around on that.

Demon had had a blast, too. More than ever before in his life, he felt like he was with his family. Not a family that had accepted him, like Hoosier and Bibi or the club, though that was wonderful. A family that he'd made. That was *his*.

They were eating fast food on a plastic table outside a McDonalds, right in front of the truck, because on the back seat, behind the driver's seat, was a box containing four kittens. One of Malachi's mousers had dropped a litter. The kittens were weaned, and Malachi didn't want so many cats overrunning his barn. So he'd said they could have the kittens if they wanted.

Tucker wanted. Faith wanted. So Demon wanted.

Hoosier was badly allergic to cats, but they weren't taking the kittens to their house. On Faith's word, they were taking the kittens to Margot's house, for Sly to look after.

Demon didn't know if that was such a great idea. Margot wasn't his favorite person on the planet, and he didn't trust her to be kind to anyone or anything. But he wasn't clear to what extent Margot would even know the kittens were around. Having not seen her himself in months, he couldn't quite conjure up an image of what she was like now. Faith, however, said it was perfect, so the kittens were going to Sly.

The discussion of what to do with their kitten windfall had brought up questions for Demon, questions he kept to himself. He might have brought them up before what happened with Kota, but now he was nervous. This second chance that he and Faith had was brand new. Only a couple of days into it, everything had slid sideways, and he felt like the floor under them still wasn't secure yet.

But if it was, how would they live? He wanted to be a family—her, Tucker, and him. Maybe, someday, a baby that was his and Faith's, too. That was something he'd thought about since the time before. But she had to take care of her mother. And Demon didn't have custody of Tucker. He was living with Hoosier and Bibi so he could be with his son. How did they make that work?

Too big a question to contemplate at dusk outside a roadside McDonalds. He smiled at Faith, holding his son. "I love you, babe."

She smiled and cocked her head like he'd surprised her.

"What?"

"You haven't called me that since…" her smile faded a little, and he knew she meant 'before.'

"Is it okay?"

"I love it. And you." She shifted Tucker's sleeping weight in her arms.

"Little as he is, he gets heavy. You want to go?"

"I'm worried he'll wake up when we put him in his seat."

"If he wakes up at all, he'll go right back to sleep. We wore him out."

She grinned. "Yeah. He's totally 'tuckered.'"

Demon groaned a laugh at her terrible pun, then stood up and helped Faith to her feet.

Tucker didn't wake up in his car seat. Demon fastened him in while Faith checked on the kittens. With their charges settled, he helped her into the front seat, then climbed in behind her and got the truck moving back to Madrone.

They rode quietly for about fifteen minutes. The traffic grew heavier the farther west they drove. Demon was mildly agitated—just aggravated by stupid California drivers and frustrated to be stuck in traffic, trapped in a cage. On a bike, he'd have been leaving these idiots behind.

Faith's hand was on his thigh, and he must have been telegraphing his declining mood, because she started to rub his leg, sliding her hand up and down as if to soothe him. He liked it, it did soothe him, and he put his arm around her again and tucked her close.

And then her hand moved far up his thigh and slid between his legs. He brought his arm back from her shoulders and grabbed her hand. Not only was his kid sleeping behind them, but just no. After the night before, he needed a minute or two to get his brain screwed back in right.

She looked up at him, but she didn't say anything. Not at first. For a few more minutes, they drove quietly, and Demon changed his hold on her hand to something affectionate rather than controlling.

"Do you think you'll ever tell me about what happened to you?" Her voice was soft and hesitant, but the question still skewered him.

He looked in the rearview and saw that Tucker was still sound asleep, his mouth open and one arm dangling over the car seat. Then Demon swallowed and took a breath. Engaging the topic at all made his heart speed up and thud. "I don't know if I can."

"But you could tell her."

Jesus Christ. She was jealous. Faith was jealous of Dakota. That was completely ridiculous.

But was it? Dakota, who was a fucking corruption of everything good in his life—of Faith—had known his most deeply-held secret. He'd given her that trust, and she'd laughed in his face. He had to trust Faith more than he'd trusted the woman who was the negative image of her. But fuck, to talk about all that with her would really let it loose in his head. He was trying to stuff it all away where it belonged.

He had to trust her with it. He owed that to her. After everything, he owed her at least that.

He pulled off at the next ramp and parked in the lot of a Chevron station.

"What are you doing?"

"I can't drive and think about this at the same time." He checked to make sure Tucker was still sleeping. "And I can't talk about it with Tucker here. But I will tell you. If you need to know, I'll tell you. But it sets everything loose in my head when I talk about it or even think about it." She dropped her head, and Demon kissed her crown. "You should know. I love you. We shouldn't have secrets."

She made a sound like a sob. "I love you. I'm sorry. I shouldn't need to know. But it's driving me crazy that she knew. It's petty and stupid of me to feel like this. But she knew you better than I do. And she gave you Tucker." She sniffed raised her head. "You know what? It really is petty. Fuck it. I don't need to know. I don't want you to have to deal with it. So forget I asked."

"Faith…" He hated the thought that she felt at any disadvantage in a comparison with Kota. It was so absurd that he might have laughed if the ground for the comparison hadn't been so treacherous.

"No. It's fine. I know enough. I know who you are, and I love you. It's fine."

He didn't believe her. He could tell it wasn't 'fine.' "Kota was like me. Grew up like me. I thought she'd understand. And I guess she did, which is how she knew how much it would hurt me to twist it up and broadcast the lie she made. She got off on making me lose my shit."

"And you don't think I'll understand?"

"I don't think you can." She tensed up, but he held her and went on, "I'm *glad* you can't. I'm glad your life was so much better. I was in awe of you from the day I met you, and I'm still in awe of you. I think you can love me because it's not in you to understand what it was like. You see something good because you can't see what's bad. I don't want you to look at me like you did last night—when you were afraid, or later, when you felt sorry for me, just knowing the little that you do. I can't deal with that."

She stared at him, her eyes wide with hurt. He didn't look away. He had to learn to hold.

"I don't know what to say to that. It feels like you don't trust me enough. But okay. I don't want to make you hurt."

"I do trust you. I *will* tell you. I just wanted you to know why it scares me."

"Okay," she said and then turned again to face the windshield.

Demon felt fairly sure he'd ruined their good day.

~oOo~

But he hadn't. Tucker and kittens saved their day.

They stopped at a pet shop and then went by Margot's house and got the kittens set up. Sly must have heard their mewing, because he was through the little pet door before they could even go out and call for him. Faith closed up the pet door to keep him inside and then made sure all the bedroom and bathroom doors were closed, too. She was going to come spend the night with Demon and leave Sly in charge until the morning.

Sly was even nice to Tucker. He must have recognized him as a baby, because he let him squat at his side and pat his head in his not-quite-gentle toddler way, and he didn't make a fuss when Tucker picked up a kitten.

By the time they left, with Tucker protesting emphatically, Sly was lying in the soft bed Faith had bought, and the kittens were crawling all over him. His eyes were at half-mast and he was purring like crazy.

Demon had never seen Sly with kittens. Faith told him that she had, in a way. Apparently, he'd carried two baby bunnies into the yard not long after Demon had left for the Nomads. Margot had let Faith help him take care of them.

It seemed like Margot maybe had a soft spot for the big old tom.

~oOo~

Tucker's car nap had screwed up his routine, so he was up until nearly midnight. Everybody in the house watched television together for a while, and Demon started trying to put him down around ten o'clock. He'd read about a library's worth of picture books before he could finally put Tucker in his crib and turn out the light.

When he went into his room to change into sweats and a t-shirt, Faith was sitting in the middle of the bed. Figuring she wanted the privacy to talk, Demon counted heartbeats for a few seconds and then sat down next to her.

But before he could think of something to say, she rose up on her knees and leaned into him.

"We don't have to talk." She planted her lips firmly on his and shoved her tongue into his mouth. He flinched back at first; the talk he'd thought they were going to have had him in no way prepared to head in the direction her kiss was taking them. But she grabbed his head in her hands and held him.

It was Faith. He loved her. He loved kissing her. He loved loving her. And his body and mind recollected these facts within a few seconds. He pulled her onto his lap. She was wearing only his t-shirt and her panties. With his hands on her bare legs, he deepened their kiss.

As soon as he did, she smiled and pulled back, kissing his cheek and jaw, moving around to his ear. Demon closed his eyes and felt her, the soft press of her full lips on his skin, the gentle sting of her teeth nipping at him. She got to his ear and sucked on his lobe, making him shiver.

"You don't have your earring anymore," she murmured.

"You're just noticing?" he teased, feeling much calmer than he'd expected to feel when he'd come in to see her waiting.

"No. Just mentioning." She nipped at him. "The scar looks like it got torn out."

"It did."

She kissed it. "That must have hurt."

"It did. Bled like a fucker. S'why I didn't pierce it again. Besides, it was lame."

"I liked it."

He leaned back and looked at her. "Yeah? You want me to do it again?"

"No. But I love that you would." Her grin lit up the dimly-lit room.

He caught her face in his hands and looked hard into her eyes. "I'd do anything for you."

For a second or two, she simply looked back into his eyes, just as deeply. Then she whispered, "There *is* something I'd like."

Feeling a hint of trepidation, he combed her hair back from her face. "What?"

"I'd like to give you head."

Demon didn't know what he'd thought she might say, but it hadn't been that. "Faith…" He moved, planning to set her on the bed next to him, but she grabbed his hands.

"Wait. I think I understand a little more why you wouldn't let me…before. But I know you had to have been with a lot of girls since. I know you've gotten head. That has to be true."

It was true, but it was irrelevant, and he didn't like the look in her eyes. This was about jealousy again, and she was ruining a nice ending to a complicated day. "Faith, come on."

"Did you let *her* give you head?"

Fuck. Suddenly Dakota Nelson was everywhere he turned, like she was haunting him. "Don't bring her in here. You're putting her between us, and that sucks."

"You did, didn't you?"

The answer was yes, so he kept it to himself. She didn't understand at all. "Faith, please."

"You did. Why not me, then?"

"It's different with you."

"Why?"

"Because I love you!" He pushed her off his lap and stood up. He wanted to get away, but he had to learn to hold. So he walked to the window and stared at his reflection in the dark glass. Counting beats. "I love you. I don't want to make you do that."

After a minute or two, she came up behind him and wrapped her arms around his waist. "I think somebody made you do that."

The shudder ran through him despite his efforts to suppress it. "I will tell you all of it, but I can't talk about us at the same time. What we have can't get wound up in all that. I will lose my shit."

"Okay. I'm sorry." She kissed his back and then leaned her head on him.

"Don't be jealous of her, Faith. You're everything. She was nothing." Demon knew then that his past—Kota, his childhood, all of it—would be between them until he answered the questions in Faith's head. Whether she demanded the answers or not, the questions were in the way. Even if it changed everything between them, even if she couldn't love him once she knew, he had to tell her. And hope for the best.

He sighed and picked up her arm from his waist, pulling her around so he could hold her. "I need to tell you everything. No secrets. I need you to know so you'll stop wondering." He looked down at her bare legs. "But put some pants on first."

CHAPTER THIRTEEN

Bibi pushed Margot into the house, and Faith followed, carrying the bag she and Bibi had packed, as well as a couple of plastic bags of crap the hospital had sent them home with.

It wasn't her mother who was coming back to this house. The days in the hospital seemed to have dulled the edges of the woman she'd been. Not that Faith really had any idea who her mother had been in the past ten years.

But for the past few days, Margot had been quiet and vaguely confused. She asked for Blue all the time and cried when no one could bring him to her. She knew Bibi—almost forty years of friendship had etched her best friend into many layers of her memory—but she only fleetingly understood who Faith was, and when she did, she thought she was still a girl. Since Faith and Margot had been in crisis during those years, it was easier, and just better, when she couldn't remember her at all.

Waiting in the house for them was Leonora Prater, who would be Margot's primary nurse. Sera was paying for one and a half daily shifts of home nursing. She'd offered to pay for three shifts, freeing Faith up entirely, but Faith wanted to try it this way first. She had no idea why, but she wanted to take care of her mother. Or at least try.

Leonora—Leo, she'd said to call her—had started working a couple of days earlier, and she had made a list of changes that needed to be made in the house. In almost no time, several members of the Horde had widened doors, built ramps, and hauled furniture and rugs to storage. They'd also installed child guards on cabinets and doors. Faith had trouble accepting that one. Her mother was becoming a child.

Because there was a notation in her file that she was prone to violent outbursts, the nurses assigned to her—Leo and a male nurse, Jose—had particular training. And they were both large people. Margot was about an inch taller than Faith and maybe ten pounds heavier. Leo probably weighed two times as much.

And Jose was built like a defensive lineman. The image of either of them taking Margot down, no matter how psycho she got, was almost laughable. If anything at all could have been laughable.

Now, Leo smiled as Bibi rolled Margot into the house. She bent down and took Margot's hand. "Hi, Margot. Do you remember me?" Leo had visited her in the hospital the day before.

Margot just smiled. And then one of the kittens, a little, snow-white girl, tumbled into the room, followed quickly by her grey tabby siblings, sister and brother. Margot saw them, and her smile grew. She tried to get up from her wheelchair, but her leg was extended in its tall cast. Faith reached down and picked up the white girl, who was trying to climb the wheelchair, anyway.

"This is Blanca, Margot." Calling her 'Mom' had only confused her, more often than not. "Would you like to hold her?"

"Please." She took the kitten from Faith's hands and tucked her under her neck. "I love babies. I didn't know you had babies here. Everything's all right, then."

Faith felt something like love, watching her mother cuddle the kitten and laugh when her whiskers tickled her face. She hadn't felt anything like love for her mother in a very long time. It hurt.

Seeing her calm with the kittens made her think that maybe she could be okay with Tucker, too. That was a huge leap, she knew. But Tucker was a sweet, beautiful little boy, who was usually quiet. Maybe Margot would like having him around. Maybe…maybe Michael and Tucker could move in here with them. When Michael got custody, at least.

Leo smiled and winked at Faith and then went behind the wheelchair. "Why don't we go into the kitchen and put some lunch together? Are you hungry?"

"I have a shoot tomorrow. I can't eat. But I'll have some coffee. Is the coffee good here?"

Leo's brow furrowed lightly. She didn't know Margot's past. But Bibi stepped up. "We had to reschedule that until your leg is better, baby. You should eat so you heal up faster."

Margot looked at the cast on her leg like she'd never seen it before. A blank mask of confusion rolled over her face, and then she smiled again, rubbing her face on the kitten. "Oh, yeah. I forgot. That was stupid of me. Okay. Can I have grilled cheese?"

"Absolutely," Leo answered.

"Watch out for the babies!" Margot admonished as Leo pushed her chair through to the kitchen.

Faith watched them go, her head in turmoil. It was always in turmoil these days. Bibi put her arm around her waist and pulled her close. "Maybe she'll come back a little, now that she's home."

"I don't know if I want her to. Isn't that awful? But she's nicer this way."

Bibi sighed. "Oh, baby. I wish I could fix what broke between you two. I guess it's too late now. But she does love you. I know her better than anybody alive. She loves you. But she hates the way she sees her failin's in you."

Faith flinched. "Jesus, Beebs. Ow."

"I said that wrong. She sees that she fucked up with you. And she's not the kind of person who can confront her mistakes."

Faith shook her head. A person who couldn't accept their own mistakes was an asshole, plain and simple. "I don't know why you love her so much. I don't know what you see in her. Or what my dad did."

"Blue was no great prize, either. I loved him, but he was a domineerin' son of a bitch. If he'd've been mine, I'd've killed him within a year. Oh, that man could not see any way but his own. Margot used to fight and fight him, but she always gave in. For years, he just rolled right over her. What he wanted, he got.

And then she finally figured him out. She figured out how to make him think what she wanted was what he wanted. Once it started to work, it became a habit. I'd say that was when she started bein' not so nice."

Bibi gave her a squeeze. "And he was always sweet to you. Sweeter even than he was with your sister. You had him tied in a bow around your finger, and it hurt your mama to see it, when she had to fight him so hard, all the time."

Pages of the past were flipping in Faith's head, and old hurts, hurts that had been aching ever since the hospital had called her about her mother's accident, began to bleed. "That's what she did to me, isn't it? It wasn't my dad. It was her."

"What good is it pickin' at that old sore? Blue was out of his head. They both were. You know that. Your daddy saw you as his baby. The thought of what Demon…well, that was too much for Blue."

"I mean the rest of it. What happened after."

Bibi stepped away and picked up Margot's suitcase. "You need to stop thinkin' about that, honey. It can't be undone, so let it be. I'm gonna unpack your mama's shit. Why don't you see if Leo needs anythin'."

After Bibi left the room, Faith picked up one of the grey tabbies. There was another kitten, solid grey, around somewhere. And Sly, too. He might have been outside, but he'd been staying close since he had a family to see to.

Standing in place, Faith tucked the kitten—she was calling this little boy Petey—under her chin.

She couldn't let it be, because it was a secret between her and Michael, and he had laid himself out to her. Because she was a stupid, jealous cunt, she'd basically forced him to tell her things that hurt him to think about. And now they hurt her, too. Maybe he'd been right to think that she couldn't understand. But he'd been wrong to worry that it would change her love for him. If anything, knowing what his life was, and knowing him now, his strength and his kindness, his capacity for love, made her love him all the more.

Now she had to tell him the thing she was holding back. She had to. No secrets—that was what he'd said, what he wanted. But Bibi was right. Her secret would hurt him. It might break him.

So she would hold onto it until she figured out a way to tell him without hurting him.

~oOo~

"Wouldn't be much to make this into a shop for you." Michael stood with her in the garage. With the help of Keanu and Peaches, they were working on clearing the mountain of junk out of this three-car space.

"Studio. I'm an artist. What I need is a studio."

"You want a welding rig in here. That's a shop, babe."

She laughed and punched his arm. "If you can make it work for me, call it what you want."

"No sweat." He hooked a finger through her belt loop and pulled her close. "It's not drywalled, and that's good. The ceiling's already vented. We can put in some fireproof insulation, improve the lighting, bring all your *studio* shit in here. And put in a steel door into the house. Take me a weekend."

"Really?"

"Sure. We can send a couple Prospects to move your shit from Venice."

"Stop calling my things *shit*."

He grinned. "I thought I could call it whatever I want." He cupped her face in his hands and kissed her. When she moaned in response to the soft but demanding touch of his mouth on hers, curving into his body and wrapping her arms around his neck, he moved his hands to her waist and lifted her up. Then he walked her to the garage wall and leaned her against it, his weight holding her up.

They made out like that for a long time, ignoring the Prospects carrying loads of her mother's junk from the garage to a U-Haul, but when Faith, unable to stop herself, began to grind on his erection, he pulled back with a groan. "Fuck, this is hard."

Arching up to tighten their connection again and feel him hard between her legs, she whispered, "Yeah, it is." Then she smiled and leaned closer to bite his lip.

"Faith…" He set her down.

"Yeah, I know," she sighed. In the week that Margot had been home, though things between them had smoothed out again, they hadn't been able to sleep together for a whole night. She stayed here, and Michael stayed with his son at Hoosier and Bibi's. They were back to stolen moments. "It's like it was before."

He frowned. "No, it's not. There's nothing wrong about us now. Things are just inconvenient."

"You're right. Sorry. My mom likes Tucker, though. And she has no idea who you are. Maybe it would work here for all of us." Margot had been mostly quiet and pleasant since she'd been home. Like a barely-acquainted houseguest who was trying hard not to make too much of a ripple in the residents' lives. Faith felt guilty for enjoying it so much, but it was peaceful.

And she didn't feel *too* guilty, because twice during the week, the Margot Faith knew had reared up and said something bitchy or just plain nasty. There was a voice in Faith's head that was suggesting that what was happening to her mother was karma.

But what did that mean for what was going on with Faith herself? Every good seemed balanced by a bad, or at least a complication.

"Let me focus on getting Tucker. If that happens, then we can figure out how we're all together. If Tucker's safe here, and your mom isn't gunning for me, then yeah, I think we can make that work."

She hugged him, feeling her own karmic scale tip toward the good, at least for now. "You want a sandwich? I'm going to check on everything inside." Not that her supervision was needed inside. Jose and Bibi were both in there with Margot and Tucker.

"Sure. Any more of that sweet tea Bibi made?"

She yanked on his kutte until he dipped his head so she could kiss his cheek. "I'll check. Hey guys," she called to the Prospects. "Sandwiches?"

"Yes, ma'am!" they called.

'Ma'am,' Faith thought. Wasn't that a hoot. Smiling, she headed into the house.

Once inside, she could hear Bibi and her mother arguing—she heard the tone but not the words themselves. Jose was in the kitchen, looking like he wasn't sure what to do. She went into the living room. Bibi stood next to Margot's chair, holding Tucker, who was quiet but looked like he was headed toward upset.

The eyes her mother turned on her were full of recognition—and anger and accusation, too.

"What's going on?" Faith asked.

"How did you do it?"

"What?" Faith knew something was really wrong—she could see the turmoil on Bibi's face—but she was clueless.

"Don't play the stupid gash with me. How did you get away with it? I was right there! How?"

"Margot, I don't—"

"Don't you call me by my name. I am your *mother*, and you will treat me with some fucking respect."

"Bibi?" Faith needed help.

"I'm sorry, baby." Bibi turned to Margot. "Margot, sweetheart, you got this all wrong."

"Shut it, Bibi." Margot turned back to Faith, her eyes searing with anger. "*I told you to get rid of it*. I stood there and watched. I made sure! How the fuck did you do it?"

A cowl of sick sorrow fell over Faith's shoulders as she understood what had Margot so upset. "Bibi, get him out of here. He doesn't need to hear all this."

Bibi nodded and carried Tucker toward the kitchen, pausing to squeeze Faith's hand. "I'm so sorry. She was playing with him, and then it all changed."

Tucker reached for Faith, leaning out of Bibi's arms. "Fay!"

She kissed his pudgy hand. "Go with Granny, buddy."

When they were clear of the room, Faith turned to her mother. "Tucker's not mine, Mom."

Margot laughed her contempt. "You lying little whore. I can see it. He looks just like his father."

Yeah, he did. But that didn't make him hers. "He's Michael's, but he's not mine. You did make me get rid of mine."

"You must really think I'm an idiot. You think I can't see?" Margot brushed her hair back in the way she always had when she thought she'd won something. "Fine, then. Your father will take care of the problem his way, then. You made your choice."

Faith had to make Michael go away before he came into the house and found this Margot. Struggling to keep memory at bay before it pulled her under completely and drowned her, she turned and headed back to the garage.

memory

Sitting on the bathroom floor, Faith pulled a length of toilet paper off the roll and blew her nose, then dropped the paper into the bowl and flushed. Not feeling ready to stand yet, she rested her forehead on the cool porcelain of the tub.

The door burst open, and her mother stood in the doorway. She tossed a box into the room. It landed on the floor and slid until it stopped against Faith's knee. Faith didn't have to look to know what it was.

"Take them both. While I stand here."

"Go away, Mom. I'm sick. I have the flu." She knew it wasn't the flu. But the past three weeks had been just fucking horrible, and she could not deal with her mother's drama on top of it all. They'd been keeping her a prisoner, not letting her out of the house at all. They'd somehow arranged with the school to put her on independent study, like she was terminally ill or something.

Her father had said he had no intention of letting her out of the house again.

Faith pretty much didn't care about anything anymore.

"Bullshit. Take the goddamn tests."

"I just peed. I don't have to go now."

Her mother came all the way into the room and filled the glass on the counter with tap water. "Then drink this, because neither of us is going anywhere until you take those fucking tests."

She drank, and puked again, and drank some more, and they waited, and then she peed. And peed again.

Her mother snatched the sticks out of her hand before the results were in. She stared at the sticks, and Faith stared at the floor.

"You stupid, stupid, *stupid* little slut!" Margot threw one of the sticks at her. "Look at that! What have you done?" She threw the other. Faith didn't bother to look; her mother was all the result she needed to see.

Then Margot stormed over to her and grabbed her arm. "Get up! Get up! We're going to see your father!"

Faith got up but pulled her arm away. "No, I'm not. Leave me the fuck alone!"

Margot slapped her across the face. Hard. And then again. Faith was too shocked to protect herself. For all her mother's faults, she'd never before hit her. The third one was a punch that knocked Faith back onto her ass. And then Margot kicked her in the stomach. The angle was odd, and she didn't connect with much force, but it was still horrible.

"Mom! Stop!" Faith cried out and curled into a ball.

Margot's voice shook when she spoke again. "Get up or I'll do worse. We're going to your father right now."

~oOo~

Her mother hadn't even let her dress. She'd dragged her out of the house in her flannel pajama bottoms and cotton camisole, grabbing the zebra throw off the couch and throwing it over her shoulders as they got to the front door. She was still barefoot.

When they got to the clubhouse, it looked empty. The men who worked in the bike shop would be over there by now, so it was too late for girls to be straggling out. And it was too early for anybody to be in for cleaning or whatever. Her high heels clicking on the old linoleum floor, Margot dragged Faith in, shouting "BLUE! BLUE! GET YOUR ASS OUT HERE! BLUE!" as soon as they cleared the front door.

Faith felt like she'd left her brain in bed at home. She'd already left her heart on the shop floor, weeks ago. She wasn't Faith anymore. All this was happening to somebody else. So she just let it happen.

It was Hoosier who came out, coming up from his office. "Jesus wept, Margie, what the fuck are you yowling about?"

Margot shoved Faith toward him, and he caught her. "HE KNOCKED HER UP! LITTLE WHORE IS PREGNANT! WHERE'S BLUE?"

"Shut the fuck up," Hoosier hissed. He looked down at Faith and brushed her sore cheek. "You okay, darlin'?" Faith shook her head, and Hoosier looked at Margot. "You do this?"

"She's *my* kid, Hooj. Watch your tone."

Hoosier stared for a second, and then nodded. Faith wasn't surprised. He'd leave it to Blue to handle. "Okay. Get in my office, and Margot, keep your fucking yap shut. I'll get Blue."

When her father came into the room, it was clear that Hoosier had told him there was trouble, but not what kind it was. He was wearing his shop coverall, and his long hair was tied back with a thin strip of leather.

He looked at Faith, but he didn't smile. Since he'd found out about Michael, Faith didn't think he'd smiled at her once. He frowned and came closer, grabbing her chin and turning her head. Then he turned to his wife. "Did you fucking hit her?"

Margot stood tall in the face of her husband's anger. "She's pregnant. That asshole knocked her up. When I caught 'em, they weren't using anything. I shoulda known."

"Did you hit her?" he asked again.

"A slap. She mouthed off. Jesus, Blue, focus on the problem here!"

He turned back to Faith, his eyes narrow. "Is it true, Faith?" He hadn't called her 'kitty cat' for weeks.

She nodded, and he shoved her away so hard she fell back, landing in an armchair.

"I will kill that motherfucker. I will skin him alive and I will kill him." He punched the tall filing cabinet, then did it again, leaving a smear of blood behind. "FUCK!"

Faith's mother closed in on her father. "She has to get rid of it."

Blue spun and faced her. "What?"

"She can't have that psycho's baby. He'll be in her life forever."

In this morning full of disorienting waves of pain, sorrow, and fear, that exchange got Faith's full attention. Her mother wanted her to have an abortion. Faith had no idea how she felt about any of this. She was sad and scared; that was all she knew. She hadn't wanted to be a mother—not yet, and maybe not ever. But if she was having Michael's baby, that meant that she hadn't lost him. That changed everything.

"Fucking Christ." He laced his fingers over the back of his neck and pulled his head down, then stayed like that for several seconds, in a pose Faith recognized as his struggle for control. Margot and Faith both watched and waited.

Faith wasn't worried. Her mother was a shrieking bitch, but her father wouldn't force her to do something like that. He loved her. And she wasn't even sure how her mother thought she could force her at all. She wasn't eighteen yet, but she couldn't believe that somebody would do an abortion she didn't want just because her mom said so. That was nuts.

"Daddy?"

At her plea, her father looked up. He met her eyes and then immediately looked away, to his wife. "Get her out of here. Go back home. I'll be there when I can. Keep your mouth shut. Do not talk to anyone. Do not do anything until we talk. And do *not* fucking touch her again. Do you understand me?"

What Margot saw in Blue's eyes must have been chilling, because she didn't fight back at all. She simply nodded and held her hand out toward Faith. "Let's go."

Faith ignored her mother and focused on her father. "Daddy, I'm sorry."

He closed his eyes. "Get out of here, Faith. Just get out."

~oOo~

Faith went to bed when she got home. She lay on her back and rubbed her belly. Michael's baby was in there. She was scared, but she felt right, too. They couldn't keep them apart now. And she knew that whatever her mother thought now, they wouldn't make her 'get rid of it.' Maybe they would throw her out. She thought that might happen.

But she remembered her father raging one night about a girl Dusty had gotten pregnant. She'd had an abortion, and Dusty had beaten her for it. Blue had said he was right to do it, because 'You don't ever take a man's child.'

So she knew it would be okay. When she heard her parents shouting at each other in the garage, she was sure of it.

When her father came in, carrying a tray with a grilled cheese sandwich and a bottle of Diet Coke, she sat up and smiled. "Hi, Daddy."

He set the tray on her desk and went back to close her door. Then he stood against it. "Your mama made an appointment at the clinic. I guess she knows somebody there, and she got you in tomorrow."

Faith's mind blanked. Was he talking about just a doctor visit? "What?"

"Your mama's right. You can't have that bastard's kid. I won't let him fuck you up more than he already did." He looked down at the foot of her bed, like he couldn't look her in the face. "So you will go tomorrow and get rid of it. And then we can try to put things back the way they belong."

"Daddy, no. I don't want—"

"Decision's made, Faith Anne. The time for what you want is long past. Now you do what we tell you, and we put this all back to rights."

"No."

"I'm not giving you a choice."

"What are you going to do? I don't want that! It *is* my choice! Are you going to tie me down and force me? Throw me out if you don't like it—I'll leave right now. I'll find Michael."

Her father, her daddy, stormed to her bed and grabbed her up by both arms. "Don't you ever talk about him in this house again. You will do as I say. And here's why—if you don't, I will kill him. I know just where he is right now. I could have him held for me with a phone call. I will kill him, Faith Anne, and I won't make it clean. Make no mistake. If you defy me, that's what will happen. You say it's your choice? So make it."

Her daddy was gone. The man whose hands were digging into her arms was somebody else. She was losing absolutely everything. It finally all hit her, all at once, and tears crashed over her. "Daddy, please!" she wailed, and he let go of her, dropping her back to her bed in a heap.

She could feel him still standing at the side of her bed, looking down at her, but she kept her face buried in her arms and let the weeping have its way with her.

"You will go tomorrow, and you will go quietly, or he dies tomorrow night."

She nodded. She had no other choice.

When he next spoke, his voice was a little farther away and broken with emotion. "I don't know where my baby girl went," he said and then opened her door and went out.

~oOo~

Margot stayed with her the entire time, holding her hand, the picture of a supportive mother. No one could see that her grip around Faith's fingers was punishingly tight.

They did lab work and an ultrasound first, and then there was counseling to confirm the pregnancy and describe the procedure, and to confirm that Faith was sure she wanted to proceed. At first, she couldn't find a voice to say the word, so she nodded. The doctor or nurse or counselor or whoever it was told her that she needed to say the word.

She cleared her throat and spoke. The woman before her cocked her head and looked hard at her, and her mother's hold on her intensified, so Faith tried again, and this time she was convincingly clear.

They let Margot stay with her for the procedure, too. On the evidence of the reactions of the nurse and a couple of other staff, it seemed like that was maybe unusual. Faith didn't care. Margot could have gone out to the waiting room and read a back issue of *People*. She had won.

With no other choice but to let it happen, Faith let it happen.

~oOo~

That night, while Faith lay in bed curled up against the cramps, Sly purring on her pillow, Margot brought her a hot water bottle and a big bowl of chocolate marshmallow ice cream with chocolate syrup and whipped cream. She left the ice cream on the desk and came over to the bed. Gently setting the hot water bottle against Faith's belly, she pulled up the comforter and then brushed her hand over Faith's head.

Sly growled quietly at her, as he always did, but she ignored him. "We fixed it, Faithy. This is better. I know you don't believe me, but it is." She left.

And Faith started to form her plan to get away.

CHAPTER FOURTEEN

"Do I need to come to you?" Demon closed his eyes and hoped the answer was 'no.' He hated going into downtown L.A.

"I don't see why at this point," Finn Bennett's reedy voice filled his ear. "I'm going to guess you won't mind me saying that this is a great stroke of luck. With Tucker's mother dead, and all of the evaluations and reports done for you and Tucker, there's nothing holding this up anymore except the court schedule. I'm going to do what I can to get us on the docket soon."

"You think I can win?"

"I don't want to get your hopes up too high. Your record is a big strike against you. But the observation evals are strong, and Tucker's caseworker and the family counselor's report both recommend reunification. I'm optimistic."

Demon grinned. Things were looking up. Everywhere he looked, things were getting good. "Okay. Thanks, Finn. Keep me posted."

"I will. Take care, Michael."

Demon put his phone in his pocket and smiled at his worktable. The cops had found and identified Dakota's body. It had taken them a couple of weeks, but her death had been ruled an accidental overdose. Case closed. Now he was Tucker's only surviving kin, and people were starting to believe he was a good father. He might actually finally catch a break.

He pulled his phone back out and dialed Faith. When she answered, his cock twitched. There was a way she sounded, answering the phone, knowing it was him, that was so...*pleased* that his chest ached with love. And maybe hope. Demon didn't really know what hope felt like, but maybe this was it.

"Hey, you," her voice smiled, "what's up?"

"Hey, babe. Talked to Finn. He thinks it's all gonna be over soon. He thinks I could get Tucker."

"Oh, my God! That's great!"

"It's not done yet, but it's the first time I really think we might be okay."

"I'm so happy for you, Michael. I love you. I love you both."

"We love you right back." He looked at the bike he was working on. He had about an hour left to finish it. "Hey—can you get away? I'll pick you up. Take a ride with me." When they'd been together before, hiding in the shadows, he'd never had her on his bike. Now, they'd had a few rides, and he couldn't get enough of it. Two of his most favorite things—the road, and Faith wrapped around him. They didn't get many chances, though, between Tucker and Margot. But it should be good now—the middle of the day. Bibi had Tucker, and Leo, he knew, was on shift with Margot.

But Faith hesitated. "Um…okay. But I'll come to you."

Okay, something was going on. She'd told him that Margot was having trouble settling in, and she thought it was better if Tucker wasn't around for a while, because he got her too excited. That made sense. He'd planned to make her a studio, but she'd put him off, saying the noise would get to her mom. That could make some sense, too. But today, Tucker wasn't a factor, and he wasn't coming over to bang around in the garage. It dawned on Michael that it had been days since he'd actually been at that house.

"What's goin' on, Faith?"

"Nothing. It's just easier if I come to you." There was a tiny, sharp edge to her answer. Defensiveness. Evasion.

"How's it easier? You make a trip here and then we ride? It's easier if I just pick you up on the bike."

A pause. "Actually, I forgot. Leo has a personal errand she needs to run today. I need to stick around. I'll just see you at the clubhouse later."

It was St. Patrick's Day, and the club was closing the shop early and having a midweek party. The heritage of the Night Horde was supposedly Norse, but that was the mother charter. Hoosier's personal heritage was half Scottish, half Irish. The charter he led, whatever its patch, partied on St. Pat's.

Demon, not much of a drinker, could have found more interesting things to do. Like ride into the desert with his old lady. But he wasn't going to fight about it with her on the phone. He wasn't going to dig into whatever had her skittish, either. Not on the phone.

He decided it wasn't worth making anything tense between them. Things were good, finally good. Her hesitation was probably just about Margot being a bitch, anyway. No point getting bunched up about that, though it would be a problem to work out when they were ready to live together.

"Okay, babe. I'll just see you later."

"Okay. I'm sorry, hon. I love you."

"Love you, too." He ended the call and put his phone away. Disappointment and a faint, lingering shade of suspicion dimmed the sheen of his good mood, but it couldn't dull it completely.

He might get his son.

~oOo~

Most of his brothers were well on their way to drunk and neck deep in pussy when Faith got to the clubhouse. The place reeked of corned beef and cabbage—not, in Demon's opinion, one of the world's best smells. But that was what Hoosier wanted: beer and corned beef. And soda bread. And Jameson.

Though Demon didn't think he'd ever actually been to Ireland, Hoosier went all out for the Irish traditions on this night of the year. He had Irish folk music blaring from the sound system, a big Irish flag over the bar, and the girls had strung plastic shamrock lights all over the Hall.

Demon thought all that was wasted on this crowd. With the exception of a greater number of hangarounds and some off-key singing along, it was just a club party. He sat at the bar and nursed a beer.

Seeing the attached Horde in the Hall with their old ladies was making him impatient for Faith. He was tired of being lonely.

Though Bibi was in club mama mode, managing the girls who hadn't gotten pulled away by patches, making sure that people were served and the food was on schedule, Hoosier, full to his eyeballs with Jameson, was on her every chance he got. She complained loudly, but she was laughing, too.

Muse and Sid were sitting in a chair in the far corner of the room, making out like teenagers. Demon laughed to himself. Sid must have gotten pretty damn drunk already. She didn't usually like to make a display like that. Muse didn't seem to be minding at all, but he wasn't getting more than R-rated. Demon figured them for the dorm soon.

Diaz had his wife, Ingrid, on one of the pinball machines. Ingrid was Finnish or Dutch or something, and her English wasn't great. She and Diaz spoke Spanish together. She didn't show up at the clubhouse often, because she worked a lot—and, anyway, she had trouble keeping up with everything going on. But she was a model and pretty comfortable being on display. She was the only old lady Demon had ever known who was perfectly happy to go to town right in the middle of everything—and didn't need tequila to get there.

Tucker was with Bart and Riley and their kids. Riley was, like, eight months pregnant or something—she looked like a tiny Goodyear blimp—so they were taking a pass on St. Pat's and had invited Tucker for a sleepover. They lived in a mansion and had every conceivable toy and game. They also had a Great Dane named Odin, and Tuck thought that dog was probably God.

Demon thought he'd like to get his son a dog of his own someday.

The most sober man in the room by a wide margin, Demon sat at the bar and watched the door, waiting, so he saw her when she walked in. Forgetting the strange roadblock in their phone call, he smiled when their eyes met. Fuck, what it did inside his chest to love her and be able to feel good about it. To love her and to have her. Years of longing and guilt were all worth it because they'd brought them here: Faith Fordham walking through a packed clubhouse, her light eyes sparkling, her smile wide with love.

It was all worth it.

She was wearing faded jeans tucked into tall, black boots. The jeans were really holes surrounded by strips of denim, with bright green lace…stockings? Tights?…underneath. He didn't know what they were called, but they were hot. Her top was just a plain white, low-cut t-shirt, and she had a black denim jacket over that.

"Hi, babe."

He held her face in his hands and kissed her. When he pulled her in for a hug, metal poked at his arms, so he looked over her shoulder at the back of her jacket. Then, curious, he turned her around.

"What's this?"

She had fashioned a set of angel's wings, spanning her shoulders, on the back of her jacket. Made of probably hundreds of safety pins. He laughed. She did love to make things out of things that were something else.

He leaned close, so she could hear him over the din. "Do you ever just see a thing for what it is?"

Smiling, she shook her head and turned her mouth to his ear. "What a boring way to see the world."

It was how he saw it, just as it was. And she was right. Her way was better. Everything about her left him in awe.

He slid his hand under her shirt and felt her bare skin twitch on his palm. "It's just you and me, babe. Tuck's with Bart and Riley. How long can you stay?"

"Jose said he'd stay over." She hooked her hands on the back of his neck. "I can spend the night."

It felt like it had been forever since they'd been able to spend a night together. And they'd only been able to spend a few so far. "Let's go back to Hoosier and Bibi's."

But she shook her head. "I don't want to take the time. You have a room here, right?"

The thought of bringing Faith into his room here gave Demon pause. He'd fucked club girls there. Not his old lady. He looked back toward the dorm, hesitating.

But she stepped closer and slid her hands under his shirt, scratching her nails over his back, and he just wanted to be with her. Right now. Wherever. Leaving his beer discarded on the bar, he took her hand and led her back.

Once they were inside, he locked the door. The wailing tones of Irish music filtered through the walls and gave a strange, rustic aura to the room. Faith was already shrugging out of her clothes. Her hair was loose and swung across her back as she took her jacket off. Following an impulse, he caught the long, dark fall in his hand and tugged her backward, to him.

She gasped and arched against him. It was the most forceful he thought he'd even been with her, excepting when he lost control, and he was on the brink of apologizing when she grabbed his other hand and pulled it around her.

Demon felt different. This night was different. For the first time, there was nothing over them—not the guilt and shame of the time before, not the awkwardness of reunion of their night in Venice Beach, not the need to be mindful of Tucker sleeping nearby. Not his past or his fear of what she would think if she knew. She knew, and she still loved him, still wanted him.

It was just them. The din of revelry around them served as insulation. In this room, they were in their own world.

And to think he'd almost talked her out of coming back here.

He pushed his hand up under her top, over the smooth, firm skin of her belly and up to her breast. Her bra was satiny, without padding, and he could feel her nipple pebble under his fingertips. He curled over her, tugging her head to the side by the hair he still had wrapped around his hand, and he pressed his mouth to her neck. She smelled like Faith, something spicy and warm, but so subtle his nose had to be almost touching her skin to be full of her scent.

She reached back, between them, and grabbed his cock through his jeans, squeezing and rubbing until a groan wrenched out of his throat, and he clutched her tightly, feeling his control start to fray. He took a step toward the bed, needing them to get naked and horizontal, but she made an agile little twist and came out of his hold to stand before him. He let loose of her hair, and it fell over her shoulder in a silken swath.

With her eyes on his, she lifted her top up and over her head, and he saw that her bra *was* satin, and hot pink. She took that off and stood topless, her hands on her hips. She stopped there, as if she were waiting, and he grinned and took his kutte off, hanging it behind him on the door. His flannel shirt and t-shirt he dropped to the floor. As he bent to untie his boots, Faith stepped up to him and put her hands on his shoulders, asking him without words to stop.

Her hands slid down over his arms, tracing every contour of muscle, all the elaborate lines of his ink, and then came back up. When they returned to his chest, she moved over every inch, stopping to draw her fingers over the lines of his old kanji. He put his hand to her neck and let his thumb rest on her identical ink.

She already bore his mark, he realized. She had for years. That understanding was so potent, his nerves flared and made his hips rock. Her eyes lifted to his, and she smiled.

"I love you so much."

Words were still hard for him at times like this, even sound itself was, and it seemed like that would always be the case. So he bent down instead and kissed her, letting his tongue tell her this way instead that they shared that love. As their mouths moved together, her hands continued their gentle exploration, downward over his ribs and belly until they arrived at his waistband.

She had his belt and jeans open and was pushing everything off his hips before he registered what she was up to. He caught hold of her elbows as she was kneeling down.

"Faith."

She stopped and stood up again, her eyes steady on his. "I love you, Michael. This isn't about jealousy. It's about making this a loving thing for you. I want this, and I want you to have it the way it should be."

It made his heart pound erratically. He'd gotten head before, plenty of times. It was different, though, when it was a club girl, just a physical thing, something she had come up to him and offered. He didn't know why that had never really stirred up his demons. Maybe because his heart had never been in it. Even with Kota, even when he'd thought they were real.

He wanted Faith kept far away from anything ugly about him.

But this didn't have to be ugly. He knew in his head that was true. Maybe he could do this. Feeling his cock lose its rigor, he swallowed. "Not on your knees."

"Fair enough." She smiled brightly. "You better strip, then, handsome, and lie down." Stepping back, she bent over and unzipped one of her boots. Demon paused and watched the way her pert little tits plumped in that position. His cock filled back out, and then some. With a brisk shake of his head to regain some focus, he rid himself of his own boots and the remainder of his clothes, and then he lay down on the narrow double bed.

Faith let her clothes fall where they would and then joined him on the bed, on her knees at his side. She loomed over him, her hair a curtain around her face, and placed one hand lightly in the middle of his chest. "Relax, baby," she purred. "I love you." As she straddled him, she bent down and kissed him. Just as he began to put the rest of it out of his head and focus just on her, the way her tongue felt and her lips tasted, the cool caress of her hair, the hot touch of her hands, she pulled away and began to kiss her way down his body—his neck, his shoulder, his chest.

Nerves caught him, and he wrapped his hands around her slender arms. "Faith, wait."

She looked up and then leaned forward, returning to let her face hover over his. "It's okay, Michael. Let me love you this way."

"I don't want...I don't want to come in your mouth"—a memory hit him—"or all over you. I hated when I did that."

Instead of backing off, or getting frustrated, she smiled. "Then don't come. Hold off until you're inside me the way you want to come."

The combination of her sultry voice and the idea in her words made him groan, and he nodded. He didn't know how long he could go before he wasn't in charge anymore, but he took a breath and let go of her arms, and she continued her journey downward.

Unwilling to see her take him into her mouth, he kept his head on the pillow and his eyes closed. So he jumped a little when he first felt her mouth—that mouth he knew so well, he loved so much, her full, soft lips—on his cock. She kissed his tip, then licked it, flicking her tongue sharply over the sensitive underside until his body was a mass of twitches and spasms. And then she took him deep.

Oh, Christ, she was good at it. He didn't want to see her bobbing up and down on him like…like…he couldn't even think it, but he knew he didn't want that image of her, so he squeezed his eyes shut. But her tongue moved, and her lips, and she sucked just exactly right, and he could feel the climax charging toward him. Fuck, it was good.

A thought crawled out of the dark: she must have done this a lot to have become so good. He hated that thought. Hated it with a black violence that frayed his control. Without his permission, his hands grabbed her head, tangling in her hair, and he raised his head and opened his eyes, feeling…feeling…heedless and intense.

She was looking at him when he opened his eyes, and she lifted up and smiled, her mouth wet. "Okay?" When he didn't answer, she moved up his body until they were face to face. His hands in her hair followed along. "Michael. Okay?"

He nodded, though he didn't know if he was.

"Can I keep going?"

He shook his head.

Her frown was brief and slight, and then she resettled across his hips and reached between her legs to hold him steady. She sat down on him, taking him into her in the way that he really wanted. Then she put her hands around his wrists and pulled his hands from her hair, setting them instead on her breasts.

This, he could watch—his hands on her breasts, the way her nipples hardened and swelled with this touch, the way her back bowed when his thumbs flicked over the tight points, the muscles in her stomach rolling as she rocked and swiveled her hips on him—all of that he wanted burned into his brain.

The face she made as she began to come—she wasn't surprised by it any longer. Now, she saw it approaching, and he could see it when she did. She bit her lip in concentration, and her attention left him. He loved that, so much, to watch her know that ecstasy was on its way and to go out to meet it. The sight both elevated his own pleasure and gave him the power to hold it off. He could wait forever to be sure she caught her bliss.

And then he recognized that he wasn't going to lose control. Not this time. He dropped a hand to her clit and massaged it in tandem with his other hand still on her breast, and she cried out and sped up dramatically, riding him hard. He could feel his finish right there, waiting impatiently, tensing the muscles of his abdomen. But it was waiting. He was always able to get her over before he lost control, but this was different. This was a calm, a lack of fight. He was completely here, in this moment with her, and that was a first. No guilt, no shame, no awkwardness, no watchfulness. No beast.

He would let her go down on him again. He could get right with that. He could be normal. He felt that now.

She came, her body tightening to rigidity, squeezing him to the point of pain. While she was still in the throes, he sat up and rolled them over. Taking charge, he adjusted their bodies so he could bend down and take a breast in his mouth as he drove into her, bringing her again to release. This time, she dragged her nails across his back.

Only then did he let himself complete, and the orgasm was more intense than he'd ever felt before. It sapped him of everything, and when it was finally over, he collapsed bonelessly at Faith's side.

"Holy shit, Michael," she panted. "That was…"

His face was buried in the pillow, and he didn't have the energy to move. But he spoke anyway. "Good?"

"Amazing." She patted his leg, which was still lying over her. "I love you."

He felt pleased and content. "Love you, too."

~oOo~

They never joined the party. They found the energy for two more goes, though Faith didn't attempt to give him head again, and he didn't bring it up. Inside her was the place he really wanted to be, his arms around her, her body around him. When they could simply go no more, they curled up together in the damp sheets and slept.

It was still dark when they were awakened by the sharp, explosive sounds that Demon knew instantly as automatic gunfire. He leapt out of bed, yanked on his jeans, and shoved his feet into his boots, not bothering to tie them. From a drawer in the small bureau, he grabbed his spare Sig and checked the magazine.

"Michael!" Faith was still in bed, her eyes wide. They'd fallen asleep without even turning out the light.

"Stay here. Don't leave this room until a patch comes for you!" Without waiting for her agreement, he grabbed his kutte off the door and left the room, turning the lock as he closed the door.

He ran out to the Hall, shrugging his kutte on over his bare chest. It was late—he had no sense of the exact time—and most of the partygoers had left or gone back to the dorm. Only the people who had passed out were still there—and the men, dressed much like Demon, who had come running at the sound of gunfire.

The gunmen were gone. They'd come in, shot up the Hall and then run. Broken glass was everywhere. Men were moaning; women were crying. Demon focused and tried to make sense. Blood. Glass. The reek of booze.

Peaches was draped face-first over the bar, dripping blood onto a barstool. One of the girls—Ember, it was Ember, fuck, she'd been around forever—was sprawled on her back near the door, one leg bent oddly behind her.

P.B. on a leather chair, his head back. What was left of his head.

A girl with her head in his lap, bleeding into a pool on the front of his jeans.

Double A, one of the Missouri patches here on loan, was struggling to his feet, his leg bleeding. He'd already been shot in that leg once before, last fall. He was helping Coco up. His jeans were open and his dick out.

Connor, Hoosier, Sherlock, Lakota, and Trick were all on their feet and armed, in various stages of undress. Lakota was bleeding heavily from a wound in his bicep. Fargo and Keanu were on their feet, too, seemingly unharmed, standing together near the kitchen, looking stunned.

Hoosier came forward from the front door, his jeans open, his bare chest covered in iron grey hair. He was dangling a large, black rubber rat from his fingers by its tail. The Dirty Rats' calling card.

"Prez?" Demon wasn't sure exactly what to ask.

"I need a head count, right the fuck now."

Demon scanned the carnage, trying to get a bead on anyone he loved unaccounted for. J.R., Diaz, and Muse all had old ladies. They'd probably gone home. Ronin never stayed late. Bart had stayed home all night with his family. Jesse...where was Jesse? And the other Missouri patch—Nolan. He was just a kid. Where was he?

As if in answer to the question Demon had only thought, Nolan came up from the dorm, barefoot and shirtless, but armed. "What the fuck?"

And then, in the far corner of the room, Sid, Muse's old lady, struggled to her feet. Her clothes were soaked with blood.

"Sid!" Demon leapt forward over the broken glass and senseless bodies until he could grab her. She only stared at him, her eyes blank.

"Are you hurt?" he asked, shaking her as lightly as his beast would allow.

She shook her head and looked down, her face shifting into a look like confused despair.

Muse was on the floor at their feet.

"FUCK! MUSE!" Demon nearly threw Sid to the side, but he kept enough grip on himself to hand her off to Connor, who'd come up behind them. Then Demon dropped to his knees.

Muse had been shot in the gut; his shirt was nothing but a pool of red. "Oh, fuck, Muse! Fuck, no!" When Demon pulled him over, he groaned, his eyes fluttering.

"Sid," he rasped. "Where's…"

That shook Sid from her fugue, and she fell to her knees at Demon's side. "I'm here. I'm okay. Oh, God. Muse, please be okay."

His face was white and shiny, making the dark of his beard stand out in relief. His lips were a terrible shade of grey. But he smiled. "I'm okay, hon. I'm okay." He groaned again. "Fucking hurts, though."

The sound of sirens filled the room, and Demon looked back at his President.

He waved that fucking rubber toy in the air. "Connor, Sherlock, Trick. Take this piece of shit thing and pay our respects to the Rats. Get out now before our company gets here."

Demon stood. "I go, Prez. I go, too."

Hoosier shook his head. "Deme, no. This'll be dirty."

He knew. God, he knew. But his best friend was lying at his feet, maybe dying. P.B. was dead. Peaches. They'd come in and shot up their home. His only home. He would be careful and try to stay out of law's reach, but he couldn't stay clean, not for this.

"I go."

Hoosier stared at him while the sirens got louder. Then he nodded and threw the rubber rat at him. "Get rid of this thing on your way. I want no link between them and us."

"I hear. Faith is back in my room. I told her to stay until a patch got her."

Hoosier nodded. "I got her. You guys get lost. Out the back. Grab what you need on the way, but move it right now. And call Ronin in with you. He was out of here early. I'll track down everybody else. Nolan—you and the Prospects, help our wounded."

~oOo~

On their way out the back, they grabbed t-shirts and weapons, enough to get them clear of the clubhouse. They rolled out low and dark and followed Connor to their locker at a twenty-four-hour storage place just outside of town. Ronin caught up with them there.

They moved carpets and boxes until they got to their stash of weapons and explosives, purchased a few months ago, when they made the call to return to the outlaw life.

Sherlock squatted next to a couple of lockers filled with components for explosives. "I've got shit pre-rigged and waiting to be armed. We can blow the fuckers out of the galaxy."

"No," Connor said. "Can't look like retaliation. That's a straight line back to the clubhouse."

"Unless it looks like the same hit."

Connor turned to Trick. "Go on."

"Can we turn this on the Castillos some way? So law looks their way, thinks they hit us both, but the players know we handled our shit?"

"AKs, then," Demon said. "Strafe 'em with AKs, like they did us. And cut the head off that fucking rubber rat, leave it for them. Cartels like cutting off heads."

Connor looked around. "Anybody touch that thing without gloves?"

"Yeah," Demon said. "Me and Hooj."

"Then that's out."

Sherlock grinned. "Not quite." He reached back for a garbage sack and rooted through it, pulling out a whole sealed bag of rubber rats.

"What the fuck?" Connor asked.

"Hey—we're beefing with the Rats. I thought they could come in handy. And I was right."

"Okay. Let's get this shit done. Lock and load, brothers."

Demon grabbed gear, wondering if tonight was the night he lost everything he'd only just gotten his fingers around. As he fitted a Kevlar vest over his shoulders, he was struck by a memory of a night not all that different from this one—an ambush, a retaliation—a night that even included Muse lying at his feet.

If the result of this night was the same, then he was about to lose it all.

memory

Demon and Muse sat astride their bikes outside a derelict warehouse, waiting and on alert. They'd been sent out early to make sure the place was secure. And it was—they were out in the middle of fucking nowhere, outside Demopolis, Alabama. Nobody around for miles. As much a danger as an advantage, depending on how the meet went.

Demon hated being so far east. It was dumb; there wasn't much about California he could really call home, but he felt like his cord was played out too far once he crossed the Mississippi. And the South was just...different from anywhere else. It was closed off somehow, and made him feel wary.

He knew Muse felt it, too, though they hadn't talked about it. He was normally just steady, all the time, but on this job he was twitchy, checking over his shoulder far more often than was warranted.

Near dusk, the rumble of Harleys came up behind them, and the contingent from the Alabama charter—Jester, the President; Howie, VP; Tug, SAA, and a couple of soldiers—rolled up behind them. Muse and Demon dismounted and walked toward the men parking their bikes.

Jester set his helmet on his bike. "They ain't here yet?"

"No, Prez," Muse answered. "No sign. Place is clear for miles—no good ambush positions unless they got a sharpshooter. That rise to the north"—he pointed—"would be the only place we don't see 'em coming."

Jester looked to the north, squinting. "Alright. If these shitheads show, I'll leave Rigger and Marcus out here with Demon. Muse, I want you inside with us. Hang back, peel your eyes. Fuckin' hate cleaning up after *el Jefe*."

Jester's sneer surprised Demon, and he cast a quick, sidelong look at Muse, and saw surprise there, too—only a tension to his eyes that most would miss. But Demon and Muse had spent practically every second of their lives together, with a couple of protracted exceptions, for years now, and Demon knew him about as well as he could be known.

Jester and Sam, the mother charter President, went way back, and Jester could always have been counted on to back Sam's play. Hearing him grouse and call Sam *el Jefe*, the nickname of the Perro head, gave Demon an ill feeling about the whole job.

Muse and he had talked over a few meals about the way the club's dealings with the Perro Blanco cartel were starting to break down. The risk was growing; cartel men were showing up to supposedly friendly meets armed to their ears, and the work was coming almost too quickly to move under the radar. But money was moving more slowly, at least outward from the mother charter in Jacksonville, Florida. Greater risk and slower reward was not a sustainable model, especially not in a club of this size. Too many Presidents who held the loyalty of their own tables. If Sam was working an angle of his own with the cartel, things would go to shit sooner or later. Maybe sooner.

Demon wasn't much of a thinker when it came to club business—he wasn't a moron, but he wasn't interested in details. He knew his job in the club was to be a blunt instrument, meant to make an impact, so he waited until someone wielded him. As a Nomad, he didn't have a home table, and was only accorded a vote at the tables he sat at maybe half the time. He tended to turn inward during table discussions and just wait to be told what to do.

Thus it had been a while before he'd noticed things getting out of true in the club. When he brought it up with Muse, they'd talked it out, but in the way of men who knew their loyalty and weren't comfortable looking for its limits. They'd decided to be wary and let things play out.

They didn't know much about this job except their part in it. Jester and his crew were meeting with some other Perro associates and handing off a reparation payment from Sam. Why Alabama had the reins on this, and why Demon and Muse had been called in—those were things Demon didn't need to know.

He needed to know where to point his gun or swing his fist. And now he did.

He didn't like that Muse was going in and two Alabama patches were on watch with him. Besides the irregularity, Demon didn't like these guys. Alabama was one of those charters Demon preferred to avoid, where the women all looked frail and frightened, a few of them looked too fucking young, and just about anything was fair game. Last night they'd had a girl face-first over the back of a couch, taking turns. She'd been passed out.

Demon had had to leave. He had no standing to protest what Jester condoned—as Muse, with his hand clamped hard on his shoulder, had reminded him—but it made him sick, so he'd spent most of the night riding around rural Alabama. Muse had looked disgusted, too, but he'd grabbed one of the healthier girls and made himself scarce upstairs in the private rooms.

When the Perro associates showed—Demon was shocked to see that they were skinheads, showing the colors of the White Guardians—rolling up in two big, blacked-out pickups with camper tops over their beds, Demon stepped back, his hands loose and ready to draw, and kept his eyes wide to take in the whole scene.

The men going inside gave up their weapons. The guards outside were allowed to stay armed. They all went in, and Demon waited, giving his Alabama brothers, and the three skinheads the WG had left outside, as much space as he could.

It all went to hell within minutes. A commotion erupted inside the warehouse, and before Demon could react, the back of the nearest pickup flew open, and two men with AKs jumped to the ground, firing. Paying no mind at all to Rigger or Marcus, Demon leapt around the corner of the rickety building and fired his Glock, taking one of the AK wielders down with a bullet to the head. He peered around the corner again, and saw Rigger fall. He shot the skinhead who got him, and then the warehouse doors flew open and the rest of the WG tore out toward the pickups. The two WG gunman still standing threw down cover fire and jumped into the back of the moving pickup, leaving the bodies of their dead behind.

Demon was inside the warehouse ahead of Marcus. Muse was down, face-first on the ground, blood forming a wide pool on the floor around him, the back of his kutte slashed open. But he was awake and trying to move. Howie was down, too, slashed in the throat. He was gone. Tug was on the floor at his side, pressing down on the wound, but it was too late. Demon could see it from where he stood.

Jester stood in the middle of it all, looking shocked and furious.

Demon went to his knees at Muse's side, but Muse pushed him off. "He opened me up, but I think everything works." He cast his eyes up to Demon's face. "Fuck, Deme. Don't lose your shit here. Count beats, kid. Hold it together."

At that moment, Jester said, "Demon. I want those bastards."

Thus wielded, Demon stood and went out to his bike, picking up the dropped AK on the way. He rode out, on the only road around, in the direction the pickups had gone. Straight toward town.

The rifle on his back, he rode fast, and he caught up, firing his Glock true and sending the rear truck into the forward one, disabling them both. Swinging the rifle forward, he ended them all on the side of the road, in sight of the Demopolis town line.

He never would remember it all. He'd never had a chance to count beats. He was back at the clubhouse before he realized that he was covered in blood. Muse's, he supposed. He went to check on him, stitched up and passed out face down on a club bed, before he bothered to wash.

But he had been seen. By the end of the next day, sitting in county lockup, he knew that much.

~oOo~

Demon picked up the phone on his side of the glass. "Hey, brother. You look good."

Muse smiled. "Not riding yet, but I'm mending up. How're you hanging in?"

He shrugged. "Did it before, and I always knew I'd do it again. Just a place to be." He actually hated being locked up, but he hadn't exactly lied. He understood the institutional life. The worst threat to him inside was his own head.

He was facing multiple life sentences. A witness had identified his bike, and then him, at the scene of the murder of six members of the White Guardians. They had little evidence other than that witness, but they were protecting the shit out of him.

Deemed a dangerous inmate, he was being held without bail and housed in prison instead of jail while he awaited trial. He had no intention of going to trial. He'd cop to the charges before lawyers starting digging into the club to prepare for a trial, but the club wanted time to get him out free and clear. To find that witness.

"You make any friends?"

Demon knew Muse was asking if he had done what was required to garner protection by the Perros, because the White Guardians wanted his head. He had. What was another murder rap on top of what he was already facing? But he hadn't been caught on that one. "I did. Not sitting alone in the mess anymore."

"Good, good. We're looking for new friends, too. Maybe somebody you've met."

Demon nodded. He hated this obscure talk, always being hyper aware of every damn syllable because people were recording and listening. He just wanted news. He'd already been in two months, and he was fucking lonely. He just wanted to sit in a diner with Muse and shoot the shit.

He needed something to occupy his mind, something that didn't have to do with whether he would spend the rest of his life in a cage. Because when he turned his mind from that, all that was left was Faith.

He hadn't seen or heard from her in years, but a whole chunk of his mind was devoted to his memories and feelings of her. He jacked off, feeling abysmally guilty, to his few memories of being inside her. The longer he was away from anything remotely like a life, the bigger the 'Faith' part of his head became. It wouldn't be long before he was consumed by her. Then, he knew he'd go mad, locked away and eaten alive by memory.

~oOo~

Muse and Tug were waiting outside the out-processing center. Tug had a van, with an empty trailer hooked up. Muse was sitting astride his Knuckle. Next to him was Demon's chopper, his kutte lying across the saddle.

They'd cut it fucking close. Almost seven months inside. Demon had given his lawyer the go-ahead to prepare a guilty plea and stave off a trial, when the witness had disappeared and the case had fallen apart.

Grinning, Muse dismounted and grabbed Demon's kutte, then came forward, with a slight hitch yet in his gait. They embraced, and Muse held out the kutte for Demon to slide on.

"You want to go back with Tug, grab some pussy?"

Demon didn't answer. Alabama club pussy wasn't his thing, no matter how long he'd gone without. He wasn't dragged through life by his dick like some of his brothers were.

"Or there's a job in South Dakota."

That was more like it. He grinned. "Good one?"

"Good bank. A little exercise."

'Exercise' was what they called it when there was somebody to hurt. He nodded. "Let's ride."

He was free. And as long as the kutte was on his back, and Muse was at his side, he was home.

Close enough, anyway.

CHAPTER FIFTEEN

"Faith. It's Hoosier, darlin'."

Faith unlocked the door. She was already dressed; she'd gotten up the second Michael had left the room, and she'd been pacing, straining her ears to try to make sense of the sounds she was hearing. It had been gunfire that had woken them up. Even if she hadn't known it right away, Michael's quick response would have made her sure of it.

Hoosier opened the door before she could, and he caught her up in a tight hug. She grabbed fistfuls of his t-shirt and held on. "Where's Michael?"

"Shhh. No questions. We got company. You were sleepin' alone back here, right? Don't know anything. You remember the play?"

She had a million questions, but she also knew what he was saying. Law was here. Michael was not. Which most likely meant he was off responding to whatever had been done here. The thought made her sick with worry, but she nodded. "Right."

"Okay. C'mon. Hold tight, darlin'. It's gonna be okay."

It was lucky that shock and horror were the appropriate responses to the scene in the Hall, because Faith was racked with both before her eyes and brain had even made complete sense of it all. The smell hit her first—the acrid, lingering tang of gunfire and the copper of blood, and the heavy, woodsy-sweet aroma of liquor. That smell, she made visual sense of first—the shelves behind the bar had been destroyed, and mingled liquor was still pooled on the floor, oozing from behind the bar.

The gunfire and blood made sense next. Black-bagged bodies were being carried out on stretchers. Faith counted four bags, but there could have been more. Four dead, and more injured. The Hall was full of EMTs, and Faith saw Michael's friend, Muse, being rolled out, his old lady following with him, trying to keep hold of his hand. Faith couldn't remember her name.

She was struck, in the midst of this chaos, by the renewed realization that this was not her club. Most of the people she'd known were gone. Looking around the room, she couldn't even be sure who was a member and who was a civilian.

A female deputy came up and began asking questions. Faith answered—her name, her address. She started to give her Venice Beach address, then caught herself and gave her mother's instead, feeling a sharp pang of loss and nostalgia for her old life. The questions were brief; she said that she had been sleeping, saw nothing, knew nothing, knew of no enemies. All of that was actually true. The only lie she told was that she had been sleeping alone.

Handed a card and freed from the deputy, Faith went looking for Bibi. If Hoosier was still here, then Bibi probably was, too. Tucker was at Bart and Riley's.

And that was another weird thing about this club. Their VP lived in a mansion and was married to Riley Chase. Another was married to a model—she'd been at the party earlier, and Faith had recognized her. That was crazy. The club she'd grown up in had had several celebrity clients at the bike shop, but they had not been hobnobbing with the rich and famous themselves.

Bibi was in the kitchen—not doing anything, just leaning against the counter, staring at the floor. When she saw Faith, she came forward, her arms out, and Faith tucked herself in for a hug.

"You okay, baby?"

"Yeah. Worried."

"I know. We just have to wait. They won't let me even make a fuckin' pot of coffee. The whole clubhouse is a crime scene."

"Did anyplace else get hit?"

"Hush, Faith. Not the time or place for questions."

"But Tucker?"

Bibi leaned back and brushed Faith's hair from her face. "He's okay. We're heading to Bart and Riley's as soon as they let us out of here. Until then, we stay out of the way and wait."

~oOo~

Bart and Riley lived in a big house deep in the foothills on the mountain edge of Madrone. Its architecture was traditional California Spanish—earthy stucco, red tile, arched doors and windows, heavy, rustic woodwork. The interior was wide and airy, with lots of two-story rooms and windows everywhere.

The décor was casual and accessible, not the chichi *Architectural Digest* ensembles Faith had been expecting. Most of the flooring was tile, but there were funky area rugs scattered throughout, and all the furniture and decorative objects were normal and kid friendly. And there were toys everywhere. Bart and Riley's daughter, Lexi, was five, and their son, Ian, was three. With two-year-old Tucker, they were the only small children in the club. But their presence was huge in this house on this night, even while they slept. Just being surrounded by the evidence of their play lightened the somber mood as the survivors of the attack on the clubhouse settled in to wait for the rest of the club.

J.R. and his wife, Veda, were there, too. The whole club was being pulled in for something like a lockdown here in this mansion.

Bart led the patches who were present into his study. Finally free to use a kitchen, Bibi gathered up the old ladies and moved in on Riley's expansive space. Riley herself sat down at her breakfast table, resting her hands on her huge belly. She really did look like she should have popped already.

Feeling the awkward unreality of walking up to a celebrity to have a little chat, Faith went over to Riley. "Can I get you anything?" That was weird, too—asking the woman of the house if she could get her anything from her own kitchen.

But Riley just smiled. "No, thanks. But help yourself."

Faith sat down. "I'm not really in the mood for food or drink."

"I hear you." She rubbed her hands over her belly.

"When are you due?"

"Just a couple of weeks. I'm so ready to see my feet again."

Riley and Bart's pending new addition wasn't something Faith really wanted to talk about. It stirred up memories and worries.

After an awkward moment, Riley asked, "How's your mom? Did they send somebody after her?"

Faith hadn't even thought about her mother. She was the only one who wasn't being pulled in. Feeling guilty, she considered whether she should ask Hoosier to send someone for her. But Margot was with Jose. And she didn't want her anywhere near where Michael might be, especially not if she might be feeling stress. "No, I think she's okay. It would really freak her out to move her in the middle of the night, and the nurse who's with her is a huge guy. She's better staying put."

Riley nodded. "It's awful, what's happening to her. It makes me so sad."

There was nothing really to say about that, so Faith didn't. She watched Bibi and Veda and a couple of club girls she didn't know making breakfast. Dawn was breaking, she noticed, the view of the mountains from the two-story windows on the other side of the table brightening with morning sun.

This, she remembered. The way life just went on, even at a time like this. Morning happened. People ate. They chatted about life and family. They didn't sit and stare at the door. They would mourn those who'd been lost, but they would do it in the background, and in ritual, together. Loss was a part of life, loss like this was a part of this life, and life went on.

At her side, Riley said, "I hope this isn't a strange thing to say, but I really love your mom." Faith turned and cocked her head. Yes, that had been a strange thing to say.

Blushing, Riley continued. "She took me under her wing, I guess, when I came into the family. She helped me understand how this world works, and she answered a lot of questions I had. Like a mentor. Or a mom, a little." She smiled. "I feel like I knew you before I met you. She talks about you and your sister a lot." The smile faded. "Or she used to."

Faith laughed, because that was funny. "I find that hard to believe. You know Margot and I went years—"

"I know," Riley interrupted. "I never asked about that, and she never said. And it's not my business. But I know she missed you, for whatever that's worth. She's been pretty unhappy for a long time. I guess a lot of it was this—what's happening to her now. But I think it was more than that, too. Anyway, I hope that wasn't me speaking out of turn. Being pregnant makes me need to mother everybody. According to Bart, it's annoying as hell."

Faith agreed with Bart. But she couldn't be snappish with this pretty little pregnant movie star, who was trying to be nice. So she put on a smile. "Well, thanks. I'm glad she helped you. She definitely knows how it works around here." Or she did, when her brain worked. Faith stood up. "I'm gonna see if Bibi needs help. You sure you don't want anything?"

"No. I'm good." Riley's expression suggested that she knew she'd crossed a line and felt sorry for it, but also knew that apologizing would only continue the awkwardness further. Faith smiled, wanting to let her off the hook. It was a queer feeling to know that other people had gotten different, better versions of her mother than she had, but it wasn't Riley's fault that was true.

~oOo~

Breakfast wasn't yet ready when the thunder of Harleys rattled the windows, and almost everybody in the house converged toward the side door. The warriors were home. Faith went over and helped Riley stand and then pushed her way to the door. Connor was out ahead; he gave her a small, sardonic smirk and then made a sweep of his hand as if he were presenting Michael to her.

She ran up and jumped onto him before he had his helmet off. He caught her and held her tightly. "I'm okay, babe. I'm good. I'm good."

Speechless, she could only nod against his neck and hold on. He moved a hand to her face, pushing her back slightly so he could kiss her.

"There's food in the kitchen," Bart said behind them. "Load up plates, then Hooj wants us in the Ke—in my study. We need a debrief."

Faith heard, and she knew Michael did, too, because he'd tensed a bit when Bart started speaking. But he didn't stop kissing her, so she stayed where she was, her legs and arms wrapped around him, their mouths linked and their tongues twining together.

Connor cleared his throat theatrically. "Okay, Skinemax. Inside."

At that, Michael put his hands under her arms and set her down. He took his helmet off and set it on his bike.

"Hold that thought. I gotta do this."

"I know. I'll be waiting."

He took her hand, and they went back inside.

Strange, but this felt *normal*. It felt *right*. This *was* her club. Faith felt like Michael's old lady, like he was really hers, more in that moment, at Bart's house because the clubhouse had been shot up, welcoming Michael home from probably killing people, than she yet had. People had died, and yet she felt secure and…and *safe*.

She felt like she was home.

~oOo~

By the time the men filed out of Bart's study, the children were awake and had been fed. Riley and Faith sat in the living room while they played noisily in the corner, which was set up like a little house, with an elaborate kitchen set and other furniture. Their fancy playroom wasn't enough, apparently.

But Faith was enjoying watching them play, and she figured that might be part of it. In a playroom, they'd be away. Here, they were in the middle of everything. The room was bright with sunshine and the happy chatter of children, and it felt good. Even during a lockdown.

Lexi, a beautiful little girl with long, pale curls, was bossing Ian and Tucker around, but they seemed perfectly content to be bossed. Faith watched Tucker stirring 'porridge' with a little wooden spoon in a little silver pot on the wooden stove while Ian set the table with plastic princess plates and teacups. So sweet, so normal. So much was normal about this strange life. There were ways in which her life alone was beginning to feel like a dream she'd had. Or like a part she'd been playing.

She had to find a time, and a way, to tell Michael the one secret that remained between them. She had to move it out of their way, nullify the last thing Margot could do to hurt them, so that they could be together and make a new life, a real life. The truth would hurt him. Bibi thought he wouldn't be able to handle it, and Faith thought she might well be right. But it was there, and it was in their way, and it had to be her who told him. If he came upon Margot when she thought it was ten years ago—that would be the absolutely most painful way to learn it, with extra layers of betrayal.

But she was afraid. He'd been hurt so very much in his life. To be the one to hurt him more? God.

Michael walked in and stood watching his son, a gentle, quiet smile on his face. He seemed more relaxed than Faith could ever remember him being. He turned to her, and his smile grew. He was—he was happy. On a morning after a night like that, even with the loss and danger, Michael was, just now, experiencing a moment of peace. Faith wanted to freeze time and let him have it forever.

Tucker saw his father and abandoned his work with the porridge. "Pa!" He trotted over, and Michael picked him up and hugged him hard.

"Love you, Motor Man. You having fun?"

Tucker nodded seriously. "Cookin' an'…an'…" Tucker swiveled his head to the corner, his forehead drawn in concentration. "Hep Lexi."

That was the longest string of words, clear words, Faith had yet heard Tucker say, and that was apparently the case for all the adults who heard him. Michael's eyes, and Riley's, too, went wide and pleased. "That's great, helping Lexi. Ian, too?"

Tucker nodded in answer to his father's question. "Uh-huh. Cookin' food."

Michael looked over Tucker's head at Faith. His eyes shone. He kissed his son. "Okay, you better get back to it. I'm going upstairs for a little bit with Faith, okay?"

He said it in the softer voice he used with Tucker, but he looked at Riley, who smiled and nodded. Michael set Tucker down, and the boy went back to his work.

"The porridge is going to burn, Tuck. You have to stir it all the time," Lexi admonished, a dainty little Gordon Ramsay. Tucker nodded and resumed stirring.

Faith stood and went to Michael. He wrapped his large hand, the skin warm and rough, around hers and led her upstairs. At the top of the staircase was a loft area that was set up like another family room, with another wall of electronics. Either Bart or Riley was really into cutting-edge tech—probably Bart. Michael led her through that area and down a hallway, like he knew exactly where he was going. And of course he would. Bart was his brother, the club VP. He'd probably been here countless times.

He led her through a door, into a small (by the standards of all the other rooms here she'd seen) bedroom. Then he closed the door and pushed her against it, leaning into her right away and covering her mouth with his.

It took her breath away—not the force or pressure, as such, but the control. Michael had always been...well, *hesitant* at the beginning of their sex, always fighting himself, always trying to give her room to back away. That normally changed when they were deep into it, but it changed because he lost the fight.

Last night, he'd grabbed her hair and tugged her back to him, and it was the most controlling he'd ever been with her. She wasn't someone who wanted to be dominated—at all—but she had found that strong move incredibly hot.

Being shoved against the door and kissed like this, like he hadn't expected ever to be able to kiss her again? That was hotter. The way he started tearing at her clothes, trying to get at her as quickly as he could? Hotter still.

This was a different Michael. Somewhere along the road he'd ridden last night, he'd cast off a heavy weight. Despite the dark of last night, he was lighter, like the work he'd been sent to do had given him something he needed.

And that was what it was. Last night had opened a valve for the thing inside him he called a beast.

Faith reached between them, too, tangling with his hands, trying to get to his clothes as he was getting to hers. He released her lips with a grunt and buried his face against her neck, still struggling with her jeans and tights. She had his jeans open, his belt undone, the buckle jingling loosely, but he had her clothes bunched up on her thighs, stuck.

She bucked, forcing him to take a step backward, and turned around to face the door. When she wiggled her jeans and tights down a little farther, she bent forward and looked over her shoulder.

He stared. Hesitation was back. And now, knowing his past so much more deeply, she understood it so much better.

"Michael."

Without a word, he stepped to her, and she felt his thick, hard cock pushing between her legs. His hand came around her hip and went to her mound, and his rough fingers slid gently over her clit and inside her, the path made swift and smooth by her arousal. He rocked his hips, and his cock pushed inside, his fingers lingering with it for just a second and then pulling back to focus on her clit.

"Oh, fuck!" she murmured, trying to be quiet. "Fuck, yes." She put her own hand over his, feeling his hand and fingers flex with strength as he gave her pleasure. "God, Michael, it's so good!"

His head dropped heavily onto her back, and his hips moved faster. His other hand grasped her hip and moved her on him, encouraging her own movements to counter his. Each time their bodies collided, the contact was deep and in that precise place where pleasure had grown so high it reached discomfort, and Faith couldn't be quiet. With her face on the door, only a couple of inches between her and the rest of Bart and Riley's house, she cried out with every crash of their bodies together.

All at once, he stopped, his body rigid. His hand between her legs moved frantically over her clit, right on the very nub, until her flaming nerves had her body twitching so much that she was moving them, forcing his cock to rub only on the singular place inside.

"Fuck, fuck, fuck, fuck," she breathed, knowing she was going to yell when this orgasm was finally done with her.

But Michael took his hand away and wrapped his arm around her waist. He picked her up off her feet and carried her, still buried deeply inside her, to the bed. He laid them both down, her prone on the bed, him stretched out on top of her. Propped up on his arms, he slammed into her once, twice—and she shouted into the pillow, a long wail that used all her breath. He kept going, and so did she.

When she was done, she felt his body taut and shaking on top of her. She opened her eyes and watched the spasms of his arm. She could feel him pulsing inside her.

He pulled out, making her whine with the loss, and lay on his side next to her, his face an inch or two from hers.

"You okay?" His skin was pink from his exertions, but his breath was barely heavier than normal.

"Holy hell, yeah," she gasped, still trying to catch her breath. "Don't take this the wrong way, but it felt different. Is something different?"

He smiled and brushed an errant, wet lock of hair out of her eyes. "I think so. I feel almost normal. If this is what normal feels like. Definitely different. Last night was fucked up. We lost P.B., and Muse is fucked up. And Peaches. But I feel…I don't know. Right, I guess." His smile faltered. "Which is pretty fucking abnormal."

She turned to her side and fitted her body with his, getting as close as she could. "No, it's not. I get it. It's normal for you. For us." She kissed his throat and realized that he was still wearing his kutte. "Is Muse going to be okay? Do you know?" Hoosier had sent the Prospects to the hospital to keep watch, but Faith hadn't heard more about the wounded.

"Yeah. The bullet missed his vital organs." Demon laughed dryly. "That fucker is a lucky unlucky bastard. Second time somebody's opened him up without getting anything important.

He's gonna look like patchwork if he keeps it up." He rolled to his back and brought Faith with him, settling her on top of him. Her bunched jeans and tights were starting to get pretty uncomfortable, but she didn't want to lose this moment.

"I'm gonna go see him when we get moving. You stay here, though. Hooj thinks families are safe, but I want you and Tuck here while I'm gone, okay?"

"Yeah, okay. I'm going to need to check on my mom, though. Leo's there, but I need to check in. But I'll ask someone to go with me."

"I'll be back in the afternoon. Wait, and I'll go with you."

"No!" Too late, Faith saw her mistake. Far too late. Michael lifted his head and looked down at her.

"What the hell is going on there, Faith?"

And now she was face to face with the time she would have to tell him.

CHAPTER SIXTEEN

When Faith put her hands on his chest and pushed away, Demon tried to hold her. But she wanted distance, and he would have had to hurt her to keep her close, so he let go. She got up and stood at the side of the bed, shimmying her tights and then her holey jeans back up.

Lying silently on his back, his jeans open and his cock out, semi-hard and still wet with her, he watched her straighten her clothes. His heart pounded heavily, but slowly, in his chest, like a medicine ball bouncing against his ribs.

Something was really wrong.

When she'd run out of clothes to fuss with, she finally met his eyes. "I need to tell you something, Michael. I need you to listen and stay calm."

The medicine ball bounced harder, picking up speed, and his hands shook as he put himself away and sat up. Why did people say shit like that? Why the fuck did they think it would do anything to him but make him upset all the sooner? The beast in his soul bared its teeth and crouched, waiting.

"Just say it."

She stared at him, her beautiful eyes wide and sad. And fearful. He could see it—she was fucking *afraid* of him. His fists clenched at that realization, and she saw them curl. She took a step back.

Fuck. Fuck. He didn't even know what was lying in wait for him, but he could feel everything inside him spooling out into a twisted knot. Everything he wanted, everything he needed, was almost in his grasp. Just moments ago, he'd felt it—he could be happy. He could be normal. And it was unraveling before he could take hold of it.

"Faith." His voice broke, but even he could hear the danger in it. "Fucking say it."

"I…don't know how." Her head was down, and she'd taken another step away. He could barely hear her. She had her arms crossed, her hands tucked at her elbows, and she was pinching herself. He knew why she did that.

Demon's face was on fire, and he knew what that meant, what he looked like. He should get out. He should run right now before he hurt her. But he was trying to learn to hold. He would never hurt Faith. Not Faith. Right?

He cast about in his mind, pushing aside the shadows that were trying to crowd in. What could it be? It was about Margot. Something about Margot. But what could be so bad? She hated him? Not news. Did Faith not think he and Tucker should move in there? Well, he wasn't so sure, either. They'd figure it out. There was nothing. He could think of nothing.

"Faith." He'd meant to make his voice a plea, but it came out a threat. Now she was back so far that she was pressed against the dresser. She dropped her head again, and when she looked up, she was crying, but there was resolve in her eyes, sidled up to the fear. Fear and resolve. Bravery. She needed to be brave for this.

Demon began to despair in earnest. His beast stood up.

"When everything happened…before…when you joined the Nomads…" She stopped and swallowed so hard he heard it. "I was pregnant."

His head full of shadow, he could see no sense in what she'd said. He stared at her, feeling dark and blank. "I don't…what?"

Her chest heaved as she took a deep breath, and a tear dropped from her jaw. He watched it hit her white t-shirt and make a spot where her pink bra showed through. "My parents…they freaked out. Michael, they made me have…they made me have an abortion."

"You were pregnant?"

She nodded. Demon's brain was being slow and stupid, but his blood was loud, hot, burning his veins. He didn't understand.

"We made a baby? You and me?" A child with Faith. Their child. Made in love.

Again, she nodded. Then she made a strange, strangled sound and took a couple of steps toward him. He stood, and she froze, her eyes wide. "I wanted to keep it. I loved you then like I love you now—with everything. It was a part of you, and I wanted to keep it."

"Don't say 'it.' Our baby's not an 'it.'" It was all he could think of to say. It seemed like an important thing to say. They could have had a baby together. He would have been nine years old. Or she. They would have made a family.

But she'd had an abortion.

He wouldn't have said he had an opinion about abortion. Until this moment, he wouldn't have thought he did. And maybe for anyone else, he didn't. Kota had never suggested it, and neither had he, and now he had Tucker. Maybe it would have been better if Tucker hadn't been born to that woman. Maybe it would have been the humane choice for Kota not to have him. But Demon knew love for his son like he'd never known before. He couldn't imagine not loving him, not having him. He was fighting with all he had to keep him.

But a baby with Faith—that baby would have been born in love and known only love, would have grown strong and happy in love. Demon's chest hurt—a searing, black pain.

"You killed our baby?"

She made a sobbing sound and closed the distance between them, but Demon thought he'd break apart if she touched him.

"Michael, please! I'm so sorry. I'm *so sorry*. I didn't have a choice. They made me."

He didn't understand. "How?"

"My dad said he'd kill you if I didn't. He said he knew right where you were and would kill you that night if I didn't."

Demon laughed. The sound grated at his throat. "I had my patch. He lost that vote. He couldn't just kill me, not without facing the same vote himself."

Faith didn't answer; she simply stared at him, her face wrenched with sorrow and that fucking fear.

"Even if he did, it wouldn't've fucking mattered. That was our baby."

"It mattered to me. I chose you. And Margot wanted to win. No matter what, she'd never have let me stay pregnant. She kicked me in the belly when she found out."

Demon's knees gave out, and he sat hard on the bed and put his head in his hands. He had to hold. He had to keep control. He had to think.

Faith knelt at his feet and put her hands on his arms. He tried to pull away, but she held on, her nails digging into the meat of his forearms. "Don't pull away, Michael. I need you with me. I hated losing our baby."

"You didn't lose him."

"I *did*. I hated what they did to us. It's why I left home. Don't you see? I know you can see, if you look. I love you. You know that."

"How did he know where I was?"

"What?"

"Blue. I was on the road. How would he even know where to look?"

"I—I don't know. I was too fucked up with everything to question him. I guess Hoosier told him, or the Nomad president? I don't know."

Her mention of Hoosier's name put another black shadow in his head. "Does Hooj know?"

Faith sat back. She stared for a few painfully long seconds and then nodded.

"Since then? And fuck, Bibi? Were they in on it?"

"They knew. They weren't part of it, but they knew."

They were the closest thing he'd ever had to parents. He trusted them with everything. With his child. His second child. "They let it happen?"

She didn't answer. Demon shoved her away—too hard, he knocked her backwards, but he barely registered doing so—and stood. With his blood scalding and his head too thick and dark now for thoughts, for anything but feelings, he left the room and went down the stairs.

Behind him, Faith called out, "Michael, no!" But only the small part of him that was still Michael heard him. The rest of him, the bulk of him that was Demon, ignored her completely.

As he walked, he saw nothing, heard nothing, his eyes trained only for what he sought. He found Hoosier in the kitchen, leaning in a corner of the counter, his arm around Bibi. There might have been other people around; he didn't know, didn't heed. Hoosier and Bibi looked at him, and he watched as interest became confusion and then alarm, but it was too late. He was there. He grabbed Bibi by the arm and yanked her out of his way. And then, with all of his might, he slammed his fist into Hoosier's face. Bones cracked, possibly his own as well as his President's, but he didn't care. Hoosier sank to the floor, and Demon fell on him in the way that had earned him his name—fierce, blazing hot, and senseless to anything but pain, delivering and receiving.

When his sense returned, his rage had not abated. But he was on his back, held down by the hands and knees and feet of his brothers, and Bart had a shotgun aimed right at his head. The room was stormy with yelling.

Still fighting against the restraints on him, he looked at Bart and then into the barrel of the Mossberg. "DO IT !" he shouted. "JUST FUCKING DO IT! DO IT! DO IT! DO IT!"

"ENOUGH!" Hoosier's voice was strong, but the word was thick and wet. "Bart, put it down."

"This is my house. There are women and children here. My pregnant wife was in here. He almost knocked her over."

Demon calmed enough for guilt to emerge from the shadows in his head. Had he hurt Riley? He lifted his head and saw Bibi sitting on the floor. Fuck. Had he hurt her? And Faith? Oh, fuck.

As he calmed, hands left him. He rose onto his elbows and turned his eyes to Hoosier, who was on his hands and knees, leaning against the lower cupboards. "You knew. All this time, you both knew. You let them do it to her." He looked up at Bart, who was still aiming a kill shot. "Just do it," he said again, quietly now.

"Put it down, Bart," Hoosier said again. Bart raised the barrel and dropped the Mossberg to his side. He stepped back, out of Demon's range.

Demon heard Faith's voice. "Tucker, no!" And then his son ran into the room.

He stopped in the middle of the kitchen, not far from Demon's outstretched legs. "PA! Bad noise! Bad noise! No, Pa!" He shook his finger like a schoolmarm.

And now his son had seen how bad his father really was.

"Get him out of here." Demon didn't say it to anyone in particular, but it was Faith who scooped Tucker up. He squirmed in her arms, calling "Pa! Pa!" as she took him away.

It was over. Everything was over. Ash and shadow, all of it. He shrugged off J.R. and Trick, the last of his brothers holding him down, and he stood. Bart raised the shotgun again, but he ignored it and looked at Hoosier, who had stood and was taking Bibi from Connor, who'd apparently helped his mother to her feet.

"You knew. You let them do it, and you never said."

Hoosier spat into the sink and wiped the blood from his mouth. His nose was swelling already. "It wasn't my place to stop it, son. And what would I have told you? How could knowing have helped you at all?"

He didn't know. He felt like there was nothing in the world that he did know, except that he had trusted and been betrayed.

Absolutely alone, Demon turned and walked out of the house.

He was just mounting his bike when Faith ran out of the house. "Michael, NO! Don't run! Please don't run! Please!"

He fired up and pulled away.

~oOo~

He'd vaguely meant to head into the desert, but he found himself coming up on the hospital instead. So, feeling numb from his vibrating nerves, he went up to check on Muse.

Keanu was sitting in the waiting room at the end of the hall. He stood when Demon came up, but Demon waved him off and went down the hall.

Muse was talking with Sid, almost sitting up. He looked pretty good for a guy who'd been gutshot less than twelve hours earlier. Sid saw Demon first and smiled. "Hey, Deme." She stood up, and he gave her a hug.

"Hey, Sid. You okay?" He felt like he was on Novocain or something. Or out of sync with time. Detached.

"I'm fine. Muse is a whiner." She smiled at her old man. "I'll give you guys a few minutes. You want me to scavenge up some more Jell-O?"

Muse groaned. "You're a cruel woman, hon."

"You love it."

"I do."

She left, and Demon turned to Muse. The first thing Muse asked was, "You take care of it?"

"Yeah. Went clean, too." Before Demon had gone to take Faith upstairs, before his life had burned down, the club had met. They'd been building goodwill in the community—in the whole county, especially with people like Sheriff Montoya—for all the years they'd had stakes down in Madrone, even when they'd been legit. Building it with deed and cash both. It was as though Hoosier had always known they'd go outlaw again. Montoya was a true friend. He was going with the story Hoosier had given him, and nobody was looking at the club for the shooting at the Rats' clubhouse. Demon was dirty again, but he was clear. They all were.

At least as far as law was concerned. What had happened the night before was an escalation, and it wouldn't die just because the Horde had fought back quickly and decisively. They'd need La Zorra to lean in if they wanted to end a full-out war with the Rats before it started.

"Muse, I'm—I have to—I..."

"Deme?"

"I'm leaving. I have to leave." He was surprised to have said it. He was more surprised that it was true. It felt true, and it felt like lead in his chest.

Muse frowned. "Leave what?"

"Town. The club."

"What the fuck? What happened?"

Demon shrugged. He couldn't say. He didn't fully understand.

"Don't fuckin' shrug at me, Deme. If you're running, have a reason."

"I'm not running. I'm leaving. I have to leave."

Muse simply lifted an eyebrow, waiting.

So Demon told him. He started at the beginning and told his friend the story of him and Faith. He'd never said it to anyone before, and putting it to words brought feeling back into his limbs. About halfway through, Sid opened the door. Muse shook his head, and she backed out and closed the door again.

Demon told him about the past, and the present, and what had happened barely hours before. "I just beat the fuck out of Hooj. He's the only father I ever had. I trusted him. I trusted them both. I can't...I have to go."

"Shit, Deme." Muse looked out the window. Some machine started beeping, and within a minute, a nurse came in and changed out an IV bag. She asked if he needed anything, and when he said he didn't, she left.

"You blame her? Faith?"

At first, hearing her tell him, he had. But not now. "No. She was just a kid. Blue told her he'd kill me if she didn't do it. I blame them—all of them. Blue and her mom most of all. But Blue's dead. And her mom—she's a woman, and losing her mind. There's nothing I can do. But I can't be around Hooj. I can't say what I'll do. I would've beaten him to death today. That's what it wanted."

"It?"

"The thing inside me."

Muse shook his head. "I love you, brother. But that's a crock of shit, and it always has been. There's nothing inside you but you. You want to find control? You get right with what's wrong."

"You say that like I can just decide."

"Can't you?"

He'd thought Muse understood. "Don't you think I already would've if I could?"

"I think it's easier to believe you live with something else inside you than to face that it's all you. I think you're afraid."

His face grew hot. "Fuck you. I'm no pussy." He turned and went to the door.

"You're running. Again. Pussies run."

Demon stopped, with his hand on the door handle.

"What do you want, Deme? Know that, and then do what you need to do to make it happen."

He opened the door and went out, walking past Sid without stopping, going down to the main floor and out the automatic doors without stopping. He was astride his bike before he realized that he had no idea where to go.

~oOo~

It was dark when he pulled back into Bart and Riley's crowded driveway. He'd ridden into the desert and sat alone on his rock until dusk. Hours. The windows of the big house were bright with light, and he could see his brothers, their women, the children—his son—moving about in the uncovered windows. Dinner was happening in there. Family dinner.

It was what he wanted. Family. Love. Home. All he'd ever wanted. He couldn't leave it behind.

Muse was right. He had to get right with what was wrong. He had to give trust, and let that trust ride. If he trusted Hoosier and Bibi, then he had to believe that they'd done the best they could. They'd kept it from him to help him. After spending a few hours on his rock, he could see how they would think that was true. They were wrong, but he could see how they thought they were right.

Maybe that was what real trust was. To see love even when it wore the face of betrayal.

The side door opened, and Faith stepped out. She was wearing different clothes—jeans without holes and a black sweater with a wide neck that showed the straps of her pink bra. He didn't recognize them, and the jeans were maybe an inch too short. Riley's clothes.

She stayed just outside the door, standing barefoot on the topmost step. Her arms were crossed under her breasts. Her hair was pulled back in a ponytail. She looked tiny and delicate. Vulnerable.

Demon dismounted and set his helmet on his bike, and she didn't move. He walked toward her, and she stayed put, except to cross her arms differently, moving them over her chest, hooking her hands over her shoulders. Like a fragile shield for her heart.

He walked to the foot of the steps and could think of only one thing to say. "I love you."

She collapsed into weeping and, nodding, wrapped herself around him. He lifted her up and carried her inside.

He would make it all right. All of it.

CHAPTER SEVENTEEN

The couple of weeks after St. Pat's was a strange whirl of comfort and chaos. Michael had come back that night, and he'd been calm. Faith would have almost called him serene, except it was Michael, and serenity was impossible for him. He had apologized to her, and to Hoosier and Bibi, and to Bart and Riley and the rest of the family, and, after hugs and handshakes, the matter had simply been dropped.

Ten years of pent-up turmoil and unhappiness had simply been bled off, as if an infected wound had been lanced. After his fury earlier, Faith didn't completely believe that it could be so easy, that Michael had simply gone for a ride and then come home and forgiven everyone—including himself—everything, and had likewise been forgiven, but it appeared to be true. He seemed at peace, and that made Faith feel a little hopeful.

That night, Michael, Faith, and Tucker had all slept together in the bed she and Michael had been on earlier.

Riley had gone into labor the next morning, and less than an hour after Bart got her to the hospital, their third child and second son had been born. Declan Bartholomew Elstad. Faith thought the poor kid would likely be in fourth grade before he could spell his own whole name. He was adorable, fair like his parents and siblings, and born completely bald.

Whatever was going on with the club seemed to have died down right after St. Pat's—at least as far as Faith could tell. No further violence happened, and the lockdown ended. The Sheriff had released the clubhouse on the morning of the second day, and the Horde had had everything back to rights within two more days—windows and furniture replaced, walls repaired, new booze purchased, the whole place cleaned.

Muse and Double A, the most badly injured of the survivors, had both been both released from the hospital within a week. Neither was riding yet, but they were healing well.

Just in time for the funerals.

Peaches' parents hadn't been thrilled with his choice to prospect. They weren't hostile to the club, but they didn't want a club funeral. Since he hadn't earned his patch yet, there was no scandal in his family making the arrangements. Three club girls had also been killed that night. Peaches and all three girls were all buried over two days, and the Horde family attended every service.

P.B. had been a patch for fifteen years. He was buried with full honors, and representatives from friendly clubs across the country came to see him put to rest. Nolan and Double A were still in SoCal from the Missouri charter, but two more members, Tommy and Dom, rode west to join them for the funeral.

Faith had been to many club funerals growing up, but she had never grown jaded. The love and solidarity among men, and women, who lived a club life was never more obvious than when they came together to mourn a brother.

And then, when it was over, life resumed. Within a day, their visitors were back on the road, Virtuoso Cycles had reopened, and everyone had returned to whatever passed for normal in a life like this.

Tommy and Dom headed back to Missouri without Nolan and Double A, neither of whom, for reasons of his own, was ready to return to the Midwest.

Faith was officially moved out of her Venice Beach apartment, and most of her stuff was in storage. She'd moved her art gear, including the pieces in progress, into her mother's garage, and she was trying to get back to work. She'd been in Madrone a little more than a month, and she felt like she was two months behind on her work. This playground piece had to be finished and ready for install by Memorial Day. It was the beginning of April.

Though it wasn't fitted out to be a real studio yet, the garage was the only place available to her. Hoosier had offered an open station in the shop, but there was no way she could work among the distractions there—the noise, the guys, Michael. So she was doing the best she could. She stood in the garage, her welding helmet pushed up on her head, scowling at the piece before her. It had been too long since she'd been able to work on it. Not in all the years she'd been away from home had she ever gone so long without working on at least one project. More than a couple of days away from her work made her twitchy, made her fear that whatever it was that made her talent would abandon her.

And maybe she'd been right. Because the snake wasn't happening.

She couldn't *see* it anymore.

That was bullshit. She was getting too much in her head. She didn't need to see the whole snake; she needed only to see the next piece of the snake. Making a disgusted sound in the back of her throat, she sat down on the concrete floor and dug through a bin of loose parts. She found one she liked and sat fondling it for a few minutes, getting to know its edges, feeling what it wanted to join with. Then she stood and found its place.

She put her gloves on, knocked her helmet back over her face and started her torch. Sometimes, you only had to see what was right in front of you and let the future worry about itself.

~oOo~

Maybe an hour or so later, she looked up from the nearly-complete third segment of her playground sculpture and jumped back a little when she saw Michael in the viewing panel of her welding helmet. He was leaning against the side of the open garage door, smiling at her. She hadn't heard him ride up. She killed the blowtorch, and he walked over before she could push up her helmet.

He knocked on the side. "This thing freaks me out."

She pushed it up. "Why?"

"Because it's a red demon's face."

She'd had a friend do a custom airbrush job on her helmet. Lots of welders—artists and commercial welders alike—customized their helmets, like the goalie masks in hockey. They spent a lot of time behind those things, and it was a way not to be obscured by them. Faith had told Jens that she wanted something 'badass,' but hadn't been more specific. What she'd gotten was crimson and macabre, something like a skull covered only by muscle. She'd never thought of it as a demon, but now she set her tools aside, shed her gloves, and took off the helmet to try to see it with Michael's eyes.

Damn. It really was a demon. "You want me to have it redone?"

"Nah. It's something, though, to see you look at me when you have it on." He bent down and kissed her, and the helmet was forgotten.

When he pulled back and smiled down at her, Faith grabbed his kutte and gave him a shake. "Not that I'm not happy to see you every single time, but what are you doing here? I thought we agreed that you and Margot should stay far away from each other." He knew everything Margot could hurt him with, so that wasn't a concern any longer. But Faith wanted him away from her toxicity, and away from the chance that Michael's massively increased hatred of Margot might explode into something that he couldn't recover from.

"I'm not going in. But I had some time, and I want to talk. How is she today? Your mom?"

Faith shrugged. "She's been all over the place, erratic as hell. She and Leo have been going at it all day. She's recognized me twice in the past few days, but the last time, this morning at breakfast, she was totally lucid and threw me out. I've been out here since." Faith led Michael to the cheap bench she'd found in her mother's mountain of crap and had kept back from storage. "What's up?"

"My court date is coming up for Tucker in a couple weeks."

"I know. I'll be there."

He smiled. "It's got me thinking—Finn thinks I'll win. I don't want to hope too much, but if he's right—I need to find a house. We can't live with Hoosier and Bibi forever, and I don't want Tucker in that tin can where my mail goes."

"You want me to help you look?"

"No. Well, yeah. I do. But I want *us* to look. For *our* place. I can't afford much, but I want a place, and I want my whole family with me." As she sat there, the thought of what he was about to ask filling her with equal parts of happiness and disappointment, he picked up her hand and made circles on her palm with his thumb. "I know you want to take care of your mom. I know it, but I don't understand it. You know Tuck and I can't live where she lives. We just can't. And all the shit she did to you and me? You said your sister would pay for her to go to a home, or have full-time help here. I guess I'm asking you to take her up on it and live with me. We can't keep doing this thing where we're together for a couple of hours and all we do is fuck because we don't have much time. I want a life with you. Don't let your mother keep us apart anymore."

"Michael, it's more complicated than that."

"It's not, babe. It's that simple. We can't really be together if you're taking care of her. Your sister will pay to have people around the clock to deal with Margot. Your mother doesn't deserve you. We deserve a real chance. It's that simple. And it's your call."

Faith knew he was right, and it sucked. She wanted to live with him. She wanted to start a life with him. But it would feel like she was leaving her mother to the wolves or something. "She's so young. She's her normal self sometimes still, and she'll be locked away with old people. Strangers. She'll know she's lost everything."

Michael looked away, out through the open garage into what passed for a yard at this crappy house. "I can't say that upsets me much. If she was a man, even in the state she's in, I'd have killed her already. If she's lonely and unhappy until she dies, that'd be okay by me." Turning back to her, he asked, "Why do you want to help her?"

Faith looked down at her knees. "I don't know. I think about it a lot. Everything you've said is right. I don't love her. Mostly, I hate her. But it makes me feel terrible to think of putting her away."

He sighed and squeezed her hand. "Okay. I love you. I'll take you however I can get you. But think about it, okay? It would help if I knew why you're picking her over us."

"I'm not!"

"You are, Faith."

~oOo~

Michael left shortly after that, and Faith stared at her sculpture for a while. Then she stared out the garage door into space for a while. Then she stared at Dante for a while. She'd only just begun to create the magnificence that was her ancient El Camino when she and Michael met. It had been complete for several years now, and she'd done some touching up and refiguring since. The car basically told the story of her life from the time she was sixteen. She and Michael were in there. Her life on her own was there. Margot and Blue and Sera were there. All of it. But nothing from this new life she was trying to start. And no room. She'd have to work over old areas to bring anything new in.

That was what Michael was asking her to do, too. Make room for something new.

She went into the house from the garage and found Leo cleaning up after lunch.

"Hey, sweets. I saw you out there with your man, so I didn't call you in. But there's tuna salad in the fridge."

"Thanks, Leo. How's—" Faith stopped and looked hard at Leo's face. "What happened?"

Leo laughed it off. "Your mother and I had a disagreement over her meal. She threw her glass at me. She's napping now, though, so all's quiet on the western front." She touched the large Band-Aid on her forehead. The pad had soaked red.

"I'm so sorry, Leo!"

"It's nothing much. Even little head wounds bleed like crazy. I think we need to switch to plastic dishes and glasses, though. And talk to her doctor about her meds, will you? She's been losing a lot of ground the past few days. She knows just enough, just often enough, to be pretty scared. Seems to me, scared with your mom comes out looking like mean."

"Yeah. She's always been her nastiest when she's afraid of something." She narrowed her eyes and took a good look at Leo's forehead. There was a lump under the bandage. "Are you sure you're okay? It looks like she really clocked you."

Leo rapped her knuckles lightly on the other side of her head. "Made of steel. It's not the first time a patient has taken their frustrations out on me. It's part of the gig with dementia care."

Faith went to the refrigerator and pulled out the plastic container of fresh tuna salad. She grabbed a loaf of sourdough from the breadbox and sat at the table to make herself a sandwich. Michael's request dovetailed with Leo's head in her thoughts. After a minute of trying and failing to make order in her brain, she asked, "If you weren't working with Margot, where would you be?"

Leo dried her hands and poured herself a cup of coffee. Then she sat at the table across from Faith. "Jose and I work for a service. We'd get reassigned, and we'd go into other patient's homes." She sipped her coffee. "Can I ask what you're thinking?"

"I'm wondering how she'd do in a home."

"Can I be blunt?"

"Sure." She'd spent a lot of time with Leo since her mother had come home. They weren't friends, exactly, but it was impossible not to feel close to someone who was going through this with her. She felt close to Jose, too, but in a different way. He was like a brother, somebody she traded shit with. Leo was close to Margot's age and had a no-nonsense maternal quality that Faith had quickly responded to. She was a lot like Bibi, actually, without the attention to her wardrobe and hair.

Still, Faith girded herself, trying to be ready to hear she was a terrible daughter.

"Your mom is slipping fast. Faster than I usually see. I don't know why, but she's losing a lot of herself every single day. In my opinion—and, you know, I'm no doctor, but I've been working with these patients for twenty years—looking at what I've seen this month or so I've been here, I'd be surprised if she had any of her present self by the end of the year."

"Jesus."

"Yeah. It's scary, I know. Don't worry about me taking a glass to the noggin. It happens. You know, in my job, I have to pay attention to a lot of subtle signs. It gets to be a habit. What's between you and her—not so subtle. I don't know what it is, except what your mom's blurted out, but I know you two have had a rocky road together. That's plain as day. It's not my place to tell you what to do. But I will say that she doesn't know you much right now. I don't think it'll be long before she doesn't know this life at all. That'll be a blessing for her, not having any more moments of knowing all she's lost. She won't remember who she's hurt, or who hurt her. Her life will get real simple, wherever she is. So if you're thinking about residential care for her, I think you should make that decision for yourself, not for her."

"I guess...I guess I want to be a better person than she is. Or was. Or...I don't know."

"Gonna be blunt again, Faith. You already are a better person."

~oOo~

That afternoon, she called Sera in Tokyo. It was the next morning there, and Sera was breathless when she answered. "Hey, Faith. I hope you don't mind if I walk and talk. I'm just getting to the office."

"That's fine. I have a question for you."

"Shoot." She moved the phone from her mouth and rattled something off in Japanese. "There a problem?"

"No. I'm just wondering if you can still foot the bill to put mom in a home."

There was no immediate response, and Faith listened for a few seconds to the noise of morning corporate bustle in Tokyo. "Did something happen?"

A whole lifetime of somethings had happened. "No. She hurt one of her nurses, but that's apparently not a big deal. It's me. I'm back with Michael, and we want to start a life."

Sera had been away at college during all the drama of the time before, but of course she knew about most of it. "Really? That's going well?"

"It is. But Mom doesn't fit into the mix. I have to make a choice."

"Well, thank GOD. Yes, you do! Have a life, for Pete's sake! Go back to the beach or do whatever you want. Of course I'll pay. I have all the contact info for the San Gabriel center. It's…three-thirty there…okay. I'll set some time aside in the next hour or so and give them a call. Do me a favor, and you call, too. They'll need a local contact."

"Yeah, okay. You're sure this is right?"

"Jesus, Faith. I don't know why you're *not* sure. Hey—we should sell her house. Can you manage that? It would be nice for those proceeds to defray some of the costs."

"I can handle that. You can set up a trust or whatever it is we should do."

Her financier sister laughed into the phone. "Yeah, I'll take care of it. I'm really glad you made this decision, sis. It's the right one. She'll get the best care, and you can move on. You left home for a good reason, remember? If you didn't come back for Dad, I don't understand why you tried to come back for Mom."

Faith was still thinking about that question when she ended the call. There wasn't an easy answer. But when she thought of sending her mother away, she had the same kind of feeling deep in her chest that she'd felt on the night she'd run away. A sense of something lost, even though it wasn't something she'd ever really had, even though it wasn't something she could even identify. That night, the feeling had slowed her limbs and made it physically difficult to leave. The memory of it still hurt, even now.

memory

Faith had parked Dante around the corner and about halfway down the block; its engine was loud and recognizable, and even though she was waiting until the house had been dark and quiet for almost an hour, her father was a light sleeper, and he might hear her start her car.

She wasn't bringing much. Though she'd been planning this for months, there was very little of her old life she ever wanted to see again. Two duffels and her backpack. And Sly. That was all. Not even any of her art stuff. That was the only thing that was really hard to leave behind, but it was too much to carry light.

She didn't have much money on her, but she had a savings account with several thousand dollars in it, and she had an ATM card. She'd stop at several places close to the house and take out what she could from each one.

At midnight, she'd turned eighteen. Her parents were planning a big party for her for that night: the kind that came with a caterer and a band. She thought it was some kind of guilt thing. Or maybe not. It was hard to imagine Margot feeling guilty for getting what she'd wanted. And Blue still could barely look at Faith. But Margot wanted this party.

It didn't matter. Faith would be long gone by the time her parents woke up.

She'd gutted it out in this house, still locked away. She was on independent study, so, with nothing better to do, she'd finished all the course work for junior and senior years and had graduated. Then she'd spent the summer working in the bike shop office, her father's watchful eye on her all the time. Bethany and Joelle had faded out of her life.

She'd waited until she was eighteen because she knew her father would hunt her down, and she knew he would find her. She'd decided to go ahead and take her uniquely recognizable car because she loved it, and she knew it ultimately wouldn't matter whether she drove Dante away from home or if she'd bought a ticket on a Greyhound, or hitched, or any other mode of transportation. He would hunt, and he would find.

But at eighteen, she had the right to stay away, and she had decided that she would call the cops if she needed to. Her parents had instilled in her a deep distrust of law enforcement, and she knew it would be a terrible betrayal to sic them on her father. But nothing like the betrayal she'd endured. So she would take whatever help she needed to stay away.

Knowing that, if her mother woke in the middle of the night, she could well open the door and peek in, Faith did the age-old trick of stuffing pillows and stuffed animals under her covers to look like a person.

The hallway floor creaked badly in this old house, so Faith slid open one of her windows and dropped her bags, then crawled through and followed them, landing on her hands and feet on the grass about seven feet below her window. It was August, and she'd had the windows open anyway, so Margot wouldn't think it strange if she did check it.

Faith gathered up her few belongings and crossed to the back gate, then went down the narrow alley and around to Dante. She felt stranger than she thought she would. For weeks, months, almost all she'd been able to think of was freedom. She'd counted the days, the hours, then the minutes until she could get away from this home that had become a prison, from these people who'd taken everything from her.

But as she hoisted her baggage into her car, her chest ached with loss and nostalgia. Her father had been her daddy. She'd always been able to talk to him. They had the same sense of humor, the same outlook, then same impatience with people. It had never really bothered her that her mom didn't have a lot of use for her, because her daddy had always been there for her. Even though that part of them was gone, as Faith prepared to leave him behind forever, she ached with the loss of him more than ever. She ached even for the loss of her mother's love, and she'd never even felt that with any particular potency.

When she had everything in the bed, she turned and went back to the house. She wasn't leaving Sly behind. Margot seemed to like him well enough, but Faith didn't trust her at all.

As she walked back down the alley, she called for her cat, calling his name and making the clucking sound he recognized as a dinner call. But no Sly. She went back into the yard, closing the gate quietly, and sat in the shadows not far from the patio, still calling, but mindful of the open windows throughout the house. Her parents' bedroom faced the front, but still.

After nearly half an hour, Faith knew that she had to go, with or without her cat. If he didn't show up, she would have to leave him behind, and lose the last piece she had of Michael.

Pinching her arms hard to stave off the sobs, still calling and clucking, Faith crossed back through the dark yard, her mother's elaborate garden, and went out the back gate. Sly never emerged from the shadows.

She hoped he was off somewhere getting laid. Or beating up another cat.

"Bye, Sly. Love you, dude." She climbed in behind the wheel and closed the door.

~oOo~

Faith had no official place to go. She wanted distance, that was all. But she knew the San Francisco art scene was cool, and she'd read several artist biographies that told stories about just landing in the city with no job or apartment or anything and just figuring it out. San Francisco was big and crowded, too, and she thought big and crowded was a better way to hide than small and isolated. So, after she cobbled together a couple thousand dollars from ATMs, she drove north.

She stopped about two-thirds of the way and refueled using her cash, and picked up a couple of packs of HoHos and a four pack of Red Bulls. By the time she crossed the Bay Bridge, the sun was coming up, and she was tweaking on sugar and caffeine.

At probably about the same time her parents were learning that she was gone from her old life, Faith was arriving in her new one.

And God, the city was gorgeous.

~oOo~

It was a typical Saturday afternoon in late September. The heavy morning fog had burned off and left a brilliant, cloudless day in its wake, warmer in the fall than it ever was in the summer on the Bay. Every tourist in California, from every country on the globe, all seemed to have decided to converge on Pier 39 at the same time. Faith was quite sure she had never seen so many people in this little shop in her few weeks working here.

Her first couple of weeks in San Francisco had been terrifying. The hotels were crazy expensive, even the shitty ones, and parking wasn't much better. She'd spent a lot of nights sleeping in Dante—which had its own set of special challenges. But she'd spent her days getting to know the city and finding the artists, especially the buskers and street artists, and she'd built up a little network. She'd graduated from car-sleeping to couch-surfing. Then she'd gotten this job as a clerk at a 'gallery' on Pier 39. It was really just a higher-end souvenir shop that sold prints and figurines, but it paid okay. She'd moved in with a coworker. Things were looking up. At least she could now reliably eat, sleep, and wash.

Dante was garaged at the back of a new friend's absurdly long garage—one long row that fit three cars. In order to get to her car, she had to make arrangements for the other two cars to be out of the garage. Luckily, she didn't need it. Walking and public transportation were all she needed, and she was glad to have her rolling piece of art somewhere out of sight. Because so far, in the seven weeks she'd been away, no one had found her—or, at least, no one had contacted her.

But as Faith looked up from wrapping her customer's glass seashell in tissue, her eyes met a familiar set of brown eyes, set in a face with the faintly emerging wrinkles of a woman who laughed often, a face framed with chocolate-brown hair, carefully cut and styled.

Bibi.

Faith froze, the wrapped seashell in one hand, the paper bag she'd been about to slide it into in the other.

"Hi, honey. You look good." Bibi spoke over the head of the small, elderly woman who was trying to buy a glass seashell.

"Bibi."

"Miss? Excuse me."

Faith started and looked down at her customer. "Oh! Sorry." She finished bagging the purchase and handed it over. "Thank you for shopping with us today." The woman nodded and turned to fight her way out of the shop.

"Cover me for a few minutes, would you?" Faith took off the canvas apron, embroidered across the bib with the shop logo and name, that served as their uniform.

Renee, her coworker and roommate, gave her a severe stink-eyeing. "Are you kidding me right now? There must be a hundred people in here!"

"I know—and that one is my mom's best friend." She nodded toward Bibi. Renee knew a little bit about Faith's home situation—not details, but enough to know that she'd left under a dark cloud and was trying to stay under the radar.

"Oh. Fu—" She looked up at the crowd of customers in earshot. "Damn. Okay, but please don't be long. It's just you and me for two more hours."

"I just need to arrange to meet her later. I promise. Five minutes."

~oOo~

Bibi was waiting for her at the restaurant when she got to the Ferry Building. She'd walked from Pier 39—thirty-eight piers. Renee had offered her a ride, but she wanted to walk and get her head straight. What did it mean that it was Bibi who was here? Well, it very likely meant that her parents knew where she was, too. Was anyone with her? Would they try to force her home?

She saw her in the window before she went in. She was alone, drinking a glass of wine and looking over the menu. When she saw Faith approach, she set the menu down and stood up. They hugged. Faith felt awkward at first, but once she was in Bibi's arms, she held on for a while.

Then they sat, and Faith just jumped in. "Do they know?"

"They do. They're not here. It's just me. I talked everybody into lettin' me talk to you first. It wasn't easy—I practically had to tie Blue down. He's been crazed since you left, baby."

The server came by, saving Faith from having to respond to that statement right away. She ordered an iced tea, and the server left, promising to be back quickly with her tea, and ready to take their order. Then Bibi crossed her arms on the table and leaned in. "The way you left, Faith. On your birthday, with that big party planned…"

"Not my party. That was Margot performing motherhood. It had nothing to do with me. What had to do with me was five months locked away in that house. And what she made me do—what *they* made me do. What my father did to Michael. That was what had to do with me. I hope she was mortified that I left on my birthday."

"Bitter's not a good color on you, Faith."

Faith sat back in a huff. She didn't want to have this conversation. "Look. I know you're on their side—"

"I'm not. I'm on the side of my family, and that's you, too."

"Can't straddle that fence, Bibi. I just need to know if I have to be ready to fight the whole club off. Is somebody going to come and yank me off the street and drag me back to L.A.?"

"That's what your father wants. But Hooj is holdin' him off. I'm here to see if you're doin' okay and to ask you what we can do to make this better. If you could see Blue, Faith. He misses you so much. Everythin' that's happened this year—it's tearin' him down. You're his baby girl."

Faith laugh, the sound choked off by looming tears. She pinched her arm and found some calm. "No, I'm not. Not anymore. He told me so himself. Unless you have a time machine, there's nothing. I'm done. Go home and tell them that I'm fine. I have a job and a place, and this is my home now. I don't ever want to see them again. Not ever."

"Faith. Please, baby. Please help me put this family back together."

"It wasn't me who tore it apart. All I did was fall in love."

Bibi laughed quietly, dabbing her eyes with the linen napkin. "Oh, baby. You're so young. You still see your life like an epic story that you get to tell. It's not how it works. Life isn't epic. It's small and made up of mistakes. I know you see that you're takin' a stand against a hurt that was done, and I see that, too. But I'm tellin' you to imagine for a second that it might be a mistake. You know the life your father leads. What if he dies before you have a chance to realize what you gave up? Can you live with that, never seein' him again, after how close you've always been?"

"How close we *were*. And yeah. I can live with it. I've already lost what we were. I'm done. I mean it. I'm young, not stupid."

"Okay, honey," Bibi sighed. She rooted around in her big handbag and pulled out a burner phone, still in its packaging. "Can we set this up, and you and me keep in touch this way?"

Faith stared at the phone like it might leap up and bite her at any second.

"Just you and me, Faith. I won't tell anybody else about it. I just picked this up here in town. Hooj doesn't even know about it—but I probably will tell him. But I won't tell anyone else, and it'll be just me on the line if you use it. And I'll call sometimes, too. Just to check in. Every couple of months or so, unless you call more."

Still, Faith could only stare.

"Please. Faith, please."

"Okay." She pulled the phone toward her. "Okay. Just you."

"Just me. I swear."

"Swear on Hoosier's life."

Bibi blinked, and then she took a breath. "On Hoosier's life, then. I swear." She smiled. "Thank you, Faith. You'll stay and eat, right? I want to send you off into the world here with a good meal."

"I eat fine, Bibi. I'm good. I really am."

Bibi reached across the table and grabbed Faith's hand. "I'm glad. But have dinner with me?"

The server was back with the iced tea. Faith picked up a menu and asked for a few more minutes to make her selection.

~oOo~

The phone that Faith had, over the years, taken to calling the Bibi Express, rang in the middle of the night. Faith pushed Tau's leg off her and got up. He groaned and rolled over but didn't wake.

She walked naked into the living room and dug the phone out of a drawer in the dresser she used as a television stand. By the time she got there, it had stopped ringing, so she stood there, looking at the screen, waiting for it to show a voice mail.

Bibi never called in the middle of the night, so Faith felt a small fizz of disquiet in her head. Something was wrong, she knew.

Instead of a voice mail, the phone rang again, Bibi's name reappearing on the screen. Faith answered. "Hey, Beeb.

Bibi's voice was heavy, like her throat was swollen. "Baby, come home. Right now."

Faith sat down on the ottoman she used like a coffee table. "What's wrong?"

"It's your daddy, hon." Bibi cleared her throat and sniffed before she went on. "He died tonight. You have to come home."

"He died?" Faith felt small and young, and she curled her upper body over her legs. "He died?" She'd left home almost six years ago, and hadn't seen or heard from her father in all that time. The distance had made him more her daddy in memory than he had been when she'd left.

"I told you it would happen, Faith. Come home. Stand with your family and say goodbye. Sera's comin'. She's already on her way."

Sera was living in New York City, a rising star in the world of international finance. Faith was still working on the Pier, but she was starting to make things happen with her art, too.

She could not possibly be within a hundred miles of her mother. Margot in grief, unfettered by her husband's control? Her daughters both before her, a ready comparison? No. Absolutely not.

"I'm not coming, Bibi."

"Faith!"

"I love you. I'll talk to you soon." She ended the call and turned the phone off.

Then she pulled her legs onto the ottoman and sobbed.

Tau came out and squatted at her side, his strong brown hands smoothing over her hair. "What is it, love?" he asked in his melodically accented voice.

She didn't love him—she didn't think she could love anyone anymore—but she was glad of him, and she was grateful he was here with her now. "My daddy died." She curled into his arms.

"Ah. I am sorry. What can I do?"

"I just want to go back to bed."

He nodded and picked her up, and he stayed in bed with her the whole day.

If she could love anyone but Michael, she would know it now, because Tau was someone who deserved her love. He was beautiful, kind, and strong, and he loved her.

But she couldn't love anyone but Michael, and she'd never see him again. She could never see him again. Not after what her parents had taken from her. From them.

Even in Tau's arms, Faith felt a loneliness as dense as the bottom of the ocean.

CHAPTER EIGHTEEN

Demon rolled his shoulders and tried not to fidget. He didn't understand how it could be true: he wore a heavy leather kutte on his back every day, but the lighter wool blend or whatever it was of his new suit felt like a goddamn straightjacket. It was the sleeves, that was it. His arms didn't fit in the goddamn sleeves, and he couldn't move.

And the tie. Christ, the tie. Men like Finn Bennett dressed like this every day, but Demon knew he was sitting here like a gorilla, embodying every cliché about uncivilized bikers with his squirming.

Finn had told him that he needed to dress 'respectfully' in court, so Bibi and Faith had taken him shopping. He was going to burn the results of that outing at his earliest opportunity.

It wasn't his first time in court, but it was his first time as an adult that he hadn't been brought in a side door wearing a jumpsuit and shackles. The only times he'd actually gone to trial for his transgressions had been in juvenile court. Then, too, he'd been shoved into some ridiculous getup and had sat there squirming next to his lawyer or advocate or whoever.

Those 'whoevers' had been court-appointed. Now, he was in family court, sitting next to the great and powerful Findley Bennett. Faith was sitting right behind him, and every now and then, usually after he'd squirmed, her hand came forward and rubbed over his back. Hoosier, Connor, Muse, and Sid were behind him, too. Bibi had Tucker in the corridor outside. She'd dressed him in a silly little suit, too, for no reason Demon had understood, except that she'd thought it was 'darlin'.'

This was it. He would either leave this building with custody of Tucker, or with no chance of ever having it.

He turned and looked at Faith. She smiled at him, her eyes sparkling with love and encouragement. God, she was so beautiful, she was so good, and she was his. Today—*today*—he might be on the path to have everything. They'd moved Margot into a home the week before. They were getting her house ready to put on the market, and they were looking for a home of their own. The life he wanted was right in front of him, close enough to wrap his arms around.

But if he lost Tucker, he knew everything would fall apart. He knew that it would break him, and he'd take everything he loved down with him.

So he faced the bench and waited.

The process was different from what he'd expected. Almost everything had been done ahead of time. Papers had been filed and counterfiled, reports had been submitted and responded to, affidavits and sworn statements and who knew what all. Finn had told him that the judge would have read the entire record before today and would likely have her ruling prepared. Today was for any final statements, and then, unless something new required further deliberation, the ruling. According to Finn, some judges did a hearing and then just emailed their ruling out later. This judge preferred all the parties to be present when she ruled.

Whatever. He just wanted somebody to fucking tell him if his life was starting or ending.

The rear door to the courtroom opened, and the state's attorney came in, followed by the guy that had been helping assemble the state's case for making Tucker a permanent ward. Sid's old boss, Harry Rucker. That was a guy Demon would have liked a few minutes alone with.

Neither the lawyer nor Rucker looked their way as they sat down. Finn turned and offered Demon a little smile and a nod. He looked pleased. Demon tried not to let that get his hopes up.

The bailiff called for the room to rise, and the judge, a woman in maybe her fifties or so, stepped up behind the bench. She sat, everyone else sat, and the proceedings were called to order.

He tried to pay attention to the legal blather that started things off, but a lot of it didn't make much sense. But then the judge nodded and crossed her arms on the bench before her.

"Before I make my ruling, each party may make a final statement." She nodded at the state lawyer. "Mr. Gomez?"

Rucker leaned over and whispered something in Gomez's ear. He nodded and stood. "Our filings are complete, and we have nothing new to add. We would, however, ask the Court to seriously consider Mr. Van Buren's violent criminal record, which includes a conviction for second-degree murder."

Finn stood. "Objection, Your Honor. The conviction to which the state's Counsel refers is a part of a sealed juvenile record."

Gomez turned on Finn. "And you know full well the seal doesn't apply in court."

"It doesn't apply in *criminal* court. This is family court. Or did you get lost?"

The judge rapped her gavel. "Okay, gentlemen. Points are taken. I am fully acquainted with the facts of this case, including the petitioner's adventures with the law. But Mr. Bennett's objection is overruled. I have the discretion to consider Mr. Van Buren's full record, and I have." She turned to Gomez. "Anything further?"

"No, Your Honor." He sat.

Demon's stomach felt twisted up. Fuck. Would his childhood fuck him up again? He looked over his shoulder; Faith looked worried, too. Oh, fuck.

"Mr. Bennett?"

At the judge's prompting, Finn stood. "Thank you, Your Honor. Our filings are complete as well. They tell the story of a man who loves his son deeply and who is doing everything in his power to help him overcome the traumatic beginnings of his life. Little Tucker was born addicted to methamphetamine. He was left in the care of an addict who neglected and mistreated him even before he was born, and that addict was allowed nearly free rein by a negligent caseworker who, as we showed in our filing and has not been disputed, falsified reports. In contrast, all of the objective parenting evaluations and observation reports of Mr. Van Buren and of Tucker show a loving father-and-son bond and a stable environment for the child to be raised in. Mr. Van Buren is as much a victim of our broken and overworked system as Tucker was a victim of his mother."

"Objection!" Gomez jumped up. "The 'system' isn't on trial. Mr. Bennett is playing out his next sound byte."

"Sustained. Let's keep the focus on the boy, Mr. Bennett."

"Of course, Your Honor. It's clear that Mr. Van Buren is a fine parent who will give Tucker a fine home. Three separate reports—including Tucker's current caseworker—recommend custody. The record Mr. Gomez would like you to consider has not had any new entries for years—since long before Tucker was born. This is a man who has turned his life around. A man who loves his son and has been nothing but stable and nurturing. The case speaks for itself, so I have nothing further. Thank you."

Bennett sat down. Demon looked at him, dissatisfied. It wasn't enough. He knew it wasn't enough.

The judge was quiet for a few minutes—or maybe it was just seconds—making some notes. Demon sat, feeling bound by his clothes and trying not to fidget.

Then she looked up. "Since there was no new information provided today, I am ready to rule." Demon expected her to tell him to stand, but she didn't. "Lots of evidence has been submitted, lots of opinions have been offered. This is always the case with child custody. But what my ruling must come down to is one simple question: in what situation is the child best served? My only interest is the child. Whether or not Mr. Van Buren was treated unfairly in the past is a concern for another court. Here, I only care if Tucker has been treated unfairly. Mr. Van Buren's criminal record is indeed…elaborate, and it tells the story of a man who has lived a violent life."

Demon dropped his head, and he felt Faith's hand on his back. Oh, fuck. Fuck, fuck, fuck, fuck, fuck.

"The state wishes me to consider the petitioner's juvenile record. I've done so. I've noted not only the murder conviction but also the mitigating circumstances attached. I've also read the observation and evaluation reports for Tucker and his father. I've seen the videos. It is clear that they have a strong bond. The state has argued that Mr. Van Buren is performing for the evaluators. I have no official opinion on that. But I do have an opinion about whether Tucker is performing. And my opinion is that of course he is not. He's a two-year-old boy who obviously loves and feels comfortable with his father."

Demon looked up. The judge was looking right at him.

"Yes, Mr. Van Buren, your record concerns me. But if the state were to take custody of all children whose parents have criminal records...well, we'd need to hire a great deal more caseworkers, that's for sure. You have paid your dues. At this point, you owe no more, and I would strongly encourage you not to accrue any in the future. Because your son needs his father. Sole legal and physical custody of the minor child, Tucker Maxwell Van Buren, is granted to his father, Michael John Van Buren. Make him proud of you, sir. And we are adjourned." The judge rapped the gavel once and then stood up.

Demon just sat there, stunned. Finn grabbed his elbow and pulled him to stand. The judge left, and the seats behind Demon and Finn erupted into rowdy cheers. Demon's back was slapped repeatedly; he rocked with the impacts but couldn't make himself connect with anything.

It couldn't be real. He would wake up and none of this would be real.

Then Faith was at his side. "Michael," was all she said. She grabbed the lapel of his stupid suit coat and tugged, and he finally moved. He turned and looked down into her gorgeous face. "Michael. He's yours. We can go home. Happy birthday."

That was right. It was his birthday. He'd forgotten.

He wound his arms around her and lifted her off the floor. Then he pressed his face against her neck and wept.

~oOo~

Riley was still home with the new baby, so the club had the party at their house. Lexi's sixth birthday was in two days, and Nolan had had a birthday a few days before, so they'd bundled all the celebrations into a big, family-friendly bash.

It was the end of April, and Bart was grilling. They had a thing on their patio like an outdoor kitchen. Sometimes, the reality that he hung out with a fucking movie star struck Demon hard. What a strange life he had.

Their pool was open, and Demon was in the shallow end with Tucker, who was wearing little yellow floaties on his arms and trying like crazy to swim. Demon didn't really dig pools. He'd never learned to swim, and the sensation of buoyancy, especially if he got into water above his waist, freaked him out a little. It was a secret he still had. But in the shallow end, serving as a climbing wall for the kids, throwing Lexi and Ian off his shoulders and dragging Tucker around in a circle through the water—that he could handle.

Faith in a bikini—that was something else entirely, and he wasn't at all sure he could handle it. It was black, with rings on the hips and between her tits, and it was spectacular. But he wanted her to put a fucking shirt on, at least. There were horny guys everywhere, and while he knew they wouldn't dare touch her, he caught them checking her out, trying to be subtle. He'd caught Double A three times now. If there was a fourth, that asshole might just get shot a third fucking time. And Demon would aim a bit in from his thigh.

When he'd asked her to put a shirt on, she'd laughed at him.

Having an old lady was going to take some getting used to. But he had her. And he had Tucker. He'd gotten his arms around it all, almost everything he'd ever wanted.

When Lexi and Ian got out of the pool and trotted off to their big play area, Demon helped an eager Tucker out of his floaties so he could run after them, his swim diaper leaving a dripping trail behind him.

He was going to have to teach him to use the toilet. He had no idea how, but he'd figure it out. He had people to help him. His son would grow up surrounded in love. He'd grow up safe and secure. Strong.

Demon lifted himself out of the water and sat on the side of the pool, looking around the yard. The air smelled of cooking cow and spicy sauce, and his stomach rumbled in appreciation and anticipation. It was a family party, so only Coco and Maria, the two most established club girls, were there, and they were helping out with food and drinks. That left a lot of unattached men with nothing to do but drink and play, so a bizarre, full-contact game of croquet was happening in the yard. Demon laughed. The way those mallets were swinging, somebody was going to be bloody before it was over.

A slim shadow was cast over his shoulder and into the pool, and then a familiar, small hand was holding a bottle of beer in front of his face. He took the bottle in one hand, and the hand in the other, and kissed Faith's palm. "Hey, babe."

She sat on the tile poolside next to him. "Hey, you. How ya doin'?"

He took a long pull from the bottle and then put his arm around his old lady. "I am good. I am the best I've ever been."

She kissed his shoulder. "Me, too."

"Pa!" Tucker was running around the pool with something in his hand. "Pa!"

"Walk, buddy. Don't run by the pool. You have to go slow and be careful." Tucker slowed to a careful, mincing step, and Demon and Faith both laughed quietly. "What you got, Motor Man?"

Tucker finally made it to them and held out a tiny pink teacup with Alice in Wonderland on the side. "Lexi made tea! And...and..." He stopped and screwed up his face. "Frumpers." He blew over the top of the cup as if what was inside it were hot, and then he presented it carefully to Demon.

He took the tiny pink—and empty—teacup and pretended to take a sip. "Yum, Tuck. Thanks!"

"Tea and frumpers?" Faith laughed.

Tucker nodded enthusiastically. "Uh-huh! For Pa! Birfday! Come, Pa!" He hooked his arms around Demon's arm and pulled.

So Demon handed his beer to Faith, then got up and took his son's hand. "Where we goin', buddy?"

"Tea party!" Tucker shouted. The Horde that were lazing around the pool hooted. Demon flipped them off when Tucker wasn't looking.

Lexi and Ian had a miniature patio of their very own, complete with a miniature outdoor kitchen and a miniature patio furniture set. The kids had set the table with Lexi's pink dishes, and there were little cookies—Oreos—on the plates. Lexi, wearing a sparkling tiara that said *Happy Birthday* in rhinestones, was 'cooking,' but there was no sign of Ian.

No, there he was, pulling Nolan over from the combat croquet game. The other birthday boy.

"Wow, guys," Nolan said. "This all looks great. Thank you for going to all this trouble."

"'Tis no trouble at all. Please join us for tea and crumpets," Lexi answered, affecting a little accent, and Demon and Nolan exchanged a look and almost laughed. She was such a prim little miss.

Tucker sat at the table, but Lexi turned and said, "No, Tucker! You should pull out a chair for the guest of honor!" So Tucker stood up and dragged a little chair back, smiling up at his father.

Demon sat. Nolan sat. And Lexi came to the table with a teapot and poured 'tea' for everyone. Sitting in the middle of a biker family party, in swim trunks, their tattooed torsos bare, they had a little birthday tea party presided over by a princess in a tiara.

Demon had never been happier in his life.

~oOo~

The party at Bart and Riley's ended around dusk, as the children began to get tired and grouchy. The single men rode back to the clubhouse to find more adult entertainment, and the families headed home. Although Faith still hadn't been sleeping with him since Margot had been moved in at San Gabriel's, because she didn't want Sly and the kittens to be totally alone at that house, on this night, she came back with them to Hoosier and Bibi's.

It wouldn't be long now and they would all be living together.

Demon put a completely zonked boy, still clutching a stuffed cow Faith had given him, to bed in his crib. Then he stood for a few minutes and watched his son sleep. His cheeks and forehead were pink; his sunscreen had worn off and Demon hadn't noticed and reapplied it quickly enough. But he wasn't overly hot, and he obviously wasn't uncomfortable.

"Night, Motor Man," he whispered and turned to go through the bathroom and into his room, where Faith was waiting for him.

She was naked and waiting in bed. She, too, had taken a little sun; he could see the faint outline of her bikini on her skin, but she had tanned, not burned. As he approached, dropping his own clothes on the way, she came up onto her knees and crawled to the edge of the bed.

When she lifted her arms to hook around his shoulders, Demon caught sight of the tiny scar on the inside of her upper arm. He put his finger on it. "How long does that last?"

"Three years. It's been in for about two." Faith cocked her head. "Why?"

He met her eyes. What he was going to say wasn't an impulse at all. He'd been thinking about it for weeks. Since before he'd learned that they had made a baby in the time before. But he'd wanted to wait to know about Tucker first. "I have almost everything I've ever wanted in my life."

She smiled and leaned in to kiss his chest, over his heart. He pushed her back gently so he could see her face again. "Almost everything. I want a house with you. I want to marry you. And I want to have children with you. Then I'll have everything. Do you want that?"

Her smile deepened and became somehow more serious. "I do. Are you proposing?"

"Yeah. Will you marry me, and make a baby with me when that thing wears off?"

"Oh, yes. And then I'll have everything, too."

Grinning, his throat feeling tight and his heart pounding, but with happiness instead of stress, he put his hands around her face and kissed her. He put everything he'd every felt for her in that kiss. She still smelled of the day—the pool, sunscreen. Sunshine. Somebody should bottle that scent.

His cock throbbed and kicked against her, and he needed more. When he moved to lay her down, though, she resisted and leaned back. "We don't have to wait a year if you don't want to, Michael. I can have it removed at any time, and then it just takes a few days to be out of my system. We can start whenever you want."

"You'd be okay with starting so soon?"

"It seems like we're starting late, really. Doesn't it?"

He nodded. "I love you so much." Then he kissed her again. As he pushed her back on the bed, he remembered the night Hoosier had told him he could come home.

Now he finally was.

memory

He felt his entry into Los Angeles almost as if he'd gone through a literal barrier. The atmosphere felt different to him. As he'd crossed into California, every mile had weighed a little heavier, but actually being in L.A., for the first time since Muse had picked him up and led him out—it was hard. It had been his home almost all his life, but it had only briefly felt like one.

Still, that brief time had been the only time he'd had one.

He was riding in alone; Muse was doing a three-year bid for aggravated assault. He'd been in for eight months and was doing his damnedest to stay out of trouble and maybe get out at half-time. That still meant nearly a year left.

It wasn't the first time Demon had ridden alone during his years as a Nomad, but he never liked it. There came a point when he was on his own where he'd gone days without talking to anyone, except to order food or take a cheap motel room. After a day or so, his head would start to get bored and snack on itself, rooting around in the dark corners for a midnight treat. Not long after that, he'd start to get twitchy. Usually somebody ended up bloody and broken when he got twitchy.

He'd spend his nights in the roughest bar he could find, knowing that he could get a good fight and bleed his line some. And he went looking for the sloppiest work he could find. All the charters knew what they were getting when they called Demon in riding solo.

But this was different. He wasn't riding to a job. He was riding to a funeral. Blue had been killed in the chaos that was swirling around the whole club's work with the Perros. Hoosier had called and asked him to come to the funeral. Demon had asked if Faith would be there. After a long pause, Hoosier had said he didn't know.

Demon didn't know if he wanted her to be there or not. He figured the odds were good that she would be; Blue was her father, and they had been close until Demon had ruined everything. Maybe they'd made up in the six years since.

He wanted to see her. He knew it would hurt. But the image of her in his mind was, despite his best efforts, fading, and at least he wanted to refresh it.

~oOo~

She wasn't there. Margot and Faith's sister were there, and hundreds of brothers and friends were there. Blue had been a member for decades. He was known and loved.

Margot paid him no mind at all, almost as if she didn't recognize him. Maybe she didn't; he was bigger, and he wore his hair much shorter, but that still seemed farfetched. He was glad, though. He kept back as far as was polite and let the funeral happen around him.

By intention, he'd arrived later than most, and he planned to leave earlier, as soon as the wake became a party. Walking into the L.A. clubhouse for the first time since he'd walked out of it in shame had hurt. Everything was the same. It looked exactly as it always had. It smelled exactly as it always had. It was as familiar as home, and it hurt Demon's insides. For the first time in his life, he understood what people meant when they talked about what it was like to go home after a long time away, the way everything was exactly as it should be and yet it all had a shimmer of newness, as if one's senses had to be reminded about the way things should be.

But this was no longer his home. He wasn't coming home. He couldn't.

His brothers were happy to see him. And Bibi hugged him for a long, long time. When she pulled back, he saw she was crying, but he didn't know if it was for him or for Blue.

There were new members, too, people he didn't recognize. Their new Intelligence Officer was a patch-in from an allied club that was getting all kinds of media attention. Demon didn't trust him. He knew Bart Elstad had been foisted on Hoosier by Sam Carpenter in some kind of trade or something, and he'd jumped over Sherlock, who'd been a Prospect when Demon had left, to take the I.O. position. It had been the main gossip in every clubhouse he'd been in for months. Demon didn't pay attention to strategy or politics, club or otherwise, but he thought it was weird to bring an expert tech guy in from outside, allied club or not.

Not his problem, however. He was a weapon. Unless he was pointed at Bart, he'd let other people worry about the man's loyalty. In the meantime, they wore the same patch, and that meant something.

The clubhouse ritual and the graveside service were quiet, somber affairs, to the extent that bikers could be quiet. A funeral like Blue's could not be discreet. The deafening blare of hundreds of Harleys filled the neighborhood air for long minutes as a near mile-long processional rode in formation to the cemetery. But once the engines were silenced, the men were nearly as quiet. In times like these, standing in the middle of a vast field of black leather, Demon could still feel the traces of family.

Even burying Blue, Demon could feel it. He held no animosity toward the man. Demon had broken their brotherhood. He had taken Blue's daughter's virginity, knowing full well that Blue would object. What he'd done in retaliation had been within his rights.

He felt differently about Faith's mother. Margot had called her own daughter a whore. Moreover, Demon had seen what was behind her anger and outrage. There had been satisfaction in the woman's eyes as she'd stood there, pointing a gun at him, at them. At her own daughter. Satisfaction and victory. Like she'd been jealous of Faith and had been pleased to be able to offer her her comeuppance. Her own daughter.

Yeah, he hated that bitch.

Feeling full of memory and lonelier than he'd felt in a long while, Demon had to go. He was trying to head out without being noticed. He'd gotten all the way out of the clubhouse and was heading to his bike when he heard Hoosier's voice behind him.

"Deme."

He turned and saw his former President leaning against the side of the building, smoking a Marlboro. "Hey, Prez." He walked over.

"You headin' out?"

"Yeah. Why're you smoking out here?"

Hoosier gave him a rueful smirk. "Beebs's on me to quit. It's hard. I'm hidin'."

Demon laughed. "I'm no rat. I got your back."

"Thanks." Hoosier took a long drag, then dropped the half of a smoke and toed it out. "You like the Nomad life?"

Demon didn't know how to answer. So he shrugged. "Ups and downs."

"I been keeping track. You and Muse are close. You have trouble on your own?"

Not understanding where the fuck this conversation could be going or how Hoosier thought it could be anything but painful, Demon shrugged again. "Ups and downs."

"Come home, brother."

"What?" He swallowed hard, his heart skittering, even as he doubted what he'd heard.

Hoosier stepped forward so that they were face to face. "No reason for you to stay away now. And we need you. Things are shit for the club all over the country, but we're the flashpoint right here. We need you. Come home."

"Home?" He knew he sounded like an idiot. He felt like one.

Hoosier put his hand on Demon's arm. "Home, Deme. Come home. This is home."

Before he had any idea something so weak and humiliating was going to happen, Demon broke into tears. He tried to stop, but then Hoosier put his arm across his shoulders, and there was no way he could stop.

CHAPTER NINETEEN

The director of the park board asked Faith to say a few words, but she was completely unprepared for that, so she had to force herself to take the portable mic thing he held out to her. It whined painfully until she pulled the mic away from the amp. Then she turned and smiled at the crowd.

Well, 'crowd' was a bit generous. 'Gathering,' maybe. There were about fifty people standing around, a lot of them families with children. But it was Memorial Day weekend, and there were lots of other people in the park who might make their way over eventually. They'd made a little event of it, with a couple of clowns doing face-painting and making balloon animals, a busker with a banjo, and a snack truck serving hot dogs and ice cream.

Faith cleared her throat and made herself speak into the mic. "I don't really have much to say. I'd rather just open the playground and let the kids in. But I am grateful that Mr. Wilson and the rest of the park board invited me to create the piece that will welcome kids to play." She looked over at Michael, who was holding Tucker and beaming at her. "Since I started working on this commission, I got a family of my own, and I'm really happy that a little boy I love so much is going to get to play here on the very first day. So thank you." There was a smattering of applause as, feeling awkward, she handed off the mic to Mr. Wilson.

Then the child who'd won the grand-opening poster contest got to cut the ribbon, and everybody went into the playground.

Faith watched as children immediately went to the twenty-foot-long snake created out of old parts and began climbing on it. *Oh, please nobody get hurt*, she muttered to herself. She'd done her research, her due diligence, taken every precaution. But as Tucker climbed up, hooking his hand into the snake's eye, Faith's heart went pitty-pat. This was what it felt like to be a mother, she realized. Fear and pride and love, all at once, blended into a single, inexpressible emotion.

She wondered if her mother had ever felt this way for her.

~oOo~

Bibi took Faith's hand, lacing their fingers together, and they went through the lobby, Bibi's ubiquitous high-heeled boots clacking on the terrazzo tile.

Sera had been right—this facility really was nice. It was arranged more like a hotel than a hospital, with high-end tile and carpet on the floors, nice wallpaper, sleek brushed-nickel fixtures. The rooms of Margot's wing were furnished like elegant hotel rooms, all the medical equipment discreetly tucked away in armoires and cupboards.

The staff was friendly and attentive, and the doctors seemed conscientious and, as far as Faith could tell, well qualified.

The residents who were strong and stable enough, mentally and physically, were taken on regular outings. It was mainly what Faith thought of as old-people stuff: gardens, museums, the Butterfly House, things like that. But they occasionally went to matinees at the little local repertory theater, too.

The facility itself offered classes and programs and had a stunning native plant garden as well as little plots that the residents could cultivate themselves. Margot, an avid, lifelong gardener, spent a lot of time working on her little private garden.

Faith's image of her mother doddering around in a circle on a bare patch of yard had proven unfounded. She felt better knowing that Margot wouldn't be spending her life in some bleak box, dwindling into nothingness. Michael didn't share her concern, or even understand it, and she wasn't sure how to explain it to him.

Yes, in all of Faith's memory, her mother had been uninterested in her at best and hostile to her at worst. But she hadn't really minded or even noticed until Sera had moved away. So there were years of her childhood in which Faith's feelings about her mother were mainly affectionate. Birthdays hadn't been forgotten, school events had always been attended, Faith had never really wanted for anything. Margot hadn't hugged her or talked to her much, but Faith had had her daddy, and that had been plenty.

But when Sera had gone off to college, Margot had had only Faith to notice, and, Faith had finally come to understand, what Margot had noticed was that her husband loved their youngest daughter a whole lot. She'd been jealous of that bond, and in her jealousy she'd tried to drive Faith down. Faith and Michael had finally given her the wedge she'd needed—hence the satisfaction in her eyes that day. Michael called the glint he'd also seen 'victory,' and Faith couldn't disagree.

But while that understanding of Margot made Michael hate her more, it made Faith pity her more. And that, her man simply did not understand.

That was okay, though. He didn't need to understand. They were good and whole, and Margot was here, in a decent place. Faith would visit her regularly until and unless doing so caused her mother too much stress. That didn't seem likely; Margot hadn't recognized her daughter in all the weeks she'd been here. Her degeneration seemed to have slowed a little, but she most often seemed to think it was about thirty-five or forty years earlier— when she and Blue had been just a new thing, and she had still been working. In porn.

Her primary nurse, Shirley, had told her and Bibi that Margot's most frequent sense of who she was made for some interesting scenes, in her room and elsewhere. Faith herself had come upon her in the garden one day, naked and draped over a bench, thinking she was doing a photo shoot. But no one seemed especially scandalized, not here in the dementia wing.

Today, she and Bibi found her in the commons, wearing a heavy sweater and leggings, despite the one-hundred degree day. She was curled prettily on a comfortable sofa, reading an old issue of *Cosmopolitan*. The center kept magazines, in library-style binders, from a wide range of eras available because, Shirley had explained, patients often found current periodicals confusing and upsetting. Dementia, specifically Alzheimer's, was the kind of disease one could fight only so much. After that, the best care dictated that patients should be allowed the world they needed, to every extent that was possible. Issues of *Cosmo* with Cindy Crawford on the cover were definitely possible.

Margot's decline had been fast—or maybe it had only seemed fast because she had been so careful, for as long as she was able, to hide what had been happening to her. Faith remembered the first time she'd gone into her mother's house. All those Post-Its, reminding her to do things that most people did almost as readily and mindlessly as breathing.

It must have been terrifying for her to know she was losing her mind, to sit alone in her house and feel it happen a little more every day.

Yes. She had sympathy for her mother. Karma or not, Faith didn't wish an end like this on her.

"Margot, baby, how you doin' today?" Bibi sat on the sofa at her side and patted her leg.

Margot closed her magazine with a sigh. "Oh, Beebs. Wow, you look tired, honey. Everything okay?"

This was a common question; Bibi, while gorgeous and youthful for sixty-one, looked a lot older than Margot thought she was.

"I'm a little tired, is all. But I asked about you."

"I'm good. Bored. I've been waiting for fucking *ever* for them to get set up in there." She looked up at Faith. "Hi, honey. You working this one, too?" She scanned Faith with an appraising eye, taking in her jeans and camisole. "Chaz is gonna give you no end of shit for wearing a bra, girl. You should take it off now, and hope the marks fade before your call. You're new, huh?"

"Um." Faith wasn't sure how to respond. Margot had never mistaken her for a starlet before. Usually, she just smiled and introduced herself. Once, she'd tried to send her off to score some coke for her.

Bibi jumped in. "She's not workin', Margot. This is Faith. She's a real good friend of mine."

Margot smiled. "Faith. That's a beautiful name. I love names like that—that are a thing you want your baby to have. Like Serenity. If I ever have a little girl, that's what I'm gonna name her. I bet your mama wanted you to grow up having faith in the world. That's a nice thing."

Bibi met Faith's eyes and gave her a sad smile. Faith's throat had constricted so tightly it ached. Pinching her arms, she blinked and swallowed, trying to make enough room for words to come through. "I don't know. Maybe. It's a nice thought."

~oOo~

"It's so…brown. Everywhere."

"It's June, babe. And it's the desert. There isn't any other color."

"Which is my point, I think. This far out? Are you sure?"

"It's fifteen miles from the clubhouse. That's nothing. There's eight acres here. We could fix up the fences and get Tucker a cow. Or a goat. Maybe some chickens. I could build a coop. And I'll tear down that old barn and put a new one up. And I could build you a shop first thing—right there." He pointed to a bare stretch of rocky dirt. It was all a bare stretch of rocky dirt, but he pointed in a particular spot and hooked his arm over her shoulders. "View of the mountains." He took a coaxing tone with that last sentence.

Faith looked around. Nothing but scrub and dust as far as she could see—until the horizon, where the San Bernardino Mountains rose up, still with just the barest cap of snow at their highest peaks. The sky was a vast, unbroken expanse of cerulean blue. She had to admit there was something beautiful in the near-perfect emptiness.

"Studio," she grumbled, unwilling to admit that there was a remote chance she'd consider this.

He grinned, seeing that remote chance anyway. "Studio, right. Not a shop. Sorry."

Faith stepped out of his hold and turned back to the house. Very remote chance. "God, Michael."

"But it could be great. Look at that porch. I can build the garage exactly the way I want it. I know it's rough inside, but…"

"Rough? Holes in the walls. Exposed subfloor. Only one bathroom, and somebody stole all the fixtures. They probably carried all the copper out in the bathtub."

His grin faded away. "Faith. I can't afford much. But I can work hard, and I can do almost everything that needs doing. What I can't do, somebody in the club can do. You know they'll all help. I know you see what things could be, not what they are. It's like you're trying not to see what this could be."

She was, and she didn't know why.

They'd had no luck finding anything in town. Part of it was their finances, which weren't dazzling. Michael had some savings, but Faith really didn't. What she'd earned from the playground commission would cover a down payment, but otherwise, she'd been living like most artists lived—feast or famine, and more famine than feast.

Madrone was a pretty expensive place to live, and Michael didn't want to raise Tucker in the kind of neighborhood there that they could afford to buy in. She agreed, of course. She was still living in her mother's house, taking care of Sly and the kittens, but that was ready to go on the market. Michael hadn't wanted to move Tucker more than once, so they had stayed with Hoosier and Bibi. They'd thought it would be just a couple of weeks. But Michael had gotten custody of Tucker six weeks earlier, and they were nowhere nearer to a real home solution.

Until Michael had come over and picked her up, wanting to show her what he'd found. Now they were way out near Joshua Tree, looking at a foreclosed property that had been on the market so long that the 'For Sale' sign was hanging by a single hook, and the agent hadn't even bothered to come out with them. He'd actually given Michael the code to the key box over the phone—which had seemed insanely reckless until they'd gotten out here and realized that there was nothing left to fucking steal. No copper wiring or pipes, no appliances, nothing.

Even taking into account the theft and vandalism, it was a house that looked like it had never been loved. No one had ever been happy to live here.

The exterior of the ranch-style house seemed intact, if uninspired. Putty-colored stucco, an indifferent asphalt-shingle roof, a long, Western-style porch across the full front. Somebody had built out the garage to be two more bedrooms. That expansion, according to Michael, had been done well, with solid HVAC and good insulation.

She sighed. "You're right. I can't get over the lack. But okay, let's go through again, and show me what you see." She held out her hand, and he took it. First he kissed it, and then he led her back into the house.

"Living room. Flagstone fireplace. Tuckpointing is solid, flue is clean. I can build some shelves on either side of it, like Hoosier has. We can put down hardwood—or probably laminate, but something nice." He led her through, walking over the exposed subfloor. "Dining room." He pointed out the wide picture window—which, at least, had glass in it. About the only thing the place had going for it was intact windows. And a low asking price. "Nice view. I can rebuild the fences, paint them. In the winter and spring, all that dead grass will be green, with a white fence and blue sky. And the mountains."

They moved on. "Kitchen. Huge blank slate. We can do anything we want in here."

Faith laughed, looking around at the apocalyptic disaster which had once been a kitchen. She didn't need him to walk her through the rest of it again. One bathroom, four bedrooms, an extra room that was long and narrow, like a hallway to nowhere. She was going to say yes to this house. Michael's outlook was so aggressively rosy, which was so new for him, that she just wanted to hug him and give him everything he wanted.

"Where are we going to live while you make this my dream house?"

He looked down at her and grinned. "Yeah?"

"Yeah. I can see it. We'll make it ours."

"Excellent!" He grabbed her and lifted her off the ground.

She cupped her hands around his face and kissed him. Before he could turn it into foreplay—no, she would not be fucking on this dirty floor—she asked, "So, where?"

He grinned, and blushed lightly—sheepish, not angry. "Here?"

"Oh, dude. No."

"It's just June. I could have most of the work done by the end of the summer. Sherlock's mom has one of those old pop-up camper things. He said it just sits on her driveway, so he's sure she'd let it sit out here for a while, free of charge."

He'd already been planning all this, Faith realized. "You want me to camp for the whole summer. In the desert. In a construction zone. You know it can get to be a hundred and twenty degrees out here, right?"

"We'll be in town during the day, and it's plenty cool at night. How about if I build your studio first? With AC."

"Michael…" He was nuts, but she couldn't bring herself to tell him no. He was just so happy, and it looked so good on him.

"Tucker would love it."

She punched his shoulder. "Oh, that's so unfair!"

He smiled, utterly without shame. Still holding her aloft, he bounced her a little. "C'mon. It'll be awesome."

"What if I'm pregnant?" They'd been trying since she'd had the implant removed. Morning sickness and camping didn't seem like they'd mix.

"If you're pregnant, I'll work double time to get it done as fast as I can. I'll get everybody to help." He leaned in and brushed her nose with his. "If you want, we can stop trying for a while."

She wasn't sure she wanted to do that, but it bore some consideration. "You are crazy. But I must be crazier. Okay. We'll camp."

He laughed, loud and wide open, and squeezed her harder. "God, I love you!"

"Remember that when I'm a sweaty, miserable bitch."

"You couldn't be a bitch if you tried."

Oh yes, she could. But she didn't disabuse him of his optimism, because he was kissing her again, thoroughly, with clear intent. When he went to his knees and laid her down, she didn't object. She hooked her legs around his hips.

The floor wasn't that bad.

CHAPTER TWENTY

Demon loved waking up like this—morning sun pushing off the night chill, slowly at first, making the canvas sides of the camper lighten and glow. Before he'd opened his eyes, that glow seeped into his head and made him smile.

The sounds of the desert dwellers beginning their day or ending their night—he liked that, too, and lay every morning still and quiet while the desert had its shift change.

Faith had been freaked out at first by the cries and yips of coyotes at night, but they never got too close. They'd have to be careful, though, if they ever got the animals he hoped they'd get—like chickens. He'd have to make sure the coop was strong and secure.

At the piercing shriek of a hawk above, getting an early start on the day's hunt, Demon opened his eyes and peered up through the mesh skylight, hoping to see.

"Morning," Faith's sleepy murmur made his cock, already thickened with morning wood, twitch. He shifted his gaze downward, to where she lay next to him, on her side, her hand on his belly.

"Morning. Sleep well?"

"Yeah. It was weird without Tucker here. Was it weird?"

"Yeah, it was." Tucker was spending the weekend at Bart and Riley's. This weekend was the last push to get the house done enough to live in, and the whole club was coming out to help make it happen. But they'd fucked three times last night, as enthusiastically as they'd wanted, after weeks of furtive grapples and stalled attempts while he slept on the other side of the camper. So Demon couldn't quite say he wasn't glad Tucker was having a likely awesome time with his friends.

Remembering their wild night, while he was already rock hard and Faith was lying naked at his side with her hand *very* low on his belly, Demon groaned. And then he remembered that Tucker was still having a likely awesome time with his friends. Away.

Demon didn't even feel guilty about being glad for that.

Okay, maybe a little.

But then Faith moved closer, right up against his side, and her hand moved lower and curled around the base of his cock, and Demon forgot about guilt entirely.

She rose up onto her elbow and loomed over him, and he pulled the cover off and let it drop to the floor. With one crooked arm under his head, so he could see, he put his other hand on her back as she took him into her mouth.

He could watch this now. Not only could he, but he loved it. She'd pause every once in a while and look up at him, smiling, and there was something in that moment of eye contact that he never saw any other time. He'd never figured out what it was, but it made him feel loved, and it was hot as hell.

It was all hot as hell, and he'd realized not long ago that he'd done something really shitty to her—in his mind, anyway—by even making any kind of connection between what the woman who loved him, the woman who was now his *wife*, did when she gave him head and any other vaguely similar experience he might ever have had. Those experiences weren't even in the same galaxy as this.

Now, he could simply feel—her lips, her tongue, her breath, her hands, the caress of her hair over his skin. She was gentle and firm, knowing exactly what touch, and when, felt best to him. She took her time, not simply getting him off, but loving him.

"Oh fuck." He was close. She hummed appreciatively at his utterance, and he said it again. She liked him to talk. It was getting easier to give her that.

He really was close. His gut ached and clenched, and he bucked his hips. Still taking her time, she eased off of him, leaving him behind with a flick of her tongue over his glans. She knew this, too—he preferred to finish buried deep inside her, with her body all around him. And he liked to hold off as long as he could. Being brought to the brink like this was exactly what he wanted.

She looked up with that sweet, private smile, and he grabbed her and rolled her over, settling between her thighs and drawing a beautiful breast into his mouth. She cried out and arched as he sucked, trapping her nipple, hard and tight with her desire, between his tongue and the roof of his mouth.

"In me," she breathed. "Oh, please, Michael, I want you in me."

Letting go of her breast and taking her mouth instead, he shifted and gave her what she wanted. Demon sank deep into her, and she brought her legs up, crossing her ankles on the small of his back. They moved together, neither frantic nor indolent, but simply in sync, every part of their bodies fitted together perfectly, gliding together, until her need overtook her. She tore her mouth from his with a gasp and began to move out of rhythm with him.

It was among his favorite moments of their sex, when Faith turned inside herself, so overtaken by the demands of her own body that she could focus on nothing else. There was a power in being there with her, helping her achieve what she needed, that he'd felt with only her. Still on the brink himself, he sped up to match her gyrations, driving hard into her until every breath she let go was a grunting cry.

The camper was rocking; he could hear their few dishes rattling in the tiny cupboard. Even in the extremity of their need, Demon could spare a proud smile for that.

She bit down on his shoulder and raked her nails across his back, and he felt her spasms embrace his throbbing length. While she was lost in the haze of her climax, he let his own need have him.

Yeah, he was definitely glad Tucker was having a likely awesome time at Bart and Riley's.

~oOo~

Connor nodded. "Aye."

"That's unanimous, then. I'll contact La Zorra and tell her that we'll pick up the eastbound route, too." Hoosier looked at Demon. "You sure, Deme? I know you need the scratch, but I want to make sure you're all in."

Demon sat forward and looked Hoosier straight in the eye. "I'm in, Prez. It's more than the money. I'm tired of sitting on the outside."

"Fair enough. I'll be glad to have you on these runs." Hoosier turned to Nolan and Double A, sitting near the end of the table. They'd been sitting at the table and voting with the SoCal charter for nine months. Demon had come to find himself surprised at reminders that they were members of the mother charter. "This expansion ups the risk, fellas. You know Show is asking after you. If you're ready to head home, it's a good time. If you're not, then it might be time to talk about changing that Missouri patch out."

"All respect, Prez, and I won't speak for A, but neither works for me." Nolan sat up in his seat. "I won't give up my patch, but I'm not ready to leave. Missouri is my home, but this is where I need to be right now."

"This about what happened to Isaac?" Lunden had been attacked and nearly killed in prison. He and Len Wahlberg had retaliated, and both of their sentences had been extended.

"They opened his throat, Prez. That was Santaveria still at us from the grave. La Zorra is taking his remaining men down—including the Castillos. I want in until it's over. If you'll still have me."

"She's the wife of the man who killed your father."

"I'm aware. David Vega ever shows up again, then I'll have some work to do. But he did what he did on Santaveria's orders. I want *every* man still working for that name."

"That's a vendetta, son. Dangerous."

Nolan didn't answer. After a moment, Hoosier nodded and turned to Double A, sitting at Nolan's side. "And you, A? You been hurt twice in our business. You ready to go home?" Hoosier was smirking, though, as he asked. Everybody at the table was. Double A and Coco had a regular thing going on—regular enough that she was off the roster.

He smiled and looked down. "I'm with Nolan. I'm good here for a while."

"Well, boys, you're an asset to this table. But you're not ours to keep, and you don't want to transfer. So let's put a date on this loan. Your family wants you home. End of the year at the latest—and I mean whether or not we got the Castillos tied up tight. Any objections?"

Nolan looked like he was going to object, but he eventually shook his head.

"Alright, then. We're adjourned." Hoosier struck the gavel on the marred surface of the Night Horde SoCal table, and the men went out to party.

~oOo~

Demon checked a side mirror on his bike for about the thousandth time and saw Keanu not far back, driving the club van. Good. He pulled onto the ramp that would lead him home, checking again to make sure Keanu had taken the exit—not that he hadn't been to their place dozens of times by now.

He checked again when he turned onto their dirt road. He didn't relax until he'd pulled up next to Dante and Keanu had parked next to him on the new gravel driveway in front of the new, three-car garage. Then, as he always did when he got home, he took a minute and just looked.

His home. What had been a sad, dilapidated, puke-brown house was now a vibrant terra cotta home with turquoise trim. He'd given Faith a cockeyed look when she'd shown him the paint cards, but it worked. And inside? Fuck, it was perfect. Not fancy—and not quite finished—but perfect.

There was still work to do, but he'd promised his old lady—his *wife*—that she'd have a house by the end of the summer, and he'd made it happen. He'd gotten the studio done first, too—also as promised. With AC.

Good thing about the AC—the summer had been the kind of hot that made special news reports. But Faith hadn't gotten pregnant yet—they hadn't stopped trying, exactly, but sleeping in a camper with a toddler hadn't made for a lot of opportunities—so she hadn't been overly uncomfortable, and the nights had been cool enough to need blankets. They'd made a campfire and cooked out every night as soon as the sun went low, and then, when the cool rolled in, they'd put Tucker to bed in the little camper and sat outside curled together under a blanket and stared up at the glittering, magnificent desert night sky.

Tucker had thought they were on a vacation all summer. So had Demon, to be honest. It had been the best summer of his life. All of his free time spent with his family, building their home.

Keanu came out of the van and went around back, and Demon dismounted. Before he could meet up with the Prospect, Faith came out of the house, trailing Tucker. Demon changed course and went up to his family.

Sly jumped down from the porch railing and wound himself around Tucker's feet, then stalked off to wherever. The kittens were more like cats now, and three of the four preferred it indoors. Only Blanca hung out in the wilds with Sly. But now that she wasn't such a baby, they only tolerated each other. Sly needed some new babies.

"Pa!"

"Motor Man!" He swept up his son and kissed his wife's cheek. "Good day?"

"Yeah! We're makin'…'chimmies!"

Chimichangas, he meant. It was a family favorite meal. "Oh, yum!"

"I wasn't expecting company, but there's plenty of food."

"The grunt's not staying. He's just delivering."

Faith narrowed her eyes. "Delivering what?"

"Come see." Taking Faith's hand, he carried Tucker to the back of the van just as Keanu finally opened the doors. The sound of tiny bleats carried into the desert air.

"What did you do?"

Instead of answering, Demon pulled her around to see inside the van. Tucker was straining in his arms. When he saw the crate and what was inside, he gasped and clapped his hands.

Two baby goats, one black and brown, the other marked and colored like a calico cat.

"They're some kind of dwarf goats. Both girls. They'll give milk when they're grown."

Faith turned, her eyes round with surprise. "You bought goats? Without talking with me about it first?"

"Adopted. They came from the shelter. Their mama"—he darted a look at Tucker, who was trying to climb out of his arms and into the van—"couldn't take care of them." The babies had been born to a doe who'd been taken in a hoarder raid. She'd died in the birth, but Tuck didn't need to know that.

The kids bleated sadly, and Demon couldn't stand it. So he set Tucker down and leaned in for the crate. "Put the feed and other stuff by the garage, and then get out."

Keanu nodded and got to work while Demon carried the crate to the front porch. Tucker was dancing and clapping as he followed. Faith was quiet, and he knew he was going to get yelled at later. But out of the corner of his eye, he saw Sly crossing back to the porch, his one intact ear high on his head. He jumped up on the railing and sat on a post, his tail wrapped primly around him. His golden eyes were intent on the crate.

"You haven't rebuilt the barn yet," Faith's voice was soft, and Demon knew she didn't want Tucker to pay attention to what she was saying. "Please tell me you don't want goats in the house."

"No, babe. It's okay." He opened the crate, and the tiny goats stepped out, bleating all the way. They'd been hand-raised, so they went right up to the human in the likeliest position for cuddles—Tucker, who was kneeling directly in front of the crate. As they tried to climb him, nibbling at his fingers and clothes, he giggled maniacally.

"Goats, Pa! They're ticking me!"

Demon walked to Faith and hooked his arm around her waist. He smiled down at their boy. He'd be three next month. Less than a year ago, he had a vocabulary of fewer than ten words, and he almost never used them. Now, he was speaking in complete sentences and chattering nonstop. Demon didn't always understand his chatter, but he usually got the gist. He was learning to use the toilet, too, and now only needed a diaper at bedtime, or when he was feeling under the weather. He was like a different child. But still his boy—no, he was *fully* his boy now. The trauma that had held him back was forgotten. And he would never have to relive it.

"They need names, Tuck. They're girls. You think you can think of good names?"

As he asked, Faith mumbled, "No, wait—ugh."

Tucker gently picked up the little calico kid, and she nuzzled his neck and nibbled his hair, which was getting pretty long. Giggling, he called out, "Elsa and Anna!"

Demon dropped his head. Damn. That stupid old movie had been on heavy rotation all summer long. "It's your fault," he muttered to Faith. "You're the one that used it to help him 'think cool thoughts.'"

"Bite me." She hip-checked him lightly. "Really, hon. What are we going to do with goats?"

"I'll get to the barn next thing. In the meantime, one of the things Keanu carried over is a portable pen. They can sleep in the garage at night, so the coyotes don't get to them, and we can bring the pen out in the day. But they've been around people since they were born. They'll be lonely too far away."

"Not in the house, Michael. Come on."

He nodded, trying to be noncommittal. Maybe goats in the house. Eventually. With a little sweet-talking. Then Sly jumped off the railing and went to check out the new kids on the porch. He was bigger than they were, but that wouldn't last long. They were a small breed, but they'd be bigger than a cat.

Sly nosed the brown one—whether that was Elsa or Anna, Demon didn't know—and the baby gave him a little head-butt. Sly popped him on the nose, keeping his claws tucked in, and the kid bounced straight into the air about six inches. Then Sly rubbed his body over the kid's legs. And just like that, he was in the middle of a goat scrum with Tucker. Sly was an equal-opportunity baby-tender.

"They won't be lonely," Faith murmured at his side.

"No, they won't be. This is a good home."

~oOo~

That night, long after Tucker was asleep in his new big-boy bed, and Elsa and Anna were bedded down with fresh straw in their new pen in the garage, Sly keeping watch, Demon went into the bedroom he shared with his wife. She was in the shower. He considered getting in with her, but she wasn't all that frisky about showers. Baths, yes, but not showers. So he closed their door and shed his clothes, then turned out all but the light on her nightstand.

Not a nightstand, really. Just a chair from the dining set she'd had in her loft. Their bedroom was a work in progress. The room had been outrageously large, and they'd given some of it up to have a private bathroom. That was great—nice tile, separate shower, tub for two, double sinks, the works. But he'd just gotten the drywall up in the bedroom, and they hadn't bought any furniture. Her bed and armoire from the loft, a couple of chairs they were using as nightstands, and a few lamps. That was about it. It looked unfinished and sparse. But he still loved it.

And she still managed to drape her clothes every damn place.

Shaking his head, he pulled her discarded clothes off the bed and put them in the hamper. Then he turned the covers down on his side. There was a small manila envelope on the sheet, just below his stack of pillows. His name was written on it, in Faith's precise, artistic printing. As the shower turned off, he picked up the envelope and tore it open.

There was a plastic stick inside. White with a blue cap. There was a little window on the side, showing words and numbers. *Pregnant*, he read, *2-3*. Two to three what? Holy fuck!

He almost ran around the bed to the bathroom door. They both preferred to knock at closed doors, but fuck that noise. He burst in. "Two to three what?! Babies?!"

She was combing out her long hair, a thick, red towel wrapped around her body. She laughed. "No, dummy. Two to three *weeks*. The test estimated how pregnant I am. I'm two to three *weeks* pregnant."

And then it sank in. "We're having a baby?"

"We are. Apparently, in thirty-seven to thirty-eight weeks."

He looked at the test stick again. Faith was pregnant with their baby.

Feeling almost as if his baby was inside that stick, he set it carefully on the counter, afraid he might drop it. Then he stepped back, still staring.

Faith came up to him and pulled him around to face her. He thought she was glowing. Pregnant women glowed, right? He saw it, in her eyes, her cheeks. She was more beautiful than ever. Sliding his finger behind the towel at her chest, he pulled it loose and let it drop. He wanted to see her belly.

It was flat as ever, but he still laid his open hand on her firm skin. His baby. Their baby.

Every hurt had now been healed. He had everything.

His eyes intent on his hand, he whispered. "Thank you."

She put her hand over his. "For what?"

"Everything."

THE END

~oOo~

COMING SOON:

Today and Tomorrow: **A Night Horde SoCal Side Trip**

Nolan has been on loan to the SoCal charter for almost a year. His home club, and his family, want him to come home. But he's not ready. He needs to know more about himself before he can go home to take his father's seat.

Analisa is a girl seeking all the experiences she can fit into the life she has left.

Together, they find exactly what they need.

Find more information and a teaser at the Freak Circle Press blog: https://tfcpress.wordpress.com/

Printed in Great Britain
by Amazon